BLACK OPS

Also by Chris Ryan

Non-fiction
The One That Got Away
Chris Ryan's SAS Fitness Book
Chris Ryan's Ultimate Survival Guide
Fight to Win
Safe

Fiction
Stand By, Stand By
Zero Option
The Kremlin Device
Tenth Man Down
Hit List
The Watchman
Land of Fire
Greed
The Increment
Blackout
Ultimate Weapon
Strike Back
Firefight
Who Dares Wins
The Kill Zone
Killing for the Company
Osama

In the Danny Black Series
Masters of War
Hunter Killer
Hellfire
Bad Soldier
Warlord
Head Hunters

In the Strikeback Series
Deathlist
Shadow Kill
Global Strike
Red Strike

Chris Ryan Extreme
Hard Target
Night Strike
Most Wanted
Silent Kill

CHRIS RYAN

BLACK OPS

CORONET

First published in Great Britain in 2019 by Coronet
An imprint of Hodder & Stoughton
An Hachette UK company

1

A CIP catalogue record for this title is available from the British Library

Hardback ISBN 9781473668065
Trade Paperback ISBN 9781473668072
eBook ISBN 9781473668003

Typeset in Bembo Std by Hewer Text UK Ltd, Edinburgh
Printed and bound in Great Britain by Clays Ltd, Elcograf S.p.A.

Hodder & Stoughton policy is to use papers that are natural, renewable and recyclable products and made from wood grown in sustainable forests. The logging and manufacturing processes are expected to conform to the environmental regulations of the country of origin.

Hodder & Stoughton Ltd
Carmelite House
50 Victoria Embankment
London EC4Y 0DZ

www.hodder.co.uk

1

The first killing took place in Dubai.

Mako Simeon was a Filipino labourer, seventeen years old. He'd arrived in the United Arab Emirates six months ago. Work was plentiful here, people told him. They were always building luxury hotels along the seafront and they needed manpower. They forgot to add that the pay was poor and the labourers accommodated in shacks where Mako would have thought twice about housing an animal. The facilities were never clean, nor were the labourers. The Dubai authorities made a special effort to keep them hidden from the tourists. Mako understood why. No doubt they made a dispiriting sight as they shuffled off the coaches that bussed them into the centre before dawn, and out again once the sun set. Nobody came to Dubai to see that sort of thing.

Mako alighted from the bus that morning with no expectation that today would be different from any other. He had his routine. The foremen allowed them ten minutes before starting work, and these minutes were precious to him. He took his packed breakfast to the far side of the building site. Here he could sit in peace, eat his sandwich and drink his water. These few minutes before sunrise were hot enough to draw a sweat, but they were still the coolest part of the day. He preferred to spend them alone. It meant nobody would hassle him to swap his breakfast for cigarettes.

He sat on a pile of bricks beneath a complex network of scaffolding, his back to the building site. In front of him was the Persian Gulf. A few ships twinkled out at sea as dawn was staining the horizon. He thought about home and when he might be able to return there. He chewed his sandwich thoughtfully, then looked down at the remnants of it in his hands. The sandwich smelled bad. *Really* bad. It turned his stomach. He sniffed it, then thought maybe it wasn't the sandwich after all. There were all manner of smells on this building site, many unfamiliar, some foul. Mako didn't want to be put off his breakfast. He carefully rewrapped his food, stowed it in a pocket, and pushed himself down from the pile of bricks. He'd find somewhere else to eat.

Mako suddenly glimpsed something in the shadows. At first he thought it was another labourer with the same idea as him: to get away from the crowd and eat breakfast alone. He could see the outline of his head and shoulders. But almost as soon as that thought crossed his mind, another caught up with it. The stench was noticeably worse here, and the person wasn't moving.

Mako squinted in the darkness. The person was sitting down, his back against one of the upright scaffolding poles. A cold dread flooded over the young Filipino labourer. He considered running back to the others, but something stopped him. He pulled his T-shirt up over his nose to mask the smell. Then he approached the figure. 'Who's that?' he said in Filipino Tagalog, his voice cracking. 'Are you okay?'

There was no reply. Mako stepped nearer. He wished he hadn't.

That the person was dead was not the most distressing thing. Mako had seen corpses before. It was the manner of the death that sickened him. The figure's neck was bound to the upright pole by a sturdy plastic cable tie. The neck bulged against the cable tie, its skin swollen and waxy. Mako could not see the corpse's wrists, but they seemed to be tied behind his back. The dead man wore a white T-shirt. In life he had been muscular, and his firm pectorals still bulged beneath the cotton. Now he saw that the material was stained dark with blood. It had dripped on to his chest from the side of his face, and the source of the blood was the corpse's ears, or that part of the head where they had once been. Horrific semi-glistening scabs had formed over either side of the head, like gruesome earphones. The two severed ears were lying on the man's lap.

Mako vomited. He couldn't stop himself. Then he staggered back, almost tripping, before sprinting back to the others, shouting wildly about the horror he'd just witnessed.

The second killing took place in Ghana.

Arron Borthwick was a successful businessman with a penchant for palm wine and black women. On his frequent trips to Accra he was able to indulge both vices. His oil interests in the country were thriving. He'd earned more in the past year than most people could spend in several lifetimes. He could easily retire, kick back and spend some quality time with his money. Certainly he *could* delegate these business excursions to somebody else. But where would the fun be in that, when he could tickle his fancy here in Africa?

It was Arron's habit to install himself in the Presidential Suite of the Intercontinental hotel in the centre of Accra. Here he could carry out his business meetings by day. By night he chose less refined surroundings. There were places on the outskirts where a man with his appetites could go. Here, for the price of one of the cheaper cocktails on the bar menu at the Intercontinental, he could engage the services of three Ghanaian women and enough palm wine to keep them going till morning.

Arron wasn't stupid. He always used a condom, and that wasn't the only protection he insisted on. He knew he was a target for kidnappers or opportunistic thieves. Whenever he stepped outside the Intercontinental, he took a guy. And because he could afford it, Arron Borthwick employed only the best. Liam Armitage had been in his service for nearly a year now. Arron's previous bodyguard had recommended him. 'Former 22, A Squadron, fucking animal in a scrap. Just make sure you pay him on time.'

Arron had only once seen Liam in action. They were leaving one of his preferred brothels when the pimp who'd supplied

Arron's girls pulled a knife on him and demanded his wallet. Arron knew Liam routinely carried two firearms: a snubnose revolver holstered above his ankle, and a harder-hitting 9mm pistol across his chest. Liam hadn't bothered to use either. He simply stepped up to the pimp, knocked the knife away with one hand, and pummelled him in the face with the other. By the time he'd finished, the pimp was unconscious and bloodied on the floor, and Arron was congratulating himself on choosing a former SAS soldier to look after him. He paid Liam a substantial bonus that week.

Today, though, he was concerned. He'd made a real pig of himself with the girls the previous night and hadn't left the brothel till sunrise, very drunk. He was lairy with one of the pimps, forcing Liam to manhandle him out of the brothel and into his black SUV. Back at the hotel, Liam deposited Arron in his suite to recover, then headed off to his own rather smaller room. Now it was 8 p.m. Arron hadn't seen his bodyguard since that morning. Normally Liam checked in on his principal every hour. Arron was worried that he'd pissed him off, and the last thing he needed was to spend precious time looking for a new BG.

He dialled Liam's number. It went straight to voicemail. Jesus, Arron thought. He must be fuming. Liam *always* answered when his principal called. He decided to head to the bodyguard's room and offer him another bonus. Five hundred should do the trick. He could hand it over in cash, no questions asked, no hard feelings.

Arron had a key card for Liam's room. Liam always insisted on it. That way, if Arron noticed anything unusual when he was alone, he had a place to hide. He knocked on the door first. No answer. He knocked a second time. Nothing. He swiped the key card, opened up, and stepped inside.

He immediately knew something was wrong. The blackout curtains were closed and the lights were off. There was a smell. Not the usual musty odour of a room occupied by a single man, but something more pungent. Arron held his breath as he slid the key card into the slit by the light switch. The lights in the room lit up. From the doorway, Arron could just see the end of the bed and Liam's booted feet.

'Liam?' he said. 'You awake? I've got a little extra something for you. Overtime.'

No reply.

'Mate?' Arron stepped into the room. As he walked forward, a fly buzzed towards him and landed on his face. He swatted it away with a wave of his arms. Then he saw his bodyguard lying on the bed. He felt his knees weaken.

Liam had been shot. Arron was no expert in these matters, but that much was obvious. A substantial portion of his head was blown away, exposing shards of skull, brain matter, viscous fluid and matted hair. A second fly crawled around the wound. The pillows had absorbed horrific quantities of blood. Liam's arms were stretched out in a crucifix position. His hands were fingerless stumps. They had leached more blood into the duvet. Clouds of red bloomed around them like boxing gloves. The fingers themselves were neatly laid on Liam's bare chest.

Arron staggered back. His breath was short, as if he'd just jumped into icy water. The room spun as he tried to get out of there. Uncertain on his feet, he collapsed against the bathroom door, then jumped away from it as if electrocuted. What if someone was in there? He hurled himself out into the corridor and galloped towards the lift, where he pressed the button incessantly until the doors opened.

On the ground floor there was a line of guests at reception. Arron barged past them and pushed his way to the outraged concierge. He was sweating heavily, and so distraught he could barely get the words out. 'Call the police,' he said. 'Quickly. And get me the British High Commission. Don't just stand there staring at me, you idiot. Do it! Now!'

The third killing took place in Florida.

Candace Sweeting was one of the best-known real estate agents in the area. She had a body that made the husbands look twice, and a friendly, confidential, easygoing nature that made the wives think she was their best friend. She used these attributes ruthlessly to gain clients and close deals. There was barely a property in this part of Palm Beach that hadn't, at one time or another, been sold by Candace.

She liked being a realtor. The money was good, sure, but that wasn't the main draw. Candace was interested in people. What better way to learn about other people's lives, she'd tell her friends, than stepping across their thresholds and into their homes. She'd seen it all. Sugar daddies in palatial residences with beauty-queen wives waiting for them to die. Greedy children ushering their dementia-ridden parents into care. Crazies with gun rooms that would give a Navy Seal a hard-on.

Candace was single and she liked it that way. It meant she could play the field just as much as she wanted, and she did so enthusiastically. Not with her clients – it would be foolish to get a reputation with the wives of Palm Beach. But she welcomed plenty of young men into her warm embrace, only to discard them as quickly as she'd picked them up. Some people had a word for women like Candace, but that didn't bother her. It was the twenty-first century, for Chrissakes. Why should the guys get all the fun?

Of course, she had to be careful. She'd learned her lesson five years previously when she picked up a guy at a sports bar on Superbowl night. They shared a few beers and she invited him back to her place. The sex was great and he was reluctant to leave in the morning. Nothing new there. Candace often had to kick them out after coffee and eggs. But when she returned from work that afternoon he was loitering on the sidewalk outside her house, hoping for a repeat performance. She asked him to leave. He got angry. She got a black eye. It was when the police were taking him away that she decided not to use her own home for her trysts again.

For a while she tried hotels but they were so impersonal, not to mention expensive. It was only after a housekeeping maid walked into a room at the Holiday Inn to find her riding the cowgirl with a pathetically grateful Math student from Florida International University, that she realised her solution was obvious and simple. She was a real estate agent! She had the keys and burglar alarm codes to twenty or thirty properties at any one time. Often the owners were out of town, and they trusted Candace to show potential purchasers around whenever it suited her. Problem solved!

There was a special thrill, she soon discovered, to making love in a stranger's house. Perhaps it was a role-play thing. Perhaps the small chance that the owners might return lent a pleasurable frisson to the encounters. Candace liked it. For the past four years she'd brought guys back to these places on a monthly basis, sometimes more often. She even, on one occasion, sold a property on the back of it. That was a good day's work.

Tonight promised to be fun. The young man in the passenger seat played guitar in a band she'd been to see that night with some girlfriends. They started chatting and Candace popped the question. Guitar man said yes. They always did. Candace already had a property in mind. A spacious three-bedroom pool home, as the property details had it, with breakfast nook, formal dining area and sunset views. Also, as the property details didn't mention, a vast double bed and the added benefits that it wasn't overlooked by any nosey neighbours, and best of all the owner was out of town for several weeks.

The owner. As Candace unlocked the door, her eager guitarist in tow, she smiled at the thought of him. A Brit, and not a bad-looking one either. Early forties, black hair on the turn to an attractive grey, twinkling blue eyes and a reserved manner. But strong, and sharp, and slightly mysterious. When Candace asked him where he was headed, he evaded the question. That was three days ago, and she hadn't been back to the house since.

She disabled the alarm, switched on a lamp in the entrance hall, and turned to her guy. They didn't mess about. Neither of them doubted why they were here. Candace's two-piece trouser suit was in a crumpled heap on the floor in under a minute. Guitar man was topless, his tight jeans unbuckled. Wearing only her expensive underwear she took him by the hand and led him up the stairs towards the master bedroom. She stood in the doorway, as though blocking it, then kicked the door open with her heel while hooking her hand round her guy's neck and pulling his lips to hers. As they kissed, she felt for the dimmer switch inside the bedroom and switched it on.

Guitar man choked, mid-kiss. It was unpleasant for Candace and she pulled back. 'Jeez,' she said. 'What the hell's wrong with you?' Guitar man didn't seem to have heard her. He was staring over her shoulder and his tanned, pretty face had drained white. She turned, then grabbed hold of him as she saw the sight that awaited them.

The owner of the house was lying on the bed. He was naked. His throat was cut and the wound had bled profusely over his chest. But this wasn't his most grotesque injury. Candace found herself staring at the man's groin. Someone had removed his genitals, leaving a gaping hole where they should be. The genitals themselves were on the carpet by the bed, a pale, bloodied mound of gristle.

Candace felt herself hyperventilating. Guitar man had already wrestled her away from him and was running down the stairs. Candace staggered back, desperate to leave this place but somehow unable to take her eyes from the horror. She finally turned and hurried down the stairs, feeling cold, ridiculous, and more than a little sordid in her skimpy underwear. Guitar man had already left the building by the time she was pulling on her trouser suit. She fumbled for her cell phone, took a moment to regulate her breathing, then dialled 911.

Ten minutes later there were four police cars parked outside, their lights silently flashing. Candace sat on a low wall in the front yard, her head in her hands, her face wet with tears, silently promising herself that she would never, *ever*, do something like this again.

* * *

The first killing took place on January 12, the second on February 3. Candace Sweeting had let herself into the spacious three-bedroomed pool home with breakfast nook, formal dining area and sunset views on March 6.

On March 9, they called Danny Black.

2

Few things travel more quickly than gossip in the corridors and squadron hangars of SAS headquarters in Hereford. If that gossip concerns the suspicious death of a Regiment man, it has extra thrust.

Danny Black heard the news about Ben Bullock, formerly of A Squadron, while he was on the range. There was a thin drizzle. It matted Danny's dark hair to his scalp, soaked into his digital camo gear and made it more difficult to group the rounds from his Diemaco accurately on the target at the end of the range. He was minutely tweaking the sights when his companion Roscoe said, 'You hear about this shitstorm in Dubai?'

Roscoe was a funny one. He'd been badged for three years, and for most of that time Danny barely spoke to the guy. But in the couple of months since Danny returned from his last op, Roscoe had latched on to him. Danny knew he had a reputation in the Regiment and was used to the other guys quizzing him about previous ops. Roscoe took that to a different level and never seemed disheartened when Danny closed down every line of enquiry.

'What shitstorm?' Danny asked. He raised the Diemaco, lined the sights with the target, and released three rounds in quick succession. They clustered precisely around the target's forehead.

'They found Ben Bullock on some building site out there. Properly fucked up.'

'Fucked up how?' Danny remembered Bullock, and not that fondly. He'd been an old-timer when Danny first joined the Regiment. In Danny's opinion, he gave the SAS a bad name.

'Well, dead, obviously,' Roscoe said. 'But they took his ears off as well.'

'Who's they?'

Roscoe shrugged. 'Dunno. Could be anyone. Fella like Bullock probably wasn't too fussy who he freelanced for.'

That was true enough. Bullock had a reputation. Danny remembered the first time he met him. It was only a few weeks after he'd passed selection, and he'd settled into the Crown in Hereford for a few jars with some of the other lads. Bullock was with another group of Regiment boys. He'd gone out of his way to pick a fight with a couple of Asian men minding their own business at the bar. They'd ended up in A & E. Now Danny thought about it, did one of them end up in a wheelchair? It was all brushed under the carpet, of course. Bullock was too good a soldier. The Regiment couldn't afford to lose him on account of one drunken night in the pub. He and Danny had crossed paths on a number of occasions since then. Danny soon worked out that the only offence those two men in the pub were guilty of was not having white skin. Bullock was a racist. Simple as that.

A racist maybe, but he wouldn't let that get in the way of earning himself a living once he left the Regiment. 'Dubai, you said?' Danny asked.

'Right,' said Roscoe.

It figured. There were plenty of opportunities out in the Gulf for a man with Bullock's skills. Oil-rich Arabs wanting the cachet of an ex-SAS man on their close-protection teams. Gun-runners needing some muscle and know-how. 'Guess he stepped on the wrong toes,' Danny said. 'Simple enough to do out there, especially for a guy like Bullock.'

'Sure. But to take his ears off? That's a bit fucking keen, isn't it?'

'Dead's dead,' Danny said. He couldn't find it in himself to mourn Ben Bullock. Not when so many of his real friends had died on ops.

'Savage, mate,' Roscoe grinned. 'Nice one.'

Danny raised his weapon and released three more rounds. They clustered in a triangle around the target's heart.

The story of Ben Bullock's grisly end followed Danny around over the next three weeks. It seemed to have caught the imagination of some of the younger guys in camp. One kid, newly badged, spread a rumour that a serial killer was targeting SAS men, until the RSM pointed out that one murder didn't make a serial killer, and would he kindly shut his fucking cakehole if he didn't have anything useful to say. But each time Danny heard Bullock's name, he remembered various other incidents that put the former SAS man in a less than favourable light. The time he'd made his presence felt to a Jewish guy in B Squadron by dumping a fistful of minced pork on his dinner tray. The rumour that he'd lit a target near Mosul knowing full well that it contained nothing more than two Iraqi children. The time he'd been photographed on the fringes of an EDF march, and had to persuade the CO that he was just in the wrong place at the wrong time.

Ben Bullock had enemies, that was sure. Danny found himself trying to work out which of them had finally caught up with him.

Not that it was Danny's problem. Like he'd said to Roscoe, dead's dead. And Danny had other things to occupy himself. Life in camp was busy, and he was glad of it. The little flat in Hereford that he called home held nothing for him. His daughter, a bright, beautiful toddler, lived with her mum, who wanted Danny to have as little contact as possible. His dad had succumbed to dementia in his old folks' home. He hadn't heard from his druggie brother for months, and a good thing too. The more he could throw himself into work, the better. He was eager to be sent out on ops, but the head shed seemed to be holding back. Perhaps the powers that be had decided Danny Black was in line for a little R and R.

He was driving home from camp one evening when he heard the news on the radio. *A former British Army soldier, Liam Armitage, has been found dead in Accra, the capital city of Ghana. It is thought that Mr Armitage was working in Ghana as a freelance bodyguard. The High Commission in Accra is helping local police with their enquiries, and Mr Armitage's family have been informed.*

Danny pulled over and turned the radio up. But the announcer had moved on to the next item, leaving Danny to ponder what he'd just heard. He knew Liam Armitage better than he'd known Ben Bullock, though he liked him just as little. Armitage was like Bullock's shadow. When Bullock was causing trouble, Armitage was never far away. No doubt they were a good team on ops, because the head shed invariably deployed them together. And for both men to turn up dead within a few weeks of each other? That was suspicious. Maybe the new recruit with thoughts of serial killers wasn't so far from the truth.

As usual, it was Roscoe who had the grisly details the following morning in camp. He sidled up as Danny was making coffee in the squadron hangar. 'You hear what happened, buddy?' He said it almost gleefully.

'Armitage?'

'Mate, he was . . .'

'Fucked up?'

'Right. Word is . . .' Roscoe looked round, as if about to impart some great secret. 'Word is, they blew his brains out and cut off his fingers.' He held up his hands and wiggled his own fingers, as though explaining to Danny what they were.

Danny spooned sugar into his coffee. 'What about his ears?' he asked.

'Nah, the ears were fine. At least, that's what I heard – which is more than you can say for Bullock, right?' Roscoe saw another mate entering the hangar, and hurried over to tell him the news.

Danny sipped his coffee, thinking hard. Bullock and Armitage, killed within a week of each other? It could be coincidence. It was in the nature of former Regiment guys to find themselves working in threatening environments. It wasn't like they had the temperament to stack shelves at their local Asda. And maybe if their bodies hadn't been mutilated, Danny would have been content to believe the two deaths weren't linked. His instinct told him otherwise. He wondered who Bullock and Armitage could have antagonised so badly. Maybe it was nothing to do with their Regiment work. They'd been out of the game for a few years now, after all. But Bullock had died in Dubai, Armitage in Ghana. Different continents, thousands of miles apart. If they'd been working on something together, their operations were truly global.

Either that, or their deaths related back to a time when they were work colleagues. Big fish in the Regiment pond.

There was a pool table on the other side of the hangar. Roscoe and a few others had spread a newspaper out on the baize. No doubt they were reading the reports of Armitage's death. The ops officer, Ray Hammond, walked past them. He was clutching an armful of folders and he paused by the guys crowded round the newspaper. He looked like he was about to say something to them, but held back. His eyes met Danny's across the hangar. Danny inclined his head inquisitively. Hammond shook his, then left the hangar.

The Bullock–Armitage situation was none of Danny's business. Over the next few days he had other matters to occupy himself. A three-day training excursion on Salisbury Plain. A HAHO training package for a bunch of guys from 1 Para that took him to RAF Lossiemouth in Scotland for a week. But in his quieter moments he found himself thinking about the two dead Regiment men, and all the times he'd seen them together. There was an operation in the Gulf of Aden, where the lads had teamed up with the SBS to go after a crowd of Somali pirates. Bullock and Armitage were first to board the ship and nailed three of the Somali kids before the rest of the team were even out of the water. They'd run a CP team for the Mayor of London on his trip to Pakistan – Bullock took delight in telling whoever would listen that if one of the locals put a bullet in the mayor, they'd be nailing one of their own. There was a training day in Belmarsh to keep their skills lively in the event of a prison riot – Danny remembered wondering if Bullock and Armitage were on the wrong side of the bars. But nothing he could recall gave any hint as to why somebody would have targeted them both, and in such a gruesome way. Bullock and Armitage may not have been Danny's cup of tea, but when it came down to it they were good Regiment soldiers who got the job done and understood the importance of secrecy and personal security.

Maybe their deaths were coincidental, after all.

It snowed at the beginning of March. The grounds of RAF Credenhill looked bleaker than ever. The guys complained about having to do exercises in the white-out, of course, but they didn't really mean it. A few inches of powder was nothing to a soldier for whom hiding out for days in an Arctic snow hole was an occupational hazard. Roscoe, though, was more vocal than the others. When Danny found himself taking a slash at the urinal next to him, he braced himself for a new barrage of complaints.

'What about the latest, then?' Roscoe said. There was something in his voice that caught Danny's attention. Normally, when Roscoe was about to share some titbit, he was almost euphoric. Today he sounded, and looked, shaken.

Danny finished his piss and walked over to the basin. 'I'm sure you're about to fill me in,' he said as he started to wash his hands.

'Ollie Moorhouse,' Roscoe said. In the mirror, Danny saw his mate shake himself off dramatically before joining him at the basin. 'Dead.'

Danny turned off the tap. He was shocked. Ollie Moorhouse was a good mate of his, back in the day. When he left the army he moved to Florida. Danny had an open invitation to his place out there, which he'd never taken Ollie up on. 'How do you know?' he said.

'Tom McKinnon, D Squadron. He's got a friend in the Palm Beach Police Department. They've kept it out of the press but ... Jesus, mate, it was fucking nasty.' For once, Danny had the impression that Roscoe didn't want to elaborate.

'What happened to him?'

'Whoever done it, they caught up with him at his house out there. They cut off his bollocks, mate. And his dick. Left them lying there on the carpet. This estate agent found them. Apparently he was trying to sell the place. Do you reckon he ...'

Danny had stopped listening. He walked out of the toilets while Roscoe was still talking. Ollie's death had just triggered a memory. He'd forgotten it, but now it was completely clear. It was five years ago, maybe six. He was new to the Regiment, and the RSM had given him a job. He was to collect a flight case full of weapons and deliver them to a safe house on the edge of Dartmoor. No more information was volunteered, and Danny knew better than to ask. He'd collected the gear, stowed it in the back of a Regiment jeep, and driven to Dartmoor that afternoon.

His destination was a disused guest house, miles from anywhere. It took hours to get there. He remembered stopping off at a village shop to buy a stash of chocolate bars and finding the jeep ticketed when he got back to it. By the time he arrived at the guest house it was dark. Four vehicles were parked outside. The ground-floor lights were on. On the first floor, darkness, with the exception of one window from which a pale light glowed. As Danny pulled up, he saw a figure at the front door. That was Ollie Moorhouse. He nodded a curt greeting as Danny stepped out of the jeep. 'Where's the stuff?'

'In the back.'

'Inside with it.'

There was an unspoken hierarchy. Ollie was an established SAS operator. Danny was the new boy. It was his job to carry in the flight case. He followed Ollie along a dark hallway with a flagstone floor, into a kitchen where two more Regiment guys were sitting with cans of lager in front of them. Danny didn't know them at the time. Maybe that was why the memory had remained submerged until now. But he was sure of it.

The two guys in the kitchen were Bullock and Armitage.

'Amazon delivery,' Bullock observed. 'Stick it by the door and fuck off back to Hereford, there's a good boy.'

Danny turned to Ollie. 'Where do you want it?' he said.

Ollie smiled. 'What he said,' he replied. 'And get yourself a beer from the fridge.'

Danny dumped the flight case of weapons and grabbed himself a drink. 'So what's the deal?' he said, indicating the house in general. 'I'm guessing this isn't a country break.'

Bullock and Armitage remained stubbornly silent. It was left to Ollie to reply. 'Training package,' he said. 'We've got a kid from the Special Reconnaissance Regiment, needs some schooling in the dark arts.'

Bullock snorted.

'Ignore him,' Ollie said. 'He's prejudiced. Even you've got to admit, Bullock, the boy learns fast.'

'He'd learn a fuck of a sight faster if he didn't have to stop and pray four times a day.'

'And he'd do *that* a fuck of a sight faster if you didn't keep hiding his prayer mat.' Bullock grinned. Ollie gave Danny an apologetic look. 'Welcome to the kindergarten,' he said.

'You two should keep your mouth shut,' Armitage said. 'Hereford want this under wraps, remember?'

'It's alright,' Ollie replied. 'I know Danny. He'll keep quiet, won't you, Danny?'

Danny shrugged. 'About what?' he said. He put his half-finished beer on the side. 'I'm out of here,' he said, and headed for the exit. Before he reached it, however, the door opened and a young man entered. He was in his early twenties, with a scraggly beard and dark skin. Danny remembered thinking he was possibly Iraqi or Afghan. He was tall and slim, but exuded a wiry strength and a fierce intelligence. He silently acknowledged Danny, then turned to the others. 'I'm getting hungry,' he said. 'Shall we get some food on?' He sounded English. If there was any accent, it was south London.

'Bacon sarnies for dinner tonight, Abdul,' Bullock said. He leaned back and took a swig from his beer without taking his eyes off the young man.

'You want to be careful, Bullock,' Ollie said. 'Sniper training tomorrow.'

'I'll take my chances,' Bullock said. 'So what do you fancy, Abdul? Streaky or back?'

The question crackled in the silence. Finally the young man bowed his head. 'I'll see you all in the morning,' he said. Strangely dignified, he turned and left.

'Bacon for breakfast and all!' Bullock called after him, sniggering at his own joke.

The atmosphere had turned sour. Danny didn't want to be here. 'I'll see myself out,' he said. He left the kitchen and headed back down the flagstone hallway to the door. Before he left the house, however, he patted down his jacket. There were two Mars bars there, left over from the chocolate he'd bought at the village shop. He thought for a moment, then climbed the stairs at the other end of the hallway. It was dark on the landing, but he saw light leaking from the bottom of a door on the left. He approached it and knocked.

'Come in.'

Danny entered. The room was sparsely furnished, almost spartan. One single bed. One chair. A table and a rattling radiator. The young man was sitting on his bed reading a book. Danny chucked the Mars bars on to the bed. 'We're not all dickheads,' he said.

The young man lowered his book. 'Thank you,' he said. He frowned, as though deciding whether or not to accept the chocolate. 'I am very hungry,' he said. 'They worked me hard today.'

'You should ignore Bullock,' Danny said.

'Maybe. Maybe not. Sniper training tomorrow, after all.'

The two men grinned. 'You'd be doing us all a favour,' Danny said. 'I'm Danny, by the way. Danny Black.'

'Nice to meet you, Danny Black. I'm . . .'

And there, Danny's memory failed him. He couldn't remember the name of that polite young Muslim who had accepted the two Mars bars so gratefully. Maybe that was because, after leaving the room and the safe house, and driving all the way back to Hereford, he'd never thought about him again. Danny was embarking on the life of a Regiment soldier. A life where staying alive meant focusing on the present and not thinking too much about the past.

But Danny thought about him now, as he left Roscoe in the toilets and marched down the corridors of SAS HQ. And he thought about him that evening, as he sat alone in his flat, a microwave lasagne uneaten on the plate in front of him, some shit on TV playing mutely in the corner of the room. He couldn't *stop* thinking about him. That young Muslim man was a link between three SAS guys who had recently turned up dead and mutilated. Did he seem the type? Not really, Danny thought, but he checked himself. Bullock had been a right bastard to him that day. And knowing him as Danny did, there was little doubt that he'd been equally unpleasant in the days before and the days after. How much abuse could a guy take before deciding that some time, somewhere, he'd make things even?

Another thought occurred to him. It wasn't easy to kill an SAS man. The vigilance and situational awareness that kept them alive on the job soon became second nature. If you wanted to kill a Regiment guy, you needed to think like a Regiment guy. And who was more likely to do that than somebody who had been under the tutelage of an SAS training team?

Danny's mobile rang and he started. He pulled out his phone. Number withheld. He answered it as cautiously as always.

'Yeah?'

'It's me.' Danny recognised the voice of Ray Hammond, the ops officer.

'Ray, what the fuck, it's nearly midnight?'

'Then you'd better get your beauty sleep. I want you in here at 06.30 tomorrow.'

'What for?' Danny asked. But he'd have to wait to find out. The telephone line was dead.

Danny had a broken night. Mutilated SAS men populated his dreams, along with a tough, wiry young Muslim soldier who repeatedly introduced himself but whose name Danny couldn't quite catch. He got up at 04.30 and went for a run, pounding the slushy pavements of Hereford by lamplight, trying to clear his head. Maybe that would ease back into his memory the name that eluded him. But it was no good. It was tantalisingly close, but still just out of reach.

Danny was back at HQ by 06.00. He could tell, as soon as the MoD policeman at the gate let him into the base, that something was happening. Three black Mercedes with tinted windows were parked up outside the main building. They practically smelled of top brass. High-ranking army personnel, perhaps. Maybe MI6. He called through to Ray Hammond. Ray came to fetch him, and led him deep into the heart of the building, towards the secure central area that was known as the Kremlin.

'What's this all about, Ray?'

'You'll find out.'

'Who's in on the meet?'

But they were passing through a set of double doors and a clerk with an armful of files was coming the other way, so Hammond kept quiet. Only a few paces later, they were outside a secure briefing room. Hammond knocked. A male voice from inside said: 'Come!'

They entered. There were three other men in the briefing room. Danny recognised the CO Mike Williamson, of course. He was wearing standard military camouflage, as he always did around camp. Williamson was that rare thing: a Rupert who was well liked among the men. He had a handsome, leathery face with a pale scar on his chin. It was a face that spoke of many years working – and fighting – in deserts, jungles and other tough climates. He spoke to the guys with respect, and he earned that respect back. Danny always thought he seemed a little uncomfortable in the office. Williamson always struck him as a man more suited to the battlefield. He sat at a large table, ignoring the cup of coffee in front of him. Two older men sat either side of him. They were familiar, but Danny couldn't quite place them. The table was covered with folders and iPads. It might be early, but this meeting had obviously been going on for a while.

The CO stood up, walked round to Danny and shook his hand. 'At ease,' the CO said. 'Have a seat. Thanks, Ray. We'll take it from here.'

As Danny sat down he saw Ray Hammond's expression, scowling at his dismissal. But Hammond knew better than to argue, and left the room.

'Danny Black,' the CO continued. 'Meet George Attwood, Director Special Forces, and Alan Sturrock, Chief of SIS.'

Danny nodded at the two men. Like Williamson, Attwood had the lined, leathery face of a soldier who had spent years in hot countries. Danny noticed that he had a disfigurement between the thumb and forefinger on his right hand, and recognised it as an old bullet wound. His hair was grey and bushy, his eyes sparkling blue. A handome bastard, but steely.

Sturrock, the MI6 guy, was the opposite. Pale, gaunt, with sunken, yellowing eyes and thinning black hair. He had the complexion of a man who rarely saw the sun. His suit was immaculately cut – Danny could tell it was expensive – and he wore his blue tie in an Oxford knot. He looked more like a guest at a society wedding than the head of MI6. His hands were in front of him, fingertips together, and Danny noticed that they were well manicured. Danny remembered seeing him on TV, asserting that the modern security services were open, inclusive and entirely above board. He'd been very convincing. But that was part of a spy's job, of course. To convince.

'You're probably wondering why we called you in,' the CO said.

Danny didn't answer immediately. He thought of Ben Bullock, Liam Armitage and Ollie Moorhouse. He thought of the old guest house in Dartmoor, and the young Muslim man sitting on his bed, thanking him for the meagre gift of two Mars bars. And unbidden, a name dropped into his head.

'I think you've called me in to talk about Ibrahim Khan,' he said.

3

The three men looked at each other. They were plainly surprised. Unnerved, even. It was Sturrock, the chief of MI6, who broke the silence. He gave the impression of a man choosing his words carefully. 'What exactly do you know,' he said, 'about Ibrahim Khan?' His accent made Jacob Rees-Mogg sound like Danny Dyer.

'I know five years ago he was holed up in a safe house with Bullock, Armitage and Moorhouse. They were providing a training package for him and they were treating him like shit. At least Bullock and Armitage were. Fast forward five years, the three SAS men end up dead within a few weeks of each other. Something's got to link them all. I saw the way Bullock spoke to Khan. Threatening to feed him bacon sandwiches, the usual shit. Armitage would have done the same as Bullock. Moorhouse was different, but maybe he got tarred with the same brush. Call it a hunch, but I reckon Ibrahim Khan's the link. It's not easy to overpower and kill a Regiment guy. Unless you've been trained up by one, of course. I think he killed them.'

Danny's accusation hung in the air. He had the impression that the three older men were uncertain about who should speak next. In the end, it was the CO. 'You're right,' he said, 'and you're wrong. We also believe that Khan was responsible for these murders, but not for the reasons you think. What we're about to tell you doesn't leave this room, Danny. You're bound by the Official Secrets Act and . . .'

'I get it, boss,' Danny said.

The CO nodded, then turned to Sturrock. 'Alan?' he said.

'Are you sure this is our man?' Sturrock said.

'He's the only remaining person in the Regiment, past or present, who saw Khan alongside Bullock, Armitage and Moorhouse,' the CO said.

'Is that really such an advantage? There must be others who can recognise him, and we can brief people perfectly well with photographic material . . .'

'He's our guy,' said Attwood. It was the first time the Director Special Forces had spoken. His voice was deep and authoritative. His words brought Sturrock's argument to a swift conclusion, but Danny could tell from the way Sturrock flinched, almost imperceptibly, that there was tension between these two. He reckoned neither of them would want to admit that the other had any kind of authority over him.

'Very well,' Sturrock said. 'If you're certain.' He put his hand in his pocket and withdrew a small plastic bottle. For a moment, Danny couldn't work out what it was. Then he realised. The guy was applying hand cream. He squeezed a little dollop into one palm, then vigorously rubbed it in. There was an awkward silence, broken only by the slight squelch of the moisturised skin. Williamson and Attwood stared straight ahead, as if too embarrassed to acknowledge what this dandy of a spook was doing.

Sturrock put his bottle of moisturiser back in his pocket and cleared his throat. 'Ibrahim Khan,' he said. 'Son of second-generation Iraqi parents. Father an engineer, mother a health worker. Khan himself was a straight-A student at school, expected to go to university to read modern languages. He applied to join the British Army instead. Passed into 1 Para at the age of nineteen.'

'Bloody good little soldier,' Attwood interrupted, to Sturrock's visible annoyance. 'We had him earmarked for the Special Forces Support Group almost from day one.'

Danny had a lot of respect for the SFSG. They were a skilled unit of operators, taken from the Paras, the Royal Marines and the RAF Regiment, who had supported the SAS and the SBS on operations since the mid-2000s, by cordoning off areas where the guys were operating, or providing extra firepower and personnel where necessary.

'He was the first British Muslim to join the support group,' Attwood continued. 'Worth his weight in gold in Helmand, working with the Afghan commandos against the Taliban. Fought as hard as any of the white guys, and it's amazing what one brown face in a British unit can do to help gain the Afghans' trust.'

'Quite,' said Sturrock. He was clearly peeved that Attwood had taken over the talking.

'Khan made a bit of a name for himself in the SFSG,' Attwood said. 'So we headhunted him for the Special Reconnaissance Regiment.'

'I never saw him around,' Danny said. The Special Reconnaissance Regiment was a covert team of special forces personnel who specialised in surveillance and reconnaissance operations that was once the remit of the SAS. They evolved from 14 Intelligence Company, the surveillance unit that supported the Regiment in Northern Ireland, and were based alongside the SAS at RAF Credenhill. If Khan had been one of them, Danny would have encountered him eventually.

'That's because ...' Attwood started to say. But Sturrock interrupted him. 'George,' he said, smiling blandly but not looking directly at the DSF. 'I know I'm always giving you fellows boring things to do out in the field, but in this instance, I think it's best that I do the talking, don't you?'

Attwood looked like he was going to argue. But in the end, he just inclined his head and said: 'We're in an office, Alan. More your domain than mine.'

Sturrock gave a thin-lipped, humourless smile at the implied criticism. His hand went for the moisturiser in his pocket, but he seemed to check himself and pressed his fingertips together again. 'It makes perfect sense,' he said to Danny, 'that you never saw Khan around. His recruitment into the SRR was part of a longer game. He spent very little time with the unit itself. When you met him at that safe house in Dartmoor, he was receiving a higher level of training from the SAS, not usually available to the SRR. Khan's ethnicity and high level of ability meant he was too good a prospect to waste. That's what Bullock, Armitage and Moorhouse were doing. It was part of an operation code-named MISFIT. Once Khan's training was complete, we orchestrated the next stage in the MISFIT plan. Namely: we kicked him out of the SRR.'

'Why?'

'For goodness sake, man, I'm getting to that. The pretext for Ibrahim Khan's dismissal was that he'd been found in possession of extremist literature. It meant he failed the vetting process and was out on his ear. He moved to London and started attending a mosque in Harlesden that we knew to be a recruiting ground for various Islamist cells.' Sturrock sniffed, then glanced at Attwood and the CO. He was plainly reluctant to divulge what needed to be said next, but neither of his colleagues helped him out. Attwood pinched the bridge of his nose before continuing. 'We have a Saudi mole in MI6.'

Danny's surprise must have registered on his face. 'Exactly,' Sturrock said. 'You are now one of only a handful of people who know that information, and if it leaks you'll be the first person we drag in to question. Understood?'

Danny replied with a small shrug.

'The mole is a low-level intelligence analyst and we've known about him from the very beginning. Nothing of any importance passes his desk, and it occasionally suits our purposes to feed him some misinformation that we'd like to pass the Saudis' way. Like it or not, they're still one of the biggest funders of Islamist activity in the UK. We gave our mole the nugget that Khan had been expelled from the SRR for suspected radicalisation, then we sat back and waited. It took about three months, but he got the tap on the shoulder just as we were expecting him to. He was just too tempting a prospect. There was the usual flirtation. Khan pretended not to be interested at first, his new friends at the mosque refused to take no for an answer. Long story short, he agreed to attend an IS training camp in Syria. After that, he was a shoo-in. IS had a British special forces-trained operator on their books, or so they thought. In reality, Khan was passing weapons-grade intelligence back to London. It's no exaggeration to say that Ibrahim Khan was our most fruitful embedded agent of the last thirty years. We estimate that the MISFIT intelligence prevented eight major atrocities on British soil, and in large part led to the downfall of IS's operations in the Middle East.'

'Right. I thought IS were pretty much dead in the water anyway.'

'By no means. It's true they've been largely eradicated from Iraq, and their positions have been weakened in Syria. Some of their members have splintered into separate Islamist groups. But they're still an active force, disparate but regrouping, and a substantial threat, both to the West and to the ordinary people of the Middle East. We ignore them at our peril. If they *have* been weakened, however, we have MISFIT to thank to a very great extent.'

Sturrock sounded extremely pleased with himself. He frowned when Attwood said: 'We have MISFIT to thank for some almighty fuck-ups, too.'

'Yes,' Sturrock said, closing his eyes. 'Yes, quite.' He seemed to gather his thoughts. 'About six months ago, Ibrahim Khan dropped off the radar. He failed to show at a scheduled meeting with his SIS handler and we received none of the prearranged warning signals to indicate that he was compromised. We discussed inserting a special forces team to extract him, but drone footage indicated his last known location in Syria was deserted.'

'Basically, we didn't have a bloody clue where he was,' Attwood said.

'We put out feelers, of course,' Sturrock continued, 'but for his own safety we couldn't be too overt about it. Snippets of chatter started to come back. It soon became abundantly clear to us that he'd flipped.'

Danny frowned. 'I don't get it,' he said. 'If IS had worked out he was a double, why not send him back to his handler with false intel for us?'

'We asked ourselves the same question. It may be that Khan's loyalties gradually aligned with IS without them learning that he was a British agent. More likely, they're just not sophisticated enough to employ their new asset against us. Most IS members are brutal, nasty and extreme, but they're not too bright. It would appeal to their world view to despatch their new convert to take revenge on the very people who trained him up in the first place.'

Sturrock opened a file in front of him and withdrew a sheaf of A4 photographs which he laid out on the table in front of Danny. He didn't have to ask what they were. Bullock, Armitage and Moorhouse looked different in death, but they were still recognisable. Even Danny, who was used to scenes of blood and gristle, avoided looking at the single picture of Moorhouse's genitals surrounded by a patch of blood-soaked carpet. 'The Ghanaian scene of crime evidence is a bit ropey,' Sturrock said. He was right. The pictures of Armitage with his fingers laid out on his chest were more blurry and slapdash than the others. 'But the Dubai and Florida authorities did a good job. The Palm Beach Police Department even found DNA evidence of Khan's presence at the crime scene. A pubic hair, believe it or not. You could say we've got him by the short and curlies.' He smiled, and glanced at Attwood and the CO for confirmation that his joke was a good one. It was not forthcoming. He cleared his throat again.

'How many other SAS men knew about Khan's training package?' Danny asked.

'One,' Attwood replied. 'You.' He smiled at Danny's refusal to show any response. 'Don't worry. We don't actually think you're a target. The real question is: who else was involved in Operation MISFIT?'

Danny looked at the MI6 chief, as if to say: him, for a start.

'Actually, no,' Sturrock said. 'Perfectly proper that I shouldn't know his name, of course,' he said quickly, as if to dispel the idea that this might indicate a lack of authority. 'I was aware of the MISFIT intelligence and I discussed it at the highest level. But I was rightly kept away from the day-to-day handling of the agent. I wasn't even aware of his name until a couple of days ago. Rule number one of running a deeply embedded agent is that the fewer people who know his or her identity, the better. In this instance, only six individuals were fully indoctrinated into MISFIT. Bullock, Armitage, Moorhouse and three others.'

'These three others,' Danny said. 'How's their health?'

'Precarious,' the Director Special Forces said. 'That's where you come in.'

Danny felt his spirits deflate. 'A bodyguarding job?' he said. 'That's what this is?' He appealed to the CO. 'Boss, I . . .'

'Relax, Black. It's not that.'

'We have men – and women, for that matter – guarding the three remaining targets,' Attwood said. 'But it's not a long-term solution. If we're to guarantee their safety, we need to deal with the threat itself. That means finding Ibrahim Khan, and eliminating him.'

The three men gave Danny a level gaze. 'I'll need a team,' Danny said.

The DSF shook his head. 'No team, Black. You know how quickly rumours spread around this place. We can't be sure Khan doesn't still have eyes and ears in the SFSG or the SRR. Maybe that was how he caught up with Bullock, Armitage and Moorhouse. This whole operation needs to be kept tight. Make no mistake: Ibrahim Khan is perhaps the most important British operative of recent times. We need to keep information about the MISFIT fiasco under wraps.'

'Absolutely,' said Sturrock. 'If word about it leaks, it'll be a massive embarrassment for MI6 and Whitehall.'

The DSF held up one finger, as if to stop Danny from interrupting. 'I don't expect you to care about that. There's another reason word of this conversation can't leave the room. The more people know, the more potential targets we create for Khan.

Bottom line, Black: it's you against him. We know your record. We think that of all our assets, you're best suited to the job.'

'Well we hope you are, at least,' said Sturrock.

Danny glanced at the pictures spread out on the table in front of him. Then back up at the older men. 'Who are the remaining three targets?' he said.

Sturrock nodded his reluctant approval of the question. 'Target one,' he said, 'is Colonel Henry Bishop. Served with distinction in Gulf War I, Scots Guards, before moving into the intelligence field in the late '90s. Operation MISFIT was his baby. He identified Ibrahim Khan as a possible asset in the first place and sweet-talked him into the whole scheme. He retired when MISFIT went dark.'

'Retired?' Danny said. 'Or asked to leave?'

Sturrock blithely evaded the question. 'He was of the age,' he said.

'He's a prize shit, Black,' Attwood said. 'Watch your step about him.'

Sturrock gave Attwood a barely suppressed glare. 'He has a country estate in Wales,' he continued. 'We've tried to persuade him to move to a more secure location but he won't have it. He knows what a headache it will be for us if Khan pays him a visit, and that we're obliged to provide whatever security is necessary to keep him safe. He has three men watching him, day and night. Good men.'

'Armed?'

'Of course. But they don't know any specific details about the threat.'

Danny looked at the pictures again. 'Khan will get past them,' he said. 'Somehow.'

'The colonel's well protected,' Sturrock said.

'Khan will get past them,' Danny repeated. 'In his sleep.'

'Well even if he does, the colonel's convinced he can talk his former protégé round.'

'Has he seen the picture of Moorhouse's bollocks on the carpet?'

Sturrock looked down his nose, as if such language was beneath him. 'Target number two,' he said, 'is Bethany White. She was Khan's case officer. She works out of Vauxhall with occasional trips abroad to meet agents. Bethany has been living and sleeping in the MI6 building for the past few nights – we have resources for that.'

'She can't stay in the MI6 building forever.'

'No, she can't. But until we find Khan, that's where she remains. She's a bloody good case officer, and was always very close to Khan. We think she'll be high on his list.'

'And target number three?'

'Christina Somers. She's a language specialist who was part of the training team alongside Bullock, Armitage and Moorhouse. Khan needed fluency in various Arabic dialects. Christina Somers is the best there is. She's in a separate safe house, not a million miles away from the colonel, as it happens.'

'And that's it?' Danny said.

'Henry Bishop, Bethany White, Christina Somers.' Sturrock ticked them off on his fingers. 'Apart from us in this room, they're the only people with in-depth knowledge of the MISFIT situation. And they're the only three that Khan knows by name and sight.'

Danny absorbed that information.

'You don't have much to go on, Black,' the CO said. 'Khan's last-known whereabouts was Syria, but that lead's gone cold.'

Danny nodded. The world was big. Ibrahim Khan was one man and he could be anywhere in it. He remembered again the few seconds of contact he'd had with his target. He saw the young man sitting on his bed, reading, calm and patient despite Bullock's taunting. His eyes fell on the photographs again. The spooks were right. He had to be found, and fast. It wasn't going to be easy. Ibrahim Khan might be a butcher, but he was also a thoughtful individual. Clever. Skilled. He wouldn't be easy to locate. The only hope Danny had of finding him, he decided, was by getting inside his head first. That meant speaking to the people who knew him.

'Tell us what you need,' Attwood said.

She's a bloody good case officer and was always very close to Khan. We think she'll be high on his list.

Danny's first move was obvious. 'I need to talk to Bethany White,' he said.

4

The briefing was over. Sturrock stood up and walked round to Danny's side of the table. Danny noticed that he wore blue socks that matched his blue tie and that he smelled slightly floral. Probably the hand moisturiser. He handed Danny a card. 'My direct line,' he said. The card had no name on it. Just a mobile number. 'You seem like a good chap,' he said. 'Call me if you need anything.' Danny knew how unusual it was for the head of MI6 to give an ordinary SAS soldier direct access, but he wasn't fooled by Sturrock's sudden smarminess. He pocketed the card, nodded, and watched the chief leave.

As soon as the door was shut, the CO scraped back his chair and stood up. 'Let's be clear, Black,' he said. 'You report straight back to us, not to him. Is that understood?'

'Roger that,' Danny said. He didn't want to get caught in the tension between Hereford and Vauxhall, but he preferred to be in contact with military guys like Williamson and Attwood, rather than some oily creep in a suit like Sturrock.

He travelled alone to London that same morning. Word had leaked that he'd been pulled in by the head shed. Roscoe was already hovering, but Danny managed to keep his distance. He checked out of the armoury a Sig P38 9mm – a good compact handgun for concealed carry around London – and shoulder holster, then hit the road.

Just after midday, having left his vehicle in the personnel car park in the basement of the MI6 building by the Thames, he found himself in the reception area being frisked by two armed security men. They felt every last fold of his leather jacket and stonewashed jeans. They examined his belt buckle and asked him to remove his shoes. They found nothing – Danny had stowed his Sig in his car. They let him proceed to an internal barrier where a young woman in a neat trouser suit was waiting for him. She had an ID card on a lanyard around her neck. 'Follow me, please,' she said. She scanned her ID card to open the barriers and Danny followed her into the MI6 building.

The building comprised a complex network of corridors illuminated by strip lighting. Although the exterior architecture of the building was modern, inside it was rather dated. Thin, worn carpet tiles on the floor. Scuffed paintwork and an out-of-order sign on one of the toilets they passed. It was also strangely silent. The men and women they passed carrying files or coffee cups paid them no attention and barely seemed to talk to each other. There was nothing to indicate that this was the beating heart of the security services. It could have been any other anonymous office block.

They passed an area where rows of people sat at computers analysing data, before going through two sets of doors that Danny's escort had to unlock with an ID card. They stopped outside a plain door. 'You can go straight in,' she said. 'She's expecting you.'

Bethany White's office was simple but comfortable, with a trace of perfume in the air. There was a small desk with a laptop, an Anglepoise lamp and a photograph in a silver frame. There was a three-seater sofa. No windows. A wall-mounted air-conditioning unit hummed noisily. By the desk was a small suitcase. Danny guessed the woman sitting behind the desk reading some papers had been living out of that for the past few days. The woman herself was tall – almost as tall as Danny himself – with blonde hair and golden freckles on her nose and cheeks. She looked up from her papers.

'Air-conditioning?' she said.

'What?'

She pointed behind her. 'It's been playing up for days, I don't know why they haven't sent someone sooner.' She was well spoken, her posh accent tempered by a slight West Country burr. She went back to reading her papers.

Danny walked past her desk and up to the air-conditioning. He thumped it heavily with a clenched fist. The noise stopped for a few seconds, then returned, even louder.

'I'd say it's fucked,' Danny said. He walked back to her desk. 'Maybe you could ask Ibrahim Khan to fix it when he rocks up.'

He knew immediately he shouldn't have said it. The woman lowered her head and inhaled deeply. Something in that movement expressed all the tension and fear she was feeling. But she recovered quickly. 'You're not the maintenance guy?' she said.

'Right.'

'Danny Black? From Hereford?' Danny nodded. 'I suppose you'd better sit down.'

'I'll stand.'

'As you please.' She neatened her papers. 'I'm Bethany White, senior operations officer responsible for the Middle East. Sturrock told me you were on your way. I understand you want to ask me some questions?' She said it with a hint of scorn. No doubt, as an MI6 case officer, she would have had contact with SAS men before, but she would have been used to calling the shots. She clearly didn't relish the idea of being questioned by a military grunt.

'I take it you know what your friend Khan's been up to?' Danny said.

'Sturrock showed me the pictures. I wish he hadn't.'

'Did it look to you like his handiwork?'

'Of course. He was forever cutting people's testicles off. That's why I liked him so much. Forgive me for saying it, Mr Black, but if this conversation is going to go anywhere, you'll have to stop asking stupid questions like that.'

'You liked him?' Danny asked, unruffled.

'Sure,' Bethany said. 'We worked together for a long time. Regular meetings.'

'Where?'

'Beirut, of course. Look, I'm busy. Didn't Sturrock tell you all this?'

'I want to hear it from you.'

'Will you bloody well sit down? You're putting me on edge, hovering over me like that.' She pinched the bridge of her nose.

Bethany had made a good attempt at appearing calm and confident when Danny walked in, but it was already unravelling. She was clearly very scared. Danny inclined his head, then took a seat on the sofa. 'When did you last sleep?' he asked.

'That's none of your business.'

'Fine. How often did you meet him?'

'Khan? Every two months.'

'Why Beirut?' Danny asked.

'He was operating in Syria. It shares a border with Lebanon. Beirut's the capital.'

'Thanks for the geography lesson. I'm guessing he didn't tell his IS handlers he was holidaying in Beirut every two months. So what did they think he was doing there?'

Danny had the impression that Bethany White was unaccustomed to revealing information about her agent. After years of protecting his identity and his movements, it must feel unnatural to open up about him. 'That's classified,' she said.

'Right,' Danny said. He pulled out his phone. 'We'll call Sturrock now and get clearance.'

'Oh, for God's sake put your phone away,' she said waspishly. 'There's a businessman there. Lebanese. He runs a successful shipping company around the Mediterranean. But he's got Islamist sympathies and he's a regular IS donor. His donations come in cash, every two months. One of Ibrahim's jobs was to cross the border into Lebanon, drive to Beirut, pick up the currency and take it back into Syria, avoiding all the border crossings and checkpoints on the way. I'd stay in the British Embassy and we'd meet for a couple of hours during each visit.'

'Not in the embassy itself?'

'Of course not.'

'Then where?'

'Hotel rooms. Never the same one twice.'

'How did he know where to meet you?'

'You sound like you don't believe me?'

Danny stood up. 'There was this guy,' he said. 'He had some information I needed, but he didn't want to give it up. I took off the little finger of his left hand. I was a bit worried he'd pass out with the pain, but I didn't have to take any more off before he started talking.' Bethany was staring at him without expression. 'Ibrahim took all ten of Armitage's fingers, and out of the three SAS men he's killed, I reckon Armitage got off lightest. Bunking down in the MI6 building isn't a good long-term solution to stop Ibrahim Khan from getting to you and doing the same thing. The only way to stop him is to catch him. If I'm going to do that, you need to tell me everything I ask. Let's try again: how did he know where to meet you?'

Bethany did a good – but not entirely successful – job of hiding her nerves. She was hesitant and stumbled over her words, but she did reply. 'His meetings occurred roughly every two months at the businessman's offices in Beirut. There was a cafe nearby where I would have a coffee. If Ibrahim's shoulder bag was on his right shoulder as he was walking up to the offices, it meant it was safe to meet later. If it was over his left, it wasn't.'

'Did that ever happen?'

'Never. Once I had the signal, I would send a WhatsApp message to a phone he kept in Beirut solely for this purpose. Don't ask me where he kept it, because I don't know. The message would include the lat and long of the hotel where we were to meet, along with the room number. The message itself was encrypted according to a one-time pad we shared. Plus the WhatsApp encryption, of course.'

Danny nodded approvingly. Bethany's tradecraft told him nothing about Khan's whereabouts, but it told him plenty about Bethany: she was experienced, careful, and knew how to operate securely and in secret. It crossed his mind that they'd make a good team: her tradecraft and local knowledge, his readiness to apply extreme violence when the situation required it.

If only she could get over her clearly ingrained notion that in a relationship between an MI6 case officer and an SAS grunt, she should be the one calling the shots.

'This businessman,' Danny said. 'How did he receive instructions about when the RVs were to occur?'

'We never found out. Our working theory was always that it was from somebody in his network of business associates.'

'It wasn't from Ibrahim himself?'

'No. They never had any contact apart from the face-to-face meetings and they only lasted a couple of minutes: hello, hand over the money, goodbye.'

'Did this businessman know Ibrahim's real name?'

'Of course not. He simply knew him as Ahmed.'

'Ibrahim must have given you other leads, too? IS contacts that he made. People we can track down to see if we have any idea where he is.'

'He gave me lots of names. But IS positions in Syria have taken a pounding. Everyone we knew who had contact with Ibrahim has been killed in air strikes or ground troop movements. To be honest with you, I thought that was what happened to Ibrahim himself. There was an IS pocket in southern Syria called Tulul al-Safa which the Syrian government forces pretty much wiped from the face of the earth – thanks to intelligence from Ibrahim himself, I should say. A few IS fighters managed to escape to other locations, but there was never any word from Ibrahim. I thought perhaps he'd been on the ground there at the time of the air strikes, and was a casualty of them, until his DNA showed up at a crime scene in Palm Beach.'

Danny pointed at the picture frame on her desk. He could only see the back. 'Who's in the photo?' he asked, abruptly changing the subject.

'My son,' she said.

Danny tried not to appear surprised. Sturrock had never mentioned that Bethany had a kid. 'How old?'

'Five.'

'Where is he now?'

'They didn't tell you?'

'Obviously.'

'He's with Christina. Christina Somers.'

Danny couldn't help registering his astonishment. Christina Somers was the third target, currently ensconced in a safe house under armed protection. 'How's that supposed to be safe? Can't he be with his dad?'

Bethany gave him a cool look. 'I don't know who his father is,' she said. 'It could be one of several men, none of whom I want to see again.' She gave him a mischievous little smile. 'Maybe that shocks you?' she said.

'What shocks me,' Danny said, 'is that he's being looked after by somebody else on Khan's hit list.'

'It's either that, or he stays with me.' She indicated the building in general. 'I can't keep him here. Christina's an old friend of mine. We go way back and she looks after Danny when I'm out of the country anyway. He's comfortable with her.'

'Danny?'

'You're not the only one in the world.' She lowered her eyes. 'I know it might sound reckless,' she said. 'But the truth is, Danny's also at risk. Christina's location is completely secret. I know where she is, and so does the chief. They've got a couple of close-protection guys, but they don't know the full story about Ibrahim. There's no way for him to find them. I'm an easier prospect. I don't intend to put my life on hold. Danny's safest with her.' Her eyes flashed as she said this. Danny found himself respecting her a little more.

'Okay,' he said. 'I get it.' He thought momentarily. 'This Lebanese businessman. What's his name?'

'Mohammad Al-Farouk.'

'Is he still in Beirut.'

'To the best of my knowledge.'

'Have you ever met him?'

'Of course not,' Bethany said. 'If he knew what I looked like, and then by chance saw me with Ibrahim, we'd be blown.'

'But he's been under surveillance?'

'From time to time. We know his general movements, where he lives, where his kids go to school, all the usual stuff. I keep my handling notes in my personal safe at the embassy in Beirut. The MISFIT intel is too sensitive to trust to the MI6 servers or the diplomatic bag. I keep it all analogue, in-country.'

Danny processed that for a minute. 'How well do you know Beirut?' he asked.

'Like the back of my hand. I must have visited it thirty or forty times, and when you're handling an agent, you need local knowledge.'

'You speak Arabic?'

'Of course.'

'Then that decides it,' Danny said.

'Decides what?'

'I need to talk to Al-Farouk. You're the best person to help me do that. We're going to Beirut.'

She stared at him. 'Absolutely not,' she said.

Danny gave her a cool stare.

'Look,' Bethany said, 'I don't know who you think you are, but if you imagine *I'm* going to be taking instructions from *you*, you can think again.'

Danny didn't reply.

'It's not safe, anyway,' Bethany continued. 'This is the safest place I can be, or so they tell me . . .'

Danny kept quiet.

'And anyway . . . I've been out of the country too much lately. I need to be within reach of my son, especially now.'

'I understand.'

'No you don't.'

'I've got a daughter,' Danny said. 'She's been in danger before, because of my job. I don't get to see her much. I know what it's like.'

Bethany inclined her head, as though reluctant to concede the point. Then, without warning, she bowed her head and put her face in her hands. Danny looked around. Here they were, in perhaps the most secure building in London, and this woman was plainly terrified for her life.

When Danny spoke again, his voice was a little softer. 'I'm going to promise you something,' he said. 'It doesn't matter whether you're in Beirut or Vauxhall, you're safer with me than with anyone else. You're a smart operator, I can tell that. So am I. We're going to fly to Beirut, we're going to interview Al-Farouk, and then we're going to find Ibrahim Khan. When we find him, I'm going to deal with him. End of problem. But I need your help. I need your local knowledge. I need your handling notes. And I need you to help me get inside Khan's head. What do you say?'

Bethany was clearly unsure. She was silent for a minute, her eyes closed. Danny supposed she was weighing up the risks and benefits. She opened her eyes. 'I want to see my son before we go,' she said.

'Deal,' Danny said. 'And I want to see Colonel Henry Bishop.' An expression of distaste crossed Bethany's face. 'Problem?'

'Not at all,' Bethany said, 'if you're a guy and you went to a posh public school. He's got an attitude towards women and plebs – his word, not mine. The only good thing about Ibrahim going off the radar was that I didn't have to make weekly reports to the colonel. He always insisted on face to face, if you get my drift.' She looked away. 'I know his type well enough, anyway,' she said.

Danny wondered what she meant, but didn't pursue it. 'We won't be there long,' he said. 'I just want his take on the situation.' He paused. 'What's *your* take on the situation, Bethany? You knew Ibrahim better than anybody. Why do you think he's doing this?'

Bethany didn't reply immediately. She stood up and turned her back to him. Danny couldn't help noticing how shapely she was. The slope of her shoulder. The curve of her hip. She was the sort of woman who men would do things for. No wonder she had found herself running agents. He wondered what Khan thought of her. 'The handler-agent relationship is a strange one,' she said. 'Officially your job is to debrief them, motivate them, and occasionally pay them. But really, your most important job is to befriend them. It's a lonely life they lead, and you become their only link to the outside world. It becomes like a clandestine affair.

You get to know each other's quirks and worries and pressure points. Ibrahim wasn't my only agent. I've run men and women all over the world. They all have moments when they doubt what they're doing. I constantly have to reassure them. To let them know that we're there for them, and their safety is our paramount concern – which it is, by the way. I never had to do that with Ibrahim. He was always calm and resolute. He knew he was fighting the good fight, and he never wavered. Not once.'

'Or,' Danny said, 'he was very good at making you think that. Seems to me, if an agent shows no sign of concern for his own safety, it means he's hiding something.'

'Maybe,' Bethany said. 'I certainly got him wrong, anyway.'

'Where do you think he is?'

Bethany stared into the middle distance. 'Sometimes,' she said, 'I think he's back in Syria. Other times, I think he's infiltrated the building and he's outside in the corridor, about to burst in on me. He could do that, you know?'

'I know,' Danny said quietly. 'That's why we need to catch him. Are you in?'

Bethany frowned. 'If I'm coming to Beirut with you, I'll need to get it cleared by Sturrock. It can take a while to get a conversation with him.' She picked up the phone on her desk.

'Don't worry about that,' Danny said. He pulled out his mobile along with Sturrock's card, put it on speaker phone, and dialled. Bethany looked astonished when Sturrock answered his phone immediately. 'It's me,' Danny said. 'We've got a lead. I need to get to Beirut and I'm taking Bethany White with me.'

5

The arrangements took less than an hour. An RAF flight to Tel Aviv was scheduled for the following morning at 08.00. Hereford arranged for it to be diverted to Beirut. That would give them time to pay the colonel a visit and look in on Christina and Danny junior, as Danny now thought of him. Bethany made some calls to ensure they were expected. Danny waited outside Bethany's office so the MI6 officer could change out of her business suit. She emerged wearing jeans, a Barbour jacket and an Alice band. Quite the Sloane Ranger, Danny thought to himself. They drew curious glances as they walked back through the corridors of the MI6 buildings and signed out.

Bethany knew the colonel's address, and she knew where Christina and her boy were being held in a safe house. She'd softened slightly, but clearly hadn't quite let go of the idea that she should be in charge. She refused to give Danny the location of the safe house. 'I'll tell you when you need to know,' she said. 'Not before. The colonel's house is on the outskirts of Brynmawr, just to the south of the Brecon Beacons.

'Says it all,' Danny said as they drove away from the MI6 building.

'I don't follow you.'

'Retired army officer sets up shop a few miles from Pen-y-Fan, where SAS selection takes place. As far as I know he never served with the Regiment, but he'll be happy for people to draw their own conclusions.'

'Trust me,' Bethany said. 'You'll draw all the conclusions you need the minute you meet him. If the MISFIT intel hadn't been so productive, he'd have been out on his ear years ago.' She plugged the colonel's address in to Danny's satnav. ETA: 17.00 hrs.

'That thing you mentioned,' Danny said, 'back in your office, about knowing the colonel's type. What did you mean?'

'It doesn't matter,' Bethany said. Danny didn't push it. They sat in silence for a few seconds. 'My father was cut from the same cloth,' she said finally. 'Military man, moved into intelligence. He was quite the legend in the Service before he retired and moved us all down to Devon. Pleased as punch when I got the tap on the shoulder at Oxford. Probably arranged it himself.'

'You didn't get on?'

Bethany shrugged. 'Let's just say he wasn't quite what he pretended to be.'

'What do you mean?'

'I don't have to answer these questions, you know?'

'I'm just making conversation,' Danny said.

'Yeah, right.' She paused again, then continued without any prompting from Danny. 'My whole life, all he ever talked about was queen and country. I went on an anti-government student march once. He saw me on TV. I thought he might disown me, he was so furious. Thought I'd fallen in with a bunch of anarchists.

'Had you?'

'Of course not. I was a history student. It's what we did. Once I'd moved up the ranks at MI6 though, looked into a few files, it turned out my dear daddy was just as grubby and morally compromised as everybody else.'

'We all have to do things we don't like in this line of work,' Danny said. 'Goes with the territory.'

'I know that. But a little authenticity would be nice, now and then, wouldn't you say?' Then she frowned and shook her head, as though she regretted having been so open in front of him.

Danny didn't have an answer for her, but for some reason the image of Ibrahim Khan dropped into his head again. Khan had seemed like one of the good guys, and from what she'd said Bethany had seen that in him too. Maybe he'd revealed himself to be another in a long line of men who'd turned out not to be what she'd thought.

They were driving along the south side of the river now, and Danny noticed a white Peugeot two cars behind. It stayed close for the next ten minutes. 'There's a . . .' Bethany started to say.

'I'm on it,' Danny told her.

He drove twice round the Wandsworth Bridge roundabout. The Peugeot stuck close. 'Clumsy,' Danny said.

'Is it him?' Bethany asked. Danny could tell she was trying to sound nonchalant. She wasn't succeeding.

'No,' he said.

'How can you be so sure?'

'Ibrahim Khan was trained up by the Regiment. He's killed three SAS guys. If he was following us, we wouldn't notice him. At least, not so easily.'

'So who is it?'

'My guess is Sturrock wants to keep an eye on us. Don't worry. I'll lose them when we get on the motorway.' When they were a couple of junctions along the M4, he did just that, pulling up on the hard shoulder while the white Peugeot went speeding past. 'Muppets,' Danny said. He waited for five minutes, then came off at the next junction and re-programmed the satnav to take them cross-country. It delayed their ETA for forty-five minutes, but it seemed to put Bethany's mind at rest. She even slept, leaving Danny to concentrate on the road, and on the task ahead of him.

Al-Farouk, the Lebanese businessman, was a lead but a tenuous one. The chance that he'd know Khan's location was tiny. He might, though, have other contacts with more information. Danny would just have to get him to talk. He hoped Bethany had the stomach for whatever that might entail. He knew MI6 officers had basic firearms training, but there was no way Bethany could be as comfortable with application of extreme measures as Danny was.

But there were others to speak to first. Colonel Henry Bishop for a start. Operation MISFIT was his baby, and it had gone sour. That was a black mark against him. Danny expected the stubbornness of a Rupert unable to admit he'd messed up. Why else would he be insisting on staying in his own home, when the threat against him was real and imminent? It was a stupid and stubborn attempt to save face. Danny wondered why MI6 were even standing for it. He was supposedly heading to the colonel's house to see if he could shed any light on Ibrahim Khan's whereabouts. In reality, Danny was just ticking boxes.

The light was failing as they returned to the M4 and crossed the Severn Bridge. The snow had returned. It swirled heavily, compromising visibility and forcing Danny to drive slower than he'd have liked. As they reached Brynmawr it was dark and below zero. Bethany was awake again. She seemed cross with herself for having fallen asleep.

Half a mile along the only road that led to the colonel's house, an SUV blocked their path. A man in a puffer jacket stood in the road, wincing slightly from the glare of the oncoming headlights. Danny came to a halt and the man walked towards the car. Danny lowered his window. 'He's expecting us,' he said.

'Names?' The man's breath steamed in the cold night air. He had snow in his beard.

'Danny Black, Bethany White.'

The man nodded. 'Drive up to the house, son. Wait by the car. You'll be searched before you can enter.'

He returned to the SUV and let them pass.

'Security's high,' Bethany observed as they drove towards the house.

'You think?' Danny said. 'We could have nailed him in about two seconds flat.'

'We?' Bethany said, one eyebrow arched.

'I. And if I was closing in on the colonel I wouldn't approach by road anyway.'

The house appeared up ahead through the blizzard: hard to make out in much detail because of the snow, but imposing – an immense outline against the dark sky, with yellow light spilling from numerous windows. Danny's vehicle crunched to a halt in front of some stone steps that led to the front door. He didn't bother to holster his weapon as he knew he'd never get it into the house. He and Bethany alighted and stood together in the driving snow, powder accumulating in their hair. The front door opened and another man emerged. He descended the steps and wordlessly frisked the newcomers, then nodded. 'In you go,' he said. 'First room on the right.'

Danny and Bethany hurried into the house. It was warm here. The snow on their clothes melted immediately. A further guard stood at the door his colleague had indicated. He stepped aside to let them in. They found themselves in a comfortable room with a welcoming open fire, thick curtains and comfortable furniture. Quiet piano music played from some floor-standing speakers. A man stood with his back to the fire, a tumbler in his hand. He had probably been handsome once, but age and booze were catching up with him. He was a corpulent man who looked like he'd eaten too many good dinners. The collar of his shirt was a little tight for his neck, and his face had a whisky-glow. He wore red trousers and a navy blazer with a smudge of food on the lapel, and a handkerchief in the breast pocket. He gave his guests a bland smile. 'Drink?' he said. It was directed more to Danny than to Bethany.

'No,' Danny said.

'You quite sure I can't tempt you? There's fuck all else to do here.'

Neither Danny nor Bethany replied. The colonel shrugged and helped himself to half a tumbler of whisky from a drinks table to the left of the fire. Danny and Bethany exchanged a quick grin behind his back. The colonel plonked himself down in an armchair, waving one hand to indicate that his guests should also sit. 'So have you found the malodorous little cunt yet?'

'No,' Danny said.

'Well, get a fucking move on, will you? I've had nothing but microwave meals for the last forty-eight hours. You'd think someone on my security detail would know how to boil an egg.' He swigged a mouthful of whisky, then peered at Bethany. 'I thought you were under close protection as well.'

'I am,' Bethany said.

'Been whisked away by a tall, dark SAS man, have you?' He raised an eyebrow at Danny. 'You're barking up the wrong tree there, my friend. Worst-kept secret in Vauxhall is that our Bethany prefers the fairer sex.' He drank some more whisky, eyeing Bethany over the brim of his glass. 'You should invite some of your lady friends round, my dear. Give us all a bit of a show. It would relieve the fucking boredom, that's for sure.'

Bethany gave no reaction. Danny stood up. He walked over to the colonel, removed the whisky glass from his hand, and poured the contents over the carpet. The colonel was clearly outraged, but with Danny towering above him, he wisely made the correct decision and didn't complain. 'They told me you served,' Danny said. 'Gulf War I?' The colonel nodded quickly, clearly a little scared of Danny, who leaned in towards him. 'That's the only reason your teeth are still in your face. Speak to her like that again, I'll do Ibrahim Khan's work for him myself. Understood?'

The colonel's red face grew redder. 'I'll call my close protection,' he said. But his bluster died on his lips. 'Just sit down, man. It was only a bloody joke. I'm more of a brunette man, in any case.'

'The only brunette you're likely to come in contact with,' Danny said, 'is Ibrahim Khan.' He put the whisky tumbler on an occasional table next to the colonel's chair and sat down again.

'Filthy little towelhead,' the colonel said. 'Wish I'd never set eyes on the bugger.'

'Do you think he was working for the other side from the get-go?'

It was Bethany who answered. 'I'd say that was impossible,' she said.

The colonel tried to interrupt. Danny held up one palm to quieten him. 'Why?' he said.

'Because the MISFIT intel was too good. If Ibrahim was working for IS from the beginning, they'd only have been passing on information of a certain quality. Correct but unimportant. Chickenfeed, we call it. Enough to make us believe Ibrahim had access to good intel, but nothing that would actually harm IS operations. We're good at identifying chickenfeed, and the MISFIT intel wasn't it. He tipped us off about major events. Troop movements in northern Iraq. A Semtex bomb at the French Embassy in London. A chemical attack on the Underground. I don't think it's an exaggeration to say Ibrahim Khan is the reason IS never gained a substantial foothold in the UK, and believe me it's not for want of trying.'

'So why did he flip?'

'Because he was weak,' said the colonel. 'Happens all the bloody time in this game. Agents are messed up in the first place. Got to be, if you want to do a job like that. A little seed of sympathy for your enemy grows over time until you start to think like them. Normally we rely on our case officers to spot the signs, and get them out before they can do any lasting damage.' He pointed at Bethany. 'She dropped the ball. Quite why you're still in post, my dear, and I'm out in the cold, is a mystery to me.'

But it was not a mystery to Danny. Bethany White was obviously sharp and capable. The colonel had gone to seed and the booze was turning his brain to jelly. They were wasting their time even talking to him. 'There's nothing for us here,' Danny said to Bethany. 'Let's go.'

Bethany didn't need telling twice. She stood up and headed for the exit. Danny, however, approached the colonel. 'Do you have family?' he said.

'Divorced,' the colonel muttered.

'So nobody else is living here?'

'Just me and the three fucking musketeers. Sure you won't have a drink? There's gin, red wine … I might have some beer somewhere …'

'MI6 offered you a safe house?'

'Damned if I'm going to bloody well …'

'You should take it. Make the call now. Get out of here. Tonight.' And before the colonel could reply, Danny knocked the empty whisky tumbler from the occasional table on to the floor. He trod on it and it cracked beneath his feet. Quickly bending over, he took a shard of lead crystal. Then he forced one hand over the colonel's mouth and pressed the shard up against his carotid artery. 'I could kill you now,' he whispered. 'Your security detail won't hear a sound. I don't need a gun, I don't need a knife, and I could gain access to this house in seconds. If I can do it, Ibrahim Khan can do it. And he will, if I don't find him first. Take the safe house.'

The colonel's eyes bulged. He was pressing himself back in the armchair, as if he could escape Danny by sinking into the upholstery. Danny stepped back and dropped the shard on to the carpet. 'Just a little word of advice,' he said. He followed Bethany to the exit. Before he left the room, he looked back. The colonel was staggering towards his drinks table. There was a desperate clinking as he found himself a fresh glass and filled it from the whisky bottle. Danny left the room.

Bethany was already exiting the building. The guard in the hallway watched Danny with a bored expression. 'What's your name?' Danny said.

'Sandy.'

'You armed, Sandy?' The guard nodded. 'Keep it cocked and locked. Don't separate yourself from your weapon for any reason.' The guard frowned and stood up a little straighter. Inside the room the colonel was draining another glass. 'You got kids?' Danny asked the guard.

The guard nodded. 'Why?'

'Get yourself off this job,' Danny said, 'if you want to see them again. Tell your mates.'

He marched along the corridor and out into the snow, where Bethany was waiting for him by the car.

6

The blizzard was worse than before as they left the colonel's residence, but they couldn't let it stop them. Their next destination was the safe house where Christina Somers – the interpreter on the MISFIT team who had given Ibrahim Khan languages training – was staying along with Bethany's son. 'I've only been there once,' Bethany said. 'Two days ago, to drop him off.' She frowned, as though trying not to dwell on a difficult memory.

'You're going to have to direct me,' Danny said.

Bethany made to plug the details into the satnav. Danny reached out to stop her. 'It's not secure,' he said. 'The satnav keeps a history. The colonel's address is easy to find out. This one needs to stay secret. Just direct me.'

Their route took them into the Brecon Beacons, down winding roads and over narrow passes that Danny knew so well. He was familiar with every square metre of these hills, and had crossed them on foot in conditions worse even than tonight. Thirty-five-degree heat. Horizontal rain. Wet fog and knee-deep snow. Men had died in these hills in their desperation to join the Regiment. He drove with care along the icy roads, keeping his gears low and braking with his engine, not his foot. He could sense Bethany's impatience as she directed him. She was obviously keen to see her boy. 'Is the colonel always like that?' he said, more to distract her than for any other reason.

'A pompous, misogynist dickhead?' Bethany said with uncharacteristic venom, and Danny found himself remembering what she'd said about her father. 'Sure. Turn left up ahead.'

Danny followed her direction. 'Was he right?'

'About what?' There was an edge to her voice. Danny realised she might think he was talking about her sexual preferences.

'When you're running an agent, do you get indications that they're having second thoughts?'

Bethany stared straight ahead. 'From time to time,' she said. 'But it isn't a precise science. Sometimes they get scared. Sometimes they get greedy. It can be hard to know what's going on in their heads.' She paused. 'People spy for lots of different reasons. Patriotism. Money. Glamour. Sometimes it's just because it's the only life they've ever known and they can't think what else to do.'

'What about Khan?' Danny said. 'Why do you think he did it?'

'Truly?' She considered the question. 'Because he thought it was the right thing to do.'

'And was there really no sign he was wavering? You can tell me, you know. Nothing you say is going to make its way back to MI6. I just want to find the guy.'

She shook her head. 'He was almost too good to be true,' she said.

'When something seems too good to be true it normally is, if you ask me.'

'Yeah. Maybe.' Danny sensed she was holding something back.

'He'll get the colonel, you know. If he doesn't move from the house.'

Bethany looked out of the passenger window and didn't reply.

The journey took a little over an hour. It was almost 21.00 when they turned down a small road in a gentle valley. Danny saw the glow of a house light about a football-pitch length away, though it was hard to be certain about distances in the swirling blizzard. 'You'd better call,' Danny said. 'Let them know we're approaching.'

'There's no mobile service here,' she said. 'They rely on a landline.'

'How many security guys?'

'Two,' she said. 'Frank and Alec. They do six hours on, six hours off.'

'Make sure they can see your hands as we approach,' Danny said.

He moved the car forward at a crawl. The tyres crunched in several inches of snow. The house came slowly into view. It was a lot less grand than the colonel's opulent mansion. Two up, two down, by the look of it. Smoke billowed from the chimney, and only the lights on the ground floor were on. A black SUV was parked out front, close to the front door and facing away from the house. Its position told Danny it was probably the security guys' vehicle: it was parked like that to allow for a quick getaway. A figure stood in the closed doorway of the house. An external light above him made the blizzard glow, and cast a long shadow away from the house. Danny could see the figure was holding something in his right hand, which was hanging by his side. A firearm.

He stopped the vehicle twenty metres from the house. 'Get out slowly,' he told Bethany. 'Put your hands in the air. Don't do anything to make him jumpy.'

They stepped out of the car, arms raised. The wind howled and the snow swirled dramatically all around them. 'Frank?' Bethany called. Her voice was muffled by the snow. 'It's me, Bethany.'

The figure approached. He wore a heavy coat and a black woollen hat. Snow had settled in his scraggly beard, and he had piercing blue eyes that almost seemed to shine in the darkness. He smiled broadly. 'Get yourself in out of the cold, my love,' he said. He had a gentle West Country accent, stronger than Bethany's slight burr, and he stowed his weapon in his coat as he spoke. 'Your lad's just having a hot chocolate. Couldn't sleep because of the wind, could he?' He looked over at Danny. 'This fella with you, is he? In you come, lad. I've got some coffee on.'

Frank led them inside, stamping his snow-covered shoes on the mat as he entered. It was a run-down place. Danny had never seen a safe house that wasn't. Gaudy ancient wallpaper covered the walls of the hallway, stained here and there with yellow patches of damp. There was a musty smell. But it was warm, and somehow far more welcoming than the colonel's austere mansion. 'This way,' Frank said.

He led them into a small kitchen. There was an old Aga against the back wall, and a little pile of washing-up by the sink. A tatty yellow roller blind covered the window. Sitting at a Formica table was a woman about Bethany's age who could almost pass for her sister – her twin, even, if her hair had been blonde like Bethany's and not chestnut-brown. Next to her was a little boy, his hands wrapped around a Thomas the Tank Engine mug. He had an unruly mop of brown hair and a slightly olive tinge to his skin. As soon as he saw Bethany enter, he jumped up and ran to her. Bethany bent down and wrapped her arms around him. She closed her eyes and inhaled the scent of his hair.

'Little lad's been asking about you all day,' Frank said.

'And all yesterday,' said the woman at the table. She stood up and offered Danny her hand. 'Christina Somers,' she said. She had a well-to-do voice, slightly husky.

He shook her hand. 'Danny Black,' he said.

At this, the little boy wormed his way out of his mother's embrace. 'I'm Danny too,' he said.

Danny crouched down to his level. 'All the best people are called Danny,' he said.

'Are you going to marry my mum?'

The other adults in the room chuckled fondly. 'I think your mum's busy enough looking after you,' Danny said.

The little boy gave him a serious nod. 'Frank and Auntie Christina look after me as well,' he said. 'And Alec, but he's asleep right now.' He pointed at the ceiling.

'It's time you were asleep too, young man,' Bethany said. She took him by the hand. 'Come on, I'll take you up.'

The little boy looked like he wanted to talk to Danny some more, but the lure of his mother was too great. 'G'night, lad,' Frank said as she led him out of the kitchen. 'Did you want that coffee?' he asked Danny, handing him a mug.

Danny accepted it gratefully. He'd warmed to Frank, but he didn't have him down as a military man. Retired police, maybe. 'What are your security protocols?' he said.

'My security protocol is I don't let the principal out of my sight.' He nodded at Christina to indicate who he was talking about. 'Except for, you know, toilet and changing and stuff.'

'That's when she's most at risk,' Danny said. 'I'm sorry, mate, but by rights you should be female. You've got to be with her at all times.'

'Do I get a say in this?' Christina said.

Danny put his coffee cup back down on the table. 'Can you give us a minute, Frank?'

Frank looked uncertain. 'Well . . .'

'It's okay, Frank,' Christina said. 'He's with Bethany.'

'Right,' Frank said. He pointed to the door. 'I'll be just outside.'

Danny waited till he and Christina were alone. 'Have you told him any details?' he said. 'Does he know about Khan?'

Christina looked uncertain, and Danny realised his knowledge of Khan was a surprise to her. 'I've been fully briefed,' he said. 'MISFIT, Bullock, Armitage, Moorhouse . . .'

Her forehead creased. 'Sturrock read me the riot act. I can't tell anyone. Not even Frank or Alec. They don't know who they're protecting me from.' She gave him a sharp look. 'Why is Bethany here? I thought she was under close protection in Vauxhall.'

'Change of plan,' Danny said, deliberately elusive.

'You're going after him, aren't you? Ibrahim, I mean. It's okay, I know you're not going to confirm or deny, but it's obvious. We can't all sit around waiting for him to come and . . .' She shuddered. 'Promise me you'll keep Bethany safe?'

'She'll be safe,' Danny said.

'I've known her for years. This business has affected her more than she's letting on.'

'Make sure you do everything your CP guys tell you to do,' Danny said.

Christina glanced in the direction of the kitchen door. 'Don't get me wrong,' she said. 'Frank's the nicest guy in the world. Alec comes a close second. But Ibrahim would run rings round them both. I spent a *lot* of time with the guy and I never met a smarter man. I mean, I know he was a good soldier and everything, but he was *smart*. He could remember everything, the first time he read it or saw it. Instant recall. Perfect mimicry of seven or eight different Arabic dialects. Spanish, German, Farsi. He should have been an academic, not a soldier. I never heard him say anything I disagreed with.'

'It would have turned out better for three SAS men if he'd stuck to his books,' Danny said.

Christina's expression darkened. 'He used to talk about them,' she said. 'The things they *said* to him ... I can't help thinking ...'

'What?'

'That they were lucky he didn't stand up to them sooner.'

'He did more than stand up to them. He butchered them.'

'Well,' she said, a hint of defiance in her voice, 'maybe they brought it on themselves.'

'You think?' Danny said carefully. Christina jutted out her chin defiantly and it occurred to Danny that of all Khan's potential targets she was the most vulnerable. As an interpreter, she wouldn't even have had basic firearms training, and she seemed to adore Khan, despite everything. He would surely be happy to use that to his advantage.

'MI6 don't think he killed them because they were mean to him,' Danny said. 'They think he killed them because they were part of the MISFIT training team. So were you. If you're thinking you're not part of Ibrahim Khan's plans, think again.'

Christina shrugged. She was obviously preventing herself from continuing the conversation. Danny felt a sudden twinge of doubt about her. She looked drained and exhausted. But somehow she didn't seem *scared*. She'd spoken about Khan with respect, and about his attack on the SAS men with empathy.

'Where are you going?' she said. 'After you leave here? Where do you think you're going to find him?'

It was not a question Danny would ever have answered, but something told him to be doubly cautious around Christina Somers. He suddenly wasn't certain where her loyalties lay. He drained his coffee. 'Wait there,' he said.

He left the room. Frank was waiting in the hallway. 'Where's Bethany?' Danny asked him.

Frank pointed towards a staircase at the end of the hallway. 'Up there, second on the left.'

Danny jerked his thumb in the direction of the kitchen. 'Keep an eye on her,' he said.

Frank nodded and returned to the kitchen. Danny headed up the stairs. They creaked noisily. He found Bethany on the dimly lit landing, closing the door of a bedroom. 'He's nearly asleep,' she said. 'Poor thing was exhausted.' She sighed. 'I don't want to leave him,' she said. There was a catch in her voice.

'I think we should move him,' Danny said.

'He's all tucked up.'

'I don't mean to another room. To another safe house. Away from Christina.'

'Why on earth would we do that?'

Danny hesitated. He had to admit to himself that it was just a hunch, but there was definitely something about Christina's attitude, and the way she spoke about Khan, that worried him. Bethany smiled. 'Christina would never do anything to harm Danny. Or me. She's just confused about Ibrahim. They got on well. It's all a shock.' She walked past Danny towards the stairs. 'I'll go and talk to her. Reiterate how important it is that her location remains a secret.'

Danny followed her downstairs. She went into the kitchen while Danny remained in the hallway. Frank joined him. 'Those women,' he said in his soft West Country lilt. 'They'll gossip for England.' He gave Danny a sidelong glance. 'Hereford Regiment?' he asked.

Danny nodded.

'You can always tell,' Frank said. 'Once you've met one or two, that is. I knew a chap once ...'

Danny held up one finger to silence him. He stepped up to the kitchen door and listened hard. He expected to hear the soft murmur of voices, but there was silence. A sharp knot of anxiety twisted in his stomach. He opened the door and burst into the kitchen.

Bethany and Christina were on the far side of the Formica table. Bethany had one hand at the back of Christina's head. Their lips were millimetres apart.

Danny remembered the colonel's boorish comment. *You're barking up the wrong tree there, my friend. Worst-kept secret in Vauxhall is that our Bethany prefers the fairer sex.* Christina pulled away, obviously embarrassed. Bethany gave Danny a 'did you have to walk in on us' look. Danny was about to murmur an apology, but at that precise moment they were plunged into darkness as the lights went out.

'Get to the ground,' Danny whispered. And when he failed to hear the sound of movement, he repeated himself. '*Get to the ground. Now!*'

He heard bodies hitting the floor. His eyes had grown somewhat accustomed to the dark. He could see the outline of the yellow blind in front of the window. Was that a shadow of movement he had seen behind it?

'Frank?' he whispered.

'Yes, lad?' Frank's gravelly voice was full of concern.

'Do you have your weapon?'

'Yes, lad.'

'Get upstairs, into the kid's room. Don't leave unless I give you the word.'

Frank didn't need telling twice. Danny sensed him heading towards the staircase. Danny himself stepped further into the kitchen, silently moving towards the pile of washing-up by the sink. He felt for a bread knife, clenching the handle in his right fist. 'Get a chair under the door handle when I leave,' he told the women. 'Then get back on the ground. Stay away from the window.'

'What are you doing?' Bethany whispered.

'There's somebody outside,' Danny said. 'I'm going to find them.'

'Oh my God . . .'

But Danny was already heading to the door. He was cursing himself for not having brought his weapon from his vehicle. To go and grab it now was impossible. He would expose himself to whoever was outside if he ran to the car. The bread knife was a distinct second best: a contact weapon that he had to be close to a target to use. But it was all he had. He held it low as he quietly opened the front door and stepped outside.

There was no moon to light his way. Even the snow was dark, though he could feel it against his face. He was dimly aware of footprints, but they were a mixture of his, Bethany's and Frank's. It was impossible to identify any extra sets. He closed the door silently and paused on the doorstep, scanning the area as best he could and holding his breath so he could better hear any external noises.

At first, nothing. Just the distant howl of the wind. Then, after a few seconds, a scratching sound. It came from his left. He peered in that direction. He could see nothing between himself and the corner of the house approximately ten metres away. He moved in that direction as quietly as possible, unable fully to disguise the crunch of snow beneath his feet. At the corner, he stopped. He listened hard. Again, nothing at first. Then the scratching sound. He consulted his mental picture of the house's layout. Along this external wall was the kitchen window. He tested the blade of the bread knife. It was blunt, but it would do the job.

Quickly, quietly, he turned the corner.

He had barely taken a step when light bled from inside the kitchen. The power was back on, and the light exposed what was making the noise: a wet, scraggly mountain sheep, such as Danny had seen more times than he could count, roaming the Brecon Beacons. It was pawing at the ground just below the window. Danny inhaled deeply, calming himself. The sheep gave him a reproachful look and went back to pawing at the hard snowy ground.

Danny carefully completed a full turn of the house, but the grounds were deserted. Back at the front, he hammered on door. 'It's me!' he shouted.

Bethany opened up. 'Trip switch,' she said. 'I found it in a cupboard.'

'What the hell do you think you were doing?' Danny said. 'You should have stayed put like I told you. This isn't a game, you know!'

'The house is safe, Danny,' Bethany said, her voice maddeningly calm. 'Nobody knows we're here, except Sturrock. Not the colonel, not MI5, no-one else at MI6, and certainly not Ibrahim. You think I'd let my son stay here if there was the remotest chance that he'd be in danger?'

Danny felt angry. Maybe a little humiliated that the threat he'd identified had been nothing but a mountain sheep. 'I need to give Frank the all-clear,' he said, and pushed past her.

'Danny,' she said when he was halfway to the stairs. He stopped. 'That thing you saw, before the lights went out . . . Me and Christina . . .'

'Not my business,' he said.

Back in the kitchen, having relieved Frank, he found himself looking at the two women through new eyes. Bethany: still capable and smart, but also complex and secretive. Christina: conflicted about Ibrahim Khan, but in thrall to her friend and, maybe, sometime lover, and also to this little boy. 'I'll be making us all a cuppa,' Frank said, clearly oblivious to the dynamics in the room.

'Don't bother about us,' Danny said. 'We have to go.'

Bethany's gaze flickered upwards. She obviously didn't want to leave her son. 'We'll be fine,' Christina said. She put one hand on Bethany's. 'I'll look after him.'

'I know,' Bethany said. She stood up and nodded to Danny. 'It's still snowing,' she said, 'and the wind's getting up. We should be on the road before it starts to drift.'

Danny shook hands with Frank. 'Keep your weapon close and don't let her out of your sight.'

'Wouldn't want to be without a nine-millimetre if I come up against one of those mountain sheep.' Frank slapped him on the arm. 'Don't worry, lad. Alec and me know what we're doing. We'll keep them safe.'

The two men waited while Bethany and Christina embraced. A couple of minutes later, Danny and his new companion were crawling back through the blizzard, windscreen wipers pumping and the heat on full. They were silent. It was almost eleven o'clock and Brize Norton, from where their flight left at dawn, seemed a long way off.

7

Danny found there was always something thrilling about an RAF base before dawn. The glow of lights on the airfield. The camaraderie of men and women reaching the end of their night shift. And for Danny, it invariably meant an operation was looming.

This morning, though, the thrill was tempered. He hadn't slept for twenty-four hours and he was filled with a growing sense of unease. The most likely place for Ibrahim Khan to be was the UK, where his targets were. Danny was heading to Beirut on the back of a hunch. An informed hunch, maybe, but what if it led nowhere? What if it merely alerted Khan? He was distracted as he entered the familiar terminal building with Bethany at his side. 'Normally,' she said, 'it's BA Business Class for me.'

'Cattle class this morning,' Danny said. 'Hope you don't mind the smell of aviation fuel.'

The terminal wasn't as busy as Danny had sometimes known it. A smattering of men and women in camouflage gear, more of them manning the base, it seemed to him, than flying out of Brize. He saw Ray Hammond almost immediately. The Regiment's ops officer was standing under a departure board. He nodded at Danny, then walked across the concourse and through an unmarked door to the right of a sign indicating the way to the gates. 'This way,' Danny told Bethany, following him.

Hammond was waiting for them in a plain waiting room with a single table in the middle and strip lighting that flickered and hummed. There were two suitcases on the table, hand-luggage size. A battered-looking British passport lay on each one, and several wodges of notes. 'You each have a couple of grand in sterling and the same in Lebanese pounds,' Hammond said. 'You'll be travelling as Mr and Mrs Tomlinson if anyone asks. Which they won't, because we've arranged for you to skip passport control both here and in Beirut.'

There was something stiff about Hammond's demeanour. He kept glancing at Bethany, and Danny realised the gruff SAS man felt uncomfortable in the presence of this attractive MI6 officer. He forced himself not to smile. Hammond wouldn't take kindly to that.

'An embassy car will be waiting for you when you land,' Hammond continued. 'Danny, are you still carrying?'

Danny nodded.

'If you need any extra hardware while you're in-country, go directly to the ambassador. He knows what to do. Anything else, Hereford's your first call. Ask for me, nobody else.'

'Have they filled you in, boss?'

'No,' Hammond said, and Danny could tell it was still a sore point. It was unusual for him to be reporting directly to the CO, and Hammond didn't like being kept out of the loop. Danny felt for him. Hammond was a good guy, and clearly didn't like the implicit suggestion that he couldn't quite be trusted with certain information.

Danny pointed at the suitcases. 'Just clothes?'

'And currency.'

Another man entered the room. He wore camouflage gear and had a 99 Squadron flash on his arm. 'Wheels up in fifteen minutes,' he said. 'If you'd like to follow me, please.'

Danny and Bethany took their suitcases and passports and turned to leave. 'Danny?' Hammond said.

'Yes, boss?'

'If this is something to do with Bullock, Armitage and Moorhouse, make sure you give the bastard one from me and the rest of the lads.'

'Roger that, boss,' Danny said, and he followed the RAF guy out of the room.

The aircraft waiting for them was a C-17 Globemaster. Its jets were humming and its tailgate was down. There was still a chill dusting of snow as khaki military vehicles were being loaded up the ramp, directed by guys with ear protectors and glowing hand signals. Their 99 Squadron escort led them to a separate air stair on the Globemaster's port side. Danny and Bethany boarded the aircraft. There was a single row of eight seats at the front of the cargo bay. The bay itself was packed with armoured vehicles, firmly fixed to rungs along the floor. The air stank of grease and fuel. To Danny, it was as familiar as home. Bethany looked uncomfortable, unsure of what to do with herself. Her nose crinkled against the smell. There was no point Danny trying to talk to her: the high-pitched whine of the jets and the trundle of vehicles being loaded drowned out every other sound, including voices. He guided her by the elbow to one of the hard seats, then stowed both their cases in lockers along the side of the aircraft. As he took his seat next to her, he saw she was clutching the armrests and her knuckles were white. It figured that she was anxious, and he wondered what worried her the most, the military flight or the prospect of their op in Beirut. A bit of both, probably.

The tailgate closed and the noise subsided a little. 'Could be worse,' Danny said now he could be heard. 'Last time I was in one of these, I had to jump out of it.'

His attempt at lightening the mood didn't work. Bethany gave him a slightly sick look, then closed her eyes and ignored him. A couple of loadies took their places along the row of seats. Five minutes later they were airborne. A minute after that, Danny was asleep.

When he woke, the Globemaster was losing height. Danny had no way of knowing their altitude, so it was a surprise when the landing gear touched down after a minute. He was used to grabbing sleep wherever and whenever he could, so he felt reasonably refreshed. Bethany looked exhausted. There were dark rings under her eyes and her face was puffy. When the aircraft came to a halt she had to steady herself as she stood up, but when Danny offered to help she brushed him away.

Local time, 12.00 hrs. The light flooding into the aircraft as the side door opened was almost a surprise. It was pleasantly warm outside, the sky a clear, cloudless blue. A black Mercedes was waiting for them on the tarmac, windows tinted. It was flanked by two dark Beirut police vehicles. A guy in his early twenties in a chauffeur's uniform stood by the Merc. When Danny and Bethany had descended the air stair, he wordlessly took their luggage and stowed it in the front, before letting them into the back of the vehicle. There was a man already sitting there. He had chunky glasses and Brylcreemed black hair brushed into a precise parting. He gave them a winning smile as they entered the vehicle. 'Mr and Mrs Tomlinson!' he announced. Then, with a slight nod of his head and quieter: 'Bethany. Lovely to see you again. You haven't visited in far too long.'

'It's only been six months, Larry,' Bethany said.

'A day without you, my dear, is like a day without sunshine.' An oily sentiment, but charmingly delivered, and Bethany didn't look displeased to have been on the receiving end. He looked at Danny and offered his hand. 'Larry Baker,' he said. 'Personal assistant to the ambassador. Welcome to Beirut. Is this your first time?'

'Do me a favour, mate? Give the two police cars their marching orders.'

Baker frowned. 'I don't think . . .'

'Seriously, mate. We're skipping passport control to keep under the radar. Last thing we need is a police escort.'

Baker looked uncertainly at Bethany. She nodded. Baker got out of the car and went to speak to the police officers. 'Like a day without sunshine?' Danny asked.

Bethany gave him a withering look, but didn't say anything.

Baker returned. 'They'll escort us off the airport, that's non-negotiable I'm afraid. Then we'll go our separate ways,' he said. Danny nodded. Baker continued to chat with ambassadorial ease. Danny had met his type before, and knew he could jabber on about nothing in particular for hours, if he needed to. 'Not the place people think it is, Beirut. Oh, sure, we have Syria in one direction and the Golan Heights in another, but that's really only half the story. Fascinating country. *Fascinating.* Lovely people, so welcoming. Beirut? Thriving! On the up! You'll see some scars from the war in the eighties, certainly, but I urge you to look beyond those.'

'I'll do that,' Danny said. He was quite certain the assistant to the ambassador hadn't seen the half of what Beirut had to offer.

'You'll have to forgive Mr Tomlinson,' said Bethany. 'He's a man of few words. I take it we're heading straight for the embassy?'

'If that's what you'd like, my dear. We have your usual room set aside in the compound.' He looked from Danny to Bethany. 'Made up for two,' he added, as though asking a question which remained unanswered.

'Is there a private entrance?' Danny asked.

'Of course. We'll be using that.'

Bethany and the assistant engaged in small talk. Danny zoned out and stared through the window. They were leaving the airport – a Lebanese police officer was waving them through a security checkpoint. The driver accelerated up a ramp and on to a busy main road that took them away from the airport and towards the centre of Beirut.

The signs of the city's violent past were impossible to overlook. Concrete walls on either side of the road, graffitied and semi-demolished. Dilapidated, derelict buildings peppered with gunshot scars from a conflict that ended thirty years previously but whose wounds still felt peculiarly fresh. There were signs of reconstruction, too: many cranes on the skyline and, the further they headed into the centre, a higher concentration of more modern buildings. And also, Westernisation: the golden arches of McDonald's, its name written in both English and Arabic. Billboards everywhere, advertising Volkswagen, Ikea and Victoria's Secret. It looked like what it was: a busy metropolis, skirting the Middle East but leaning to the West.

As the car pulled off the highway and into the heavy traffic of central Beirut, Danny found himself looking at people in the street. They were as varied as the architecture. Bearded hipsters and fashionable young women walked side by side with older men and women in sober, sometimes traditional, clothes. The capital clearly had its share of poverty too. Beggars were abundant on the streets, sometimes what looked like whole families of them. Danny zoned back in to the assistant's voice. 'Of course, Lebanon has accepted well over two million Syrian refugees. A sticky old situation, especially as Hezbollah has supported the Syrian regime during the recent troubles. The refugees have increased the country's population by more than half. But when a humanitarian catastrophe unfolds on your doorstep, what else can you do?'

The British Embassy was a modern, glass-fronted building facing on to a broad, busy road. The Mercedes drove past it and hooked a left down the next side street. Here there was a high wall, topped with razor wire, and a solid steel gate where the Mercedes stopped while the driver phoned through for access. A minute later, the gate slid open and the Mercedes entered the perimeter of the embassy compound. They approached another barrier, manned by three British soldiers carrying MP5s. One of them pressed his face up against the tinted window of the Merc. He recognised Baker, and ushered them through the barrier. 'Welcome,' Baker said. He opened the car door and they all stepped outside.

They found themselves in an enclosed square with high buildings on three sides and the razor-wired wall on the fourth. Most of the square was taken up with a lawned garden, neatly manicured, though its effect was somewhat spoiled by the presence of the barrier and the armed guards on its perimeter. To their left was the rear of the embassy itself, where three embassy staff loitered, smoking cigarettes and gazing incuriously at the new arrivals. Bethany pointed at the building covering the side of the square opposite the barrier. Two more soldiers guarded the entrance. 'Ambassador's residence,' she said. 'Back entrance, obviously. We'll be quartered over here with the rest of the embassy staff.' She pointed to the building on their right, opposite the embassy itself.

'I can leave you to get settled in, my dear?' Baker said.

'Of course, Larry. Thank you.' Bethany seemed genuinely fond of this slightly patronising embassy official.

He handed them both an ID card in a plastic housing on a red lanyard. 'This will get you access to anywhere in the compound, with the exception of the ambassadorial residence. If there's anything else you need, please don't hesitate. Perhaps you'd both like to join me for supper this evening?'

'We'll be busy,' Danny said. 'But thanks.'

Baker politely inclined his head and walked in the direction of the embassy.

'That man,' Bethany said, 'sets my teeth on edge.'

'I thought you liked him.'

'I pretend to.'

'You're a good actress.'

'First rule of embassy work: butter up the pompous men to get what you want.' She smiled ruefully. 'First rule of any work, for that matter.'

The driver of the Merc gave them their luggage. Danny followed Bethany towards the embassy staff quarters. From the outside, the building was grey and austere. Inside, it reminded Danny of a cheap hotel. They walked across a deserted, air-conditioned communal area, all sofas and pot plants, and Bethany used her ID card to open a door that led into a tidy, brightly lit kitchen area that smelled of cleaning products. There were two doors leading off it. She led them through one of them. 'This is us,' she said.

They were in a comfortable living area. Sofa. Armchair. TV. Coffee table. Three pictures on the wall, one of the Tower of London, the second of the Beirut coast, the Med a deep, attractive blue. The third was a satellite image of central Lebanon, from Beirut to the Syrian border, presented in a mahogany frame like a piece of art. 'My bedroom,' Bethany said, pointing at a door. 'The bathroom's through there too, en-suite. Couch. That'll be yours, as long as we're here.' She said it with a raised eyebrow, as though expecting Danny to protest. Was it his imagination, or did she seem a little disappointed when he failed to comment?

Mind on the job, Danny, he told himself. Mind on the job.

'Where are your handling notes on our guy?' He made a special point of not saying his name out loud. Anybody could be listening.

'There's a secure MI6 office in the main embassy building.'

'Why don't you go and get them?'

'You want to come?'

'No,' Danny said. 'The less people see of me, the better. I'll wait here.'

It was in Danny's nature to search every room where he was likely to stay for any period of time. When Bethany left, he did just that. This self-contained apartment was not to his liking. The only exit was the one that led to the shared kitchen area. There were no windows in Bethany's bedroom or the adjoining en-suite bathroom. He quickly unscrewed the bulbs in each of the five lights he found dotted around the place, searching for concealed listening devices. Nothing. In the en-suite, he pulled out the recessed lights and felt behind the mirror over the sink and in the cistern of the toilet. By the time Bethany returned, he'd satisfied himself that the apartment was secure. He switched on the TV in the main room just in case, found a noisy Arabic music channel, and led her into the bathroom. He closed the door behind them.

'Well,' Bethany said. She was clutching a bundle of Moleskine notebooks bound with an elastic band. 'This is all very intimate.'

'Don't mention our guy's name,' Danny said. 'If he's as influential as you say, he could have ears inside the embassy. I'm pretty sure this bathroom's secure, though.' He indicated that she should sit on the toilet while he perched on the edge of the bath. 'What have you got?'

'Give me a moment.' She flicked through her notes, muttering under her breath and occasionally referring back to a previous page. Finally she nodded and closed the book. 'I kept pretty detailed surveillance notes. If anything happened to Ibrahim, Al-Farouk would have been our first port of call, so I needed to know his daily movements and any weaknesses that would have given us opportunities to blackmail him. He's a man of habit, which is good for us. He's also pretty clean-living, which gives us less leverage.'

'But there are regular payments to IS,' Danny said.

'Right,' she said. 'As far as his daily schedule goes, he attends the first call to prayer at the Al-Omari Grand Mosque in the central district every day. Without fail. He has a chauffeur, who drives him there from home each morning and picks him up when morning prayers are over.'

'Do you have pictures?'

Bethany nodded. She opened a second notebook, the pages of which were interleaved with photographs.

'Old-school,' Danny observed.

'I told you. We keep everything to do with the MISFIT operation analogue, and in hard copy.' She flicked through the notebook and handed a particular photograph to Danny. It showed a black SUV with blacked-out windows, the image too blurred to tell what make, from which a Lebanese-looking man in a grey suit was emerging.

'That him?' Danny asked.

'Yes.'

Danny sized him up. Broad shoulders, but small, and he looked out of shape. He wouldn't present a problem if it came to it.

'Always the same car?'

She consulted her notes again. 'Yes,' she said. 'I've got the reg number. From the mosque he heads to the office. It's overlooking the harbour on the northern edge of the central district. Once he's in there, we've lost him until evening. He never comes out. People come to him.'

'People like Ibrahim Khan.'

'Right.'

'He goes home at night, though?'

'Seven p.m., on the nose. The chauffeur takes him back.'

'Family?'

'Wife, three children, all girls. They're kept pretty well under wraps. He's that kind of hardliner.' She looked up from her notebook. 'I want to make something clear,' she said. 'I won't countenance any threat to the wife and daughters. There's no evidence that they share our man's extremist tendencies. They're innocents.'

'They're the best leverage we have,' Danny said. 'Threaten the kids, he'll tell us everything we want.'

'That's not how I want to do things.'

'It's not up to you.'

'Then count me out.' Bethany stood up.

'Sit down,' Danny said wearily. 'Fine, we'll leave the family. But it means we'll have to use other methods on the target, you understand that?'

She nodded.

'Do we know anything about his chauffeur?'

'Glad you asked,' Bethany said. 'His name is Abdullah Dimitri. I've reason to believe he's an IS plant. He took the chauffeuring job about eighteen months ago. My suspicion is that he's in place to keep tabs on our target and report back on him to his IS handlers.'

'What makes you think that?'

Bethany removed two more photos. One was of the same vehicle, the black SUV. The chauffeur was opening the rear door. The image was taken with a telephoto lens, and the chauffeur's face was very clear. She handed him a second picture. It was taken in the desert. Three men in orange jumpsuits were kneeling in a line. Behind them, carrying a vicious-looking scimitar and wearing all black, was the same man. There was no doubt about it. Their faces were identical.

'Our target's chauffeur is an IS executioner? Seriously?'

'It's not so surprising. Lots of them try their hand at it. It's a rite of passage, almost, a way for them to prove their loyalty. Then they get moved on to other roles.'

'Does anybody else know about this?'

'The colonel. It's the kind of operational information we keep under wraps. It wouldn't play well if anybody found out we'd identified one of these guys and done nothing. I'm not saying it doesn't leave a bad taste in the mouth, mind you.'

'I don't know about you,' Danny said, 'but in my book, cutting off people's heads makes our chauffeur kind of expendable.'

'Expendable?'

'Yeah. Permanently.'

'I'm not comfortable with that kind of talk,' Bethany said.

'That's why you do your job and I do mine,' Danny replied. He fixed her with a steady stare. 'This is a black op, not a vicar's tea party. You need to get used to the idea that Ibrahim and the people he's fallen in with don't share your sense of fair play.'

'Don't patronise me,' she said. 'I understand the situation. You realise the Lebanese authorities won't countenance any foul play on their territory by a foreign agent? They've got enough difficulty keeping Hezbollah in line.'

'Then I'll make sure I don't get caught,' Danny said. He had another look at the pictures of the chauffeur. He was a different proposition from Al-Farouk. Lean, young, tall. Danny could handle him, but he'd take a bit more force. 'Where's our target's home?' he said.

Bethany hesitated. 'I said we're not hitting the family.'

'And I said I wouldn't. Just tell me where he lives.'

She consulted her notes. 'There's a residential area to the south-east of the city centre. It's as plush as you'd expect. Gardens, staff quarters, the works.'

'Security?'

'Of course. Extensive.'

'Then the easiest time to hit him is when he's in transit. Early morning's too risky. If his staff expect him at work, they're going to start asking questions if he doesn't turn up. If we get him to call them, it's still going to look suspicious if he instructs them to cancel a day's worth of meetings. So that leaves the evening journey from the office back home. From what you've said, the wife and kids are submissive. They're less likely to act on their own initiative.'

'Definitely.'

'Then that's decided. We'll target him on the journey home.'

'When?' Bethany said.

Danny gave that a few seconds' thought. They should probably wait twenty-four hours. It would give them time to put in one round of surveillance on the target as he headed home that evening. If Danny was following SOPs, that would be the routine call. But something didn't feel right about waiting. Ibrahim Khan was out there somewhere, planning his next hit. Perhaps it would be the colonel? Even worse, perhaps his next stop would be the little safe house in Brecon. He found himself thinking of Bethany's little boy. Khan had shown himself to be ruthless and sick. And clever. MI6 thought Christina and Danny Jr were under the radar, but it really wasn't so difficult for information to leak. The longer Danny waited, the closer his target would be to his next strike. If that strike harmed the kid, Danny wouldn't forgive himself.

Decision made. 'We do it tonight,' he said.

8

According to Bethany, the target's chauffeur was likely to pick him up at 19.00 hrs. It was now 14.00. They had five hours to make their preparations.

Danny examined carefully every photograph Bethany had of the target's vehicle. It was a black BMW X5. Five doors and heavily blacked-out rear and side windows. Registration number B 759375, and the equivalent written on the plates in Arabic. Bethany had three pictures of it. In the first, it was leaving Al-Farouk's home, through a set of secure gates flung wide open. In the second, it was waiting outside the Grand Mosque, the blue minarets just visible in the out-of-focus background. It was the third picture that interested him. Here, the X5 had parked up in a dedicated parking spot outside Al-Farouk's office. A time code stamped on the image stated that the photograph had been taken at 18.57 hrs. 'That's the regular pick-up spot?' Danny asked.

'As far as I know.'

'We need to go and look at it. How long does it take to walk there?'

'Fifteen minutes, if that.'

He stood up and moved over to the satellite picture of Lebanon on the wall. Beirut was a massive urban sprawl halfway down the Mediterranean coast. To the east, the city boundary merged with a vast forested area. There were few main roads. Danny identified a river running north–south. Beyond that, to the east, a mountain ridge. Danny pointed at the forested area and the river. 'Do you know this terrain here?' he asked.

'A bit.'

'What does that mean?'

'I know it a bit, okay?' She sighed and pointed to an area on the western bank of the river. 'There's a disused farmstead here. You can't see it on this map because the trees have overgrown it. It often gets flooded in the winter so it's no longer any use to anybody. Ibrahim and I identified it as a place we could meet if he ever felt his cover was blown. It's deserted. Nobody ever goes there.'

'Are the roads that lead to it busy?'

'No.' She pointed at a main road heading east to west, across the mountain ridge. 'Once you get off this main supply route that leads to the Syrian border, you're pretty much on your own.'

'Do you know how to get there? To the farmstead, I mean.'

'I was Ibrahim's handler. Of course I know how to get there.'

Danny nodded. 'Okay,' he said. 'Let's go and check out Al-Farouk's office.'

'I need to change first,' Bethany said. She went into her bedroom. When she emerged again, she was dressed similarly to Danny. In jeans, a white T-shirt and a leather jacket. Danny found himself wondering which was the real Bethany: the Sloane Ranger with the Alice band, or the altogether more sophisticated woman standing in front of him. He reminded himself that she was an MI6 trained agent. She was clearly adept at presenting to the world whatever version of herself most suited her circumstances.

They stowed their embassy ID cards in their jeans. Danny gave his Sig a once-over and placed it, cocked and locked, in his jacket. Bethany eyed the weapon anxiously but didn't say anything. They left the accommodation block, before walking across the central square and into the main embassy building. Bethany led them confidently across the bustling reception area, where embassy staff were dealing with British nationals' passport problems and other queries. Nobody seemed to pay them any attention as they exited the building from the front and took an immediate right.

It was clear that Bethany knew the back streets of Beirut well. She avoided the main thoroughfares, and led Danny through a network of tiny winding streets, packed with artisan stores, tiny workshops, hip restaurants and coffee shops, and more than a few tourist traps. Arabic pop music blared out from various quarters, and a smell of grilled meat hung in the air, making Danny hungry. These little cobbled streets were run-down, but thronged with Lebanese and tourists alike. Danny sensed that he was blending in okay, although Bethany's striking features and blonde hair drew more than a few glances from some of the men.

Then, suddenly, they were out of the network of tiny streets and facing a busy main road. On the other side was an enormous concrete building. Glass was missing from its many windows, its fascia was bullet-riddled and scarred. At the very top of the tower were the remnants of a sign: Holiday Inn. The building looked like it had been removed from a war zone and plonked here in the middle of the city. But then, Danny reminded himself, Beirut had been a war zone not so long ago. Bethany saw him staring up at the building. 'The locals see it as a monument to the war,' she said. 'It was the scene of a great deal of fighting back in the seventies. They say a thousand people died in that building. A lot of them were thrown from the top. It was looted and scavenged after that. I quite like that it's still there. You know, to remind everyone.'

Danny's attention had already moved on. 'Which way to Al-Farouk's office?'

She pointed along the main road. They headed north. Danny could smell sea air amid the exhaust fumes. A forest of modern tower blocks gleamed up ahead. The road led to the port. Expensive yachts. Glamorous pedestrians strolling the boardwalk that followed the seafront. The afternoon sun shimmered on the Med. Danny had operated all across the Middle East, in brutal deserts and war-torn towns. This part of Beirut couldn't have been less like those barren, unwelcoming environments.

They crossed over to the boardwalk, heading west towards the office blocks that looked out to sea. After five minutes, Bethany stopped. She nodded towards a tall, mirrored block on the other side of the road. 'That's it,' she said. 'Al-Farouk has the thirteenth floor. That's where Ibrahim used to meet him to collect the money.'

Danny checked the area in front of the block. There was a neatly kept garden with palm trees swaying gently in the breeze coming in off the Med. He immediately identified the parking space in front of the main entrance, which he recognised from Bethany's surveillance photo. 'Have you ever been inside the building?' he asked.

'Once. The first time Ibrahim met with Al-Farouk. I wanted to be on site in case there was a problem.'

'What's behind the main entrance?'

'Big foyer. Marble floor. Sofas. Reception desk. You have to report there if you want to get through a security barrier to reach the upper floors.'

'Toilets?'

'What?'

'Are there toilets you can use without approaching reception?'

Bethany closed her eyes, clearly picturing the layout. 'Yes,' she said finally.

'Okay,' Danny said. 'Way I see it, we have two options. Option one: we get ourselves a vehicle, follow Al-Farouk as his driver takes him home, drive into the back of him, and when the driver gets out to deal with it, we carjack them.'

Bethany gave him an 'are you insane?' look.

'Yeah, I agree,' Danny said. 'We might not find the right moment to make the hit, our car could be identified. Too many things can go wrong. So I guess it's option two.'

'Which is what?' Bethany spoke carefully, clearly worried that option two would be even riskier.

'You saw how the side and rear windows of Al-Farouk's car were blacked-out?'

'Yes.'

'Big mistake that, if you think someone might target you.'

'Why? It keeps him anonymous, doesn't it?'

'Sure, but sometimes you don't want to be anonymous, if the threat's already in the vehicle.' Danny looked her up and down. 'That two-piece suit you were wearing in your office yesterday. Did you bring it with you?'

'Yes,' she said carefully. 'Why?'

'Are you comfortable with a handgun?'

'I've had firearms training. Look, Danny, I don't like the . . .'

'How's your Arabic?' he interrupted.

'Fluent. I had Christina as a teacher.'

'Good. That's sorted then. Let's get back to the embassy and change. I'll explain what we're going to do while we walk.'

He turned and headed back along the boardwalk. He heard Bethany give a little shout of impatience, and couldn't swear that she hadn't stamped her foot. But then she was beside him again, walking fast to keep up with his pace. She listened wordlessly as he explained his strategy to her. And fair play to her, Danny thought. She let him finish what he was saying before she told him he was completely crazy.

But Danny wasn't crazy, and by the time they reached the embassy, Bethany had come round to his way of thinking. He was confident in his plan, because he knew how men's minds worked. They seldom saw women as a threat. Beautiful blonde women like Bethany White even less so. And if the man in question was an IS operative, whose belief system had at its very core the idea that women were inferior? That was a strategic advantage just waiting to be exploited.

Back in their embassy apartment, Danny waited in the sitting room while Bethany changed into her two-piece suit. She emerged with her hair tied back and a little make-up on her face, soberly applied. 'It'll do,' Danny said.

'Flatterer,' Bethany replied.

Danny held up his handgun. 'This is a Sig Pthirty-eight nine millimetre,' he said. 'It's important you look like you know how to handle it, if you're going to appear a genuine threat. The first thing you need to know . . .'

'Just give it me,' Bethany said. She took the Sig from Danny's grasp, expelled the magazine, checked the lip, reloaded it and cocked the weapon, all in about five seconds. Then she smiled at Danny. 'Anything else you'd like to mansplain to me?' she said.

Danny shook his head. 'Nothing,' he said. He took off his jacket, removed his holster and threw it to Bethany, who caught it one-handed. She removed her jacket, donned the holster and stowed the pistol. When her jacket was back on, Danny could just make out a slight bulge where the weapon was, but only because he was trained to see it and he knew it was there in the first place. To a passing glance, Bethany was just a Western woman in a business suit. Danny checked the time: 18.03 hrs. 'Let's get moving,' he said. 'Don't forget your dark glasses.' Bethany lifted them from the breast pocket of her jacket to indicate she had them.

It took fifteen minutes to return to the seafront. The sun was setting and there was a chill in the air, but still enough of a glare for Bethany to warrant wearing sunglasses. The seafront boardwalk was still busy, and several yachts had moored close to land. Danny walked twenty metres behind Bethany. They looked too peculiar a couple, with Bethany in her business suit and Danny in his jeans and leather jacket, to be seen side by side. Not that Bethany went unnoticed. Heads turned as she passed. Not ideal, but at least it meant Danny himself was as good as invisible.

Danny had to hand it to Bethany. She had a certain flair. As she approached the section of the boardwalk opposite Al-Farouk's office, she showed no hint of nerves. Nobody would have thought that two hours previously she'd been telling Danny he was insane and refusing to go through with his plan. It had taken some fast talking from Danny just to get her to consider it. He'd already told her once today she was a good actor. Right now she was owning the part.

There was a low wall between the boardwalk and the seafront. Danny perched on it while Bethany crossed the road and walked with great confidence towards the office block. Without looking back, she entered via a revolving door.

Time check: 18.50 hrs. There was no sign of Al-Farouk's chauffeur in front of the building. Danny pulled his phone from his pocket and made a show of aimlessly staring at it and occasionally typing. Even here, in Beirut, there was nothing so ordinary as someone engrossed with their phone. In fact, he'd opened WhatsApp and he knew about now Bethany would be in a cubicle in the ladies' toilets, phone out, waiting for his message.

But he wasn't sending it yet. Al-Farouk's driver hadn't arrived.

18.53. Nothing. Danny looked left and right along the main road. It was full of traffic, but the vehicles were mainly old rust-buckets. A smart black SUV would stand out. There was no sign of it.

18.55. Danny sensed someone watching him from the other side of the road. He glanced in their direction. It was a Lebanese woman, mid-twenties. She looked embarrassed that she'd been caught watching him. She lowered her head and walked away.

18.56. Visual contact. A black SUV was approaching from the right. Distance: fifty metres and closing. Danny forced himself to focus on his phone, only watching the SUV in his peripheral vision. He avoided looking directly at the vehicle as it drove straight past him, but he noticed with satisfaction that all the windows, with the exception of the front windscreen, were so heavily tinted it was impossible to see inside.

The vehicle made a U-turn across the traffic and pulled over in front of the building, coming to a halt in its regular parking spot.

Danny typed a single-word message: 'Go.' He pressed send.

18.57. No sign of Bethany. They had three minutes till Al-Farouk appeared. If they didn't get this done before then, the moment was lost. Their only remaining option would be to bundle Al-Farouk into his own vehicle as he approached. That would be clumsy and, more to the point, obvious. It would be much better for Al-Farouk to enter his vehicle willingly, and find Danny waiting for him. 'Come on,' he muttered to himself.

The seconds dragged by. No sign of her. Danny considered sending another WhatsApp. He told himself to hold his nerve. She knew what she was doing.

18.58. Bethany appeared in front of the office block, her sunglasses propped up glamorously on her forehead. They'd done one job already, disguising her from any CCTV in the office block foyer. Now they had another job: to make her look, in the eyes of a man disposed to see her in such a way, like a Western bimbo thinking only of her appearance.

Danny moved, crossing the road as Bethany approached the X5. He was gambling that the chauffeur of the vehicle would be extremely reluctant to open his window to a Western man of Danny's gait and stature. But an insignificant woman who'd just emerged from Al-Farouk's office block? That was a different matter. Danny upped his pace. He had to coordinate himself properly with Bethany, so they both reached the X5 at about the same time.

Time check: 18.59.

Bethany was at the driver's window. Danny was approaching the car from behind. Distance: fifteen metres. He saw Bethany rapping on the driver's window. No response. She rapped again. Danny couldn't quite see the window itself, but he knew it was descending because Bethany bent down to its level, one hand feeling for the holster inside her jacket. Nobody else would have noticed her withdrawing the pistol. It was a small movement, easily concealed. But Danny noticed, five metres from the rear of the vehicle. And the chauffeur would have noticed too, because about now, the pistol barrel would be almost touching his face. And Bethany would be instructing the driver, in flawless Arabic, to unlock the vehicle.

Danny was three metres away when he heard the clunk of the central locking. Feigning nonchalance, he opened the rear passenger door, driver's side. He slipped into the back seat and sat immediately behind the chauffeur, closing the door behind him. He reached forward, unclipped the seatbelt, and forcibly wrapped it round the chauffeur's neck, pulling tight. 'Get in,' he told Bethany through the open window.

Bethan concealed her weapon and walked round the front of the vehicle. For Danny, this was the riskiest moment. He knew the chauffeur was likely to be armed. Sure enough, now he was no longer at gunpoint, the driver suddenly reached inside his jacket. Danny was fast enough to grab that arm and yank it back. Bethany entered the vehicle by the other rear passenger door and slammed it shut. She handed the Sig to Danny, who now let the seatbelt choker loosen and pressed the barrel of the pistol into the back of the chauffeur's head. Danny examined him in the rear-view mirror. He was young, mid-twenties maybe, with a sharp black suit and a tidy haircut, and easily recognisable from his photo. A bead of sweat trickled down his right cheek. His expression suggested both outrage and fear.

'Al-Farouk's coming,' Bethany said, her voice tense.

Now that he was armed, Danny had more options. He reached over and felt inside the chauffeur's jacket. A weapon was holstered there. Danny removed it – it was a Browning 9mm – and handed it to Bethany. 'Tell him to let his boss into the car as usual. Tell him I'll have my weapon trained on him at all times, and a round from this pistol will easily shatter glass and enter his body. Also tell him I like shooting IS monsters like him. His only chance of surviving this is to do exactly what he's told.'

Bethany looked a little disapproving, but she translated. Danny picked out Al-Farouk through the heavily tinted window of the X5. He took an instant dislike to the Lebanese businessman. Al-Farouk wore a pinstripe suit, slightly too small for him. Grey hair, balding. Skin like a prune and sharp, mean little eyes. He had his phone out and was texting as he walked, paying no attention to his surroundings.

The chauffeur opened the driver's door. Now was the difficult moment. If he decided to run, this would turn into exactly what Danny didn't want: a street tussle, overt and a matter of record. But he felt confident it wouldn't come to that. Everything had happened as quickly as he'd planned. The chauffeur was disoriented and scared. He wouldn't be thinking straight.

Al-Farouk didn't even look up as the chauffeur stepped from the car and opened the rear passenger door. If he had, perhaps he'd have noticed the wild look in his man's eyes. The Lebanese businessman was still engrossed with his phone as he ducked down to enter the car. It was only when Danny grabbed him by his collar and tugged him hard into the passenger seat that he realised something was wrong. He made a strangled sound, but by then it was too late. Danny leaned over him and pulled the rear door shut. The chauffeur stood on the pavement, obviously conflicted. He wanted to run, but was scared. Danny leaned forward, restraining the struggling Al-Farouk with one arm and pointing his weapon through the open driver's door with the other. He nodded to indicate the chauffeur should get back into the car. That was all it took. The IS man took his seat and shut the door. He gripped the wheel firmly, like a kid on a rollercoaster. He had one gun pointing at the back of his head and another – his own Browning held by Bethany – pointing at his midriff.

It had all happened in less than ten seconds. Only now did Al-Farouk react. He started shouting aggressively in Arabic, and reaching out to open the passenger door again. Danny didn't mess about. He moved his weapon to his left hand, clenched his right fist and slammed it hard into Al-Farouk's face. There was a splintering crack as the businessman's nose broke. Blood and mucus spurted down his face. As his initial outrage gave way to pain, he bent down, his face in his hands. Danny shifted his pistol back to his right hand and pointed it at the driver, his left hand pressing down on the back of Al-Farouk's head to keep him bent double and immobilised.

Danny didn't bother trying to speak Arabic. He knew the chauffeur would understand what he was telling him. 'Drive,' he said.

9

The chauffeur started the engine and pulled out into the traffic, cutting up another vehicle that beeped long and loud. The chauffeur swore under his breath, but he was obviously rattled and his full attention was not on his driving. 'Direct him,' Danny said. 'You know where we're going.'

Bethany delivered some instructions in Arabic. The chauffeur didn't seem to register any kind of response, but he kept driving.

'Tell him if he makes me nervous, I'll shoot him and do the driving myself. If he does what he's told, I'll let him go free in two hours.'

Again, Bethany translated. The chauffeur nodded curtly, keeping his eyes on the road. Danny noticed his knuckles were white from gripping the steering wheel. He yanked Al-Farouk back up to a sitting position. The businessman's face was a mess. Blood was still oozing slowly from his nostrils. Some of it had clotted on his upper lip, and some smeared where his chin and cheeks had touched his trousers.

'You and me are going to have a nice little chat,' Danny said.

'Who are you?' Al-Farouk demanded. His English sounded excellent.

'I'm the guy,' Danny said, 'who's going to cut your bollocks off and send them to your children if you don't do exactly what I say.'

'I demand that you . . .'

Danny whacked him on the nose again, not so forcefully this time, but hard enough to feel the broken bone shifting under the skin. Al-Farouk gasped in pain. He was still clutching his phone. Danny took it from him and switched it off. 'First things first,' he said. 'The only person making any demands is going to be me. My first demand is that you shut the fuck up and don't make any sudden movements. If you do, I might forget I need to talk to you and put a bullet in your face instead.'

Al-Farouk turned to him in horror, as if he was looking at a monster. He said nothing. Blood was flowing freely again, dripping off his chin.

The traffic through central Beirut was slow. A fog of exhaust fumes seemed to hover over the city, glowing faintly in the deep red of the setting sun. They crawled away from the coast, past the concrete shell of the Holiday Inn and the road that led to the British Embassy. A tense silence enveloped the car each time they stopped at a set of lights or a junction. Everyone was clearly thinking the same: these would be the best opportunities for Al-Farouk and his driver to hurl themselves from the vehicle and run away. So whenever the vehicle stopped, Danny nudged the back of the chauffeur's head with his weapon, and kept a steadying hand on Al-Farouk. Neither of them tried anything stupid.

Bethany, the Browning in her hand still pointing at the chauffeur's midriff, gave regular directions in Arabic. It occurred to Danny that perhaps the greatest humiliation for their IS chauffeur was to receive instructions from a woman. But he knew what was good for him. He kept silent and did as he was told.

Twenty minutes passed. Half an hour. Night fell, and headlights burned as they penetrated the suburbs of Beirut. The city became gradually less built-up, Danny's perception of it limited to streaks of light in his peripheral vision as cars passed in the other direction.

And then, near-darkness. A full yellow moon hung in the sky above them, bright enough to illuminate the line of a mountain ridge in the distance. To their left and right, trees. Vehicles in the oncoming direction passed at a rate of two or three a minute. And soon, less frequently than that.

All the while, Danny said nothing. He knew his silence would intimidate his captives all the more. When Al-Farouk dared to whisper a simple question – 'Where are you taking us?' – Danny growled at him to keep quiet. He could feel the Lebanese businessman trembling next to him. Experience suggested it wouldn't be long before his captive pissed himself.

Bethany instructed the chauffeur to turn left off the main road. A couple of minutes later they found themselves on a forest path, tall umbrella pines on either side of them. The X5 juddered slowly over the rough ground. The terrain – perhaps thirty klicks from the centre of Beirut, with no sign of human habitation anywhere – seemed to escalate Al-Farouk's terror. He was positively shaking now, and not without reason. Danny was inserting them into this unpopulated, hidden terrain for a reason. Al-Farouk was clearly sensing that it might not end well for him, and that suited Danny just fine.

The forest grew thicker on either side, the track narrower. They were heading downhill and the X5 was struggling. Danny was on the point of asking Bethany how much further they had to travel when she spoke to the chauffeur. They turned off down a narrower path to the right, trundled along for a further minute, then came to a halt. The vehicle's headlights illuminated the gable end of a tumbledown stone building. The roof had collapsed and vegetation was growing over the stonework, as if the forest was reclaiming it. At Bethany's instruction, the chauffeur killed the engine but kept the headlights burning. A blanket of deep silence covered them.

Danny could smell the businessman's fear. It was a stench of sweat and halitosis brought on by his anxiety. He knew their captives would try to run, given the chance. It was what most people would do in his position. He kept his weapon trained on the driver and looked at Bethany. 'Get Al-Farouk outside,' he said. 'If he tries to run, shoot him in the knee.'

Bethany exited the car, holding the chauffeur's handgun. She walked round the front and opened Al-Farouk's door. 'Out,' Danny told him. Al-Farouk wriggled awkwardly out of the vehicle. He was obviously thinking of running – his eyes darting here and there into the forest – but Bethany cast a strangely imposing figure in the darkness, and he remained where he was.

'Now you,' he told the chauffeur. He nudged the gun against the side of the man's head to give force to his words. The chauffeur hesitated. Danny knew he was considering his options. It was Danny's job to make sure he didn't have any. '*Get out!*' he shouted.

Danny's raised voice clearly scraped at the chauffeur's frayed nerves. He started, then scrambled to open the door. Danny exited the vehicle at the same time, keeping his weapon firmly trained on his target. Once they were standing outside the vehicle he indicated with his gun that they should move to the patch of ground between the X5 and the building, illuminated by the car's headlights. Danny and Bethany ushered their hostages in that direction. Then Danny forced them to their knees, so they were five metres from the car bonnet and squinting uncomfortably in the beam of the headlights.

Danny took up position with his back against the car, standing between the two headlights, knowing it would make him appear a sinister silhouette bearing down over them. He could see their faces clearly: dazzled, blinking and scared. He turned to Bethany, who was standing just outside the light cone from the car. 'You might want to look away,' he said.

'I'm fine,' she said, though her voice cracked as she said it.

Danny turned his attention back to his hostages. 'Okay, Al-Farouk,' he said. 'Up until a couple of months ago, you were meeting an IS representative once a month in Beirut. You knew him as Ahmed. At each meeting you'd give him a cash donation to the IS cause.'

'I don't know what you mean,' Al-Farouk said.

'Oh,' Danny said. 'Maybe we got it all wrong.'

Al-Farouk nodded enthusiastically. 'All wrong, yes,' he said.

'Shit,' Danny said. 'After all this trouble we've gone to.' He turned to Bethany. 'I guess we'd better kill them, in that case.' He stepped forward a couple of paces, his pistol secured in two hands, and released a single round directly into the head of the chauffeur.

The effect on Al-Farouk was immediate and profound. The retort of the weapon – stunningly loud in the silence of the forest

– made his whole body start. His eyes clenched shut and remained that way for a full five seconds, so he didn't see the chauffeur slump to the ground. He must surely, however, have felt the warm spatter of blood and brain matter as it showered him and his smart suit, spraying his already bloodied face. When he finally opened his eyes he stared first at Danny, who now had his gun pointing in Al-Farouk's direction, then to one side at the bleeding, mutilated corpse of his former driver. He whispered something in Arabic – a prayer, maybe – then squinted up at Danny. 'Please,' he whispered. 'No . . .'

'Sorry, pal,' Danny said. 'If you don't know anything about Ahmed, you're no good to me.' He strode a couple of paces towards Al-Farouk, his weapon outstretched.

'I know him!' Al-Farouk squealed. 'I know Ahmed! I know him!'

Danny stopped, but didn't lower his gun. 'You're lying,' he said. 'You're just telling me what I want to hear. Sorry buddy, it's curtains.'

'I swear I am not. *I swear it.* He has dark hair, a thin beard like a boy's. He comes every two months, to my office. I give him money and he takes it away. That's all I know, I swear . . .'

'He's still lying.' Bethany's voice was severe in the darkness.

Al-Farouk's eyes rolled. He shook his head. Danny stood right over him. 'Who told you when to expect Ahmed in your office?' he said. 'And take my word for it, pal: you're one wrong answer away from a bullet in the head.'

'Adnan Abadi,' Al-Farouk whispered.

Danny glanced across at Bethany. She shook her head to indicate that she didn't know the name.

'Where do I find him?'

Al-Farouk closed his eyes again. He was clearly reluctant to say anything. Danny grabbed him by his shirt collar and dragged him over to where the chauffeur's corpse was lying in a spreading pool of his own blood. When Al-Farouk opened his eyes again he was presented, close up, with the grisly sight of the chauffeur's shattered head. It was too much for the businessman, who loudly vomited all over the dead body. Danny let him finish, but didn't let him move from the proximity of the corpse. 'Where do I find him?' he repeated.

He couldn't make out the answer at first. Al-Farouk was half speaking, half retching. He asked the question for a second time, and only then did Al-Farouk make sense. 'He is an olive farmer. His farm is between Damascus and Homs.'

It was as if giving up that piece of information had entirely drained Al-Farouk. He collapsed, foetus-like, on the ground. Danny stepped away and walked back to the car, aware that Bethany was watching him intently. He reached into the vehicle and killed the headlights, shrouding them in thick, impenetrable darkness. 'Did Ibrahim ever mention this Adnan Abadi guy?'

'No. But that's hardly surprising. His handlers would have exercised basic separation of information.'

Danny nodded. 'I think he's telling the truth,' Danny said quietly, so only Bethany could hear him.

'Did you have to kill the chauffeur?' she said.

'Of course. If we let him go, he'd have gone straight back to his bosses. They'd have worked out what we're doing. Ibrahim would have a description of me, and he'd know you're out in the open.'

She looked like she was trying to find fault with that argument, but couldn't. 'We need to verify this intel,' she said. 'I have some contacts who . . .'

'Leave it to me,' Danny said. He pulled out his mobile. The service was weak out here, but there were a couple of bars. 'Watch him,' he said. 'Don't take your gun off him. I don't want to be scrabbling around in the forest trying to find the fucker if he decides to make a run for it.'

Bethany didn't look pleased with that prospect, but she didn't complain. Danny had to hand it to her. She might not like what he was doing, but she was dealing with it. He crossed over towards the dilapidated building, out of earshot. For a moment, he considered whether he should contact Sturrock or Hereford. Then he remembered how insistent the CO had been about reporting directly to him. He dialled his access number into Hereford. The call was answered immediately. '*Go ahead.*'

Danny had no call sign, and he knew he didn't need to speak his name. He simply told the voice at the end of the phone what he wanted. 'Do me an ID check. Adnan Abadi. He's an olive farmer, north-western Syria. Does he exist, is he on our radar, does he have extremist links to anybody else in the region? It's urgent.'

'*We'll call you back.*' The line went dead.

Danny knew Hereford would work fast. He stayed put and looked back in the direction of the car. The moon was visible through the treetops. It cast silver beams on to the forest floor, half illuminating the car. Bethany was perched on the bonnet. She was capably holding the weapon in two hands. Al-Farouk was sprawled on the ground on all fours. Danny found himself staring intently at Bethany. She barely moved. Danny sensed that her revulsion at the chauffeur's killing had dissipated. Now she seemed calm. Danny was weirdly reminded of Ibrahim Khan himself, and the way he sat on his bed all those years ago. Quiet, tranquil, unflustered. It struck him that of all Ibrahim's potential targets – the three SAS men who'd humiliated him in training, the arsehole of a colonel who ran the MISFIT operation, the translator who furnished him with the linguistic tools he needed to operate deep under cover – his most difficult prospect might be Bethany White, his case officer. She'd acted skilfully this evening. She was a good operator.

Danny heard a sound off to his left. Bethany clearly heard it too, because like Danny she instantly moved her weapon in that direction. Danny scanned the terrain ahead of him. Just behind the tree line he saw the shape of an animal, about the size of a fox, slink back into the darkness. He exhaled slowly, lowering his weapon. Bethany turned hers back to Al-Farouk, but Danny could tell she was now looking across at him. He almost thought their eyes met, but that was impossible. He was completely in shadow.

His phone vibrated. He answered immediately. 'Go ahead.'

'*We have confirmation. Adnan Abadi is a former Syrian government minister. He had a diplomatic position in the UK when he was younger . . .*'

'So he speaks English?'

'Presumably. He was pushed out by the Syrian regime because of suspected sympathies with IS when they were dominant in the area. He's an influential guy so it was difficult for them to do anything more permanent. We do know his brother was a high-value IS commander, believed killed twelve months ago in a Russian air strike.'

'Is there any evidence that Abadi has direct IS links?'

'Nothing concrete, but the CIA and Mossad have him on their watch list. He's a player.'

It was all Danny needed to hear. 'Get everything you have on him sent through to the British Embassy in Beirut for the personal attention of Bethany White.'

'Roger that.'

Danny finished the conversation and killed the call. Then he walked back across the open ground towards Bethany. She gave him an enquiring glance. Danny nodded. He turned to look at Al-Farouk. The businessman was a mess. He was crouched on the ground like a frightened child, his arms covering his head. There was an occasional mew of terror. It was a pitiful sight.

'I'm going to finish him,' Danny said.

Bethany put one hand on his gun arm. 'You don't have to,' she said. 'I'd prefer it if you didn't.'

'We don't have a choice.'

'Sure we have a choice. It's easy. One phone call. We get MI6 to pay some money into his account, easily traceable back to them. We let Al-Farouk know if he steps out of line, we'll leak details back to Islamic State. He'll know their punishment will be far worse than anything we'd ever come up with.'

Danny shook his head. 'It's not secure enough. He's seen us both. He can describe us. That's gold dust to Khan.'

'He's got kids, Danny.'

'Yeah,' Danny said. 'So do you. So do I.'

'Listen, this isn't the first time I've worked alongside one of you people. I call the shots, and I say . . .'

'No, *you* listen,' Danny cut in. 'If Ibrahim Khan decides to come looking for him, how safe do you think his wife and kids will be then?'

'Are you *seriously* trying to tell me you're doing it in their best interests?'

'I'm just giving you a different way to think about it, if you want. It doesn't matter either way, though. We've got what we need from him. Now I need to clean up. Turn your back.'

Bethany looked like she was trying to find another argument, but she couldn't. Danny approached Al-Farouk. The Lebanese businessman looked up. His face was smeared with a mixture of mud, blood and tears. Danny could see the moon reflected in his eyes. 'Please,' Al-Farouk whispered. 'My little ones . . .'

There was nothing to be gained from waiting. Danny raised his weapon.

'Not in the head, I beg you,' Al-Farouk said. He started to cry again. '*Not in the head . . .*'

Danny saw no reason not to grant the man his dying wish. He lowered his weapon a little so that it was aiming at the chest area. Al-Farouk closed his eyes and whispered the words '*Allah-u-Akbar*'. Danny squeezed the trigger twice in quick succession. The shots echoed loudly around the forest as Al-Farouk slumped to one side on to the ground.

10

They left the bodies where they were. Bethany assured Danny that few people ever came to this location. That was why she and Ibrahim Khan had chosen it. It would be days, weeks even, before anybody came across Danny's victims.

The vehicle was a different matter. They needed it to get back into central Beirut, but it was crawling with their DNA by now. They couldn't drive it into the embassy compound, not if they wanted to keep their night's work under the radar. The Lebanese police would be searching for it as soon as Al-Farouk was reported missing. 'I know a place,' Bethany said as she removed Danny's holster and gave it back to him. She was surprisingly calm, given what she'd just witnessed. If she was angry with Danny for nailing Al-Farouk, she was professional enough not to show it. Danny was grateful for that. It had been a long day, and he wasn't in the mood for a grilling by the ethics committee.

'Where?' he said.

'It's an underground car park in the Sabra district. It's run by a Palestinian guy. He'll keep it under wraps for as long as we pay him. If the money runs out, he strips the plates and sells it in Syria or Gaza, but it won't come to that. I'll notify MI6 and they'll get some of our fixers along to clean the vehicle out and make it disappear.'

'Will they know it's anything to do with MISFIT?'

'Those guys don't even know what MISFIT is. They just do their job.'

They drove in silence out of the forest and on to the main road. Danny drove soberly back towards Beirut. The last thing he wanted was to draw the attention of the police. He followed Bethany's directions into a run-down suburb. Compared to the seafront, it felt like a different city. Bleak concrete blocks. Groups of young men, their heads wrapped in black and white keffiyehs, loitering on street corners. Arabic music blared from open windows. If the harbour was rich Mediterranean, this was poor Middle Eastern. It wasn't a place for Danny and Bethany's white skin and expensive car.

The parking lot was down a narrow, dead-end side street. Danny felt uncomfortable entering it, but Bethany assured him this was the right way, and she seemed to know what she was talking about. There was nothing to indicate what the premises were for: just a heavily padlocked metal double door with an unmarked intercom on the right and a separate pedestrian entrance a little further along. Danny pulled up while Bethany exited the vehicle and spoke into the intercom. A man appeared at the pedestrian entrance. He was squat and overweight, with several days' stubble and a couple of missing teeth. He seemed to recognise Bethany, though he registered no pleasure at seeing her. He glanced through the driver's window of the X5, giving Danny a cursory and unimpressed glance, then took a key from his pocket and unlocked the double doors. He swung them open and indicated that Danny should drive in. Danny loosened the Sig in his holster and placed it on the dashboard where their unsavoury-looking host could see it, then drove in.

The garage was dark and stank of fuel. There were five other vehicles. One of them was jacked up with no wheels or doors. Danny parked up alongside it, took his weapon and exited the car. Bethany was wordlessly handing over a sheaf of bank notes to the man. He counted them suspiciously, then crammed them into his pocket. The transaction was done. He stared at Danny. Not at his face, but at his hands. Danny realised they were blood-spattered. 'Ask him if there's somewhere I can clean up,' he said to Bethany.

Bethany made the request and the man pointed to a door at the far side of the garage. Behind it was a foul toilet and a small sink where Danny tried, without much success, to scrub the blood off his hands in a trickle of cold water. He returned to Bethany with his hands in his pocket. 'Let's get out of here,' he said.

They exited the garage. Back on the main street, people stared aggressively from behind their keffiyehs, especially at Bethany with her blonde hair and crumpled business suit. Danny, however, allowed his holster to show, and that was enough to ward off any unwanted attention. After five minutes they turned on to a larger thoroughfare and managed to flag down a taxi. It was a mustard-yellow Toyota, stinking of incense, with garlands and religious icons draped across the dashboard. The driver kept staring at them in the rear-view mirror as the radio played Arabic music that to Danny's ear was indistinguishable from the stuff he'd heard on the streets. It took them ten minutes to reach the vicinity of the embassy. Bethany told the driver to stop a couple of streets away, and paid him more than he asked for. They waited for the taxi to drive out of sight before covering the final couple of hundred metres on foot and entering the embassy compound by the side entrance. The guys on duty recognised them, but examined their ID anyway. They were clearly curious as to where Danny and Bethany had been, but knew better than to ask any questions. Danny kept his bloodied hands out of sight.

It was just before eleven when they reached their apartment. The door was slightly ajar. Danny held out one arm to stop Bethany entering, then drew his weapon. He approached silently. There was a light on inside. He gently kicked the door open, clutching the weapon two-handed. The main room was as they'd left it, with one exception: there was a box file on the coffee table. The door to Bethany's bedroom was also open. Danny moved stealthily towards it, then violently kicked it open.

Larry Baker, the ambassador's assistant who had met them at the airport, was leaning over Bethany's bedside table, opening the drawer. He spun round when he heard Danny enter, then clutched both hands to his chest. His glasses slipped down his sweaty nose.

'G-G-Good grief, man,' he stuttered. 'Will you please put that bloody thing down?'

'What are you doing?' Danny didn't lower his gun.

Baker flushed. 'I'm . . . I'm just checking everything's okay with the room.'

'The ambassador's assistant does the housekeeping these days, does he?' Danny said. 'Times must be hard.'

Baker was almost purple with embarrassment now. 'I brought you some documents,' he spluttered. 'London sent them through a few minutes ago. They're in a box file . . .'

'. . . on the coffee table. Yeah, I saw. Any documents from London in Bethany's underwear drawer?'

Baker's expression went from embarrassment to outrage and back again. Danny was almost certain he'd been rooting around in here for some kind of cheap sexual thrill. The ambassador's assistant made a few spluttering sounds. Danny considered toying with him a little longer, but it was late and he was tired. 'Get the hell out of here,' he said.

Baker clumsily closed the drawer. He muttered to himself as he pushed past Danny and exited the bedroom. Danny followed. 'It's okay!' he called to Bethany, who entered the room.

'Larry?'

Baker waved airily at the box file on the coffee table. 'Just delivering some documents, my dear,' he said, unable to hide how flustered he was. 'I'll be off now.'

He scurried out of sight.

'What *was* he doing?'

'You don't want to know.'

Bethany made a sour face, but didn't seem to be taking it too seriously. She pointed at the box file. 'Is that the intel on Adnam Abadi? Your friends at Hereford have worked fast.'

Danny locked the door from the inside. 'You should get a shower,' he said. 'I've got some reading to do and some calls to make.'

Bethany looked faintly amused. 'Have you seen the state of you?' she said. Danny looked down at his clothes. He hadn't noticed in the darkness, but it wasn't just his hands that were bloodstained. There was spatter over the lower part of his jeans too. 'You clean up first,' Bethany said. 'Please, you look like a butcher.'

She wasn't wrong. Danny went to the bathroom, which was en-suite to Bethany's bedroom. He stripped, and stared at himself in the mirror. There were scars all over his body, like a map of his past battles. He felt unclean. There was a very particular kind of filth associated with the aftermath of a killing. A combination of sweat, cordite, blood and dirt. It required extremely hot water. He turned the shower on, waited for it to reach its scalding maximum temperature, then stepped inside. His skin smarted, but he endured the heat. He scrubbed his hands particularly hard. Pale pink water sluiced down the plug hole. Only after five minutes did it run clear.

There was a bath sheet hanging on the towel rail. Danny wrapped it round his waist and walked into the bedroom, expecting it to be empty. It wasn't. Bethany had undressed and was wearing a white dressing gown, loosely tied at the front. She was standing by the bed and as Danny walked in she gave him an overtly appreciative look, then walked towards him. Her lips were slightly parted, and a tendril of blonde hair tumbled over her forehead. The golden freckles on her nose and cheeks looked especially alluring.

Danny was surprised. Since walking in on her embrace with Christina the interpreter back at the farmhouse in Brecon, he'd assumed the colonel was right: for Bethany, guys weren't on the menu. But she had a kid, he supposed. Maybe the menu wasn't limited to one choice. Maybe it was unusually long. He put one hand on her hips. She smiled, then removed it. 'Look but don't touch, Danny,' she whispered. She stepped to one side and pointed at the cupboard next to the door. 'There are blankets in there,' she said. 'To make the couch comfortable.' She disappeared into the bathroom.

Danny stood there for a few seconds, smiling ruefully. He was finding it hard to get the measure of Bethany White. She was scared but brave. Flirtatious but untouchable. She disapproved of Danny nailing Al-Farouk and his driver, but now it was done she seemed completely unconcerned. He shrugged. It was for the best. What would his old mate Spud have said, if he was here now? *Don't dip the quill in the company inkwell, buddy* . . . Not that Spud would ever have taken his own advice.

Danny left the bedroom, found some clean clothes in his suitcase, and dressed. He took a seat. He was as tired as hell. He closed his eyes for a moment, inhaled slowly, then reached for the box file on the coffee table and examined its contents. There wasn't much. In fact, the intel was so scant it crossed Danny's mind that somebody at the other end might be holding back on him. Three photographs, black and white and taken with a telephoto lens, of an elderly man with round glasses, wearing a traditional dishdasha, like a Middle Eastern Ghandi. There was a newspaper clipping from the *New York Times* about an air strike near Aleppo, reporting the probable death of an IS commander called Mohammed Abadi – that would be Adnan's brother, Danny assumed. Good riddance to bad rubbish. There was a satellite map with an area circled on it – agricultural land – and some lat/long figures scrawled next to it. As briefing documents went, it was distinctly lacking in hard information. If the CIA and Mossad were interested in this guy, their intelligence gathering had been poor. Or maybe this was the limit of what they were prepared to share with MI6.

Whatever, it was all the information Danny needed. He had a phone call to make. He switched the TV on. It was still tuned to the Arabic music channel he'd used earlier. He turned it up to mask the conversation he was about to have.

It was impossible to tell if Ray Hammond was relieved or peeved to hear from him, because he was as abrupt and unemotional as ever. 'What's that shit in the background?' he demanded.

'MTV, Lebanon style.'

'What do you need?'

'I have to get into Syria,' Danny said. 'The north-west area, between Damascus and Homs.'

'The lat/long location we just sent through to the embassy?'

'Roger that.'

'It's pretty fucked up round there.'

'I know. I'll need gear, and some guys to make the border crossing. I'll need to be tooled up, so I don't want to risk getting caught at the border or checkpoints on the main supply routes. Can you get me a team out here?'

'No can do,' Hammond said.

'Boss, I . . .'

'Forget it, Black. We're running on empty. We'll get you some freelancers.'

'Do you have any in-country?'

'I'll find out. Stay by your phone.' The line went dead.

Bethany entered the sitting room. Her hair was wet and scraped back from her face. She was still wearing her dressing gown but she no longer emanated flirtation. She sat opposite Danny and nodded at the box file. 'What you got?'

'Not much. A few photos. A location.' He paused, then stood up, took the box file and led Bethany back into the en-suite bathroom, where he felt they could speak more freely. It was steamy and humid. Bethany sat on the toilet seat again, while Danny perched on the edge of the bath. 'I have to get into Syria.'

'Adnan Abadi's olive farm?'

He nodded.

'You'll need a visa to cross the border.'

'Yeah, I don't think I'll be bothering with that.'

She nodded. 'It's dangerous. There are parts of Syria that are more or less safe, but there are still bombing campaigns in certain areas and you don't want to run into government forces if you're not supposed to be there.'

'I know,' Danny said. 'I was in Syria eight years ago.' He frowned. That operation hadn't ended well. He'd almost put it from his mind. 'Adnan Abadi is our only lead. I have to speak to him.'

'Then we'll go,' Bethany said confidently.

'No,' Danny replied. 'Not we. I.'

Bethany expressed no emotion. 'You want me to head back to the UK?' she said, her voice level. 'Just when we were beginning to get to know each other?'

Danny didn't get the chance to answer. His mobile vibrated. It was Ray Hammond. 'What have you got, boss?' Danny asked.

'You sound like you're in a fucking swimming pool now.'

'Bathroom. What have you got?'

'A team of three former SF lads working for CNN in Beirut. One from 22, one SBS, one Delta. They take news crews across the border into Syria and they've done a couple of private jobs moving CIA operatives in-country. They've got all the gear and the local knowledge. They're your best bet.'

'Put me in contact?'

'Already done,' Hammond said. 'They're expecting you at 06.45 tomorrow. RV outside the Grand Mosque. MI6 is going to wire them a payment on account. Tell them whatever you need.'

'Roger that. Do you have names for me?'

'Joe Ludlow, left A Squadron about the time you joined. Mike Rollett is the SBS lad. Bradley Guerrero from Delta.'

'Copy. What do they know about me?'

'Your name, and that you need an escort. I have some further intel on Adnan Abadi.'

'Go ahead.'

'A few months ago, the Syrians bombed the last IS stronghold in the south, and they took out a contingent of the militants. But not all of them. We don't have anything concrete, but we have access to a few CIA reports that suggest some of the militants who survived sought sanctuary with Abadi. You can expect his place to be heavily guarded.'

'Right,' Danny said grimly. He hadn't really expected less, but it was useful to have his suspicions confirmed.

There was a pause. 'How's it going out there, Black?' There was something probing in his voice. Hammond was clearly trying to pump him for information.

'Good,' Danny said, evading his real meaning. 'Grand Mosque, 06.45. Joe Ludlow, Mike Rollett, Bradley Guerrero. I've got to go, boss.' He hung up.

'So?'

'I'm meeting with some guys who can help get me into Syria.'

'And what am I supposed to do?'

'For now, nothing.'

'Do I go back to London?'

Danny shook his head. 'No. I can't promise to keep you safe there. I've got a hunch that when I find Abadi, Ibrahim won't be far away. The closer we are to him, the higher the chance he'll find out what we're doing. I want to be able to get back to you quickly. Also, if we send you back to the UK, it's easier for people to find out where you are, and I won't be there to protect you. You need to stay in Beirut.'

Bethany chewed the nail on her right thumb, deep in thought. 'Okay,' she said finally. 'I'll stay here in the embassy.'

'No,' Danny told her. 'That won't do.' He patted the box file on his lap.

'I don't get it,' Bethany said.

'Baker just walked in here. He might have been more interested in the contents of your underwear drawer than anything else' – Bethany made an 'ew' face – 'but it means we don't know how many people have access to this room, or even how many people know you're here. It's not secure.'

'Danny, this is the British embassy.'

Danny gave her an amused look. 'Do you know and trust everybody who works here? Do you know and trust every British citizen that rocks up here on a daily basis? Ibrahim Khan's a British citizen for a start.'

'But surely he wouldn't make an attempt on my life with so many people around?' Bethany said.

'Tell that to Al-Farouk and his driver,' Danny said.

Bethany had no answer to that.

'My job is to keep you safe,' Danny said. 'If I can't be with you night and day, I need to make sure you're somewhere nobody else can find you. Tomorrow morning, I'm going to RV with the team that'll take me across the border. We'll make arrangements. I want you to know what they are, because if things turn to shit and I don't make it back out, you have the intel to pick up the trail. When that's done, we'll book you into a hotel.'

'There's a decent place not far from here I sometimes use.'

'Forget it. All the decent places will require a passport or some sort of ID. We don't want to give that. We'll need a back-street doss house where they won't ask any questions. Only two people in the world are going to know where you are: you and me. While you're there, you keep your room locked from the inside and you don't leave. Not for any purpose.'

'It seems a bit over the top,' Bethany said.

'If I'm not there with you, we're still running a massive risk.'

Bethany stared at him. 'How long do you think you'll be?' she said.

'Four days,' he said. 'Maybe three. Less if I can. It's not a place you want to stay for long.'

She nodded silently. Danny stood up. 'I'm going to get some sleep,' he said. 'It's going to be a long few days.' He headed towards the bathroom door.

'Danny,' Bethany said.

'Yeah?'

'Thank you. I mean it.'

Danny nodded curtly and left the en-suite and the bedroom. Back in the main room he killed the music channel and unfolded his blanket. He checked his weapon, placed it under the sofa that was to be his bed for the night, and switched off the lights. He stood in the darkness, listening. He could hear Bethany moving around in her bedroom. A pale frame of light surrounded the door. Along the bottom edge, Danny could just make out the shadow of Bethany's feet. He knew she was standing just on the other side. Was she thinking of joining him? Maybe he should knock softly. Maybe he should rejoin Bethany in the bedroom. This time tomorrow, he'd be preparing for an insertion into a war zone. A night in Bethany's bed was a far more attractive prospect than a night on the couch.

Look but don't touch, Danny. Bethany had made herself quite clear. And anyway, the shadows of her feet were no longer visible. The light disappeared. She'd switched it off.

Danny returned to the couch and pulled the blanket over his clothes. Soon he was asleep.

11

Danny slept badly and woke long before dawn, his muscles aching and his mind whirring. It was just gone five when he finally threw off his blanket and pulled on some clean clothes from his suitcase. He could hear Bethany moving around in the bedroom. 'You up in there?' he called.

She entered the room, fully dressed now. 'Comfortable night?' she said.

'Not really. I could use a coffee.'

'Me too.' She looked around the room. 'Are we coming back here?'

Danny shook his head. 'Get all your stuff,' he said.

Bethany packed a rucksack with her purse, passport, make-up, hairbrush, and a few items of clean clothing. Danny grabbed his passport, money and weapon. He took the intelligence sheets from the box file, carefully folded them and stowed them in a pocket. That was all he needed, for now. They left their suitcases where they were.

The embassy compound was deserted, apart from the two armed guards at the side entrance, who let them out with enquiring glances but no awkward questions. The early morning call to prayer rang out over the rooftops of Beirut and there were a few cars on the main thoroughfares. At Danny's request, Bethany led them through some tiny, maze-like side streets before bringing them out on to a square where the Grand Mosque was situated. It was a large, sand-coloured building with impressive arches, tall minarets and blue domes. Sections of the mosque were cordoned off by metal railings, and there were already police officers patrolling the area. Morning worshippers hurried up the steps into the mosque. On the opposite side of the square, a small cafe was open. It was warm and inviting, and felt a million miles from the rough slum where'd they'd ditched the X5 the previous night. The cafe was surprisingly busy and bustling, given how early it was. Danny and Bethany took a table on the pavement outside – the only free one of eight or nine. Bethany ordered them small cups of thick, black coffee and a plate of sweet cakes. They ate ravenously. Danny checked the time: 06.30 hrs. He looked towards the mosque.

'How will you recognise them?' Bethany said.

'I just will,' Danny told her.

And he did.

The three SF guys didn't appear at the same place and time, but Danny hadn't expected them to. They would be as cautious of him as he was of them, to start with at least. From his vantage point outside the cafe, he clocked the first guy as he entered the square from the north-east. He was tall, with short dark hair and a moustache that extended down the sides of his mouth. He was dressed in jeans and a North Face jacket, zipped up. Everything about his gait told Danny that he was carrying. He stood at the foot of the mosque's steps, arms folded, scanning the area. So far, Danny didn't think he'd noticed him. He tried to work out which of the three guys this was, and immediately settled on Bradley Guerrero, the Yank from Delta. It was the moustache. Something about it said Alabama, rather than Hereford or Poole.

The second guy walked straight past Danny and Bethany without seeming to notice them. It was the bulge at the bottom of his trousers that gave him away: he clearly had a snubnose holstered there. He was older than Danny expected, early fifties maybe, but he had a face that looked like it had been chiselled from granite, and a sturdy, rugby-player's physique to match. This was Joe Ludlow, he decided, the former SAS man. Hammond had said he'd left the Regiment around the time Danny started, and he looked about the right age. He took up position ten metres along from the cafe. Danny saw him catch the other guy's eye:

confirmation, if he needed it, that these two men were operating together.

Time check: 06.37. Danny hadn't clocked his third guy yet. As Bethany ordered more coffee, he scanned the area. He saw him a minute later, climbing out of a taxi fifty metres to Danny's three o'clock. Similar in build to the first guy, with a nose that had obviously once been broken and dark glasses, he paid the cab driver and walked straight past Danny and Bethany as he approached the second guy. They spoke briefly.

'Stay here,' Danny said. 'I'm going to make contact.'

He stood up and walked up to the two guys. They gave him a distinctly unfriendly look. 'Ludlow?' Danny said. 'Rollett?'

It was plain they didn't like the fact that Danny had recognised them so easily. He didn't blame them. Escorting news crews across the Lebanon–Syria border wasn't child's play. But equally, it wasn't serious Regiment work. It would be easy to become a bit soft. Three guys, on form and on ops, would never have allowed themselves to be so obvious.

'Who's asking?'

'You know who I am,' Danny said. He looked over the road at the first guy. 'Is he joining us?'

'He'll watch.'

Danny held out his hand. 'Danny Black,' he said. The other two seemed to relax a bit. They shook his hand and introduced themselves. Danny had got their names bang on. 'Let's walk,' Ludlow said.

Danny glanced over at the cafe. Bethany was still sitting there, her face alert.

'Nice,' Rollett said. He put his dark glasses up on his forehead and stroked his misshapen nose. 'Wouldn't mind a crack at her myself.'

'You're barking up the wrong tree, mate. You armed?'

He nodded.

'Then do me a favour, take my seat next to her. Anyone tries to approach her, scare them off.'

'You the jealous type?'

'Just do it, mate. Me and Ludlow are going to stay in sight. If anything goes noisy, we'll be there.'

'You expecting things to go noisy?'

'We're not here for the sightseeing.'

Rollett nodded and headed towards the cafe. Danny and Ludlow started to stroll around the square. 'I had Hammond on the blower last night,' Ludlow said. 'Told me the square root of fuck all. What's going on?' He wiped his nose on his sleeve, and Danny saw he had a black tattoo extending down his arm on to the back of his hand. It looked like the head of a wolf.

'I need to get into Syria. There's an olive farmer I want to have a heart-to-heart with.'

'Oh yeah? Thinking of going into the olive oil business?'

Ludlow's questioning was aggressive. Danny felt he'd got off on the wrong foot. He shouldn't have made them feel like their SOPs were rusty. But nor did he want to give them too much information. 'He's got some intel I need. Have you operated in the area between Damascus and Homs lately?'

'Sure.'

'What's the situation there?'

'Volatile. Government forces have retaken most of western Syria and they know there are still pockets of resistance, various rebel groups lying low, Islamist sympathisers with links to IS, Al-Qaeda and various other splinter organisations. They keep a pretty firm grip on the situation.'

'Can you get me into Syria?' Danny said.

'You can get yourself into Syria, pal. Easiest thing in the world. Your granny could do it. Go to the embassy, get yourself a visa, the Masna border crossing's just a couple of hours from here. Twenty minutes wait this side, twenty minutes the other side, you're all good. There are a few checkpoints on the way, but as long as you're clean . . .'

'Is that what you tell your news crews when they want to get in under the radar?' Ludlow didn't answer. 'It takes days for the Syrians to agree a visa, and I don't want my face on their paperwork. Also, I'm not going to be clean. I don't want the border or checkpoint guards paying close attention to the gear I hope you're going to supply me with.'

'What do you need?'

'The full English. I want to be prepared for whatever we might come across. Can you sort that for me?'

'It's possible. Won't be cheap.'

'MI6 is footing the bill. They've wired you money already. You don't have to worry about that. You just have to worry about getting me in and back out again.'

'Why us? Hereford could mount an airborne insertion in their sleep.'

'Do you want the job or not?' Danny said.

Ludlow sniffed, then wiped his nose again. For some reason, Danny found his eyes drawn once more to the tattoo. There was nothing decorative about it. It looked to Danny like a mark of pure aggression. Ludlow looked around the square. 'You'd better come with us,' he said. 'We've got a place where it's easier to talk.'

'How far?'

'Ten minutes. Go get the chick and follow us.'

Bethany was plainly unimpressed by whatever conversational gambits Rollett had attempted. She sat cross-legged, facing away from him. Rollett had a schoolboy grin on his face, and was stroking his broken nose in the same way as before. When Danny told them they were leaving, she did nothing to hide her relief. She even managed to appear rather prim as she stood up and left a note on the table to pay for their breakfast. 'Ignore Rollett, darling,' Ludlow said. 'He's got a potty mouth. You go ahead, Mike. I'll show them the way.'

Rollett was still grinning as he left. 'Don't leave me alone with that man again,' Bethany said. 'Where are we going?'

'Follow me,' Rollett told her.

The streets were getting busier. They had to weave in and out of rushing pedestrians as Rollett led them in a direction that Danny estimated to be approximately south-east, into an area that was by no means as low-rent as the place they'd been last night to dump the car, but was still decidedly down-market. They stopped at a tower block. The fascia of the block itself had a chunk of concrete missing between the second and third floors, and bullet holes from automatic fire. Rollett led them up a bare, echoing staircase to the sixth floor and into a flat where Rollett and Bradley Guerrero, the Delta guy, were waiting for them, sprawled out on a couple of sofas, legs apart, bottles of water in their fists. This was obviously an apartment where men lived. It wasn't untidy – these were military personnel after all – but it was completely functional. The sofas didn't match, the walls were bare and the TV had pride of place. Against one wall was a stack of scuffed flight cases. They bore stickers that read 'Press', 'CNN' and, in a couple of instances, 'BBC'. They were clearly intended to look like camera gear, but Danny suspected that in reality they served a different purpose.

Guerrero had ditched his North Face jacket and wore a grey shirt, the top few buttons open. He eyed the newcomers with apparent suspicion. Neither Rollett nor Ludlow spoke. Danny could tell they were waiting for Guerrero. He was the leader of this mismatched trio. He suddenly stood up and a broad, likeable smile crossed his face. He held out one hand. 'Brad Guerrero.' An accent straight from the deep south of America.

'Danny Black.'

Guerrero looked at Bethany. 'And this is?'

'You can call her Jane.'

Guerrero didn't immediately reply. There was tension in the air. The Yank had a challenger for his position of authority, who was withholding information. Danny stood firm. These three freelancers needed to understand that he was in charge now. Guerrero inclined his head. 'Pleased to meet you, Jane,' he said.

'Me Tarzan,' Rollett muttered, but nobody paid him any attention, least of all Bethany.

Guerrero turned back to Danny. 'I need to get into Syria,' Danny said. 'Covertly. With weapons. No official border crossings.'

'Crawling with Lebanese border police on this side, friend, and Syrian government troops on the other. Not to mention Russian special forces, here and there. Where exactly are we going?'

Danny unfolded the satellite map with the lat/long location and handed it to Guerrero. Guerrero glanced at it, then fetched a small, scuffed flight case from the pile at the back of the room. When he opened it up, Danny realised it was a laptop. He typed in the lat/long numbers, reading them out loud as he did so. Then he sat back and looked at the screen. 'You don't want much, do you, friend?' he said.

'Can you do it?'

He looked at Bethany. 'Is she coming?'

'No. Can you do it?'

Guerrero didn't answer immediately. When he did, it was with a slow nod of the head. 'You want the lil' lady to hear all this?'

Bethany was about to retort, but Danny silenced her with a glance. 'It's fine,' he said.

Guerrero shrugged. 'You're the client,' he said. 'Getting across the border itself isn't the biggest issue. There are plenty of stretches where it's just a fence – rolls of razor wire, about a metre high, strung between pickets. The locals have smuggling routes for moving commodities in and out of Syria and Lebanon – weapons, alcohol, drugs, whatever there's a market for. They cut through the fence and move across the border that way.'

This was not new to Danny. He'd crossed borders this way before and it gave him confidence that Guerrero and the others knew what they were talking about.

'The border guards fix the holes up again, but they tend just to use normal barbed wire for repairs so the fences are easier to cut through where they've patched it up – a pair of wire cutters will do it. You don't want to mess around cutting the rolled razor wire without protective gear and plenty of time. But the authorities have taken to digging in anti-personnel mines around the weak spots. Guess they like to make things a bit spicier for guys like us.'

'You have mine-detecting equipment?'

Guerrero jabbed one thumb over his shoulder at the flight cases.

'And you know where the current weak spots are?' Danny asked.

'We have a little team of guys,' Guerrero said. 'Lebanese. They drive up and down the border every few days and mark the weak spots on a map.' He pointed at the laptop. 'This area here, where we'll want to make the crossing, our fixer there is a guy called Barak. He's good news. Lebanese, but knows the Syrian terrain well and he can translate. We should take him with us.'

Guerrero spoke with confidence and expertise. Danny liked him. He could tell Ludlow and Rollett were the muscle in this trio. Guerrero could certainly handle himself, no doubt about that. But he had the brains to back it up. He was also already talking like he was on-side. This was a done deal. 'What about transport and weapons?' Danny said.

'We have a Hilux here with press markings. Weapons, we can't safely keep here in Beirut. The authorities pretty much know who we are, but we can't keep up the pretence of being press employees if we're toking assault rifles. We have weapons caches dug into the ground at strategic points along the border. We'll collect them before we make the crossing.'

Danny nodded. Guerrero was inspiring even more confidence. 'What about timings?' he said. 'I want to get to my guy as quickly as possible.'

Guerrero looked at his laptop again. 'We can get to the cache in about three hours,' he said. 'We hook up with Barak, make the crossing tonight. I advise that we lie up during the day. We don't want to be stopped and asked difficult questions. We've got some NV goggles so we're good for night-time driving.'

'Roger that,' Danny agreed. 'How long from our lying-up point to the target.'

'Another three hours. Maybe four, depends on how we go. You should expect to close in on your target at dawn in two days' time.'

Danny looked at each of his team in turn. 'When we reach our destination, it might go noisy. There's a chance my guy will have some IS militants guarding his place. You fellas comfortable dealing with that?'

The three men stared back at him. They didn't answer directly. They didn't need to. Their grim, resolute expressions told Danny everything he needed to know.

'Do you have enough heavy weaponry in your cache to put in a decent distraction while I find my guy?'

'Gimpy, Minimi, AKs,' Ludlow said. 'Heavy enough for you?'

Danny pointed at the laptop. 'Can I look at that?' he said. He sat down next to Guerrero and examined the satellite image on the laptop screen. The lat/long numbers had pinpointed a ringed compound in the centre of an agricultural area. Danny couldn't make out any entrances in the compound wall, but a single road led to it from almost precisely due south, from which he surmised that the main entrance was on the southern edge of the compound. The agricultural land completely surrounded the compound, and the crops – olive trees, Danny supposed – were grown in neat lines, like vineyards. The compound itself comprised several buildings. Guerrero pointed at two large blocks in the western half of the compound. 'I'd say this is some kind of processing facility,' he said. 'These blocks here are most likely the living quarters, but we won't know for sure till we're on the ground.'

Danny pointed to the area north-east of the compound. 'This looks like raised ground,' he said. 'When we arrive, I want you guys to put in a firing position there. Open up and draw them out. That'll give me a chance to enter the compound and find my guy.'

If the others felt uncomfortable about purposefully picking a firefight with a bunch of IS militants, they didn't show it. If anything, Danny sensed they were more eager to get moving. Ludlow and Rollett looked fierce, like attack dogs on a leash, ready to pounce. For men trained to fight, years of escorting news crews from place to place could grow monotonous, Danny supposed. Guerrero looked more thoughtful, like he was still weighing up the pros and cons of the operation. Danny turned to him. 'We can discuss it some more when we're on the road,' he said. 'Jane and I have something to sort out. You make contact with Barak and get together any gear you think we'll need. I'll be back here at midday. You'll be ready to go by then?'

'We're always ready to go, friend. We'll see you back here at midday.' He smiled at Bethany. 'You and Jane have a good morning now,' he said. 'And don't do anything I wouldn't do.' Ludlow chuckled. Rollett openly eyed Bethany up and down, stroking his nose. Guerrero reclined on the sofa, watching them.

'Do you trust those guys?'

'Trust is the wrong word,' Danny said. 'They're pros, and they're getting paid. They want to stay alive just like I do. They'll do a job for us.'

'What about the fixer? He could be anyone.'

'I'll work that out when I meet him. But Guerrero's right. Local knowledge will get us in and out faster and safer.'

'That Rollett character is obscene. You should have heard what he said to me in the cafe.'

'I'm not hiring them for their table manners. Guerrero's got them under control and they'll know what to do if we run into trouble.' He looked back over his shoulder at the tower block. He wondered if Guerrero and the others were watching them leave. Probably, he decided. 'We need to get you to a hotel,' he said. 'It can't be anywhere you've stayed before, or that you've ever mentioned to Ibrahim. And I don't want MI6 to have an inkling where you are either.'

'I know somewhere,' Bethany said. 'I identified it as a safe place when I first started coming to Beirut, in case I ever needed a place to lie low.'

'Have you ever mentioned it to anybody?'

'Nobody.'

'No contacts? No friends?'

Bethany gave a cynical laugh. 'Friends?' she said. 'I work for MI6. I can't tell anyone what I do, who I am, where I'm going. I don't *have* any friends, Danny.'

'I just need to know . . .'

'When are you going to realise I know what I'm doing?' Bethany interrupted. 'I've never mentioned it to anybody, okay? It's a couple of miles east of here. We'll need a cab.'

Danny had told Bethany that wherever she stayed, it couldn't be fancy. The hotel they found themselves approaching forty-five minutes later, having been dropped by a cab a couple of blocks away, certainly was not. It was called the Hotel Faisal and situated in a litter-strewn street between a convenience store and a boarded-up building. Its frontage was brick. There had once been a window here, but it was filled in with bricks of a different colour. Danny checked for CCTV cameras, but did it out of habit rather than necessity. This was a place where someone could go off-grid for a bit.

Before entering the hotel they went into the convenience store, where Bethany bought food and bottled water to last her several days. Danny had been expecting an argument when he reiterated that she wasn't to risk leaving her hotel room while he was away, but he received none. 'I understand, Danny,' she said. 'I'm not going anywhere. Believe it or not, I don't want to be killed either. Just get back over the border as quick as you can. I'll be going stir-crazy.'

The reception area of the Hotel Faisal was dingy and deserted. A pot plant was dying in one corner, next to an empty vending machine. The room tariff behind the counter was all in Arabic. They had to ring the brass bell three times before anyone appeared to help them: a corpulent, sweating Lebanese man with a roll-up hanging from the corner of his mouth. He approached the desk, but then a telephone rang in the adjoining room. He muttered something under his breath before abandoning them again to answer the phone. When he returned a minute later, Bethany did the talking, her Arabic fluent and convincing, as the ash fell from his cigarette to the floor. The man looked lasciviously at her, and Danny had the impression this was an establishment where rooms were often rented by the hour. But they were renting a room for several days, and the guy greedily counted the notes Bethany gave him, payment in advance, before handing over a key attached to a chunky wooden key ring. Then he nodded at the staircase at the far end of the reception area.

Bethany's room, number 35, was on the third floor at the far end of a corridor that smelled of body odour and cigarettes. TVs blared behind the doors of a couple of the rooms they passed, and behind the third was the sweaty, grunting sound of a man having sex. The room itself had little to recommend it. A double bed with a couple of thin blankets. A wardrobe and table with a pencil and notepad, where Bethany neatly laid out her food and water. A TV on the wall. A tiny toilet and shower cubicle that hadn't been cleaned since the last person used it. If Bethany was in any way put off by her surroundings, it didn't show. She moved immediately to the window, which overlooked a grim courtyard full of junk, and checked the window locks before drawing the heavy curtains. Danny checked the lock on the bathroom window, before examining the security arrangements on the main door. There was the main lock, and a feeble-looking security chain. Neither would be good enough to withstand a persistent intruder. There was a hook with a wooden door wedge hanging from it. Danny held it up. 'Put this under the door while it's locked,' he said. 'It'll make it a lot harder for anyone to enter.'

'Nobody knows I'm here,' she said.

'Right. But this isn't exactly the best area of Beirut. There could be opportunists. Can you move that table?' Bethany had a go at shifting it: it was heavy, but it moved. 'If you get worried, use it to block the entrance. If you need ballistic protection, get the mattress up against the door.' She frowned as he spoke. 'Take this seriously, Bethany,' he said. He scrawled his access number to Hereford on the notepad. 'Keep your phone switched off. Only turn it on in an absolute emergency. I don't want anyone using it to trace your position. It means I won't be able to keep in touch. If I'm not back in four days, call this number. Tell them where you are and do what they tell you.'

'But you'll be back in four days, right?' She sounded genuinely concerned.

'Sooner,' Danny said, 'if I can. Where's your weapon?'

She gave him the chauffeur's Browning. Danny checked it over, then cocked and locked it. 'Keep it close,' he said. 'By your bed if you're sleeping, in the bathroom if that's where you are. Don't let anybody in, no matter what they say, unless it's me or you have an order from the guy on that number. No house-keeping, no nothing.'

'Okay, Danny, I've got the message.'

'Good. Because believe me, if Ibrahim Khan locates you here, he isn't going to announce himself. He's going to . . .'

'I know him better than you do.' She had a slightly waspish edge to her voice. 'And in any case, the only way he's going to find my location is if you give it to him. And you're not going to do that, are you?'

Danny didn't immediately answer that question. He knew that, under torture, there was a limit to the amount of time any man could withstand interrogation. If he was caught by IS, he would have to hold out until he knew Bethany had made her escape. But he saw no point in telling her all this. She was anxious enough as it was. 'Four days,' she said eventually. 'No longer.'

There was an awkward silence. Danny, not quite knowing what else to do, held out his hand. Bethany didn't take it. Instead, she embraced him. Her waspishness had disappeared. 'Maybe I made a mistake last night,' she whispered into his ear.

They unwrapped themselves from each other's embrace. Bethany looked demurely at the floor. 'I'll be fine,' she said. 'Go on. Leave. I'm tired and I need some sleep. Get back soon.'

Danny nodded. He turned his back on her, left the room and closed the door behind him. He stood there for a moment, listening for the sound of the key in the lock and the security chain, then the wedge being slid under the door. He checked the time. 11.20 hrs. He needed to get back to the team. But something had unnerved him and he couldn't quite work out what it was. He looked down the corridor. There was nobody there. He was certain they'd entered Bethany's room completely unobserved. He stepped up to the door again and listened closely. No sound. He pictured Bethany lying on her bed, eyes closed, her weapon on the floor beside her.

Maybe I made a mistake last night.

Danny couldn't deny those words gave him an urgent thrill. He liked Bethany. He liked her pluck and her complexity. He liked that she didn't seem put off by the darker side of his job. Maybe, when this business with Ibrahim Khan was over . . .

But not now. Now he had business to take care of. He stepped away from the door, walked along the corridor and down the stairs. The reception area was empty again. Danny let himself out and checked left and right. Nobody seemed to be paying him any attention. He headed back into the streets of Beirut, hailed a taxi and retraced his steps back towards the apartment where Guerrero, Ludlow and Rollett were waiting for him.

Bethany White stood at the door to her room. It was locked. The security chain was engaged. The door wedge was tightly fitted. She hadn't yet heard his footsteps receding. She knew he was there, in the corridor, inches away, listening. She breathed calmly and didn't move.

Footsteps. Light, but just audible. He was leaving. She remained where she was for a few more seconds, then walked back into the room. She entered the en-suite shower room, pulled back the mildewed shower curtain and switched on the shower. But she didn't undress. Instead, she returned to the room and emptied her rucksack bag on to the bed. Passport in the name of Tomlinson, phone, money, make-up, hairbrush, clean clothes. When the bag was empty, she lifted a flap at the bottom to reveal a second mobile phone. She switched it on and waited for it to connect to a local network.

Bethany had been well trained at the MI6 field training centre at Fort Monckton in Portsmouth. She knew how to handle weapons, operate under cover identities, and tell when she was under surveillance. Her tradecraft was good and in one respect it was excellent. She had the facility to learn and remember phone numbers, because there were few actions less secure than writing them down or storing them on a device.

She recalled the number with ease and dialled it on her second phone.

Five rings, then someone picked up but didn't answer.

Bethany closed her eyes and drew a deep breath. 'You don't know me,' she said, 'and I don't know you. But I have some information, and I think it might be of interest. Do with it what you will.'

12

Guerrero, Ludlow and Rollet were well equipped. When Danny presented himself in their apartment again at midday, they had laid several sets of blue body armour and a selection of helmets on one of the sofas. 'Take your pick, pal,' said Ludlow.

Danny chose a set of body armour and tried on three Kevlar helmets before selecting one that fitted right. Rollett chucked him an ops vest. It was empty to start with, but Guererro threw him a med pack and some waterproof matches. 'We'll fill you up with ammo when we get to the cache,' he said.

'Where's your vehicle?' Danny said.

'There's a basement parking lot here,' Guerrero said. 'We've been loading up while you've been seeing to your little lady. She's quite a babe. Maybe you can give me her number when we get back.'

'Join the fucking queue,' Rollett said. 'I reckon I was in there.'

'Not sure you're her type,' Danny said.

'What do you mean?'

'One dick too many.'

Rollett's eyes widened. 'You fucking kidding me?' The others started laughing. Rollett shook his head in disbelief. He was almost blushing. 'I could fucking turn her,' he said belligerently.

'Have you spoken to Barak?' Danny asked Guerrero.

'Sure. He's ready to RV with us at 19.00.'

'Where?'

'There's an old Palestinian training camp about ten klicks from the border. Saw a lot of activity back in the eighties, and it's on the edge of Hezbollah territory.'

'What's the risk of contact?'

'It's possible, but nobody goes to this training camp now. Barak will meet us there. Even if Hezbollah come nosing around, the bigger threat is when we cross the border. Syrian government patrols, Russians – there's even a risk of Spetsnaz units helping out the Syrians.'

'I want to avoid firefights,' Danny said. 'We don't want to leave a trace of where we're heading.'

'Agreed,' Guerrero said. 'Take your body armour and ops vest off. We'll stow it in the back of the Hilux and put it on when we're nearer the border.'

They headed down the concrete stairwell of the building two abreast. Danny found himself next to Ludlow as they descended. 'So what's the craic from Hereford?' he said. 'I heard something on the grapevine that my old mucker Ollie Moorhouse came to a sticky end.'

'You knew Moorhouse?' Danny asked carefully.

'Course. We did selection together. Last time I spoke to him he'd just bought his gaff in Florida. Fuck knows where he got the money. So what happened to him?'

'I dunno,' Danny said. 'I heard he'd died, that's all.' It didn't sit well, keeping facts from his team. But Danny felt he knew Ludlow's type well. He was a blunt instrument, and while he felt he could trust him and Rollett to operate skilfully in enemy territory, he wasn't sure he could trust them to keep their mouths shut. So for now, at least, the less they knew the better.

The Hilux was parked in a corner of the underground parking lot. It looked like it had been well driven. The chassis was dented here and there, the paintwork covered with a thick layer of dust. But the tyres looked new and sturdy, with deep treads. That told Danny it was in decent nick. The word PRESS was written along the side, the back and on the roof. The rear of the Hilux, where all their gear was stashed, was covered with a sturdy green tarp. Guerrero rolled it back a little so Danny could dump his body armour and ops waistcoat, then tied it up again.

They got into the vehicle. Guerrero took the wheel, Danny the passenger seat. Ludlow and Rollett took the back. Minutes later, they were negotiating the streets of Beirut. There was a rugged military GPS unit on the dashboard, with an LCD display that gave lat/long coordinates and altitude statistics. Danny could tell, though, that for now Guerrero wasn't using it. He clearly knew this city as intimately as Bethany. He avoided the traffic jams that clogged up the main roads by a series of shortcuts, and soon they were free of the centre and heading towards the outskirts. The press vehicle drew the occasional glance from passers-by, but that was to be expected. Once they were closer to the border, this would surely be a less infrequent sight.

The team drove in silence as their urban surroundings became rural. Guerrero navigated up into the hills surrounding Beirut, along winding roads lined with olive trees and fruit groves. There were far fewer vehicles up here in the hills, and any houses they passed were old at best, tumbledown at worst. It felt as if they were leaving the modern world behind.

Their first destination was the weapons cache. They were two hours out of Beirut when Guerrero pulled up by the side of the road to allow a vehicle behind to pass, then turned unseen down a rough track that led downhill into an area of waist-high gorse bushes. Hidden from the main road, they pulled up. Rollett took up position at the back of the Hilux, keeping watch back up the track. Danny, Guerrero and Ludlow removed entrenching tools from under the tarp. Guerrero and Ludlow pulled out a scuffed aluminium camera case with the CNN logo painted on the side in black. Danny carried the entrenching tools and his companions the case as they followed a rough animal trail through the gorse bushes. A hundred metres from the vehicle was a patch of bare earth dotted with large flat stones. An observant eye might have noticed that the dusty ground had been disturbed – there was a slight mound by three of the stones – but this location was so remote, and the mound so small, that no passer-by would think of examining it. The three SF men got to work with their entrenching tools, digging out the hard earth in small chunks.

Danny's entrenching tool was the first to hit something hard and unyielding, about a foot beneath the surface. The guys continued to scrape around it. Ten minutes later, they revealed the lid of a large flight case. Guerrero loosened the lid, pulled it away and laid it to the side of the hole. 'Howdy, sweethearts,' he said as they looked down.

The flight case was a perfect little armoury. Four AK-47s with IR sights – 'We always keep a spare, so you're in luck, friend,' Guerrero said as they pulled them from the earth. The AK was hardly Danny's weapon of choice, but these had clearly been locally acquired, and it was better than nothing. Ludlow removed a general purpose machine gun with bipod, which he lay on the ground before leaning in and extracting a Minimi and its attendant box magazine. 'Belt of two hundred,' he said to nobody in particular, tapping the box magazine like it was an old friend and laying it by the Minimi. These two pieces of hardware were a reassuring sight. Danny especially favoured the Minimi. Belt-fed or magazine-fed, it was a halfway house between the Gimpy and an assault rifle. It came with a bipod but could be carried and fired like a rifle, with extra range and a higher degree of accuracy.

The bottom of the flight case was covered with brown boxes of ammunition: a couple of belts of 7.62 NATO rounds for the Gimpy, boxes of 7.62x39mm for the AK-47s and a couple of M16 5.56 magazines for the Minimi.

'You keep yourself well kitted out,' Danny said.

'It's Syria, friend,' Guerrero said, as if that explained everything, which it did.

They transferred weaponry to the camera case, closed up the empty flight case and infilled the hole. Ludlow cut a few branches of gorse and used them to swipe away their footprints. They carried the full camera case and entrenching tools back to the Hilux, where Rollett was still keeping watch.

'Anything?' Guerrero asked.

'Fuck all,' said Rollett. He peeled back the tarp and helped them load the camera case back on to the Hilux.

Within minutes they were back on the road. Danny was hotter than before and covered in a thin film of dust, but he felt more secure now. It was reassuring to have the necessary hardware stowed in the back. 'How far to the RV point?' he asked Guerrero.

'Thirty minutes,' the American said. Danny checked the time: 15.30 hrs. The RV was at 19.00. They'd have time to kill.

Ten klicks further on, their route took them off the main road again. The track Guerrero followed this time was a lot rougher than the one that led to the cache. Danny had the impression it was seldom used. The Hilux's engine complained as Guerrero forced it in first gear across the rough earth and over heavy ruts in the terrain. Only after twenty minutes of this did their destination come into view.

The former Palestinian training camp to which Guerrero had driven them was a mismatched collection of single-storey buildings. Each building was individually painted in a bright colour – blue, green, red, yellow – strangely lending them the aura of a child's nursery. That aura was punctured somewhat by the bullet holes sprayed up against the walls of each building, and by the fact that the training camp had evidently received a bomb strike, long ago, with the evidence still plain to see. There was a crater at the centre of the camp, a good ten metres in diameter and a couple of metres deep. Some buildings were reduced to rubble, now reclaimed by hardy foliage. On the far side of the camp was what looked to Danny like a former firing range. The rusted frames of metal targets were still lined up at one end, although the once-open ground in front of them was now strewn with debris and weeds. Danny imagined that thirty years ago, this place would have been buzzing with the activity of Palestinian militants, their heads and necks wrapped in red and white keffiyehs as they gave instruction to idealistic civilians from all over the region. Now it reeked of disuse, a relic of Lebanon's violent past.

It was a perfect rendezvous point for a team wishing to stay under the radar: it was out of the way and afforded cover if they needed it. It was surrounded by hilly ground covered with wild trees and foliage. If they needed to disappear for any reason, they could do so in a matter of seconds.

Guerrero parked the Hilux on the far side of a green-painted building, out of view of the track they'd used to approach. They unloaded the aluminium camera case, opened it up and withdrew the AK-47s. Each man took a rifle, stripped it down and checked the moving parts. Satisfied that his rifle was fully operational, Danny loaded the weapon. 'We good to put a few rounds down?' he asked Guerrero.

'Be my guest, friend,' Guerrero said. 'Nobody for miles around here.' The Yank gave him a night sight with IR capability, which Danny fitted to his AK. He stepped away from the building. To his eleven o'clock was a gnarled old olive tree, its trunk thick and its branches heavy. Danny raised his weapon and trained the sights on a knot almost in the middle of the trunk. He released three rounds in quick succession. He could tell they had landed in a close group, but the group itself was a couple of inches to the right of the knot. He made a fractional adjustment to the sights and released another three rounds. They landed precisely, splintering the knot and throwing shards of bark into the air. Satisfied that he was properly zeroed in, Danny turned back to the other guys. They had completely removed the tarp, and were now pulling out their body armour and ops vests. Danny did the same. He pulled on the protective gear and stashed more ammo into the pouches of his ops vest.

Guerrero was busying himself with a personal comms system for the four men. He assigned the correct frequency to each radio pack, then handed each of the guys their own set, along with earpiece and boom mike. Danny fitted his mike to the helmet he'd chosen back in the Beirut flat. They performed a comms check, then powered down the radio sets to preserve their battery life. 'You got satellite comms?' Danny asked. Guerrero tapped his ops vest. 'Iridium sat phone,' he said. 'Never leave home without it. Stays with me, though, friend. My toy.'

Danny didn't argue. As long as he knew they had some means of contacting the outside world, that was okay by him.

The others zeroed in their weapons while Danny performed a quick recce of their location. He heard the occasional scurry of wild animals as he entered the multicoloured buildings. Their interiors were dilapidated, filled with old furniture and junk that was slowly rotting away. He wondered how many terrorists this place had spat out in its day, and how many of them had been brought to book by one of the special forces organisations his new team represented. A good number, he imagined.

Back at the vehicle, Guerrero handed him an MRE – sausage and beans – and a canteen of water. 'It's no Big Mac,' he said in his American drawl, 'but it keeps us going.' It was the food, even more than the weapons and personnel, that made Danny feel he was with a regular military unit rather than a group of freelancers. He ate the unappetising cold sludge gratefully, then hunkered down by the nearest wall and waited for the RV time.

Danny was anxious to get moving but the hours passed slowly. Guerrero was keeping watch on the track in. Rollett had the bonnet of the Hilux up and was tinkering with the engine. Ludlow spent a good hour sharpening a knife. The dull, regular scrape of the blade against a stone rang out metronomically as the sun started to set. It only stopped when Guerrero called: 'We got company!'

Danny, Rollett and Ludlow moved at once, engaging their weapons and taking up positions that faced towards the access track. Danny knelt in the firing position by the corner of one of the buildings, aware of Guerrero doing the same behind a pile of old oil drums to his right. A Land Rover was approaching, kicking up a cloud of dust that looked red in the setting sun. It came to a juddering halt fifty metres from their position. There were several seconds of silence, then a figure emerged.

He was a curious-looking man. He was thin and even taller than Danny, with a shock of silver hair. At first Danny assumed he was old, but his gait and movements were young, and his face, though tanned, was not lined. He was probably no older than thirty, and had friendly, sparkling eyes. He held his hands up in the air. 'My friends!' he shouted with only the hint of an accent. 'Will you put down your weapons? I have good things for you!'

Guerrero was the first to show himself. He stood up from his position behind the oil drums and approached the newcomer, his weapon now slung across his chest. The two men embraced. Guerrero turned and indicated to the others that they should approach. Danny did so with care. Guerrero and the others might trust this guy. It didn't mean Danny had to. Truth was, he'd seldom met a fixer he *did* trust. As he drew near, both the Yank and the newcomer seemed to sense Danny's wariness. 'This is Barak,' Guerrero said. 'Barak, this is our client we told you about. The one who has business over the border.'

Barak's smiling face became a little more serious. He held out one hand. 'I am pleased to meet you,' he said. 'A friend of these gentlemen is a friend of mine!'

Danny nodded wordlessly. Barak turned back to the Land Rover and fetched something from the front passenger seat. He returned with a plastic carrier bag full of rolled-up flatbreads, which we handed out among the men. 'First we eat,' he announced. 'Then we travel.'

The flatbreads were filled with a spicy meat paste and tasted a hell of a sight better than the MRE Danny had wolfed down a couple of hours previously. The team tore into them. Barak ate his more slowly, watching Danny thoughtfully as he chewed. There was something unsettling about the way he didn't stop staring at Danny, even when Guerrero started pumping him for intel. 'Have you recce'd the crossing points?'

'Of course, my friend,' Barak said, running one hand through his silver hair.

'Where's the nearest?'

'Beyond the village of Massak.' He frowned. 'We would do well to avoid that place. There are tensions there, between Hezbollah and the Christians. We do not want to become involved in that.'

'You know a route around the village?' Danny asked.

'Certainly,' said Barak. 'It will not be a problem. It will add maybe one hour to the journey. Did you enjoy your food?'

Danny didn't like the way Barak was trying to change the subject. He looked over towards the Land Rover. 'Did anybody see you coming?'

'Nobody. I am very careful.'

Danny stepped up to him. 'Not so careful that you didn't stop off on the way to buy flatbreads. I'll ask you again: did anybody see you coming?'

The question hung there between them. 'You do not trust me, my friend?' Barak said, his voice suddenly much quieter. 'That is alright.' He bowed slightly to the others. 'I will leave you to find someone else who you do trust.' Without another word he turned his back on them and started walking back to his vehicle.

'Barak!' Guerrero called. 'Wait up, buddy, just one minute!' Barak stopped, but didn't turn. Guerrero looked at Danny. 'Listen to me, friend.' There was a sudden edge to his voice. 'You want to cross the border by yourself, be my fucking guest. But Barak there is part of my team, and without him we don't have a business out here. Do you have any idea what kind of grief those Hezbollah crazies would give him if they thought he was helping us? Say the word and we'll leave you here by yourself. You can fucking walk to Syria. But if you want our help, you go and make it right with him.'

Guerrero's reprimand crackled between them. Danny looked around. The setting sun cast long shadows across the disused training camp. Barak had almost reached his vehicle. The other guys were all looking at Danny intently. Their body language told him they were right behind Guerrero. Danny realised he'd messed up, questioning Barak's loyalty. And he'd messed up even more by getting on the wrong side of Guerrero. The American knew what he was about. While Danny might not fully trust the fixer, it was clear Guerrero did. For now, that would have to be good enough.

He walked over to Barak. 'That bread thing was pretty good,' he said. Barak inclined his head, a silent, reluctant thank you. Danny offered his hand. 'I just need to make sure this operation goes right. No hard feelings?'

Barak flared his nostrils, but then smiled. 'No hard feelings, my friend.' He shook Danny's hand. His palm was limp and rather sweaty. He turned and raised his arms in a friendly gesture, as if nothing had happened. 'It will be dark in one hour,' he announced to the others. 'We should wait until then.'

'At least,' Ludlow said. 'I say we don't move until 23.00. Fewer people about.'

'Agreed,' Guerrero said, a note of finality in his voice. 'Barak, get your Land Rover out of sight. One vehicle's easier to smuggle over than two. We'll bring you here to pick it up once we're back in Lebanon.'

Barak did as he was told. The rest of the guys returned to the Hilux. Rollett took a long piss up against a nearby wall. Ludlow lifted a jerrycan of diesel from the back and refuelled the vehicle. Nobody spoke. The tension had not yet dissipated, and Danny had a gnawing anxiety that this evening wasn't going to go quite the way he'd planned. Maybe he should call the whole thing off. Return to Lebanon. Contact Hereford and insist they send him a fresh team. If they could all RV in Cyprus, they could insert into Syria by air . . .

No. It would take days to arrange that. A week, even. Anything could happen in that time. Adnan Abadi could move from his current location. Ibrahim Khan could strike again. He thought of little Danny Jr, and of Christina Somers. He hadn't been certain about her loyalties, but had taken Bethany's word for it that she was clean. Now he was taking Guerrero's word for it that Barak was trustworthy. He couldn't shake the uncomfortable sensation that an op supposed to be watertight was springing leaks.

The quicker he followed up this latest lead, the better.

Barak had parked alongside the Hilux. The sun was sinking fast and a bright moon was rising. Time check: 19:47 hrs. Just over four hours till the off. 'I'll keep stag,' Danny said.

Guerrero nodded his agreement. Danny walked across to the far side of the training camp and took up position by a mound of rubble where he could keep watch on the road in. He felt more comfortable by himself, and was certain the others felt the same.

Darkness fell. Danny quietly cursed the bright moonlight that illuminated the terrain all around, because it would illuminate the team too, once they were on the move. But it was what it was. They would deal with it. He passed into the quiet, watchful trance that always accompanied an extended period of surveillance: highly tuned into his surroundings, but hardly aware of the passing of time. Everything around him was still. There was a sea of stars and the distant croak of cicadas. But no movement. No enemy personnel. No threats.

Maybe they'd be in and out of Syria without any incident. Or maybe this was the calm before the storm.

Movement. Guerrero was approaching. Danny checked the time. 22.55hrs.

'Okay,' Guerrero said. 'We're loaded up and ready. It's time to go.'

13

The team retook their usual positions in the Hilux, with Barak sitting between Ludlow and Rollet in the back. Danny had his assault rifle stowed barrel-down in the footwell. The rest of the guys had laid theirs between the two front seats. Danny watched the old Palestinian training camp fade from view in his wing mirror as Guerrero manoeuvred the vehicle back up the rough track towards the main road. The moon was bright enough to drive by. Guerrero had a set of NV goggles on his helmet, but he needed neither those nor the headlights as they carefully crossed the difficult terrain. At Barak's instruction, they turned left on to the main road, lit the headlights and headed north-east.

The road was almost deserted. Every couple of minutes a car approached from the opposite direction, but there seemed to be nobody behind them. The countryside, whizzing past in Danny's peripheral vision, was becoming sparser. Fewer trees, more scrub-land. There was the occasional broken-down vehicle by the side of the road and, here and there, the lights of a house or a village off in the distance. But the light pollution was minimal which meant that when, after twenty minutes, a glow appeared in the sky up ahead, Danny knew they were approaching a larger settlement.

'Massak?' Guerrero said.

'Yes,' Barak replied. 'We will come off the road in about one kilometre.'

Their route, when they came to it, was not an actual road or even a rough track. Barak instructed them to kill the lights and pull off to the right by a squat, solitary tree. The terrain took them uphill for about five hundred metres, then over a steep brow and down towards a stream that meandered in a direction that Danny took to be roughly east. The water level was low, but wide enough to reflect the moon in its surface as the team grew nearer. Once they were on its bank, Danny saw it was about four metres wide, and moving sluggishly. Give it a couple more months and it would evaporate completely in the sun. 'Follow the water,' Barak said. 'It'll eventually turn to the south, but by the time it does that, we'll have bypassed Massak. But go slowly and keep the lights off. There are border guards in this area, and sometimes skirmishes.'

Guerrero didn't move out of first gear. The moonlight was bright enough to drive by, but not to see the terrain ahead in any detail. More than once, the tyres came across a rock in the road big enough to throw them off course. If they'd hit those obstacles at speed, they'd have found themselves upside down in the stream. Every five minutes, Guerrero brought the vehicle to a halt and killed the engine. He and Danny would leave the vehicle and listen hard for the sound of vehicles. There was nothing. Just the gentle sound of the water's sluggish flow down-river, and the occasional creak from their own vehicle as the engine cooled down. When they were moving again, Danny focused to his left. The glow from the lights of Massak was off to his ten o'clock. It felt they were moving past it only slowly. 'These border towns,' Guerrero said after they'd been driving for a further fifteen minutes, 'can be a fucking mess. They've taken in more Syrian refugees than they can really deal with, and . . .'

'*Hit the brakes!*' Danny hissed.

Guerrero's reaction was immediate. The Hilux came to a sudden halt and the engine died. Up ahead and to their two o'clock, on the other side of the stream, the terrain followed an upward gradient. Beyond the brow of that raised ground, Danny had seen moving beams of light. Headlights. Three sets, he estimated. Distance to the brow: maybe a hundred metres. He felt for the rifle stowed in the footwell. Guerrero grabbed his from between the seats. 'Wait,' Barak hissed. 'I do not think they will come this way. The terrain on the far side of that hill is not good for vehicles.'

They sat in absolute silence, watching the headlights. They were growing brighter, closer, lighting up the midnight air. But Barak was right. At no point did they crest the brow of the hill. A minute later their glare subsided as the vehicles moved, by Danny's estimation, to the south-east. And then they were gone.

Nobody spoke for a full two minutes, until they were sure there was no longer any risk of being seen. Only then did Guerrero start the Hilux again and continue his slow, measured path along the stream. They travelled for a further half hour without incident before the stream meandered sharply to the right. The glow from the lights of Massak were behind them now. 'We can turn back to the road here,' Barak said. 'That way.' He pointed to a gulley between two gentle inclines off to their eleven o'clock. Guerrero altered their trajectory but moved as slowly as ever, keeping the engine noise down and the vehicle's traction good. Fifteen minutes later, they emerged on to the main road.

'We are about two kilometres from the crossing point,' Barak said. 'The road will take us half that distance, then we must go cross-country again.'

'We'll need to scout the approach for anti-personnel mines,' Guerrero said. He looked over his shoulder at Ludlow and Rollett. 'You good with that, boys?' Ludlow and Rollett nodded. 'It's their speciality,' Guerrero added.

'Is the crossing point visible from the road?' Danny said.

'No, my friend,' Barak replied. 'The terrain is hilly. We can stay out of sight while the ground is swept for mines.'

Guerrero allowed himself the use of the Hilux's headlights while they continued down the main road. They encountered no other vehicles. He killed the lights again at a sharp bend to the left, where Barak told them to go off-road again. Guerrero carefully negotiated a couple of hillocks, then stopped. By the light of the moon they could see, fifty metres in the distance, the silhouetted outline of the border fence. It had an unwelcoming air: high, impenetrable, the thick bundles of jagged razor wire looking even from this distance like sentries waiting to maim anybody who approached.

As soon as they stopped, Ludlow and Rollett left the vehicle and pulled back the tarpaulin at the rear of the Hilux. Rollet removed some minesweeping apparatus – a metal detector with an individual headset. Ludlow grabbed a sturdy pair of wire cutters and a canister of spray paint to mark a safe passage on the ground to the border fence. 'I'm going to keep watch on the terrain back towards the road,' Guerrero told Danny. 'You watch the open ground here. Barak, stay where you are.'

'Yes, my friend.'

They exited the vehicle. Guerrero disappeared into the hilly terrain. There was something reassuring about the American watching their backs. He instilled confidence. Danny considered removing the keys from the ignition to stop the fixer taking charge of the Hilux. He elected not to: Barak was touchy enough as it was and, besides, it was more secure for the team if any of them could drive the vehicle in an emergency. He took his rifle, positioned himself in the firing position in the moon shadow at the front of the vehicle, and watched Ludlow and Rollett sweep the approach.

They moved forward slowly, Rollett panning the detector over an area a little wider than the Hilux. Every couple of metres, Ludlow sprayed a short white line on either side of the path they had cleared. Danny surveyed the area through the IR sight on his AK-47. Apart from his two unit mates, there was no movement on either side of the border.

Five minutes passed.

Ten.

Danny was on edge. The longer they remained in one place, the higher their chance of being seen and challenged. But he knew this process couldn't be rushed.

Rollett and Ludlow were fifteen metres from the border fence when Rollett suddenly stopped and raised one hand. Danny watched them carefully. It was clear that Rollett had seen something. Danny found himself holding his breath as the ex-SBS guy skirted carefully around whatever buried object his detector had found, with Ludlow spraying a white line around its perimeter. It looked to Danny to be roughly circular and about a metre in diameter. He felt a ferrous tang in the back of his throat at the thought of what would have happened if the Hilux had hit that device. He'd seen guys get fucked up by a landmine before. It was a bad way to go.

Having passed the obstacle, Rollett and Ludlow continued at the same ponderous speed. Danny saw no indication that, having located one mine, they were less cautious. The opposite was true. Knowing the area had been booby-trapped, they seemed twice as vigilant. It was a relief when they finally reached the fence.

Ludlow went about his business with the wire cutters. Through his IR sight, Danny could see that this part of the fence had already been breached. Rather than rolls of razor wire, it was patched with single strips of cable, easily snipped. Ludlow did just this, and in less than a minute he'd opened up a gateway from Lebanon into Syria.

Their work wasn't done. It was possible there were mines on the far side of the border too. Rollett and Ludlow continued their minesweeping. Danny lowered his weapon and ran back towards the road. He found Guerrero lying prostrate on the brow of a small hillock, watching the road and its surroundings. 'We're through,' Danny said.

'They find anything that goes bang?'

'Yeah. They're sweeping the Syrian side now.'

Guerrero got to his feet. 'Funny kind of way,' he said, 'locating a mine is a good thing. It means the border patrols are less likely to be in this area.'

'That's one way to look at it.'

Guerrero grinned and held up his fist. Danny gave him a fist bump. 'Any time you're looking for work, Danny, you know where to come, right?'

'Right.' Danny smiled.

They jogged back to the Hilux. Barak was still waiting for them in the back seat. Rollett and Ludlow were ten metres beyond the border, still minesweeping. Guerrero took the wheel. Danny jogged along the path between the white lines. He slowed up as he approached the white circle on the ground where Ludlow had marked the mine. The proximity of the device made his skin prickle, but he stood his ground as Guerrero drove in his direction and, at Danny's marshalling, round the dangerous patch of ground. Once Guerrero had cleared the landmine, Danny jogged after the vehicle. As he drew close to the border, he saw rolls of razor wire that had been cut away from the fence on either side of the white lines, rusting, sharp and evil. And as the Hilux trundled over the border, he stopped for a moment. One more pace and he'd be back in Syria. It wasn't a country that held good memories for him.

But the trail he was following led in this direction. He took the step. Lebanon was behind him now.

Rollett and Ludlow were returning to the Hilux. 'We're clear,' they called. They replaced their gear in the back of the vehicle and everyone retook their seats.

'Good work, guys,' Guerrero said as he turned the engine over. 'Barak, give me the coordinates of the lying-up point?'

Barak handed him a slip of paper. 'It is about one hour,' he said, speaking quietly as if there was a chance of being overheard. 'Continue east from here. If we head in a straight line, we will not meet any roads.'

For the first time in the journey, Guerrero turned his attention to the GPS unit on the dashboard. He added the coordinates. The display gave him a bearing of 43 degrees and a distance of 43.8 klicks. There was no map. Guerrero edged the vehicle forward and adjusted its direction so they were heading towards the lying-up point. Then he brought his night-vision goggles down from his helmet.

The team headed further into Syrian territory. Danny tried to clear his head, but somehow couldn't. He thought of the colonel, drunk and blustering in his austere mansion, surrounded by armed guards but weirdly alone. He thought of Christina and Danny Jr, holed up out of the way, hoping they were anonymous enough and safe enough to stay beyond Ibrahim Khan's reach.

And he thought of Bethany, lying low in a bleak Beirut hotel room, waiting for Danny to return with intel on the man who wanted to kill her. Was she really as well hidden as he'd hoped?

He felt a moment of crushing uncertainty. In one part of his mind, he knew he was following the right – the only – lead. In another part of his mind, he couldn't shake the feeling that here, in the vastness of the Syrian countryside, he was looking for a needle in a haystack. Khan was just one man, and the world was big. What if right now he was two thousand miles away, hiding out on the bleak moors of the Brecon Beacons? What if he was hunting his quarry on the streets of Beirut?

'You're looking pensive, friend,' Guerrero said. 'Want to tell us all what you're thinking?'

Danny didn't. 'Just drive,' he said.

It was 23.00 in the UK, and the colonel was drunk. He always was at this time of day, and indeed at any time of day. Each morning he woke in fear: the cold, debilitating fear that can only be felt by a person who knows his life is under threat.

At first a couple of mouthfuls of Scotch with breakfast was enough to help him rationalise his fear. Ibrahim Khan wouldn't really be interested in him. The little bastard had just been settling scores with a few SAS men who'd given him some stick. Those Hereford fellows were little more than legalised hooligans anyway. And, the colonel persuaded himself, Khan wasn't *that* skilful an operator. Just some jumped-up little towelhead who thought he was good with a gun.

Gradually, though, those two mouthfuls of whisky weren't enough. They wore off quickly and the doubts kept creeping in. Why would the security services put three armed guards on his doorstep, unless they genuinely thought his life was at risk? Those chaps were under-resourced enough as it was. It took a half bottle to beat that thought into submission, and to keep him sane through the long, slow afternoons.

But night-time was the worst. The house was old. It creaked. And once the sun had set, in the colonel's head every creak was a footstep, coming nearer. He spent every evening in his drawing room, cocooned by Glenfiddich, Bach, and the knowledge that an armed guard was permanently stationed at the door. At ten o'clock he would stagger up to bed and lock himself into his bedroom. His guards assured him they had the landing covered all night, but he suspected they slept for at least some of it. As the effects of the whisky wore off, and the fear mounted in his thorax, he would sit at the window, one finger parting the yellowing net curtains, and stare out across the countryside.

He was there now. His room was dim, lit only by a bedside lamp with a low-wattage bulb. He could see more of his reflection in the window than he could of the outside. His red, jowly face and haunted eyes. It was hardly a face he recognised. He'd been a soldier once, lean and eager to hunt. But now the soldiering in his blood had been replaced by booze.

The colonel was staring at that strangely unfamiliar reflection, more than at his extensive grounds, when he thought he saw movement in his peripheral vision. A cold electric shock of fear zapped through him. He pulled his finger back from the net curtains and let them shut. He tried to breathe in and found that, for a moment, his lungs were refusing the intake of air. He could hear the crunch of hurried footsteps on the gravel below his window. He staggered over to his bed and, for some reason he couldn't quite fathom, fumbled at the beside light and switched it off.

Darkness. Silence. He didn't know if it made him feel better or worse. There was a faint cracking sound from the ceiling. That was just the natural movement of the house, he told himself. There was only the loft above him. Then his eyes were drawn to the loft hatch in the ceiling, and what started out as a comforting thought became chilling. He was paralysed with fear, unable to move from the edge of his bed, his skin clammy and his stomach sick. He thought he could hear movement in the corridor outside. Footsteps, getting louder. For some reason he thought of Bethany White, and that damn arrogant SAS man who had visited for the precise purpose of putting the shits up him. The colonel could hear his voice now. *MI6 offered you a safe house? You should take it. Make the call now. Get out of here. Tonight.*

Damn, right now he wished he had.

The footsteps stopped outside his room. Silence again. The colonel's hands were shaking. He clenched his fists to try to steady them, but then the room started to spin. Booze or terror, he didn't know.

A thump on the door. He started.

'Everything alright in there, sir?'

The colonel frowned. It was the voice of one of the men. He couldn't remember his name. He cleared his throat. 'What?' he demanded, feigning a sleepy crack in his voice.

'It's Sandy, sir. Just checking everything's alright.'

'For God's sake man, you woke me up. Can't a fellow get a night's sleep around here? Just . . . bugger off, will you?'

A pause. 'I'll be out here if you need me, sir.'

The colonel tried to express his outrage at being treated like a child, but couldn't quite manage it. He harrumphed a little, and spluttered, but then fell silent again.

He wished he'd brought a bottle up with him. Without Dutch courage it was going to be a long night. He continued to sit on the edge of his bed, staring blankly into the darkness.

Christina Somers couldn't sleep. Nothing new there. Her nights had been broken ever since she heard the dreadful news about Ibrahim. To think a man whom she'd liked so much and respected so well, a man of such fierce intelligence and apparent loyalty, could be capable of such horrors. It had shifted Christina's world on its axis. Sometimes, in the dead of night, she would fantasise about what she might say to him, if they found themselves face to face again. They had bonded before, over a shared love of the languages in which she had instructed him. Surely she'd be able to appeal to him. To talk him round. To find the old Ibrahim buried deep inside the monster he'd become.

But then she thought about what he had done, and her idealism was replaced by the gnawing fear that had become her near-constant companion. Fear not only for herself but for little Danny, and of course for Bethany. Christina wondered where she was. She hadn't liked the look of that man Bethany was with. Or maybe, she was honest enough with herself to admit, she hadn't liked the way he looked at her and she looked at him. Jealousy, it turned out, could be an even stronger emotion than fear.

She turned over her duvet and opened her eyes. The door to her bedroom was half open. Frank had insisted on it, ever since Bethany and her SAS man had been here. A sharp rectangle of light cut into her room, surrounding the shadow of Frank whom she knew was sitting on a chair in the corridor, probably reading one of the paperback detective novels he liked so much. He was a reassuring presence, a bit like having a kindly uncle nearby, albeit an uncle with a handgun holstered to his chest. But the reassurance only went so far. She knew, beyond question, that neither Frank nor Alec would be any kind of a match for Ibrahim, if he found out where they were.

The thought chilled her.

The screaming, when it started, was sudden and intense. It was little Danny, and he sounded as if all the horrors of the night had descended upon him at once. Christina felt a blinding flash of panic and hurled herself from her bed, sprinting to the door in her pyjamas, dread thoughts unfolding in her mind. Danny was still screaming: '*NO! GO AWAY! NOT ME! GO!*', his voice a high-pitched and panicked shriek. Frank had stood up, but was struggling to loosen his handgun from its holster. There was no sign of Alec. Christina hurled herself past Frank towards the half-open door of Danny's room on the other side of the corridor. '*LEAVE ME ALONE! GO AWAY! GO!*'

'*Get back, girl!*' Frank roared, and she felt his hand on her left shoulder, pulling her back.

'*IBRAHIM!*' Christina shrieked. '*NO! LEAVE HIM!*'

Frank had barged in front of her. His handgun was raised to eye level and he held it with both hands. He advanced on the door and kicked it open. Danny screamed even louder. His terrified voice seemed to echo inside Christina's head. She clenched her eyes shut, waiting for the sound of gunfire …

It didn't come.

The screaming had stopped.

She opened her eyes. Frank was inside the room. There was a sudden silence. Alec appeared at the far end of the corridor, bleary-eyed and half dressed. 'What the …'

Christina held up one hand to silence him. She crept to the open door and, with great trepidation, looked in.

Danny was sitting up in bed. His face was white, his adorable mop of hair dishevelled. Frank had perched on the edge and, having laid his firearm to one side, put an arm around the boy. He was talking to Danny in a quiet, calming whisper. He looked up at Christina and smiled. 'Nobody called Ibrahim in here,' he said in his soft West Country accent. 'Just a young man who's woken himself up with the night terrors.'

Danny looked at Christina and the sight of her made him burst into tears again. 'I want my mum,' he wailed. 'I miss my mum.'

'You're not the first little boy to say that, are you now?' Frank said consolingly. 'Don't you worry about it, lad. Your mum'll be home before you know it.'

It was all Christina could do, a hot flush of relief spreading through her, to stop herself articulating the thought in her head: *I miss your mum too. I want to know when she's coming home.*

Standing there in her pyjamas, she wondered where Bethany was. What she was doing. And if she was safe.

Bethany White lay in the darkness.

She was fully clothed and fully awake. There were no lights on in her room, but her eyes had adjusted to the dark and she was staring at a crack, faintly visible, in the ceiling. There was a film of sweat on her forehead, but her breathing was shallow and steady. She was calm. The food she had bought from the convenience store sat uneaten on the table. A bottle of water, half drunk, was on her bedside table. Next to it was the handgun. Cocked and locked.

Although her room was quiet, the hotel was noisy. Over the course of the day and night, she had heard shouting in the streets and in nearby rooms. She had heard the creak of plumbing and the thump of heavy footsteps in the room above. A woman had screamed, but it hadn't lasted long. Doors banged frequently enough for it to be clear that these rooms were being rented out for only short periods. She wondered if, having been here now for twelve hours, she was already the longest-staying guest.

Each new noise, however, kept her alert. Each time she heard a shout, she tried to determine whether it sounded closer or further away than the last one. Each footstep was a potential approach to her locked door. More than once, she had grabbed her handgun at the sound of creaking floorboards outside. And she grabbed it now, because that was what she had just heard.

Slowly, so she made no noise, Bethany swung her legs over the side of the bed. She listened again. Silence. Maybe she had imagined those footsteps in the first place. She crossed the room, treading softly, and placed herself by the door. She listened closely where it met the door frame. There was no doubt: she could hear breathing.

Her handgun was by her side. Now she raised it so it was shoulder-high and pointing up. The breathing on the other side of the door was fast. Wheezing.

A knock on the door. Bethany started.

'*Salam*,' she said, uncertainly. *Hello.*

'*Salam*. I have brought some wine. Perhaps you would like some.' Bethan recognised the voice of the man at reception. A sour expression crossed her face. She lowered the gun.

'I want to be left alone,' she said. 'Go away. Don't disturb me again.'

The heavy breathing didn't stop. The reception guy coughed chestily. 'It is good wine,' he said. 'I bought it specially.'

'Leave me alone,' Bethan reiterated.

The reception guy mumbled something she couldn't hear, but then the sound of breathing stopped and his footsteps disappeared down the corridor again.

Bethany glanced down at the door wedge that Danny Black had told her to fit under the door. The guy knew what he was talking about, no question. She wondered where he was now. Somewhere on the Syrian side of the border, she guessed. At least he should be, if he and his team were on schedule.

She walked back to her bed, laid her weapon on the bedside table, and lay down again to stare at the ceiling. She wondered if she should leave. It would be easy to do. But not the right thing, she decided. She needed this room, squalid and dark and simple though it was. And if the reception guy's ardour got the better of him? Bethany had dealt with worse.

She took a deep breath and closed her eyes. Get some sleep, she told herself. You have a busy time ahead.

14

To start with, the terrain on the Syrian side of the border was flat and sparse: a vast, empty plain of hard-packed earth and low, wiry scrub. The area was not without towns and smaller settlements. Because the land was flat, Danny could see the glow of built-up areas in the distance. Their line of travel, however, avoided those areas. In that respect, at least, Barak's itinerary was a good one.

After an hour's driving, however, the terrain became more undulating. It meant that the team was less easy to spot but also that they were unable to see for a great distance in any direction. Guerrero continued to drive blind, relying on his night-vision gear. For Danny and the others, it was a journey in the dark.

Forty-five minutes later they were travelling along the furrow between two raised areas, when Guerrero braked suddenly and without warning. Danny didn't need to ask what the problem was. With his night-vision goggles, Guerrero was more sensitive to light than the rest of them. He must have seen something.

The team moved like a single being. Each man opened his door and exited the vehicle with his weapon, silently falling down on one knee into the firing position. Danny immediately saw what had alerted Guerrero: moving beams of light, just like those they'd seen on the other side of the border, over the raised ground to his eleven o'clock. He panned his weapon in that direction just as the beams of light stopped moving and disappeared. There was the sound of a vehicle's doors opening and slamming shut. Then voices. Danny tried to estimate how far away they were. Thirty metres. Maybe a little more. He was certain of one thing, though: they were speaking Russian.

He wasn't the only person to notice. 'Ain't no regular Russian troops operating in this neighbourhood,' Guerrero said quietly over comms. 'We got ourselves some Spetsnaz.'

'I don't want this going noisy,' Danny said. 'Hold your fire unless I give the . . .'

He was unable to finish his sentence. A figure appeared on the brow of the hill. In the fraction of a second after it appeared, Danny saw it was military personnel. He could see the outline of a Kevlar helmet, and the bulge of a kneepad on the right knee.

Then he heard the gunshot that killed the man.

It came from Rollett's rifle.

'*What the fuck . . .*' Danny hissed.

The shot was true. The target collapsed on the far side of the brow.

'Get in the car,' Guerrero barked. The team did as he said, closing their doors as he turned the engine over, knocked the vehicle into gear and lurched ahead.

'I told you to hold your fire!' Danny bellowed at Rollett.

'No fucking point,' Rollett said. 'You think they were just going to ask us nicely what we were up to and then let us go? It went noisy the moment he saw us. This way, they're one down before we start.'

'Will you motherfuckers stop arguing?' Guerrero said.

Danny forced himself not to retort. There was no point. The contact had happened.

'What are the Russians even doing in this neck of the woods?' Danny said.

'Surveillance,' Barak said. He sounded very tense. 'Looking for anti-government militants.'

Danny caught a gleam of headlights in the rear-view mirror. 'They're following us,' he stated.

'How many?' Ludlow said.

'I don't know,' Danny said. 'I didn't get the chance to recce, remember?'

Guerrero accelerated. The vehicle bumped and rattled over the rough terrain. Danny caught another glimpse of headlights behind them: two sets, maybe? It was momentary and he couldn't be sure. They had a decision to make: continue the contact, or hide. Guerrero clearly had the same thought. 'They'll comb the fucking area for us, if we try to hide,' he said. 'Gotta take them out.'

'Fuck,' Danny muttered. A trail of bodies was exactly what he didn't need, if he was to stay under the radar, and taking out a Russian SF team brought with it a whole new set of problems. But the Yank was right. Try to hide now, they'd be dodging these soldiers for the next forty-eight hours. 'You think we're leaving tracks?' he shouted.

'Ground's pretty hard,' Guerrero replied. Danny had to hand it to him: he sounded calm.

'Accelerate harder,' Danny said. 'When I give the word, pull off to the right and loop back round. We'll get behind them and attack from the rear.'

Guerrero nodded. He clearly understood what Danny had in mind. Danny looked back over his seat. 'Get down,' he told Barak, who was blocking his view. Barak lowered his head. Rollett and Ludlow faced forward, their faces coldly expressionless. Through the rear window, Danny caught another glimpse of headlights. His brain was making a raft of fine calculations. How far away were the enemy vehicles? About a hundred metres. Were they using night-vision? Unknown. Could they see the Hilux by the naked eye? Possibly, even though Guerrero was driving without lights. If they were going to loop back, they had to do it when the undulating ground put them out of sight.

The headlights disappeared as the Hilux entered a dip in the road. They reappeared two seconds later as the Russian patrol moved on to higher ground. They disappeared for a second time as the Russians dipped down.

'Now,' Danny said.

Everyone was violently thrown around as Guerrero yanked the car to the right. For a moment, Danny thought he'd lost control. He felt the left-hand wheels leave the ground and the change in momentum seemed to spin the vehicle on its horizontal axis. But then Guerrero regained control and drilled the Hilux along a dip in the undulating terrain before making another ninety-degree turn and continuing back the way they'd come, camouflaged by raised ground between themselves and the road.

'Stop,' Danny said. Guerrero hit the brakes. Danny wound down his passenger window and heard the sound of the Russian vehicles speeding past.

He looked over at Ludlow and Rollett. They were also winding down their windows. 'Ready?'

'Ready.'

'Go,' Danny instructed.

Guerrero hit the gas and forced the Hilux over the raised ground back on to the road. As soon as they were over the brow of the hill, Danny knew the patrol would have noticed them. But they weren't likely to expect an SF manoeuvre like this, so Danny's team had the element of surprise. Another ninety-degree turn and they were directly behind the Russian convoy. It was definitely two cars, Land Rovers perhaps, Danny could see that now. The nearest was twenty-five metres ahead of them, the furthest ten metres beyond that. Guerrero was flooring the Hilux, and they were gaining on the targets. Danny manoeuvred his assault through the window and leaned out. He was aware of Ludlow doing the same from the rear window on the other side. He set his weapon to automatic fire, aimed at the rear of the furthest target, and fired a burst while Ludlow opened up on the nearest target.

Shooting from a moving vehicle: it was a mainstay of the SAS fast-driving course. Danny and Ludlow made no mistake. The back tyres of both vehicles burst, and the rear windows shattered. The two Land Rovers spun to a halt, broadside on. Guerrero hit the brakes while Danny and Ludlow released another burst, spraying the sides of the vehicles with rounds. Rollett, who was sitting behind Danny, exited the vehicle. He fired short bursts of suppressing fire at the Land Rovers, shattering their windows and peppering them with rounds. It was impossible to tell how many enemy targets there were, or how many they'd hit, but the Russians wouldn't be able to fire back while the unit kept them pinned down. So long as Danny and the guys dominated the situation completely, this could only really end one way.

Guerrero exited the vehicle and joined Rollett in advancing on the Land Rovers, firing bursts alternately with him. Danny grabbed a fresh magazine from his ops vest and reloaded. He could hear some screaming in one of the Land Rovers, but then there was another burst from Guerrero and the screaming stopped. Danny and Ludlow advanced behind the other two, firing short bursts towards the furthest target. Guerrero and Rollett were at the windows of the first Land Rover now, and firing single shots point blank at the occupants. Distance to the second Land Rover: ten metres. There was movement on its far side. Two figures had thrown themselves out of the vehicle. They were sprinting away from it, but must have known they didn't have a chance. Danny picked them off with brutal ease, two single shots in the back. As the rounds hit their bodies, a shower of blood burst from the entry wound before they fell to the ground with dull thuds.

Ludlow was aiming his weapon in through the open windows of the second vehicle. 'Clear!' he shouted.

'Clear,' Guerrero echoed. And suddenly there was complete silence.

In addition to the two guys Danny had nailed, there were three more corpses in the first Land Rover. Two of them had taken shots to the skull. One of them, the driver, had bled out from the side of his neck and was slumped over the steering wheel. Both engines had stalled and the interiors of the two vehicles were a gory, blood-spattered mess.

'Fuck's sake,' Danny hissed, and kicked the first Land Rover in frustration.

'We didn't have a choice,' Rollett grunted.

'We had a fucking choice,' Danny spat back. 'We could have talked our way past them, spouted the press line, paid them off, anything. Now anybody with half a brain can join a straight line between our crossing point and this fucking meat market and work out which direction we're travelling.'

Rollett shrugged awkwardly. 'Nobody knows we're here,' he said, clearly unconvinced by his own words.

'You sure about that?' Danny railed. 'You want to bet your fucking house on it? Word gets back to the Russians that six of their guys just got hit, they'll be all over us like a fucking rash. Drones, the works. If they decide it was Syrian rebels, they won't fuck around, they'll have fast air here . . .'

'Hey,' Guerrero interrupted. 'If we're talking drones and fast air, I'd say now was a pretty good time to get the hell out of here.'

As usual, he was right. The firefight had been noisy. It could have alerted anyone in the vicinity. They ran back to the Hilux and took their places again. Barak was visibly shaken up: his silver hair was ruffled and there were beads of sweat on his forehead. Guerrero hit the gas. They drove round the two shot-up vehicles and past the corpses on the ground. The GPS unit indicated they were still heading in the right direction. 'Do you know anywhere else we can lie up?' Danny asked Barak tersely.

Barak's air of confidence had left him. 'No,' he said. 'This is the way I always go.'

Danny looked back over his shoulder. There was no sign of lights or anyone following them. 'What's your call, friend?' Guerrero said.

Danny gave it a few seconds' thought. 'Keep going,' he said. 'We'll head for the lying-up point. Anyone follows us, we'll deal with them.'

Guerrero nodded. 'For what it's worth, I agree.' The team continued through the Syrian night in tense, unfriendly silence.

If the unit was being tracked, they couldn't tell. They met no vehicles and passed no settlements. It didn't put Danny at ease. Someone might be watching them by more covert methods, and they wouldn't know about it. It was a relief to reach the lying-up point, but it was also a concern. While they were a moving target, they were more difficult to hit. Motionless, they could be sitting ducks.

At least the LUP was acceptable. Barak's GPS coordinates had led them to a wadi, a dried-up river bed in theory, although it had a narrow stream of water trickling down its centre at this time of the year. It had cliff-like banks, four metres high, and deep overhangs where it was possible to conceal themselves. And Guerrero was able to enter the wadi by means of a tributary stream that led down on to the river bed. From the confluence, they continued 150 metres along the wadi and parked up where the overhang was particularly deep. Guerrero backed up against the side wall, ready to leave in a hurry if necessary, then killed the engine. He looked round at the unit. 'This hasn't gone the way we wanted,' he said, 'but we have to suck it up. Any of you guys don't feel you're part of the team any more, say the word and you can walk back to Lebanon.'

It was clear who his words were directed at. Rollett said nothing. Danny grunted his agreement. 'We need to keep stag,' he said. 'Two hours on, two hours off. Me and Ludlow will go first.'

There was no argument. Danny and Ludlow exited the vehicle and headed in opposite directions away from the Hilux. Danny took up position behind a boulder that was almost as tall as the overhang. From that position, he could see back along the way they'd come, towards the tributary. He hunkered down to keep watch.

It was cold. He could feel the chill air in his lungs. The moon had set and here, in the overhang of the wadi, it was pitch dark. Every few minutes he made use of the NV sight on his AK-47 to scan the area, but there was no movement. They were, so far as he could tell, alone and unwatched.

Two hours passed slowly. A grey dawn was breaking when Guerrero quietly approached. 'You'd better get some z's, friend,' he said.

Danny was glad to be relieved. He was about to trudge back to the Hilux when he stopped. He'd heard something. A dull, clunking sound. It was on the terrain above them. 'You hear that?' he whispered.

Guerrero nodded tersely. They stood still, listening hard. The sound had stopped. For a full thirty seconds there was silence. Danny was on the point of walking away again when the sound returned. It was a little louder this time, and more than a single clunk. Several: dull, and semi-melodious.

'Livestock?' Guerrero said.

Danny nodded.

'Maybe they'll walk on by,' Guerrero suggested.

'Maybe,' Danny said. 'Maybe not.' He pointed at the narrow stream of water trickling down the middle of the wadi. Livestock needed water. If some local shepherd or goatherd was leading them across this rough terrain, there was every chance they would lead their animals down into the wadi to drink.

Ludlow's voice came over the comms system. '*We got company . . .*'

'Roger that,' Danny said. 'Hold your positions. They might just carry on.' As he spoke, a man's voice drifted over the wadi. It was musical, like a chant, the voice of an old man singing to his animals. So far as Danny could tell, the voice's owner was almost exactly above the overhang.

And then there was a second voice: the voice of a child.

Danny and Guerrero exchanged a long look. Having a kid in the mix changed things.

The noise moved on. The clunking of the livestock's bells faded and the old man's voice drifted into nothingness. Danny stayed there with Guerrero, but he relaxed a little. And when, after half an hour, there was no sign or sound of the livestock, the man or the kid, he returned to the Hilux, lay out on the hard floor behind its rear wheels, and closed his eyes.

Two hours later he was on stag again. Two hours after that, sleeping. The day passed uneventfully, regulated by these metronomic two-hour periods, until the sun started to set.

And that was when the sound of the old man's melodious voice returned.

As before, Danny had just reached the end of his watch. The wadi was flooded with the intense red light of a Syrian dusk. The sound of the voice drifted towards him on the still air. He could tell from its direction that the old man was already on the wadi floor. He spoke into his comms. 'There's someone in the wadi.'

'*Who is it?*'

'Wait out.' He had just seen movement. Three goats appeared in his field of view, about thirty metres distant. Another four followed and then, in traditional dress, his back slightly bent and a staff in his hand, came the goatherd. He called to the goats in that chanting voice, and they seemed to obey his command, trotting in a line towards the stream that ran along the centre of the wadi. As the animals drank, the goatherd sat on a boulder. He unwrapped something from a pack on his back – food – and started to eat. Then another figure appeared, half the goatherd's height. It must be the kid he'd heard that morning, Danny thought to himself. The goatherd offered the child some food, but the offer was not accepted. Instead, the boy started wandering along the stream in the unit's direction, occasionally kicking the water into a shower.

'Shit,' Danny whispered.

Guerrero: '*What is it?*'

'The old boy's staying put with the goats, but we've got a child walking our way.'

'*Fuck it.*' Rollett's voice. '*Take them both out.*'

'No.' Danny and Guerrero contradicted him in unison.

'*He's just some Syrian kid,*' Rollett said. '*He'll probably be bombed to fuck before his next birthday anyway. We should nail both of them before they have a chance to bollocks things up for us.*'

Danny found himself sneering in distaste at Rollett's words. He wasn't shocked. He'd met plenty of guys in his line of work who wouldn't think twice about shooting a kid. It didn't mean he had to agree with them. He'd seen children being killed in Syria last time he was here. He wasn't about to add to their number if he didn't have to, and he was glad that Guerrero seemed to agree with him. 'Hold your fire,' he said.

The kid was wandering further up the wadi. Distance: twenty metres. He was humming something as he kicked the water, and was clearly oblivious to the four concealed men, heavily armed, who were watching him. Oblivious, that is, until he was ten metres from Danny's position, when he looked up and peered along the wadi. He squinted, not in Danny's direction, but at the Hilux which he had obviously just seen parked up under the overhang. He inclined his head for a minute, then shouted out and sprinted back towards the goatherd.

'*Put him down!*' Rollett said into the comms.

'HOLD YOUR FIRE!' Danny shouted. And because he knew they were compromised and couldn't tell what Rollett's next move was likely to be, he burst out from his hiding place behind the boulder and chased after the kid.

The boy was wiry and fast, but not as fast as Danny, who grabbed him when he was ten metres from the goatherd, quelled his wriggling arms with one hand, and put the other over his mouth to stop his screams. The goats were agitated: they bleated anxiously and crowded away from the water where they'd been drinking. The old goatherd jumped to his feet with surprising speed and shouted out in alarm. But he quickly fell silent, because running towards him, their weapons engaged, were Guerrero, Ludlow and Rollett.

Danny kept hold of the kid while the three others descended on the goatherd. Rollett got to him first, lowered his weapon and grabbed him round the neck with the crook of his arm. Danny sensed that the old man was suffering from Rollett's disappointment at not being able to make a kill. Whatever. They had some decisions to make. He looked over at the goats. They each had a length of rope around their necks. 'Tether them,' he told Ludlow. 'We'll get these two back to the Hilux. We need Barak to translate.'

After their initial struggle, the old goatherd and the boy quickly became compliant. Danny and Rollett dragged them up the wadi with Guerrero close behind. They found Barak anxiously wringing his hands by the Hilux, his silver hair faintly pink in the light of the setting sun. Guerrero threw the goatherd to the ground. Danny went easier on the kid, who scurried up to the old man, tears in his face. He looked back at Danny in absolute terror and for an uncomfortable moment Danny was reminded of Bethany's son, Danny Jr, back in the UK. He wanted to give the kid some reassurance, but that wasn't possible: for now, they needed to be frightened. 'Ask them where they live,' Danny told Barak, 'and when they're expected back home.'

Barak put the question. The old man answered in a terrified stutter. 'Ten hours' walk from here,' Barak translated. 'Their family expect them back tomorrow night. They were going to sleep the night here in the wadi, then carry on in the morning.'

Danny turned to Guerrero. 'You believe him?' he asked.

'Who knows, friend?' Guerrero said.

'Who cares, more like,' Rollett said. 'We should just nail them now, then get out of here. If we let them go, first thing they're going to do is leg it to the nearest settlement and raise the alarm.'

'He's got a point,' Guerrero said, and Danny had to concede that he was right. Rollett's solution was a simple one. The ex-SBS man had a fierce glint in his eyes as he waited for the others to come round to his opinion.

'Put your weapon down,' Danny said quietly.

'Fuck's sake,' Rollett spat. 'Guerrero?'

'Put it down,' the Yank said.

With two of his unit against him, Rollett didn't have a choice. He lowered his weapon. 'What's the plan, friend?' Guerrero said.

Danny thought it through. If he was going to leave the old man and the boy here, he couldn't leave them alone to escape and raise the alarm. He didn't want to leave Guerrero with them, because of all the members of the unit, the Yank was the one whose abilities and temperament he trusted the most, and who he wanted by his side. And he couldn't leave Rollett or Ludlow here for the opposite reason: he didn't trust them to do what he said, and keep their captives alive.

Which left Barak.

The fixer was watching Danny intently. Danny had the feeling that their Lebanese guide knew what conclusion he'd come to. Barak frowned, looked down at the goatherd and the boy, then back at Danny.

'It's two hours to the target, right?' Danny said to Guerrero.

'On a good run,' Guerrero said. 'Three max.'

'And we can navigate it without Barak?'

'If we have to.'

Danny turned to Barak. 'You know what I'm going to ask you?'

'I have an idea.'

'I want you to stay here with these two. We're going to tie them up, but you need to make sure they keep quiet. We'll pick you up on the way back. When we return to Beirut, I'll see you get paid triple.'

Barak contemplated the suggestion. He had a calculating expression that Danny didn't quite like, but Danny's choices were limited.

'Do I have a choice?'

'Sure,' Danny said. 'We do it this way, or our new friends have an early night.' He removed his handgun and pointed it at the old man and the boy.

Barak winced. 'The goats will make a noise,' he said. 'What if they attract people?'

Danny turned to Rollett. 'You got a knife?'

'Yeah.'

'Deal with the goats.'

Rollett didn't need telling twice. He marched off down the wadi. Barak watched him go with a slightly sick expression.

'Have you got what we need to restrain them?' he asked Guerrero.

Guerrero nodded and headed over to the Hilux.

Danny was alone with the two hostages and Barak. 'We're going to head further up the wadi and find you a better place to hide,' Danny said. 'We'll gag these two to keep them quiet. There'll be no reason for anyone to find you. We'll be back some point tomorrow night. If you're here, you get paid. If you're not here, or I get any hint that you've revealed our destination to anybody, you'll go the way of the goats. Do we understand each other?'

Barak plainly didn't like being spoken to in this way, but he didn't flounce off like he had at the disused training camp. He simply jutted out his jaw and said: 'We understand each other.'

It was almost dark now. A goat squealed on the edge of Danny's hearing, then fell silent. Guerrero returned with cable ties and masking tape. He wrapped the tape around the mouth and head of the old man and the boy, then bound their wrists behind their backs. He and Danny forced them further up the wadi, with Barak accompanying them. A hundred and fifty metres further along they found a crevice in the wall of the wadi, big enough to take them all. They forced the hostages into it, then cable-tied their ankles. The old man was frail, the kid tearful and terrified. It was grim work, but Danny told himself this was the only way their hostages could stay alive. It was a temporary measure, then they could go home.

Guerrero and Danny shook hands with Barak. His palm was clammy and he wouldn't look Danny in the eye. 'You still don't trust him?' Guerrero said as they hurried back down the wadi towards the Hilux.

Danny didn't have an answer to that. This was their only option, if they weren't going to nail the old man and the kid.

It was fully dark now. They continued to where Ludlow had been tethering the goats. Rollett had slaughtered them all. He and Ludlow had hidden six of the corpses in crevices around the wadi. As Danny and Guerrero approached, they were dragging the seventh along the wadi. Danny watched them stuff the dead beast into a hole on the far side of the stream. Their hands and clothes were smeared in goat blood when they returned, but it didn't seem to bother them. 'We're making a fucking mistake,' Rollett said. 'We should kill the Syrians and take Barak with us.'

'Not happening,' Danny told him. 'We're doing this my way or not at all.' He checked his watch. It was 20.03 hrs. 'We leave at midnight. That gets us on target somewhere between 02.00 and 03.00. I want to catch my guy while he's sleeping. If we're quick, we can get back to the wadi before sunrise.'

'Personally I want to catch your guy while these IS militant guards you're expecting are sleeping,' Guerrero said. Danny had to agree with that. 'I think it's about time you told us a bit more about what's going on, friend.'

The three men stared at Danny. They were on edge, and Danny knew he couldn't get away with keeping them entirely in the dark. Nor did he feel comfortable telling them everything. 'The target's name is Adnan Abadi,' he said. 'He has historic links to IS, and I think he might know the location of a guy I'm trying to find.'

'Who's the guy you're trying to find?' Rollett asked.

'I can't tell you that. I'm sorry.'

'Is it something to do with Ollie Moorhouse?' Ludlow asked.

'What makes you think that?' Danny said carefully.

'You shut me down pretty quick when I asked about him earlier. So is it?'

Danny nodded. He was surprised Ludlow had managed to join the dots. There was a pause, then Ludlow said: 'That's good enough for me.'

'Who's Ollie Moorhouse?' Rollett said.

'Ex-Regiment guy,' Ludlow said. 'Turned up dead a few days ago.'

'What's the chick got to do with it?' Guerrero asked.

All eyes were on Danny. 'We think she's next on the list. I can't tell you any more. I'm sorry. But I do know that when we get there, Abadi's going to be reluctant to talk. We won't have much time. We'll have to be persuasive.'

'Oh, I think we can be persuasive, friend,' Guerrero said. He looked back towards the Hilux. 'I say we get some food inside us. Nothing I hate more than fighting IS scumbags on an empty stomach.'

'Roger that,' Ludlow growled. Since learning they were on the trail of someone who'd nailed an SAS guy, he had a new eagerness about him. And even Rollett seemed less surly all of a sudden.

Together, the unit returned to the Hilux, ate cold MREs, and prepared for the next part of their journey.

15

Beirut. 11.15 p.m.

For Bethany, the day had passed in a meditative trance. She ate small amounts, and regularly. She spent the rest of her time lying on her bed, breathing deeply, keeping her mind clear and her heart rate down.

The hotel was quieter during the day than at night. It was getting noisy again now. The slamming of doors, the shouting of voices. To her relief the reception guy seemed to have got the message, and hadn't banged on her door since she'd sent him away the previous night. She wondered if he'd tried it on with any other guests. Probably not, she thought to herself. This wasn't the sort of place where women routinely stayed by themselves.

She stood up and stripped, peeling off the dirty clothes she'd worn since yesterday morning. She stepped into the shower cubicle. The seals were covered in mildew and the shower curtain was streaked with dried soap. Bethany didn't care. She ran the shower as hot as it would go and thoroughly cleansed her body and hair.

Back in the bedroom, she stood naked in front of the mirror, water dripping from her skin. A man was shouting in one of the nearby rooms. Somewhere in the distance she could hear the low beat of music. She blocked those sounds out and remained standing until her skin was dry. She towelled her hair and brushed it well, then laid out the clothes she had packed in her rucksack. There were two T-shirts, one white, one black. A clean pair of jeans. Attractive underwear. She selected a matching black set, put it on, then took her make-up bag back to the mirror. She did not, under ordinary circumstances, wear much make-up. At Fort

Monckton, the MI6 training centre, they'd explained that more often than not it made a woman more conspicuous. Bethany generally aimed for the opposite effect. But not tonight. Tonight she would have eyelashes thick with mascara, statement eyebrows, full red lips and eyeliner wings. She applied it all carefully, then stood back and appraised the result. It was perfect. She looked hot.

She chose the black T-shirt. It was a little tighter, and showed off her figure to better effect than the white one. The jeans hugged her thighs and accentuated their shapeliness. The little white pumps completed the outfit perfectly. There was a perfume bottle in her make-up bag. She didn't apply any of the contents but she did hold it up to the light. It was slightly cloudy, which was as it should be. She stowed the bottle back in the make-up bag.

She looked around the room. It wouldn't do. The half-eaten packets of food on the desk looked a mess. She collected them up and put them out of sight in the bottom of the wardrobe.

The handgun was still on the bedside table, next to the mobile phone she'd promised Danny Black she would keep switched off. Bethany considered them for a moment. The handgun was bulky. Impossible to carry it covertly in the clothes she was wearing. The wardrobe wasn't a secure enough hiding place. She took the weapon into the shower room and lifted the top of the toilet cistern. It was only half full of water, and there was space to rest the gun on the internal mechanism. She did this, then replaced the cistern lid.

Back in the bedroom she turned her attention to her rucksack. Apart from her British passport in the name of Tomlinson it was empty, or at least it appeared to be. She lifted the flap at the bottom to reveal the second mobile phone. She switched it on and placed her other phone in the rucksack before folding up her dirty clothes and stuffing them in. She opened up a zip on the outside of the rucksack and withdrew a thick wodge of Lebanese pounds, bound with an elastic band. She peeled off several notes, pocketed them, and returned the currency to the rucksack, which she stowed with the food in the bottom of the wardrobe.

Bethany surveyed the room, then smoothed the bedclothes. It was hardly comfortable accommodation, but she wanted it to be as inviting as possible. She took the key from its wooden fob and put it in her back pocket, along with her Lebanese mobile. She turned the TV on, then stood at the door and listened. She could hear nobody in the corridor, so she unlocked the door, stepped outside and locked the door again behind her.

She walked swiftly along the corridor to the stairs, hyperaware of the noises in the rooms she passed. She moved unseen down to the ground floor. From the stairwell she could see out into the reception area. The reflection of the reception guy was visible in the front window. It meant she couldn't simply walk out unseen. So she removed her mobile phone and dialled a number. The phone emitted a ringtone. A fraction of a second later, the hotel phone rang. She saw the guy's reflection as he moved into the adjoining room to answer it, and heard his voice on her mobile. That was her cue to exit the building. She strode through the reception and out the door. Only when she was in the street did she kill the phone call.

It was good to be outside. She'd been cooped up in that little room for what, thirty-six hours? Bethany had deep reserves of patience, but even she was beginning to feel the strain of her enforced solitude. She walked with great confidence through this rough area, ignoring the looks she got from men and women alike. She knew where she was going, and she walked quickly to get there.

Horsh Beirut was one of the few open spaces in this city dominated by buildings and traffic, a miniature forest surrounded by tarmac and tower blocks. Bethany had spent many a slow afternoon there, shading herself under the trees from the fierce summer sun on her frequent trips to make contact with Ibrahim. It was to Horsh Beirut that she now walked. It would be closed to the public at this time of night, of course, but she didn't need to get in. It was the perimeter of the park that interested her. It took half an hour to reach it and another ten minutes to walk round to its northern edge. A concrete and wire fence surrounded the park, keeping people out at night, but here there was a tree with a thick trunk growing through the pavement just outside the perimeter. It was a little after midnight when she reached it, and there was a surprising amount of traffic and passing pedestrians. She loitered by the tree for a couple of minutes, waiting to be certain she was unseen, before sidling into the area between the trunk and the railings. Here, at head height, there was a deep, hollowed-out knot in the tree. Bethany reached inside. After a few seconds, her fingers touched plastic. She pulled out a ziplock bag, wrapped tightly in gaffer tape. It was slightly damp and covered in dirt. But it was there where she had left it, at least two years ago.

Clutching the package, Bethany crossed the road and ducked into a deserted side street. Here she picked away at the gaffer tape round the package and tore into the ziplock bag. It contained three passports: one British, one French, one Armenian, all in different names. She discarded the packaging and flicked through the passports to check they were intact. The expiry dates were nine months, twelve months and fifteen months hence, and the photographs were unmistakably her, although the picture on the British passport showed her with brown hair. She slid the documents into her back pocket, relieved to have them in her possession.

Because like any agent worth the name, Bethany White always had an exit plan.

But not yet. The time wasn't right.

And anyway, the night was young.

She headed west, to a little place she knew.

Five minutes to midnight. Danny and Guerrero had just checked on Barak and the Syrians. Amazingly, the kid was asleep, his head on the bony lap of the goatherd. The old man had refused even to look at Danny or Guerrero. Barak was obviously scared, but making an effort not to seem so.

'He'll keep them there,' Guerrero said as they walked along the wadi. 'He's in too thick with us guys now to let anybody else get their hands on them.'

The night was still. The moon had risen and the stars seemed much brighter than the previous evening. They took their places in the Hilux, their weapons close to hand. Guerrero turned the engine over, flipped on his NV, and the Hilux crunched its way out of the wadi.

They drove slowly and in absolute silence, guided only by the GPS unit. It was work that they'd all trained for, but still: Barak's absence was noticeable. Without his knowledge of the terrain, they were driving blind in more ways than one. Danny constantly scanned the darkness, checking for lights or movement. He saw nothing and nobody. Somehow that only made the acrid taste of anxiety at the back of his throat more intense. The area was suspiciously deserted. Did that mean somebody was on to them? Were they being covertly tracked? Was their own black op being trumped by a black op of somebody else's design?

It was impossible to tell. All Danny could do was maintain his heightened state of awareness and be ready for an attack, if and when it came.

They continued to drive slowly through the night.

Beirut had surprised Bethany when she first started coming here. In her mind it was always synonymous with war, and it had indeed suffered its share of violence. But it was very far from being the shell-shocked city under constant bombardment that she remembered from the news as a child. It was metropolitan and even, in places, subversive, if you knew where to go.

Her destination was a nightclub called La Lanterne. The French name attracted a cosmopolitan crowd, and Bethany had never known it to be anything other than heaving, no matter what day it was. Tonight there was a queue along the pavement, and two broad-shouldered Lebanese bouncers operating a strict one-in, one-out policy. It took Bethany half an hour to gain entrance, during which time she smiled politely at the two persistent American guys in the queue who didn't seem in the least dismayed when she failed to respond to their advances.

The music inside the club was relentless and deafening. The lighting was neon and ultraviolet. Bethany squeezed through sweaty crowds of scantily clad clubbers towards the long bar at the far end of the club. She had to shout to make herself heard, and she paid for her vodka and tonic in cash, of course. Then she stood facing the dance floor, with her elbows on the bar, and watched.

The dance floor was a gyrating mass of bodies, pressed close. There were men dancing with women, men with men, and women with women. She chose this club for that very reason: when it came to sexual preferences, anything was acceptable, and everybody knew why they were here.

She sipped her drink slowly, declining several advances from men of different nationalities with a curt shake of her head. Instead, she picked out various women on the dance floor and tried to make eye contact. A tall, dark-skinned woman with a purple streak in her hair caught her gaze and smiled coquettishly. Bethany didn't return the smile, and looked elsewhere. A white woman, wearing little more than a bikini on the top half of her body and with a full sleeve of tattoos on her left arm, made a gesture that Bethany should join her. But she had a lip ring and a stud in her nose, and was a little too short. Two younger women, barely older than eighteen, had been kissing nearby. Now they were hand in hand, and one of them made a 'come here' gesture to Bethany, who turned away and sipped her drink.

It was only then she noticed the woman standing next to her.

She was about Bethany's height and build, and like Bethany she had blonde hair, though hers was perhaps a little longer. She was white, in her mid-twenties, and dressed to party, with a little black choker around her neck and a strappy top that revealed more than it hid. She gave Bethany a smile that pretended to be shy, but which was plainly the very opposite. And when she made a 'would you like a drink?' gesture, she received a smile in return that gave the same message.

It was impossible to talk. The music was too loud. Bethany and her new companion downed their drinks quickly. Then Bethany allowed herself to be led on to the dance floor, deep into the thronging heart of the crowd. Writhing bodies tangled all around her. The bass of the music vibrated her core. Her new companion pressed herself up against her.

They danced.

Thirty minutes passed uneventfully as the solitary Hilux trundled across the uninhabited Syrian terrain. The GPS showed they were fifty klicks from their target.

An hour. Thirty klicks.

Ninety minutes. Fifteen klicks.

'Stop the car,' Danny said.

Guerrero hit the brakes and killed the engine. 'What?' he said.

'Does it seem weird to you? We haven't seen anybody since we left.'

'I told you, Barak knows his shit. He gave us a good route. We're behind schedule. We need to keep going.' He started up the Hilux again and continued to follow the trajectory marked by the GPS.

Time check: 01.30 hrs. They were eight klicks from the target and the terrain had changed. Even in the darkness, Danny could tell the area had become greener and more fertile. The ground was softer, the low, dry scrub juicier and abundant. Guerrero had to manoeuvre the vehicle around vegetation that appeared in their path. The terrain became less undulating and gently sloping. And when the GPS indicated they were five klicks from the target, Guerrero stopped again. 'There's a road up ahead,' he said. Danny exited the vehicle and used the night sight on his weapon to scan the surroundings. Guerrero was right. The road was about three hundred metres away, perfectly straight and, by Danny's judgement, followed a north–south trajectory. The unit was approaching it from the west. Danny visualised the satellite map he'd examined on Guerrero's laptop back in Beirut. There was just a single road heading from the south into Abadi's compound. This was it. He estimated it would be only another kilometre before they hit the olive groves surrounding the compound.

There wasn't time to cover the ground on foot and they couldn't drive through the groves. The road was their only option.

Time check: 01.50 hrs.

'Let's get on to it,' Danny said. 'I want to hit him quickly, give us chance to get back to the wadi. We can't wait any longer. We'll drive to within a klick of the compound, then we'll advance on foot.'

Guerrero nodded his agreement. They trundled across the rough terrain, on to the road, and headed north.

It wasn't a well-made-up road. The ground only felt slightly different under the tyres: just as bumpy, but noisier and a little more gravelly. There were no other road users and, as Danny had predicted, they were soon surrounded by olive groves. The terrain sloped gently up on either side and the gnarled old trees were planted in regular lines.

Distance to target: four klicks. There were now occasional outbuildings among the olive groves to the side of the road: squat stone sheds, which Danny assumed were there for machinery, or to give farm workers a place to shelter in the summer. Each time they passed one, he felt an anxious prickle of the skin. Those outbuildings were perfect cover for anybody watching the road. He told himself that Adnan Abadi's people had no reason to be watching for them, and his confidence was bolstered by each building they passed without incident.

Distance to target: three klicks.

Two klicks.

Fifteen hundred metres.

'*STOP!*' Danny roared suddenly.

Because of the darkness, he only saw the bump in the road when it was five metres in front of the Hilux, and by then it was too late. Instinctively, he grabbed the steering wheel and yanked it to the right. Guerrero shouted something as the vehicle swerved, but his shout was immediately drowned out by an explosion.

Danny knew they were fucked. The ferocity of the detonation was like nothing he'd heard or experienced before: a sickening, ear-splitting crack that jarred the bones in his body and sent a white-hot flash across his brain and vision. Or maybe that was the flare of the IED that he'd seen in the road at the very last minute, and which they'd just hit.

The Hilux overturned. Danny thought the end was seconds away. He couldn't see anything – nor could he do anything to prevent the inevitable. It was just a matter of self-preservation. Knowing his head was protected by the kevlar helmet, he crossed his arms over his abdomen to protect his vital organs and waited for the roof of the Hilux to hit the ground. It connected with a thump that sent another horrific jolt through his body, and filled his hearing with the sinister, angry sound of buckling metal. He felt his helmet connecting with the crushed roof of the Hilux and for a moment thought they'd come to rest in that upside-down position. But the force of the blast had been immense and the vehicle continued to roll, its chassis, from the sound of it, being crushed like tinfoil before it came to rest in an upright position again.

Tactical thoughts punched his mind. They were fifteen hundred metres from the compound. Out of sight, but within earshot. Abadi's people would have heard the explosion. But those thoughts were suddenly displaced by the screaming. It came from Guerrero. He was evidently in agony. The dust inside the Hilux cleared and Danny saw something he'd never forget. The driver's side of the Hilux had taken the brunt of the blast. The door was no longer attached to the chassis, and the front of the bonnet on the driver's side was torn and demolished. The windscreen had shattered – in the explosion he hadn't even heard the sound of it disintegrating – and the steering column was ripped away. But it was Guerrero, not the Hilux, who was in the worst state. Both legs were missing below the knee. His upper right leg was smouldering. There was a nauseating stench of burning flesh and hair. And the blood. Jesus, the blood ...

Guerrero was screaming inhumanely. His NV goggles were still lowered. Danny lifted them and saw an expression of insane fear and panic. He looked over his shoulder. Ludlow was dead. No question. He'd been on the same side of the car as Guerrero and had taken the full force of the blast. The skin on his face was burned away. Danny could see patches of skull and a scorched network of damaged blood vessels. A shard of jagged metal was protruding from the side of his head.

Danny's reaction was instinctive. He ripped his med pack from his ops vest and withdrew a tourniquet. 'Give me yours too!' he shouted at Rollett, who was right behind him. If Guerrero had any chance of survival, these were it. He quickly wrapped his tourniquet just above the knee of Guerrero's left leg, which seemed to be bleeding the worst. He tightened the tensioning stick as hard as he could. Guerrero screamed even louder. That was a good sign. It meant he could feel the pain and he was breathing. Already Danny's hands were covered in his blood, but he kept tightening the tourniquet until the bleed slowed to a gentle ooze.

Rollett was holding out the second tourniquet. Danny grabbed it and started to apply it to the other leg, twisting hard, ignoring Guerrero's screams.

'*Movement!*' Rollett barked. '*Three o'clock!*'

'Put them down!' Danny had to shout to be heard over the screaming. There was gunshot from outside. Four rounds. One of them hit the side of the vehicle. '*PUT THEM DOWN!*'

Rollett was already on the case. He was facing sideways across the rear seats, his AK-47 raised. He released a round through the side window, which was astonishingly still intact. The glass exploded outwards and Rollett immediately followed it up with several short, targeted bursts. Danny had to trust to his companion's skill if he was going to tend to Guerrero. He kept twisting the second tourniquet, harder and harder, until he couldn't ratchet any more. His ears were ringing with Guerrero's panicked screams and the deafening noise of Rollett's AK-47. His lungs were full of smoke and the acrid stench of burned flesh and hair.

And then, suddenly, complete silence, apart from three sets of heavy breathing in the Hilux.

'Targets down,' Rollett said.

'You sure?'

'I said targets down, didn't I?'

Guerrero had stopped screaming and the tourniquets were doing their work, but he was clearly going into shock. His body was shaking. One hand on his neck told Danny his pulse was rapid and weakening. He was looking at Danny in terror. Danny, his hands covered in blood, forced a grin. 'We're going to get you out of here,' he said.

Guerrero couldn't reply.

'You know what that was?' Rollett said, his voice high-pitched and tense.

'Yeah,' Danny said.

'It was an ambush. It was a *fucking* ambush. They were *fucking* waiting for us!'

He was right. An IED in the middle of the road. Gunmen in wait to provide attacking fire after the hit. It was a classic manoeuvre and they'd driven right into it.

Guerrero groaned. Danny wished he had a morphine shot to give him. His eyes were rolling.

'So who was it?' Rollett said. His voice sounded accusatory, almost as if he suspected Danny of compromising the mission himself.

'Barak,' Danny said.

'Fuck off, he could have been in the car with us.'

'What if he tipped someone off after we left him. He knew our itinerary.' He cursed under his breath. 'It's my fault. I didn't trust the fucker the moment I saw him.' Sweat was dripping into Danny's eyes and he felt a cold creep of fury at the mistake he'd made.

A moment of silence. Then . . .

'*Fuck!*' Rollett said in the back seat.

Danny didn't have to ask what the problem was. He could see it well enough: headlights approaching from the direction of the compound. Three sets. Distance, maybe seven hundred metres. Difficult to tell in the darkness. But one thing was clear: this ambush wasn't over. Abadi's people – because it was surely them – were closing in.

'Get the Gimpy!' Danny shouted. 'Stop their approach.'

'What about you!'

'I'm staying with Guerrero.'

'He's fucked,' Rollett said. But he didn't argue. He opened the passenger door and exited. In the cracked rear-view mirror, Danny saw him running round to the back of the Hilux and then, twenty seconds later, sprinting to the side of the road. Looking over his shoulder, Danny saw why. There was a slight bump on the area between the road and the olive groves. It offered some protection as a firing point.

The headlights were approaching fast. There was no gunfire from the Gimpy. Danny reckoned they were five hundred metres away. 'Come on,' he hissed. '*Come on!*'

Suddenly, the machine gun burst into life. Its effective range was eighteen hundred metres, so Danny expected it to do some serious damage if Rollett managed to land the rounds accurately. The night air lit up as red tracer rounds, one in every five, burned a path directly towards the approaching convoy. Danny removed Guerrero's NV sights and clipped them to his own helmet while the Gimpy fire continued to rip through the air. As he lowered the sights, the red tracer turned to glowing green projectiles, and Danny could see the convoy much more clearly. There were two vehicles at the front and one behind. Rollett's Gimpy fire had ripped into one of the front vehicles: Danny watched as it swerved into the centre of the road and collided with the vehicle next to it. That swerve told Danny the driver had been hit. Rollett kept the rounds coming. They continued to rip catastrophically into the front two vehicles. Danny was certain the occupants, however many, were being ripped to shreds.

But it was the third vehicle that alarmed him.

Danny could see that, unlike the other two, it was an open-topped technical. And although it was still perhaps four hundred metres away, he could tell there was some kind of top gun rigged to it. He could just discern movement there, and he knew they were about to come under fire.

There was no time to explain to Guerrero. He pulled his companion by the waist so that he was lying across the front seats of the Hilux. The engine block would give him some protection from the incoming fire about to rain down on them. Danny himself burst out of the vehicle and ran round to the back. There was a momentary lull in the bursts of fire from the Gimpy. Danny knew Rollett, who had no NV, was unlikely to have seen the top gunner. He roared at him: '*INCOMING! HIT THE THIRD VEHICLE! THEY'VE GOT A TOP . . .*'

He didn't finish, because at that moment, the incoming fire commenced.

The tracer rounds had been effective in helping Guerrero land his rounds accurately. But there was a downside: they'd pinpointed his position for the top gunner. So when the enemy opened up, he didn't aim for the Hilux. He aimed to neutralise the threat of the machine gun. He aimed directly at Rollett's position.

Danny saw it happen through his NV. The rounds from the top gunner's machine gun peppered the ground around Rollett, causing little explosions in the earth. Rollett was about to counter-attack when one of the incoming rounds slammed into the top of his shoulder.

The counter-attack never came because there was nobody to launch it. Rollett was slumped face down on the ground. Danny knew he was dead.

There was a sinister silence. The top gunner's fire had stopped. Danny was drenched in sweat. He gave it ten seconds, then peered round the back of the Hilux. He saw the technical had turned to the side of the road so it could bypass the two other vehicles Rollett had mashed up with his Gimpy. Danny assessed his options. He was in darkness. He could get to the Gimpy now without being seen. The enemy would no longer be expecting gunfire from that position, and the Gimpy would give him more firepower than the Minimi in the back of the Hilux.

Decision made.

Crouching low, he sprinted the fifteen metres that separated him from Rollett's Gimpy position. He threw himself down alongside his dead unit mate. Rollett was a mess. The round had drilled deep into his shoulder blade and the wound had spewed several pints of blood. Danny rolled him out of the way and took up position at the Gimpy. There was still half a belt of ammo to be fed into the machine gun, which was hot from the rounds that had already gone through it. Danny placed his sticky, blood-soaked hands on the body and the trigger and checked out the position of the technical. It was in front of the two other vehicles now, and approaching. Danny fixed his attention on the top gunner, but now he couldn't see him. It looked like he'd got into the vehicle, or was crouching low for protection.

Bad move, Danny thought, because now he had a direct, unopposed line of fire on the technical. He'd seen the kind of damage the Gimpy had wreaked on the other vehicles – they were smoking, twisted heaps behind the technical – and he was ready to inflict the same.

He would just let it get closer, because the nearer it was, the more damage he could do.

The technical trundled slowly towards them, its headlights glowing bright green in Danny's NV.

Distance: three hundred metres. Did they think they'd eliminated everyone in the Hilux? Possibly. If so, they were in for a surprise.

Distance: two hundred metres. Danny frowned. Now it was closer, he realised there was something strange about the shape of this technical. It was weirdly box-like, and he suddenly realised what he was seeing. Rough sheets of metal had been welded to the sides of the vehicle, and to the front. There were holes cut out for the headlights and a mesh grille over the windscreen. It was a homespun armoured vehicle, but those sheets of metal would be effective. The Gimpy wouldn't have the same effect on it.

Danny tried to work out how many enemy targets he could expect. At least two: the driver of the vehicle and the top gunner. Possibly more. He had a call to make. Should he fire and give up his position, in the hope that the machine-gun rounds would penetrate the armour? Or did he require a different strategy?

He removed his trigger finger from the Gimpy and turned his attention to Rollett's dead body.

The shoulder wound was still leaching blood. Danny inserted his right hand into the wound. It was warm and wet, and he could feel the shoulder blade. He scooped out a fistful of gore and plastered it over his own neck and the side of his face, before going in for another handful and repeating the process. One man's blood and tissue looked no different to another's. Danny's grim make-up would make it look like he'd been shot.

The technical was 150 metres away now. Danny crawled back to the Hilux, pressing himself hard against the ground so he'd remain unseen by the approaching enemy. He removed his NV goggles, cast them to one side and took his pistol in his right hand. He lay on his side behind the Hilux, his fake wound visible, his weapon concealed under one arm. He fully closed one eye and half closed the other.

Then he waited.

From his prone position Danny could see under the Hilux but couldn't establish the advancing technical's exact position. All he knew was that headlights were getting closer and brighter and that the engine – a rough, low diesel growl – was growing louder.

And then, suddenly, it was idling.

A minute passed. Danny could hear voices, and then the sound of doors closing. Peering below the undercarriage of the Hilux, he saw two sets of legs blocking the beam of the technical's headlights. He estimated they were twenty metres beyond the Hilux, and they were approaching.

Danny inhaled deeply and held his breath. It was crucial that he remained utterly still. Through his half-open eye, he saw one of the sets of legs stop almost directly in front of the Hilux. The second set was walking round to its left-hand side. Five seconds later, he came fully into view.

The target wore a red and white shemagh round his head and neck. Jeans and T-shirt. No body armour, but an assault rifle held loosely across his chest. He stopped five metres from Danny's position, and Danny knew his fake wound had done the trick because the target stood there without raising his rifle to fire.

Danny moved suddenly. He rolled on to his back, raised his handgun and released a single round into the target's face before he even had the chance to register his surprise. Then he rolled on to his side again, arm outstretched, the handgun at ninety degrees, parallel to the ground. He released two more rounds in quick succession beneath the undercarriage of the Hilux. His marksmanship was on point. The rounds slammed into each of the legs. The target fell. Danny winced as more light from the vehicle hit his retina, but he kept his aim true. Within a second he had a direct line of sight on his enemy's head. He squeezed the trigger and the target was eliminated.

Two guys down. The vehicle was no longer advancing, which suggested to Danny that he'd taken out the driver. But he reckoned the top gunner was still in there.

There was no sign of anyone else approaching. Danny scrambled to a kneeling position and moved over to the rear of the Hilux. The tailgate was down and the tarp was peeled back. He had direct access to the Minimi, which he grabbed. There was no time to set up the box magazine, so he took a standard M16 mag and loaded it. The Minimi was larger than a regular assault rifle, and heavier. It had a shorter range than the Gimpy – about eight hundred metres – but for this job it was fine. Danny felt his arm muscles straining as he hauled it from the back of the Hilux. There was a sudden deafening burst of fire from the technical. Sure enough, the top gunner was back in position. Danny crouched behind the Hilux, still holding the Minimi. Heavy rounds splintered into the vehicle and ricocheted off on to the ground all around. One round even thumped into the dead body of the guy Danny had shot in the face, making his limbs flap momentarily.

Sweat dripped from Danny's forehead into his eyes. He blinked heavily to clear it. The gunfire stopped.

Silence.

Danny only had a single mag. It meant he only had one chance. He needed guile as well as firepower. Moving slowly and silently, he reached out for the NV goggles he'd discarded on the ground.

He breathed calmly for a few seconds. Then he threw the goggles to his right.

The top gunner's response was almost immediate. A brutal burst of rounds exploded on to the ground where he'd seen movement. Danny moved in the opposite direction, to the left of the Hilux. He thrust himself up to his feet, raised the Minimi to chest height, and fired.

The top gunner was just visible behind the technical's headlight beam. He'd clearly seen Danny, and was rotating his mounted weapon from the right-hand side of the Hilux to the left. But he wasn't fast enough. A full clip of 5.56s spewed from the Minimi and slammed straight into him. The top gunner fell backwards and his gunfire stopped.

And then there was silence again.

Danny was gasping for breath. He threw himself back behind the Hilux and waited for any more sound of movement or attack. The technical was still turning over, but there was no other noise. Danny gave it two minutes, checking the view underneath the Hilux. There was no sign of personnel approaching, nor any indication of further threats.

He dropped the Minimi, re-armed himself with his handgun, and stepped round the Hilux. The air was a pungent brew, stinking of cordite and burning flesh. He edged carefully round to the driver's door and looked in to see what kind of state Guerrero was in. His unit mate was still on his back, with the horrific, bleeding stumps of his legs pointing towards Danny who knew, even before checking, that he hadn't survived. He reached in and grabbed his wrist, checking for a pulse. Nothing.

The rest of his team were dead. Danny was on his own.

16

Bethany's hair was wet with sweat and her eardrums were numb. They hadn't left the dance floor. They hadn't even spoken. Bethany didn't know her pick-up's name or nationality. It was only when the young woman dragged her from the floor, put her lips to Bethany's ear and shouted, 'Let's get some fresh air!', that Bethany knew for sure she spoke English.

Fresh air, of course, wasn't the only thing on the young woman's mind.

Her name was Sophie. That, at least, was what she told Bethany as they stood outside the club sharing a cigarette. Was she telling the truth? Probably not, and she most likely knew Bethany was lying when she introduced herself as Krystal. Sophie stubbed the cigarette out on the floor. 'We could go back in,' she said, 'or . . .'

'Or what?' Bethany asked, a flirtatious smile on her lips.

'Or, you know . . .' Sophie said. 'Go somewhere else.'

Which was how they ended up in the back of a taxi, giggling each time the taxi driver gave them a disapproving look in his rear-view mirror. Sophie was a little tipsy and Bethany was good at pretending. It was gone three in the morning when they pulled up at the end of the street where Bethany's hotel was situated. She gave the cabbie a good tip and watched his vehicle disappear before turning to Sophie and saying: 'This way.'

'I don't know this part of town,' Sophie said. She appeared a bit unsure. La Lanterne had been in a glamorous area. This was anything but.

Bethany gave her a shy look. 'I like to stay somewhere where people don't ask questions.' Sophie burst into giggles again.

Bethany took out her mobile phone and dialled the hotel's number. She knew Sophie would just assume she was checking her messages. As they approached the entrance to the hotel, she saw the reception area was empty. They entered in time to hear the reception guy answering the phone in the adjoining room. Unseen, Bethany led Sophie to the stairwell, then killed the call.

The hotel was quieter than usual. TVs were playing in a couple of rooms, but it was otherwise silent. As they walked along the corridor towards Bethany's room, Sophie seemed nervous again. Outside the door, Bethany took her gently by one arm. 'You okay?' she said.

Sophie looked at the floor. All her lightheartedness had suddenly disappeared. 'I've never done anything like this before,' she said.

Bethany put one hand on her cheek. 'There's a first time for everything.' She removed the key from her pocket and unlocked the door. The room was just as she left it: the TV playing quietly, the bed newly made, the little perfume bottle on the table. As Bethany locked the door again, Sophie walked further into the room. Turning, Bethany saw her holding up the perfume bottle as though she was about to apply a squirt.

'Leave that,' Bethany said, her voice level. And when Sophie looked chastened, she added. 'It's a present for my mum.' She walked up to Sophie, took the bottle from her, replaced it on the table and then put one hand behind her head, entwining her fingers in the curls of her hair. Sophie was trembling a little with apprehension, but she also had a faint smile.

Their first kiss was tentative and short, a mere brushing of the lips. But their second kiss was more meaningful, a foretaste of things to come. When it was over, Bethany turned off the main light, so the room was lit only by the glow from the TV. When she returned, Sophie had already kicked off her shoes. She allowed Bethany to brush her fingertips lightly along her neck, then raised her arms as Bethany peeled off her top. She was wearing nothing underneath. She closed her eyes, inhaling sharply and excitedly as Bethany kissed her breasts. She made no complaint as Bethany undid the button on her jeans. When they were loosened Sophie wriggled out of them and stood before Bethany wearing nothing but a silk g-string. 'Aren't you joining me?' she asked.

'Lie on the bed,' Bethany told her.

Sophie did as she was told. Bethany stood at the foot of the bed and started to strip: T-shirt first, then jeans. She allowed Sophie to enjoy the sight of her in just her underwear, before unclipping her bra and dropping it to the floor. She joined Sophie on the bed, crawling hungrily towards her and kissing her again. Their hands started to explore each other, and the lovemaking began in earnest.

Silence.

Rollett's body lay dead by the Gimpy. Guerrero and Ludlow were dead in the mangled Hilux. There were two dead gunmen on the ground, more in the technical, the two other vehicles in the distance, and in the olive groves. Danny – breathless, sweating and wired – evaluated his options amid the bloodbath. He was about a kilometre from the compound. Adnan Abadi, and whoever was with him, would certainly have heard the firefight. They would have been expecting the sound of gunfire, so they wouldn't necessarily know their guys had been overcome. Danny had two options: withdraw or advance. He was hard-wired to keep pressing forward, but he needed to do it quickly before they worked out what had happened.

The Hilux was out of action. He had no option but to move on foot.

He scavenged ammo from the ops vest of his dead unit mates, and also Guerrero's sat phone which was blood-smeared but hopefully still working. Then he left the road.

The olive groves, planted in straight lines, provided a path that ran directly parallel to the road. Still carrying his rifle, Danny sprinted, breathing deeply to keep his blood aerated, and confident of his fitness. The olive trees were a blur as they passed. The thump of his footsteps and the beating of his heart seemed unnaturally loud. His thoughts were all over the place: the shock of the ambush, the fury at Barak, the horror of watching his team killed. He tried to put all that from his mind. His focus was Adnan Abadi. He hadn't come all this way, and gone through all this, to lose his one link to Ibrahim Khan.

The compound came into view three hundred metres up ahead. Its circular exterior wall was white and it glowed faintly in the moonlight. It was also about four metres tall: unscaleable without assistance. Where the road met the wall there was a wooden entrance gate, wide enough for two vehicles side by side, but shut and, Danny had to assume, locked.

He reached the perimeter wall and stood silently for a minute, listening carefully. There was no sound inside the compound. If the noise of the firefight had panicked its occupants in any way, Danny heard no evidence of it. Maybe the compound was empty. Maybe Abadi had sent all his guys out to deal with the threat, and was here by himself. Whatever the situation, Danny wouldn't know until he was inside.

He skirted round the perimeter wall. The olive trees were planted up close to it, some within five metres. He was on the north-eastern edge when he came to a tree that, although it was no closer than the others, had branches that sprawled somewhat further. He repositioned his rifle so it was now slung across his back, then scrambled up the olive tree and along a sturdy branch that took him within three metres of the perimeter wall. He was only a couple of metres off the ground, and it was still a decent jump – up and across – to the top of the wall. Danny didn't think about it too hard. He hurled himself to the wall and slammed against it, just managing to claw his hands over the top edge. He hauled himself up and, seconds later, jumped down into the compound. He crouched low, taking stock of his surroundings.

He was behind a low building, perhaps twenty metres in length, made from bare breeze blocks with no visible windows. There was still absolute silence. He moved anticlockwise around the perimeter wall until he reached a position where he had line of sight on the main entrance. There were two guards about twenty-five metres away. They were both on one knee, side by side, about five metres in from the gate. One was in the firing position. The other was speaking urgently into a radio and getting no response. He dropped his radio and raised his weapon. They'd obviously heard the sounds of the ambush and subsequent firefight, but clearly didn't know what the hell had happened out there, and were expecting the worst.

Beyond them, parked up along the inside of the perimeter wall, were three trucks. Danny silently pressed himself against the wall of the long, low building and assessed his options. It seemed clear to him that those two guards had heard the firefight and were expecting an attack. It was equally clear to him that in all probability those two guards were the only remaining defence in the compound, otherwise there would surely be others marking the entrance. Taking these two out now was a risk, but an informed one. There was a good chance it would leave him alone in the compound with Adnan Abadi, wherever he might be.

The guards were as good as dead, even before Danny had them in his line of sight again. He raised his weapon, set it to semi-automatic, and aligned his crosshairs with the skull of the closest guard. He moved his finger from the trigger guard to the trigger itself, inhaled, and held his breath for the moment it took to release the round. The retort of the weapon echoed across the compound as the target slumped heavily to the ground. Danny kept his cool. The second guard didn't. Panicked by the sudden attack, he was clumsily trying to raise his own weapon while looking around blindly for the shooter. Danny released a second round, aiming this time at the chest since his head was moving. It was just as effective as the first, and the guard crumpled to a heap as the echo of the gunfire dissipated into the Syrian night.

Silence again. Danny put himself back in the cover of the low building and waited for half a minute, his senses heightened. Everything was still. He crept quietly round to the end of the building and surveyed the compound at large. Opposite him were two adjoining buildings. Guerrero had identified them as a processing facility. Danny agreed. There was an open door on one of them, high-up windows, and an old tractor parked outside.

Maybe that was where the olives were sorted or pressed. To his right, at the end of the long, low building, was a smaller unit. This had windows at eye height, and there was a dim light inside. It struck Danny as a domestic dwelling, and he decided that should be his next stopping point.

Even though there was no sign of external threats, Danny moved stealthily. The long building cast a moon shadow. He kept in its camouflage as he pressed forward in a northerly direction, his footfall practically silent. He stopped five metres from the entrance to the target building, and listened.

Nothing.

Danny was just giving some thought how to best enter the building – by the main entrance, the windows, or perhaps by moving round to locate a back entrance – when suddenly the door burst open. A figure appeared, silhouetted by the light inside. The light was behind the figure, so Danny couldn't make out his face. Whoever it was, however, had a thin frame and was plainly panicked. Danny could see his shoulders rising and falling with breathlessness. He stood there, peering out, for a few seconds. Then he ran.

Danny assumed he was heading for the trucks. Certainly he was sprinting in the direction of the exit. It would have been simple for Danny to put him down with his rifle, but it was clear to him this wasn't a guard. It was the person being guarded. As the target ran, Danny launched himself towards him. They connected with a brutal thump halfway to the exit. Danny heard the wind being painfully knocked from the target's lungs as he grappled the man to the ground. He roughly rolled him on to his back, sat on his chest to immobilise him, grabbed a clump of his hair, and put one hand over his mouth. He examined his face in the moonlight. It was an elderly man, but he had a strange bumfluff beard like a teenager. He smelled bad enough to make Danny want to hold his breath. It was the little round Gandhi glasses, wonky on his face, that gave Danny a positive ID: this was the man whose photograph he had seen at the embassy in Beirut. This was Adnan Abadi.

Abadi was trying to writhe and wriggle away, but he was thin and old and it was like restraining a child. Danny dragged him up to his feet. Abadi's escape attempt had confirmed one thing: there were no more guards. This was a guy who had sent armed men out to defend him. If he was trying to escape alone, his defences were down. He dragged him back to the building he'd burst out of, throwing him so roughly through the open door that he ended up sprawled on the ground again. Then he kicked the door shut behind him and took in his surroundings.

The front door entered on to a large room. There were carpets on the floor and what Danny presumed to be Islamic scriptures on the wall. It was dim. The light he'd seen through the window came from various candles and the screen of a laptop on an old wooden desk. There were cushions scattered around, a TV against one wall, and a door leading to the rest of the house. The intel from the UK had indicated that Abadi was a former Syrian government minister, but this didn't look like a government minister's dwelling. It was much simpler than that.

'You speak English?' Danny said.

Abadi pushed himself up into a sitting position and straightened his glasses. He looked glazed – it crossed Danny's mind that the old boy might even be stoned – and stroked his bumfluff beard. He nodded.

'You know all your guys are dead?'

He nodded again.

'Good. So you know what's going to happen to you if you don't do exactly what I tell you. That ambush killed three of my men. I'm not feeling generous. I'm going to ask you some questions. If you don't give me the answers I want, I'll kill you and find someone who can. Do you understand?'

'I understand,' Abadi said. They were the first words he'd spoken. His voice was as thin as his body, and it shook as much too. Danny knew that fear – real fear – was impossible to feign. Adnan Abadi might be stoned, but he was also fucking terrified. He looked up at Danny like he was a monster, and that suited Danny perfectly.

'You know the name Ibrahim Khan?'

Abadi stared at him.

'I said . . .'

'I know it,' Abadi whispered. 'Yes, I know it.' He stroked the bumfluff again.

'Where is he?'

Abadi blinked at him. His eyes widened. Then, suddenly and quite unexpectedly, he started to giggle.

For some reason, Abadi's laughter infuriated Danny more than anything else. A surge of anger burst through him. He strode up to the old man, grabbed him with one big hand by his neck, ripped him up from the floor, and pressed him hard up a section of wall where an Islamic scripture was hanging. The scripture fell loosely over Abadi's head and Danny had to rip it away again to look the old man in the eye. Abadi's stench caught the back of Danny's throat. 'What's the big fucking joke?' he growled. 'Where is he?'

Abadi's face was flushing. The giggling had stopped. 'You came all the way here to find Ibrahim Khan?' he gasped. 'You will never find him. Ibrahim Khan is dead. He has been dead for six months.'

Danny stared at him. 'What are you *talking* about?'

'Ibrahim Khan. He was a traitor. His body was torn apart and he was burned to ash.' Abadi's eyes had the wild-eyed glint of a fanatic. 'He was a traitor, and he paid a traitor's price.'

Danny felt lightheaded. He threw Abadi to the floor again. The old man couldn't be telling the truth. It was an impossibility. Bullock, Armitage and Moorhouse had all been killed in the past three months. Ibrahim Khan's DNA had been identified in Florida. Abadi was mistaken, or lying. Danny would have to turn the screw a little tighter to find out what was really going on.

He approached again, but something made him pause. Abadi's glasses had steamed up and he was grinning insanely at him. There was something triumphant in his face. Danny had conducted enough field interrogations to have developed an instinct about these things, and something told him that, at the very least, Adnan Abadi *thought* he was telling the truth.

'They butchered him,' Abadi whispered, as if taunting Danny. 'They put him in a cage and they filled his blood with adrenaline so he was unable to pass out. They removed his ears first, so he could no longer hear the false words of the infidel. Then they took his fingers, so he was unable to fight back. They removed his genitals, to unman him, and then his eyes, because they wished him to see what was happening while they punished him. And finally they burned him alive, to return his body to the dust where it belonged.'

Abadi's words rang in Danny's head. He remembered the pictures of the three SAS men's bodies. Bullock, his ears sliced off. Armitage, his fingers removed. Moorhouse, his genitals separated from his body and lying on the carpet by the bed where he lay. Abadi was claiming that Ibrahim Khan had suffered the same brutal tortures. And he believed he was telling the truth . . .

But if Ibrahim Khan had died six months ago, who was responsible for these killings? Who had the skill, the strength and the stomach to overpower three ex-Regiment soldiers, and carve them up in such a sickening fashion? Who had managed to misdirect MI6 and Danny himself so spectacularly?

Adnan Abadi grinned at him, plainly enjoying his confusion. Danny could find no words. A crowd of questions ricocheted in his mind as he tried to make sense of the information Abadi had just imparted.

But he couldn't.

The bedclothes were on the floor. Bethany and Sophie were still entwined on the sheet. Sophie's kisses were as intense as they'd been all night. She showed no sign of flagging.

Bethany suddenly knelt up on the mattress.

'What is it?' Sophie said. She looked worried.

Bethany put a hushing finger to her lips. Then she crawled, naked, to the end of her bed, where she picked up her own bra and knickers. She handed them to Sophie. 'Put them on,' she whispered in her ear. Sophie looked confused. 'It's my thing,' she said. 'I want you to dress up as me.'

Sophie bit her lower lip, smiled, and took the underwear. She wriggled into the knickers and put on the bra.

'Nice,' Bethany said. She threw her the black T-shirt.

'It smells of you,' Sophie said as she put it on. 'I like that.'

Bethany picked up her jeans from the floor and gave them to Sophie. She pulled them on. 'Do you want me to do them up,' she said, 'or leave them undone?'

Bethany walked round to the side of the bed and knelt on the floor next to her. 'It's up to you,' she said. She leaned in to kiss her. Their lips touched and then their tongues. Bethany stroked her hand up Sophie's thigh, over her breasts, and came to rest on the soft skin of her neck. Sophie shivered with pleasure and made no complaint when Bethany did the same with her other hand.

And at first, when Bethany started to strangle her, Sophie almost seemed to like it. She made a little whimpering sound, and goose bumps appeared on her skin.

Bethany pulled her mouth away from Sophie's, both hands round her neck. Sophie's eyes were wide. It was clear to Bethany that she was beginning to doubt that this was what she wanted. 'Stop it,' she whispered.

But Bethany didn't stop. She tightened her grip.

Sophie's arms started to flail. She grabbed hold of Bethany who, still naked, hauled her body on to her one-night-stand's. With Bethany's weight on her abdomen, there was nothing Sophie could do. Her legs kicked uselessly. She tried to scream, but she didn't have the breath to do it, and her voice was feeble and dry. Her face was turning red, her neck thickening slightly under Bethany's grip. Her eyes, which reflected dim, flickering light from the TV, were bulging.

And now the flailing of her limbs was less frenetic and her eyes were rolling in their sockets. Bethany did not loosen her grip. Even after Sophie's eyes rolled upwards and her body fell still and her breathing stopped, she kept her hands firmly round her neck, keeping them there for a full two minutes after all signs of life had gone.

Gingerly, she released her grip, as if half-expecting the dead woman to spring back into life again. She stood up and walked, naked, to the wardrobe. She found her make-up bag in her rucksack and took it into the shower room, where she removed the make-up from her face, returning the dirty cotton-wool pads to the bag. She walked back into the room and collected Sophie's clothes from the floor. They were too skimpy to wear around Beirut without attracting attention, so she folded them up and packed them away in the rucksack, before putting on her old clothes that she'd been wearing before going to the nightclub.

She switched the main lights on. The woman's body already looked cold and waxy. Then she turned her attention to the perfume bottle on the table. She carried it over to the corpse, then unstoppered it and carefully removed the pipette applicator. A drop of liquid fell from the pipette on to Sophie's chin, where it fizzed and left an angry red mark. Taking great care not to get any of the liquid on her own skin, she trickled it from the bottle over the woman's face. The result was instant. The skin bubbled and blistered. The liquid merged with pink body fluids and dripped down the side of the disfiguring face on to the bedclothes. The woman's eyebrows and eyelashes burned away into nothing. An acrid, chlorinated stench filled the room and for a moment Bethany was worried that it might leach out into the corridor. But the smell faded quickly as the fizzing chemical subsided, its work done.

The woman's face was no longer recognisable. The skin had peeled away to reveal a mush of tissue underneath. The eyes looked as if they had been gouged. The lips that Bethany had been kissing just minutes ago were strips of congealed blood melting into Sophie's teeth. But the hair looked like Bethany's, and the clothes were hers. Anybody coming across this sight and expecting to see Bethany would certainly assume it was her. And when they found the passport in the name of Tomlinson, which Bethany was now slipping into the back pocket of the corpse's trousers, and reported that back to MI6, there would be no room for doubt. At least for a little while.

She carefully stoppered the empty perfume bottle and put it back in her make-up bag. She returned the half-eaten packets of food to the table, then stowed everything else in her rucksack. By the time she was done, there was nothing in the room but the food and the body.

Bethany listened at the door. There was silence outside. She unlocked the door, slipped into the corridor and locked it again. Rucksack on her shoulder, she headed back along the corridor and down the stairwell for a final time. She didn't need to do her trick with the phone because the reception area was empty. She exited the hotel unseen.

Dawn had arrived, grey and cold. The streets were almost deserted. Bethany directed herself to a very narrow side road entirely devoid of pedestrians. Here she found a drain grille and posted one of her two phones into it. She didn't need it any more. Danny Black certainly wouldn't be phoning, if everything had gone to plan. And if it hadn't, she'd bought herself some time.

She double-checked her fake passports and her anonymous phone. Then she shouldered the rucksack again and directed herself to the nearest main road.

Ten minutes later she was in a taxi, heading to the airport.

17

'How do you know all this?'

Danny had lifted Abadi to his feet. The old man had started to giggle again. He was definitely either stoned or insane. He was grinning, his eyes gleaming. Danny pressed his handgun hard into Abadi's skull to focus his attention. 'How do you know all this?' he repeated. 'How do you know how Khan was killed?' A suspicion was growing in Danny's mind that Abadi was leading him on after all. Maybe he'd heard about Bullock, Armitage and Moorhouse. Maybe he was trying to lay a false trail.

'I saw it happen,' Abadi whispered.

'You were there?'

'No. They recorded it. I've seen the film.'

A beat.

'Do you still have it?'

'Yes.'

'Here?'

'Yes.'

'Show me. Now.'

'You're too weak. You won't be able to watch.'

'Listen to me, buddy. You're one wrong word away from getting the full treatment. Show me the fucking footage or you'll be the next one to get your bollocks ripped off.' He saw Abadi's gaze flicker towards the computer on the other side of the room. 'Is it on that laptop?'

Abadi nodded.

'Put it on.' He threw Abadi in the direction of the laptop. The old man staggered towards it. Danny watched as he navigated to a folder of Quicktimes and clicked on one of them. Dark, juddery video imagery appeared on the screen. Danny forced Abadi to the ground and kept his weapon pointing at him as he watched the footage unfold on the screen.

He recognised Khan immediately, even though the quiet, unassuming young man whom he'd last seen sitting on his bed in a remote farmhouse looked very different. He wore a beard, for a start, and his hair was long, almost shoulder-length. He was dirty and he was naked. He was also, as Abadi said he would be, sitting in a padlocked cage, not much bigger than a large dog crate – in fact, it might have been a dog crate. He was crouched and cramped and gripping the bars. His skin was smeared brown with his own excrement. He looked spaced out, as if he'd been drugged.

There was a cut in the footage. The crate was open and Khan was outside it, still naked and kneeling. A figure dressed in black and wearing a balaclava was next to him. He had an evil-looking hooked knife and was chanting a prayer in Arabic. Khan was shaking, but seemed unable to move. The figure stopped chanting. He grabbed Khan by the head, yanked it to one side and, with a swift and sudden movement, sliced off his right ear.

It didn't bleed as much as Danny expected, and Ibrahim Khan didn't scream. Maybe he was too pumped full of drugs for either outcome. His eyes rolled, however, and he looked like he might collapse if the hooded figure hadn't grabbed him by the other ear and, with the bloodied knife, quickly whipped it off.

Another cut in the footage. Ibrahim Khan was tied to the crate, kneeling in the doorway, his arms spread out as though crucified, his wrists bound to the bars. His ears were bandaged. A black-clad figure – it might have been the same person as before, or another one, Danny couldn't tell – stood by his right hand with a long-handled chain cutter. There was no preamble. He took Ibrahim Khan's little finger in the blades of the cutter and lopped it off as easily as a gardener pruning a rose bush.

There was no doubt Khan felt it. His body started and he appeared to inhale sharply. But again, there was no scream. Danny felt a seed of respect germinating for this man. And although he knew what was coming, Danny could not take his eyes from the atrocity as it unfolded. The removal of Khan's remaining fingers took less than a minute. Only the thumbs were troublesome. The black-clad figure failed to cut them at the joints, so the bones audibly splintered and it took a couple of goes to remove them. Blood seeped from the wounds, slow and viscous as it dripped on to the floor. Khan stared ahead, his face etched with horror and pain, but with an apparent determination not to beg or crumble.

Cut.

Khan's butchered arms were still strung to the cage but he was no longer kneeling. His legs were spread open in front of him. His head was leaning back so his face was out of view. The black-clad figure was kneeling between his legs. Thankfully, it was impossible to see what the figure was doing, but Danny didn't need to. Khan was struggling with his restraints now, but weakly. There was life in him, but it was draining fast.

Cut.

Khan was in the same position, bound to the cage. His body was fully visible now: the bandaged head, the stumps where his fingers should have been, the excoriated genitals. His skin was smeared with his own blood and his head hung back. The black-clad figure reappeared. He had a different knife this time, not curved but long and straight with a hooked, serrated edge. With one hand he grabbed Khan's hair and straightened his head. Then, with not even a moment's hesitation, he stabbed the knife into his left eye. Khan's body shuddered, as if electrocuted, as the figure twisted the knife a quarter turn then pulled it out, bringing with it a gelatinous trail of gore. He wiped the gore on Khan's shoulder, then repeated the operation on his other eye.

Cut.

Khan was back inside the cage. He was on his back and not moving. It was impossible to say if he was dead or not, but it seemed likely. The figure had a jerrycan of fuel which he was sloshing through the bars of the cage on to Khan's body. There was at least a gallon of fuel. Danny could almost smell it. Sickened by what had gone before, he felt something like relief when the figure disappeared from shot and a burning rag was thrown into the cage. The fuel ignited immediately and it was only then, when Khan's body writhed for a few seconds, that Danny realised he had still been alive before they burned his body.

Not now though. What remained of him did not burn well, but quickly became charred and smouldering.

The footage finished.

There was silence in the room. Danny, no stranger to atrocity, felt nauseous nonetheless. A single question was foremost in his mind: if Khan was dead, who had been killing the SAS men in the MISFIT team? He looked down at Abadi and had to suppress the urge to nail him there and then. The old man was huddled on the floor, clutching his knees, almost childlike. Danny felt a rising sense of panic. He was alone in the wilds of Syria, and everything he thought he knew had just turned out to be wrong. What was his next move? Should he confiscate this laptop and get back to Beirut to show Bethany? Should he contact Hereford, or MI6?

He cocked his head. MI6. With the extent of their intelligence networks, how come they hadn't even heard a rumour of this grisly snuff video? That thought led to another. Nobody made footage like this just for the hell of it. It was an act of terror and politics. These home movies served a purpose: to appal, to publicise, to terrify. They were made to be disseminated, and when that happened the intelligence services of every major power would be all over them.

But not this one. Why?

Abadi wasn't telling him everything.

He looked coldly at his prisoner. 'Why did they do this?'

'Because he was a traitor.'

'I don't mean why did they kill him. Why did they film it? Nobody in the West has seen this footage. What's the point of it?'

Abadi's glasses had slipped down his nose. He looked above the lenses up at Danny. 'What makes you think nobody has seen it?' he said. 'The most important person has seen it. The person it was made for.'

'Who?' Danny said.

'His wife.'

Danny stared at him. 'You're wrong,' he said. 'Ibrahim Khan didn't have a wife.'

'No. *You* are wrong. Before Khan was sacrificed, he confessed. He had a wife and he had a child. This film was made to send to her. To torment her, because his greatest betrayal was marrying an infidel Western woman, and spawning a son with her.' Abadi sneered. 'He deserved every moment of his punishment. Every second of pain. Every . . .'

But Danny had stopped listening. A nightmarish thought was growing in his mind. And that thought had a face. It was the face of Bethany White.

For an instant, he was back in the Brecon Beacons. The lights had just failed and Danny had left Bethany and Christina in the kitchen while he went to search the exterior of the safe house. He'd told the woman to block the entrance to the kitchen and get down on the ground, away from the window. Bethany had been scared, or so it seemed, and for good reason: they had all been thinking the same thing, that Ibrahim Khan had found them. But Bethany hadn't done as Danny said. She had located the trip switch in the kitchen cabinet and turned the electricity back on. They had argued. *The house is safe, Danny. Nobody knows we're here, except Sturrock.* But how could she have been so certain Khan wasn't on site? Why would she take such a risk, especially with her boy in the house?

Unless, of course, she knew the power outage *couldn't* have indicated Khan's presence, because she knew Khan was long dead.

He remembered Baker, the assistant to the ambassador, rooting through Bethany's bedside drawer. Was it really, as Danny had assumed, because he was a sad old bloke in a suit, because he had some pathetic sexual fascination with her? Or was it because he mistrusted her in some way?

And then he saw Bethany in Beirut, stylish and confident, walking from Al-Farouk's office building towards the IS chauffeur in the X5. Danny's entire strategy that day had been centred around a single assumption: that the chauffeur would be so blinded by his own prejudice that he wouldn't see a woman as a threat. And with a cold sensation in the pit of his stomach, he found himself wondering if he himself had fallen into the same trap. He heard Bethany's flirtatious words. *Look but don't touch, Danny . . . Maybe I made a mistake last night . . .* Had she manipulated him so thoroughly? Had she flirted with him as a means of keeping his eye off the ball?

He swore under his breath. This was paranoia, nothing more. He was inventing a conspiracy theory to fit the facts. Could he really believe that Bethany was married to Ibrahim Khan? That her little boy, Danny Jr, was Khan's kid? Danny Jr's face rose in his mind: the unruly mop of brown hair, the olive tinge to his skin. He realised, with an icy certainty, that the kid's features were not unlike Khan's. He hadn't noticed it before, but why would he? Bethany had been evasive about the boy's parentage. Now he thought about it, did he really believe a woman so in control of herself as Bethany would not know who the father of her child was?

And then it hit him.

The ambush.

There was no doubt about it: Abadi's men had known they were coming. It was a set-up. Textbook. Apart from Guerrero, Ludlow and Rollett, only two people in the world knew they'd be approaching that location at that time: Barak the fixer, and Bethany. Danny had assumed it was Barak who'd betrayed them, but what if . . .

He had one more question for Adnan Abadi. It was perhaps the most important question of all. He bent down, pulled him to his feet again, and threatened him once more with his handgun. 'Someone told you we were coming,' he said. 'Who was it?'

At first it looked like Abadi wasn't going to answer, and Danny would have to become more persuasive. He moved the barrel of the weapon from Abadi's cheekbone to his eye socket. 'I don't know,' he whispered. 'I received a call from my contact in Damascus.'

'When?' Danny said. 'Exactly when?'

Abadi hesitated.

'*When?*' Danny hissed.

'Midday, or perhaps a little later. Not yesterday, but the day before.'

Danny hurled him to the floor as the confirmation took hold. Abadi and his men had been tipped off just after Danny left Bethany in the anonymous Beirut hotel room, but well before Barak knew he wouldn't be accompanying the rest of the unit all the way to Abadi's compound. So it couldn't have been Barak: why would he set up an ambush on a vehicle in which he knew he would be a passenger? It would be suicidal.

Bethany White knew where they were going and when. Everything fitted. She knew Danny was on the trail of Ibrahim Khan, and she knew where that trail would lead. And so she'd set him up. She'd sent him to his death, so the trail would die with him.

But Danny wasn't dead, and the trail had just taken an unexpected fork. He didn't know what Bethany was up to, but he was determined to find out.

He thought of Bullock, Armitage and Moorhouse, and their grisly deaths. Would Bethany have been capable of that? She'd certainly been unmoved when Danny nailed the chauffeur, and although she'd argued that they should spare Al-Farouk's life, and feigned concern for his family, she hadn't been traumatised by the sight. No, she was accustomed to death. Both witnessing it and, Danny was fast concluding, administering it. All the time he'd been hunting for the killer of the three SAS men, she'd been right by his side.

And now what was she doing? Lying low in Beirut? No way. She had a job to finish. The death of Ibrahim Khan, her secret husband and the father of her son, was being avenged in kind. She'd been inflicting the same torments Khan had received on those people who, for whatever reason, she blamed for his death. The colonel and Christina were the only two remaining people who'd been indoctrinated into operation MISFIT from the start, and Bethany White was one of the few people who could approach them without suspicion. Now she assumed Danny was dead, he calculated she'd certainly be making plans to do just that . . .

A noise, outside. It sounded like a door closing. Danny cursed under his breath. He'd let his guard drop while interrogating Adnan Abadi. 'Who is it?' he hissed.

Abadi grinned. 'Reinforcements,' he said. 'Put your gun down now and maybe I'll tell them to be kind.'

The threat failed to hit its mark. Danny yanked the power lead from the laptop, tucked the computer under one arm, then lifted Abadi to his feet with the other. He dragged him roughly across the room to the main door. 'Goodnight,' he said, before opening the door and pushing Abadi from the dim interior into the outside.

The gunfire was immediate. It was so dim the gunmen couldn't have known who they were hitting at first. Three single shots, each from a different weapon, slammed into Abadi, knocking him on to his back over the threshold of the door, keeping it open. From the sound, Danny estimated the shooters were approximately ten metres from the entrance to the room. He took up position behind the door, placed the laptop on the floor, and waited.

The first enemy target to enter had the swaggering confidence of an untrained man. He was plainly not expecting Danny's sudden attack. Danny grabbed the IS attacker from behind, one arm round his throat, the other staying his trigger finger. He pulled him silently back behind the door and strong-armed the life out of him. The attacker went limp and collapsed silently to the floor. Outside, somebody shouted a question in Arabic and received no response. Danny saw a figure approaching through the crack between the door and the wall, and he knew he couldn't pull the same trick twice. He raised his handgun and, as the target appeared, dispatched a single shot into the back of his head. The attacker collapsed in a dull heap.

Silence.

Danny knew there was at least one more gunman, and he remained calm as a burst of rounds entered the room from just outside the door, ricocheting off the far wall. There was a pause of a few seconds, before a second burst split the air. Only then, when he clearly felt his adversary was subdued, did the third attacker approach. Danny saw his body pass the crack in the door, but didn't wait for him to fully appear. Instead, he fired a burst of his own, straight through the door, when he knew the target was on the other side. The wood splintered violently and there was a thud as the third attacker collapsed on top of Abadi's dead body.

Silence again.

Were there more hostile targets? Danny didn't know, but he couldn't hear anything. Abadi was dead. He had no reason to remain in this compound a second longer, and every reason to leave: more reinforcements could arrive at any time. Stepping out of the room was a risk – there was only this exit – but it was one he'd have to take . . .

He grabbed the laptop with one hand and hauled the first gunman – the one he'd throttled – up from the ground with the other. He manoeuvred him into the doorway. He stood there in the dim room, behind the two other fallen bodies, for a full thirty seconds, protected by the corpse. There was no attack. He decided he'd have to risk it, and was about to let the corpse fall, when a single round was discharged from outside. It penetrated the corpse's right arm and slammed straight into the body of the laptop Danny was still holding, shattering it completely. At the moment the round was fired, Danny saw a muzzle flash in the compound outside, directly to his eleven o'clock. He moved instinctively and lightning-fast, letting the corpse fall at the same time as he engaged his assault rifle and fired a burst in the direction of the shooter. He knew he was on target because of the screams, wild and almost inhuman, that echoed around the compound. Danny crouched down behind the pile of bodies on the threshold and waited for the screams to fade into a death rattle, which they did in about half a minute. And once more there was silence.

Danny cursed. The laptop was fucked. He couldn't allow that to slow him down. He had to get out of here. He left the computer on the ground and, scanning the area outside the room, stepped into the compound. There was no sign of movement. He sprinted to the old tractor parked up outside the two adjoining buildings and used it for cover while he surveyed the path to the exit. The main gates were open. The two men he'd shot on his arrival were prostrate in front of them. The three trucks were still parked up along the inside of the perimeter wall. Danny sprinted up to them. None was locked, but nor did they have keys in the ignition or anywhere to be found. He located a jerrycan of fuel in the back of one of them. Other than that, they had nothing to offer except that they were old – old enough to be hot-wired if necessary.

Breathless, Danny assessed his options. More IS militants could arrive at any moment. There had been two firefights that could have been heard from miles around. He might only have minutes to get away. He certainly couldn't stay here. Perhaps he could drive back in the direction of the Lebanese border. He could try to find Barak. Unlikely. He had no satnav and no maps. He could be stopped at any time. Barak would have to fend for himself. Danny had Guerrero's sat phone, which meant he could call in to Hereford, tell them what he'd learned, and request an exfiltration. He was surrounded by olive groves that extended several klicks in either direction. He could get to their perimeter, well clear of the compound, and lie low while waiting for a pick-up.

He decided to do just that.

He grabbed the jerrycan of fuel. It was heavy, but he'd need it. He jogged to the exit, checked for threats and, seeing none, left the compound. He skirted clockwise round the perimeter, then headed west into the olive groves. Dawn was breaking, the sky lightening. It had been a long night's work, but it wasn't over yet. The jerrycan became increasingly difficult to carry as he ran through the stunted forest of olive trees. His energy was sapping fast but he'd been here before, in training and on ops, and that thought gave him the confidence that he was able to carry on.

He had run for about three kilometres when he reached a deep irrigation trench running at right angles to his line of travel. Beyond it was about thirty metres of open ground before the olive groves started again. It was a good place to stop: the open ground presented a landing zone for a chopper, and he could hide in the trench. He hauled himself into it and let the jerrycan fall. Every muscle, and both lungs, burned. He gave himself a minute to recover before pulling out his sat phone.

He knew, as soon as he switched it on, that he had a problem. The battery level indicator was low. He might only have a few seconds to talk. Certainly no more than a minute. He had to prioritise what information he imparted. He dialled his access number into Hereford. A voice answered. '*Go ahead.*'

'I'm three klicks west of the target location with three men down. I need an exfil. Get me the boss, now.'

'*Wait out . . .*'

The line hissed and crackled.

Ten seconds passed. Twenty. A voice. Mike Williamson, CO of 22. '*Go ahead.*'

'Ibrahim Khan is dead. He has been for six months. He didn't kill Bullock, Armitage and Moorhouse. Bethany White is at the Hotel Faisal in Beirut. Room thirty-five. You need to apprehend her immediately. I think she's complicit in the murders. Boss, do you copy? Boss?'

The line was dead.

Danny swore. He didn't know how much intel had been transmitted. The sat phone was bricked. He had no other means of making contact with the head shed. All he could do now was wait. The Regiment wouldn't be sending him a pick-up by day, of that he was sure. They needed the cover of night if they were to breach Syrian airspace. Danny quickly collected several armfuls of fallen olive branches and constructed a lying-up position in the ditch. He needed to keep well out of sight until nightfall.

By the time the sun was fully above the horizon, Danny was camouflaged under a blanket of branches and foliage. His mind turned to Bethany White. Had he really been so wrong about her? Had she really played him for such a fool? She was beyond question a smart operator. But was she smart enough to outfox three SAS men, and of sufficiently strong stomach to kill them in such brutal ways?

But something didn't add up. Ibrahim Khan had been a highly successful double agent. In the end, his cover was blown and he'd paid the price that he must surely have known would be exacted if IS found out the truth about him. He knew the risk he ran, and so did Bethany. Why, then, would she be exacting revenge on the MISFIT personnel? Was it simply because Khan had told her how unpleasant his SAS training team had been to him? That hardly made sense. There must be more to it than that.

He thought of Sturrock, sitting in Hereford and applying moisturiser to his manicured hands, and how insistent he was that word about the MISFIT fiasco shouldn't leak, for fear of embarrassing MI6. But was it just fear of embarrassment, or was it something else?

And then he thought of Ibrahim Khan himself. Subdued. Calm. Grateful for the simple kindness of a couple of chocolate bars. The young man Danny had met all those years ago had put himself out in the field and risked unimaginable danger. When the end came, his bravery and loyalty to the UK had been repaid with unspeakable horror and suffering. The video footage of Khan's torture and death replayed itself in Danny's mind as he lay beneath his camouflage, sweating in the heat of the morning sun. He felt an unfamiliar emotion: guilt, for having believed that Ibrahim Khan had been one of the bad guys. The opposite was true. Khan was a hero, and Danny owed it to him to find out what had happened.

And that meant catching up with Bethany White, the woman who had tried to kill him, and almost succeeded. The woman who was responsible for the death of three SAS men and, if Danny didn't stop her, had more killings ahead of her. Maybe she had the same opinion of Khan as Danny did. But that sure as hell didn't put them on the same side. He wondered where she was now. Still lying low in the Hotel Faisal like he'd warned Hereford? Somehow, Danny doubted it. Beirut held no real interest for her and with Danny out of the way, she could be anywhere in the world by now. It would be down to him to find her. He couldn't do that stuck in a ditch in the backwaters of Syria.

He steeled himself to wait. The day couldn't pass quickly enough.

18

07.00 hrs

Bethany had learned at Fort Monckton, the secure MI6 training facility, that the first rule of counter-surveillance was deception. If you suspected somebody was watching you, the skill lay in making them look the other way. It was an elaborate game of smoke and mirrors, and she was good at it.

When she arrived at Beirut International Airport, she headed straight to the British Airways ticket desk. Even at this early hour there was a queue, and it took twenty minutes before she reached the immaculately uniformed female assistant who gave her an air stewardess's smile and asked how she could help. Bethany noticed the security camera on the back wall and made no attempt to shield her face from it. She brightly asked about evening flights into Heathrow, fully aware that her lips could be read by the camera, and the assistant's computer search would be a matter of record. 'There are seats on the six p.m., Madam, but only business class I'm afraid.' Bethany thanked the woman, told her she would return when she'd firmed up her plans, and then left. She didn't know for sure that MI6 would be looking for her – it would surely take several days for them to learn or even suspect that Danny Black was dead – but if they were sniffing around, that should put them off the scent.

Now she had a choice. She wouldn't be flying directly to London. If there was a surveillance order on her, they'd be watching the flights in from Beirut. She had to travel elsewhere first. Europe was out, as was the US. MI6 had reciprocal agreements with half of Asia and even a good proportion of Middle Eastern and African nations. But there was one country, of course, where this was by no means true.

She headed to the Aeroflot desk.

The queue here was half as long, but the security measures twice as stringent. Two cameras looked down on the desk. But that was okay. While MI6 had access to security camera footage for pretty much every UK-based airline around the world, Russian airlines were a very different matter. Intelligence sharing between Moscow and London was practically non-existent. She could safely land there without alerting MI6 to her whereabouts, and if anybody was looking out for her at the UK border, their eyes wouldn't be on the Russian flights.

Bethany used her Armenian passport to buy tickets on the 11.30 flight to Moscow. As Armenia was a member of the Commonwealth of Independent States, its passport holders didn't require a visa to enter the Russian Federation, and since Armenia was a short hop from Lebanon her purchase was unremarkable. While she waited for her flight to be called, she visited a chemist, where she bought herself a pair of cheap Jackie O sunglasses and a box of hair dye, chestnut brown. She stowed the hair dye in her bag, bought a cup of much-needed coffee and a sandwich, then headed to her gate.

She slept on the plane as it travelled north-east. Thirty thousand feet in the air, this was one of the few places she felt she could relax. Sure, there might be difficulties at the Russian border, but there was no point stressing about that now. If she'd learned one thing, it was this: rest while you can. She covered her eyes with the complimentary blindfold and ignored the air steward's offer of an in-flight meal. Almost before she knew it, the four-hour flight had passed and the wheels were hitting the tarmac. Local time: 17.10 hrs.

She experienced a twinge of anxiety as she queued at passport control. In her experience, Russian immigration officials were even less welcoming than American ones. The square-jawed man who scrupulously examined each page of her Armenian passport was no exception. He appeared disgruntled that he could find no valid reason to delay her. Bethany thanked him with a polite *bol'shoy spasibo*, then headed calmly out on to the arrivals concourse. There was a free internet station here. She took advantage of it, checking the time of the next flight from Moscow into a regional UK airport – not Heathrow or Gatwick, where security was that bit higher. There was a 23.30 flight into Manchester via Paris, arrival 01.00 local time. It was possible to buy tickets online, so she should be able to get one later at the desk.

It was dark outside, and cold. Bethany waited five minutes at a taxi rank, then directed a cab to the nearby airport Novotel. She paid for one night in advance, cash, using her Armenian identity. As soon as she was in her room, she stripped, showered and washed her hair. Then she opened up her packet of hair dye and massaged it into her scalp. As she waited for the dye to do its work, she stood naked in front of the bathroom mirror. For a moment, she was transported back in time. She was in a hotel room like this, anonymous but comfortable enough. She was naked, fresh from the shower, and the door had just opened. Ibrahim had entered, also wearing nothing. He stood behind her, enclosed her body in his arms and kissed her neck.

Bethany loved him most when he was naked. His body was fit and strong, of course, his brown skin soft. But he seemed so appealingly vulnerable. The body of a man, the aura of a child.

'I want to come home,' he'd whispered to her. 'I don't want to do this any more. I want to be with you, and to know my son.'

These were the words Bethany had longed to hear. She almost didn't dare respond, in case she said the wrong thing and he changed his mind.

'Will you tell them?' Ibrahim said.

Bethany nodded.

'And will you tell them about us? And about our son?'

'No. Not yet. They won't like it. Better to wait until they've sorted out a new identity for you, and a financial package. They can be petty.'

'You know best,' Ibrahim said with a smile. 'You always know best.' He squeezed her and she felt goose bumps all over her body.

As she stood in the Moscow Novotel with her hair turning dark, the goose bumps returned at the memory. That was the last time she'd seen him, at least in person. It was four weeks later that a young woman bumped into her as she exited Vauxhall underground station and pressed a USB stick into her hand before disappearing into the crowd. Bethany clenched her eyes at the thought of the images that USB stick had contained. The frightened message from Ibrahim explaining how he'd been compromised. The tearful apology that he'd been forced to tell his IS tormentors all about her. And the sickening vision of the horrors inflicted on him before his death.

She opened her eyes again. Those recollections had turned her complexion pale as death. Her eyes were like flint. For some reason, she thought of Danny Black, bare-chested in their quarters at the embassy in Beirut. She remembered the scars on his skin – so different from the perfect body of her Ibrahim – and his pathetic air of sexual expectation. It angered her and she drew several deep breaths to quell that anger, because she had enough stored up, deep inside her, for a whole lifetime.

And she couldn't be distracted. Because what was her love for Ibrahim worth if, now he was dead, she failed to avenge him? For his sake, for her sake, and for the sake of their child.

She washed the dye out of her hair and pulled out the tangles with a flimsy hotel comb. Then she returned to the bedroom, opened up her British passport, and compared her reflection in a mirror to the dark-haired version of herself in the document. The resemblance was precise. She nodded with satisfaction, dressed, and headed back to the airport to buy a ticket to Manchester.

Night fell over the olive grove. The temperature dropped. Danny waited for full darkness before cautiously moving out from his lying-up point. His muscles ached, his belly was empty and his throat was raw with thirst. But the day had at least passed without incident. Some time in the early afternoon he'd heard fast air passing somewhere in the vicinity, but there was no indication of any nearby threats. The discomfort he could deal with.

It was a clear night. A bright moon and a full, startling canopy. He crouched down in the ditch and listened hard. The exfiltration team only knew his rough location: three klicks west of the compound. When the time came, however, they'd need a little help to pinpoint him. For now, he had to listen hard for the sound of a circling chopper.

Time dragged. It was 23.02 hrs when he heard it – the distant but familiar sound of rotor blades on the edge of his hearing. He got to work immediately. The exfil team would doubtless be breaching Syrian airspace without permission, and they wouldn't want to fuck around. He grabbed the jerrycan of fuel he'd confiscated from the compound and emptied most of its contents over the pile of olive branches, reserving a little to pour a two-metre trail the length of the ditch. He discarded the empty tin, then removed the waterproof matches from his ops vest. He lit one and ignited the trail. The fuel and olive branches immediately ignited and a thick, greasy pall of smoke rose into the air. Danny climbed out of the ditch, stood on the flat, open ground, and waited.

It took the chopper less than a minute to arrive, drawn like a moth to the signalling fire. Danny stood on the flat ground of the makeshift landing zone, marshalling the chopper – a Merlin – to the ground. As soon as its landing gear touched down, a side door opened and a loadie in camouflage gear and headset ushered Danny in with an urgent gesture. Head bowed, one hand protecting his eyes from the swirling dust, Danny sprinted to the aircraft and climbed inside. The familiar stench of grease and sweat common to all military aircraft hit his senses. It was oddly comforting. The Merlin rose from the ground before the door shut, turning 180 degrees as it gained height. It had been on the ground for no more than fifteen seconds and was now accelerating west, nose dipped, lights extinguished, engines thundering. Danny glanced through the open door at the terrain below. The chopper was flying low. The expanse of olive groves was illuminated by the moon, but from this angle he had no line of sight in the direction of the compound itself. He wondered if anybody had found the scene of devastation he was deserting and he thought about

Guerrero, Ludlow and Rollett and their mauled corpses. He felt a bitter taste in the back of his throat. They knew the risks they were running, but still . . . to lose men on an operation was the worst. That was three more deaths he could chalk up to Bethany White when – if – he came face to face with her again.

The loadie was giving him a disgusted look and Danny remembered he still had Rollett's gore plastered to his face. 'Where are we headed?' he roared over the noise of the engines.

'Cyprus,' the loadie shouted back. It made sense. The tiny Mediterranean island was 150 miles off the Lebanese coast and hosted a major British army base.

'ETA?' Danny asked.

'Ninety minutes, all being well.' The loadie seemed tense. Danny didn't blame him. Syrian airspace was not a safe place to be.

'I need a secure line to Hereford. Can you sort that for me?'

'Not while we're airborne. You'll have to wait till Cyprus.'

End of conversation. Danny suppressed a wave of frustration. There was no point succumbing to it. He put his back up against the webbing on the side of the helicopter and let the chopper carry him west.

Buying the ticket presented no problem. Her passport was fine and she paid for her economy seat in cash. She cleared passport control without any difficulty, the Russian officials seeming far more relaxed about letting people out of the country than welcoming them in. It was when she reached the departure gate that alarm bells started to sound in her head.

There were perhaps a hundred people waiting for the flight, but it was quiet at the gate. The occasional tannoy announcements in Russian seemed particularly resonant. Bethany stood apart from the others, standing close to the floor-to-ceiling window that overlooked their aircraft and several others. She could see her own reflection in the glass – dark-haired and tired – and she could also see three officials, standing about ten metres behind her. They were talking quietly to each other, and one of them kept pointing in Bethany's direction. Or was he pointing at the plane? She couldn't quite tell.

She inhaled slowly to quell her nerves, then glanced left and right. Apart from the people at this gate, the area was deserted. If she moved away now, she would be conspicuous. And where would she go? It was impossible to leave the airport now she was through passport control.

Stay calm, she told herself. Nobody knows where you are. Nobody knows *who* you are. She turned away from the glass and went to sit next to a woman whose daughter was asleep on her lap. They smiled at each other. 'She looks exhausted,' Bethany said. Casual conversation would make her look less suspicious.

'We should have taken the earlier flight,' the woman said. 'It'll take her days to . . .'

'Ladies and gentlemen!' An English voice over the gate tannoy. 'I'm sorry to announce that we have a technical difficulty with our aircraft tonight. Technicians are on their way to try to resolve it, but in the meantime we'll be unable to board. Tea and coffee will be made available while we wait.'

A wave of disappointed muttering passed through the crowd. The woman said something to Bethany, but she didn't hear it. The alarm bells were too loud. Was there really a technical problem with the plane? She hadn't seen any mechanics down on the airfield when she was looking through the window. Was this just a ruse to keep her in place? Were the authorities – British, Russian, Lebanese – on to her? Or was this a genuine, innocent delay? She tried to rationalise her situation. If they'd wanted to confine her, surely they'd have let everybody board, and then keep them in situ. And she told herself again there was no way anybody could know where she was.

'I said, do you think they'll put us up in a hotel?'

Bethany blinked at her neighbour. 'I'm . . . I'm not sure.'

Her panic was replaced with frustration. This delay was a problem for her. She had work to do in the UK. A job to finish. She had, it was true, arranged her affairs in Room 35 of the Hotel Faisal in such a way that she might buy herself some time in the event that Danny Black had failed to keep her location secret. But still, she needed this flight to leave, and soon.

The Russian airport officials were looking at her again. She tried hard not to catch their gaze, to look normal and unconcerned. A woman was approaching with a trolley of hot drinks. Bethany turned to her neighbour. 'Let me get you a cup of tea,' she said.

'We've exited Syrian airspace!' the loadie shouted at Danny. His relief was evident. Danny looked out of the window of the Merlin. He could see the chopper's shadow, cast by the moon, black against the blurry terrain beneath. They were gaining height now they were in what Danny assumed was Lebanese airspace. He inferred that the head shed had cleared this part of their flight path with the Lebanese authorities.

And then, in an instant, they were over the Med. The sea looked surprisingly rough given the clarity of the night, the curling foam of the waves illuminated by the bright moon. The ride was suddenly turbulent, so turbulent that Danny found himself picking out the location of the chopper's EPIRB emergency locator beacon in the event of a landing on water. But the Merlin was skilfully and safely piloted. Thirty minutes later they were over ground again, flying over the island of Cyprus. The British airbase glowed warmly in the distance. The chopper circled it to the north, then touched down.

The loadie opened up the side door. Danny exited immediately. A beige Land Rover was waiting for him thirty metres from the landing zone, a green army guy standing by it. As Danny ran up to the vehicle and climbed into the passenger seat, the green army guy did a double take at the state of him, then took the wheel. 'There's a C-17 on standby, ready to transport you back to Brize,' he said. 'I've got to put you on a secure line to Hereford first.'

'Do it quickly,' Danny said.

The Land Rover sped away from the LZ, past two well-lit aircraft hangars, towards a collection of Portakabins that had been cordoned off by a roughly built breeze-block perimeter wall. Danny knew this to be the area reserved for special forces operations. A soldier in camouflage gear stood guard by the entrance. He recognised Danny's chauffeur and waved them through. The lights were off in all the Portakabins bar one. Danny jumped out of the vehicle, ran up to it and entered.

There was one man in here. Danny recognised him vaguely, but knew he wasn't Regiment. SBS, maybe? 'Danny Black?' he said. Danny nodded. 'Jesus, mate, you look like shit.' He pointed to a telephone at one of the desks in the room. 'It's a secure line,' he said. Without another word, he left the Portakabin, closing the door behind him. Danny perched on the edge of the desk and dialled his access number into Hereford.

'*Go ahead.*'

'Get me the boss.'

'*Wait out.*'

There was a ten-second pause before the CO's voice came on the line. '*She's dead,*' he said.

Danny blinked heavily. 'Who?'

'*Bethany White.*'

'What are you talking about? Of course she's not dead.'

'*Room thirty-five, Hotel Faisal. MI6 passed your intel on to the Beirut police force with a request for them to apprehend the occupant. They found Bethany White's body. The working theory is that Ibrahim Khan got to her before the police did.*'

For a moment, Danny doubted himself. Could he have got all this wrong? He shook his head quietly to himself. 'Ibrahim Khan's dead, boss. Very fucking dead. I've seen video footage of his murder. They tortured him first, took off his ears and his bollocks and his fingers. All the things that happened to Bullock, Armitage and Moorhouse. It's not Khan that's been on the rampage, it's somebody avenging his death. I think it's Bethany White. She'd married him secretly. Khan's the father of her kid. She's behind the killings.'

'*You're not hearing me, Black. Bethany White's dead. It's textbook Khan – he disfigured her after he killed her.*'

'How?'

'*We're not sure yet. Acid, probably.*'

'So they can't make a positive ID of her face?'

'*It's her, Black. Blonde hair, same height. I've seen the photos. It's definitely her.*'

'Have they run her DNA?'

'*It's in progress, but it'll take some time.*'

'Boss, you've got to believe me, it's not Bethany White.'

'*They found her passport, Black. The Tomlinson one. It was in her pocket. It's her.*'

'She's played us all like a fucking instrument . . .'

'*That's enough.*' A beat. '*Danny, you need to get back home. There's a plane waiting for you. Board it now.*'

It was the use of his Christian name that alerted Danny. That, and the sudden tightness in the CO's voice as he issued his order. It wasn't just that Williamson didn't believe Danny. He didn't quite trust him, either. Danny kept his voice level. 'Roger that, boss,' he said, and he put the phone down.

Danny hesitated for a moment. He tried to see the situation from the CO's perspective. MI6 thought Bethany was dead. They thought Khan had killed her. And they thought Danny was the only person who knew her location. That put him under suspicion. He looked at the door. It was closed, but he knew that when he opened it, the SBS guy wouldn't be alone. The CO was insistent that Danny board the C-17. He wouldn't be leaving it to chance.

It occurred to Danny that, right now, he had the advantage. If he struck quickly, he could overcome whoever was waiting for him outside the Portakabin. But where would that leave him? Alone in a British military base, and under even greater suspicion than before. No. If he had any chance of stopping Bethany White's killing spree, he needed to be where he had no doubt she was headed next: the UK, where the colonel was under armed guard and Christina Somers was looking after Bethany's son in a supposedly anonymous safe house.

He stood up, walked to the door and opened it. He was right: four guys were there, two on either side. They looked uncomfortable, as if they'd been given an order they didn't much like. But it was clear to Danny they intended to obey it. 'No need for any aggro, lads,' Danny said. 'I'm getting straight on the plane.'

He stepped down from the Portakabin, flanked by two guys on either side, and marched back to the Land Rover.

Twenty minutes later, he was airborne again.

At Moscow airport, midnight came and went. The passengers waiting for the flight to Manchester became fractious. Several of them surrounded the stewardesses at the gate, demanding more information, but there was none to be had. Bethany quietly kept her head down. She had no desire to draw attention to herself. The enthusiasm of the more belligerent passengers for an argument soon waned, and they joined the others, some of them sleeping in awkward positions on the hard airport chairs, some looking at their phones, some staring into the middle distance. Bethany occasionally got up to stretch her legs and to check on any progress down on the airfield. There were two maintenance vehicles at the far end of the aircraft, each with a flashing orange light.

She walked up to the two stewardesses, who were quietly talking to each other. 'Is there any news?' she asked.

One of them gave her a thin-lipped smile. 'As soon as there is, Madam, we'll make an announcement.' She wasn't masking her irritation very well, and Bethany had a sudden surge of her own. She had a series of momentary flashbacks. She was applying acid to the face of her one-night stand in Beirut. She was unmanning an ex-soldier in his house in Florida. She was dismembering the fingers of another military man in the best hotel in Accra. She was cutting the ears from a third in Dubai. It was strange how, when you'd done it once, you had a recurring taste for it.

Something must have shown on her expression. The stewardess recoiled. 'Is everything alright, Madam?' her companion asked.

Bethany forced her facial muscles to relax into a smile. 'Of course,' she said. 'Everything's fine. I'm sorry, I don't mean to hassle you . . .'

As she spoke, a man appeared from the air stair leading to the plane. He nodded at the stewardesses, who visibly relaxed. One of them moved to the intercom. 'Ladies and gentlemen, please accept our apologies for the delay. Flight RK235, destination Manchester via Paris Charles de Gaulle, is now ready to depart . . .'

She repeated her announcement in Russian as the passengers roused themselves and formed a queue.

Bethany was the first person to board. Twenty minutes later she was staring blankly out of the window as her transport back to the UK accelerated down the runway and launched itself into the air.

19

06.00, Brize Norton.

The C-17 Globemaster, whose sole purpose on this flight was to transport a single SAS soldier from Cyprus to the UK, thundered along the runway, its wheels bouncing twice before it decelerated to taxiing speed. It came to a halt a hundred metres from the terminal building itself, where three ground vehicles awaited it: an unmarked white Transit van and two police cars. Danny Black was half expecting them, but their presence was still a blow. They confirmed that he was under suspicion.

He had no option but to approach the Transit. His heart sank when the side door slid open and he saw who had been dispatched from Hereford to accompany him back to base, his breath steaming in the early-morning air. It was Roscoe, the lad who first told him about Bullock's death, and who was a constant source of questions that Danny never wanted to answer about his time in the Regiment. Like an eager puppy, he couldn't hide his pleasure at seeing Danny as he walked up to greet him. But there was wariness, too. He felt obliged to take Danny lightly by the arm and guide him in the direction of the Transit. The C-17's engines were still powering down, so it was too noisy to speak. A single look sufficed, however. Roscoe gave him his space, and Danny climbed into the van with no more misplaced encouragement.

There was a bench along either side of the van. Danny and Roscoe sat opposite each other as the vehicle sped across the airfield. There were no windows and the driver's cab was blocked off. They could only see each other by a dim yellow light, and Danny had to depend on his sense of the vehicle's movement to judge what was happening. They didn't slow down for any passport control procedures, though their speed varied as they exited Brize Norton. A minute later they were travelling at a constant velocity, clearly on a regular main road.

'The boys in blue taking us all the way?' Danny asked.

''Fraid so, mate,' Roscoe said. 'MI6's instructions. CO didn't like it, but the spooks pulled rank.' He licked his lips with anticipation. 'So where you been? Word back at base is that you . . .'

'Here and there,' Danny said.

As usual, Roscoe did not appear remotely disheartened that Danny had shut him down like that. A wild idea crossed Danny's mind. Perhaps Roscoe would help him get away from this little convoy transporting him back to base. But what would Danny do then? Make his way to the colonel's house and warn him that Bethany White was on her way and that she had plans to do things that would sicken him just to imagine? He could well imagine how badly that conversation would go. Perhaps he could head to the safe house, where Christina was looking after Bethany's son. MI6 thought Christina was on Khan's hit list. Did that mean that she was on Bethany's? Would Bethany really leave her son with the woman she intended to murder? Danny didn't know. She was surely unhinged, driven to the extreme by grief and the horror of what had happened to Khan. Danny didn't feel confident predicting her next movement, but he was sure of one thing: at some point, she would collect her child. He'd seen the way she embraced the little boy. Bethany White had feigned many emotions over the past few days, but she hadn't feigned that.

'Can't do it, buddy,' Roscoe said. He must have noticed Danny eyeing the mechanism on the side door. He sounded regretful.

Danny smiled. 'Wouldn't ask you to, mate,' he said.

'You're not thinking of doing anything stupid, then?'

'Mate, I spent yesterday lying in a ditch in Syria. Whatever they've got waiting for me in Hereford will be a fucking vacation.' He sniffed. 'You said MI6 were on site. Any idea who?'

'Pale fella. Thinning hair. Weasley little cunt.'

'Sturrock,' Danny said. 'He's the chief.' Danny wished he hadn't said it. Roscoe's face lit up at this titbit: the presence of the head of MI6 at a debrief for Danny Black, escorted straight off a C-17 with a police guard, was as juicy a piece of gossip as Hereford had heard in months. Danny reflected that Sturrock waiting for him at Hereford didn't bode well. Danny was being recalled under a cloud. He knew the CO hadn't believed his reading of events, but the presence of the chief of MI6 at his debrief suggested there was more to it than that. There would be no police convoy or SAS chaperone if he wasn't under suspicion in some way.

The head shed was making a mistake. Danny had to be free if he was to have any chance of catching Bethany. And if Roscoe wasn't going to help him, he'd have to do it on his own.

Which meant putting his chaperone at his ease. He smiled again. 'Shame we've never found ourselves on ops,' he said. 'You and me. You've got more about you than some of the halfwits they've put me with.'

Roscoe visibly preened at the compliment. 'That'd be awesome, mate,' he said, more like an enthusiastic puppy than an SAS man. 'Maybe when all this is ironed out . . .'

'Right,' Danny said. 'Look, do you mind if I put my head down? It's been a long couple of days. I'll tell you about it some time, as long as you promise to keep it quiet.'

'Course,' Roscoe said. 'Go ahead.'

Danny closed his eyes and pretended to sleep. But he listened hard. He was hyperaware of the sound of the Transit's engine as the vehicle shifted through the gears, sped up and slowed down. He breathed slowly. He stayed still.

And then, then minutes later, when the vehicle came to a halt, he struck.

Roscoe barely knew what had hit him. Danny launched himself across the Transit van and cracked his left elbow into Roscoe's right cheek. He had no desire to cause the guy any permanent damage, but he needed to stun him. The force of the blow knocked Roscoe on to his side. Danny lurched to the side door of the van, unlocked it and slid it open. Daylight flooded in, making Danny wince. He saw they'd stopped – presumably at lights or in a traffic jam – by a forested area, and he felt a surge of optimism: it was good terrain to get lost in. He launched himself from the Transit, ready to sprint into the trees. But the instant his feet touched the ground, he was pushed forward. Roscoe was on his back, and the momentum knocked him to the ground. He felt one strong arm round his throat, and immediately the lights and sirens from the two police cars burst into life.

Danny struggled, but he knew his reckless escape attempt was over. Roscoe's weight, heavy on the small of his back, was too much to overcome, and Roscoe knew what he was doing. He kept the pressure on Danny's throat while two police officers ran towards them from their vehicles. A moment later his hands were being cuffed behind his back and Roscoe was pulling him to his feet. A bruise was already emerging on Roscoe's face and there was blood dripping from his nose. 'Get in the fucking van,' he said, and he pushed Danny roughly in the direction of the door. A second push forced Danny back inside. He was aware of a brief conversation happening on the side of the road, then he was joined not only by Roscoe but also by one of the two police officers, who slid the door shut with a resounding bang. 'What the *fuck* are you playing at?' Roscoe asked, wiping blood away from his lip as he spoke.

Danny didn't answer. He just stared into the middle distance, silently cursing himself for making such a stupid move, for failing to execute it properly and for underestimating his chaperone.

'Fucking psycho,' Roscoe muttered as the Transit van moved off again.

09.00.

Flight RK235 from Moscow to Manchester via Paris Charles de Gaulle touched down, several hours late, to the sarcastic cheers of several passengers who thought they'd never make it home. Bethany White kept her relief to herself. It was tinged, in any case, with the anxiety of having to make it past another passport control official. A British one this time. She reassured herself as she de-planed and walked with the other passengers to the immigration booths. So far as the British authorities were concerned, her location was either unknown somewhere in Beirut, or she was dead. Certainly they wouldn't yet have had time to realise that the body in Room 35 of the Hotel Faisal was not hers. She estimated that for another twelve hours at least, her anonymity remained.

Which meant that her work had to be completed today.

The official who examined her passport was male, but Bethany didn't attempt to flirt with him. She waited calmly as he scanned her document and checked her photograph. And she made very sure not to look relieved when he handed it back and allowed her into the UK.

The Transit van came to a halt and there was a tap from the driver in the cab. 'We're here,' Roscoe said. 'Wait there.'

He climbed out of the van, leaving Danny alone with the police officer, who looked less than thrilled to be in that situation. Roscoe reappeared thirty seconds later. 'Out you get. You know where we're going.'

'Holding cell?'

Roscoe nodded. 'You know we can do it one of two ways, right?'

'I thought we were mates, Roscoe,' Danny said. He knew he sounded like a dick, but he was angry, and he was panicked, and he was about to endure the humiliation of being put behind bars in the guard room of RAF Credenhill, like a common criminal. The holding cells were for anyone causing trouble on site or off, and it was an indignity to find yourself incarcerated there.

As he stepped out of the Transit van, his wrists still cuffed behind his back, he couldn't help but look at the sky. The clouds were dark and boiling. A storm was threatening. The air was cold but full of moisture. For a split second, Danny gave thought to another escape attempt, but his options were non-existent. The guard room was situated just next to the main entrance barrier. The entrance was normally guarded by an MoD policeman. This morning he had three Regiment guys as back-up. Five other guys, all of whom Danny recognised, were dotted around the Transit van. They had the demeanour of men who didn't like what they were doing, but were going to do it anyway. Any thoughts Danny had of controlling his next move faded. He had no option but to follow Roscoe into the guard house.

There was one guy at the desk – Tim Saxton from A Squadron. His eyes widened at the sight of Roscoe's bloodied face. He stared at Danny, then pointed at the door that led to the holding cells. Danny walked through it to avoid the ignominy of being ordered there by Roscoe. A minute later he was in the holding cell, sitting on a red plastic stool fixed to the floor. 'You need to sort your shit out,' Roscoe said before leaving. 'But I'll see what I can do to get you out of here.' Danny almost felt like laughing. He knew Roscoe's influence with the head shed was precisely zero.

He sat alone with his thoughts, and waited.

Bethany had no physical driving licence corresponding to the identity of her dark-haired alter ego. But she'd bought the false identity from the very best the dark web had to offer, and she knew the DVLA would have the name on file. It only took a call from the girl at the car-hire desk to confirm. She paid for two days' rental of a Honda CR-V with cash and walked briskly to the pick-up location. She patiently allowed the Mancunian guy there to mansplain to her how to drive it, and agreed with a solemn nod that it was important to check the paintwork for any scuffs. If she'd been anything other than attentive to his patronising explanations, she'd have rendered herself memorable. Having indulged him, she drove away safe in the knowledge that she had been instantly forgettable.

She had some shopping to do. Leaving the airport, she followed signs to the city centre, where she parked up in the Trafford shopping mall. She walked straight past Next, New Look and Top Shop. She ignored Apple, Jo Malone and Starbucks. Her destination was John Lewis. She headed through haberdashery, lingerie and toys until she reached the houseware section. She stood by the rice cookers and looked around somewhat aimlessly. A clean-shaven young man with short red hair approached her. 'Can I help you at all?' he asked.

Bethany smiled at him. 'Thank you,' she said. 'Perhaps you can. I've decided to treat myself to some new kitchen knives. My old ones are dreadful.'

The young man inclined his head in an old-fashioned manner. 'If you'd like to come this way,' he said, 'I'll show you what we have in stock.'

The CO entered the holding area. Danny stood up immediately. 'Black, what in the name of . . .'

'Boss, it's not what it looks like. You need to let me out of here . . .' But as he spoke, Sturrock entered. Danny knew from a glance that he was moving in for the kill.

The MI6 chief's eyes looked yellower and meaner than before. He reeked of suspicion and looked like Danny felt: exhausted. 'I think,' he said with the wary confidence of a man who knows his immediate threat is safely behind a locked door, 'we'll debrief you where we can keep an eye on you. Would you like a lawyer present, Black?'

Danny ignored him and addressed the CO. 'You need to let me go. She's . . .'

'*Would you like a lawyer present?*'

Danny turned slowly to face him. 'I don't need a lawyer,' he said.

'Then *talk!*' Sturrock snapped. 'I want to know every detail of what has happened.'

The CO nodded mutely. Danny suppressed his anger. Then he started to talk.

He told them everything. How they'd abducted, questioned and eliminated Al-Farouk. How they'd requested intel on Adnan Abadi and made contact with Guerrero, Ludlow and Rollett. How Danny had installed Bethany White anonymously in the Hotel Faisal before crossing over with his team into Syria. He told them how they'd left Barak, and how they'd been ambushed on their approach to Abadi's compound. He told them how his team had been KIA, and how he'd raided the compound alone.

The CO was completely expressionless as Danny spoke, but already Danny could tell that Sturrock didn't believe what he was saying. Danny wasn't surprised. Pen-pushers seldom understood what happened on the ground. He recounted what he had learned in Abadi's compound, and what he had seen: the gruesome video footage of Ibrahim Khan's final hours. Sturrock was openly shaking his head by this point. When Danny explained that the laptop had been destroyed, Sturrock muttered: 'How convenient.' And as Danny finished talking he snorted derisively. 'I've never heard such claptrap in my life,' he said. 'Perhaps you've forgotten that Ibrahim Khan's DNA was found at the murder site in Florida? Hard for him to be in Palm Beach when he'd been killed six months before by Daesh, wouldn't you say?'

'Perhaps you've forgotten,' Danny said, 'that he was married to Bethany White. Not so hard for her to source a DNA sample, wouldn't you say?'

Sturrock wagged his finger. 'Oh no,' he said. 'You're not going to twist it, Black. We have Bethany White's body, and as soon as we've positively identified it, you're going to have some explaining to do.'

'I've told you everything.' He appealed to the CO to back him up, but Williamson kept quiet.

'No you haven't,' Sturrock said. 'You haven't explained, if you and Bethany White were the only two people in the world who knew that she was staying at the Hotel Faisal, how did Ibrahim Khan know how to locate her?'

Danny stared at him in disbelief. 'Haven't you listened to a word I've said? Ibrahim Khan is *dead* . . .'

'And there's one other thing you haven't explained. When we first brought you in to talk about this operation, you knew we were after Ibrahim Khan before we even told you. How could you have known that? How could you *possibly* have known that?'

Danny stared at him in dismay as he realised what Sturrock was implying. 'I worked it out,' he said. 'It wasn't so hard.'

'Not so hard,' he said, 'if you were aware of it in advance. By your own admission, you knew Ibrahim Khan . . .'

'I met him once.'

'So you claim,' Sturrock said, and it was clear from the tone of his voice that he thought Danny was lying. He turned to the CO. 'He tried to escape. He attacked a fellow soldier. He's plainly not telling us the truth.' He enumerated these points by raising three fingers. 'This man stays under lock and key until I give you the word. Is that clear?'

'I think you're barking up the wrong tree,' the CO said.

'*Is that clear?*'

The CO glanced at Danny. 'Perfectly clear,' he said.

'I know what you Regiment types are like,' Sturrock said, his voice suddenly dangerously quiet as he continued to address the CO. 'Watching each other's backs even when you're in the wrong. Well, not on my watch. My instructions come straight from Number Ten, and this man stays right where he is until I've got to the bottom of this, otherwise *you're* looking for a new job.'

Sturrock turned and made to leave the room. 'What's got you so nervous, Sturrock?' Danny said before he could exit.

Sturrock stopped. 'What are you talking about?'

'You told me Ibrahim Khan is killing members of the MISFIT team because he was turned by IS. I think you're lying about that.'

Sturrock's eyes narrowed, but he didn't say anything.

'You want to ask me how I know you're lying about that?'

Again, no answer.

'Because I know he's *not* killing the MISFIT team. So whoever *is* doing it, they're doing it for a different reason.'

A heavy silence fell over the holding cells. Sturrock's discomfort seemed to fill the room. 'You don't know what you're talking about,' he said finally. 'There's no doubt Ibrahim Khan killed those men. And you . . .' He jabbed his forefinger in Danny's direction. 'You're just digging yourself deeper into a hole of your own making.' Sturrock looked at the CO. 'He stays where he is, no matter what.' He strode out of the room without looking back.

'Boss . . .' Danny started to say, but the CO raised a finger to silence him.

'Is there anything you want to tell me?' Williamson asked. 'Off the record?'

Danny stared at him. 'Tell me you're not thinking what *he's* thinking,' he said. 'The only contact I've ever had with Ibrahim Khan was that one time, years ago. You believe me, right?'

'I don't know what to think just now, Danny. But you're not giving me much to go on. What was that shit with Roscoe? Forget about being returned to unit, that's a court martial offence.'

Danny had no answer. But he did have a request. 'Do me a favour, boss,' he said. 'Make some calls. Find out Bullock, Armitage and Moorhouse's official times of death. MI6 will keep a detailed record of their agents' movements, right? If they know exactly where Bethany White was at those times, beyond any doubt, then I'll drop it. But they won't. She'll have dropped off the radar at those times. I promise you.'

The CO didn't look keen. Making enquiries of this nature behind Sturrock's back was a serious breach of protocol. But he nodded. 'I'll see what I can do,' he said. Then he followed Sturrock back into the guard room, leaving Danny alone in the holding cell.

'The decision you have to make,' said the sales assistant, 'is whether to go for German, French or Japanese. The edges are all ground at different angles.'

'As long as they're sharp,' Bethany said, and there must have been something in her voice that sounded unusual, because the young man looked at her oddly. Bethany smiled at him. 'I find it's more about how they feel in the hand,' she said. 'Could I have a look at a few?'

They were standing at a counter at the far end of the department. There was a glass cabinet behind it, filled with a display of kitchen knives. The sales assistant unlocked and opened it. He pulled down a selection of knives and laid them in a line on the counter. 'At this end,' he said, 'French. Everything up from a paring knife to a large chef's knife. What will you be using your knives for mostly, do you think?'

'Meat,' she said. She picked up the largest of the black-handled French knives. 'It's a little heavy,' she added, weighing it in her hand. 'I think I prefer something more subtle. This one, perhaps.'

'A Japanese filleting knife,' the sales assistant said. 'For fish, mostly. Or for carving.'

Bethany picked it up. The blade was long and exquisitely sharp. The knife was moulded from a single piece of metal, and felt good in the hand. 'I'll take this,' she said. 'And something shorter.' She pointed at a German knife with a curved three-inch blade.

'Certainly, Madam.' He hesitated. 'These are quite specialist knives. Perhaps you'd like to look at more of an all-rounder?'

Bethany was about to refuse, when it struck her that to walk away without a regular chef's knife would be conspicuous. She selected a five-inch blade almost at random, and allowed the shop assistant to carefully package up her knives. 'Will that be all, Madam?'

'Yes,' Bethany said. The sales assistant started to put the purchases through the till. 'Actually, no. I'm cooking a roast tonight. I don't suppose you sell butcher's string?'

'Of course, Madam. I'll go and fetch it for you.'

'Two rolls, please.'

'A large joint is it, Madam?'

'Yes,' Bethany said. 'Very.'

Two minutes later she was walking back through the Trafford Centre, her John Lewis bag in one hand. She only had a couple of hundred pounds left in cash now, but that would be enough. She paid for her parking and, when she was back in the car, unpackaged the knives and stashed them in the glove compartment where they were easy to access. A couple and their young son squeezed past her car as she was doing this. The adults were too tall to see in, but the boy's head was at just the right height to see her with the three knives in her hand. He looked momentarily alarmed, but Bethany gave him a reassuring, motherly smile. His expression relaxed and he trotted after his parents.

Bethany cached the knives, leaned back in the driver's seat and took a deep breath. The boy had reminded him of her own son. That expression of curiosity. That adorable innocence.

And as always, when she thought of her boy, she thought of his father, and of the things they did to him. The thought made her palms clammy and her skin prickle. A numb determination passed over her. Soon, she would have finished what she'd started. She would do right by Ibrahim. She would avenge the love of her life and the father of her child. She and little Danny would be able to live out their lives in peace.

But none of that could happen while the architects of the MISFIT operation were still alive. Which meant two more people had to lose their lives.

It would happen today.

Thirty minutes later she was on the motorway, heading south. The weather grew worse, the sky turning from pale grey to almost black. There were distant rolls of thunder.

A storm was coming.

20

Danny was scared, and Christina didn't blame him.

It had been dark outside all afternoon. The clouds rolled in after lunch and settled stubbornly over the safe house. They had to turn all the lights on inside just to see around the house. The thunder started at around three. Each time it boomed, Danny grabbed hold of Christina a little harder as they sat on the squashy old sofa in the front room, listening to the wind whistle down the chimney into the empty grate. He had quite a grip for a child, and Christina had never known him more interested in the story books she'd read him all afternoon. That was his way of taking his mind off the real world and they were a good distraction for Christina, too. She'd been on edge since the moment she'd woken up, and she could tell Alec and Frank were nervous too, though they'd never have admitted it. Every half hour, while Alec kept an eye on Christina and Danny, Frank made a tour of the house, checking each room. He didn't normally do that. When Christina asked him if everything was okay, he said, 'Of course, my dear,' in his gentle West Country accent. But then he went back to prowling round the house.

There was an especially loud roll of thunder. Danny whimpered, then started when it was followed by a flash of lightning. 'Don't be scared,' Christina told him. 'It's only a silly old storm. We're nice and safe inside, and the sun will probably come out tomorrow.'

'I want my mum,' Danny said.

'I know, love. You'll see her soon . . .'

Another roll of thunder and a flash of lightning. There was a loud bang. The lights in the front room where they were sitting flickered, then died. They were plunged into half-light, half-darkness.

'What's happening?' Christina whispered, her voice stressed.

'Stay where you are,' Frank said. He didn't sound gentle any more. 'Alec, watch them.'

Christina and Danny gripped each other on the sofa. Danny buried his head in her chest, and she put one arm around his shoulders to comfort him. His body was shaking with tears. Alec stayed by the door. His eyes flickered between the two windows that looked out on to the grounds. Christina didn't find it reassuring. He looked like he was searching for somebody.

A minute passed. The lights switched on again. Frank reappeared. 'It's alright,' he said. 'It's just the trip switch again. I think there must have a been a power surge from that there lightning.' He held up a cordless phone handset. 'I think the landline's down too. I can't get a dialling tone.'

Alec chewed his lower lip. 'I could drive somewhere,' he said. 'Report it.'

Frank considered that for a few seconds, then shook his head. 'Best we both stay here,' he said. 'They'll get it sorted out soon enough.' He walked over to Danny and ruffled his hair. 'Don't you worry about a silly old storm, my little lad.' He looked at Christina. 'Nor you neither,' he said.

He left the room just as another crack of thunder rolled overhead. Alec took up his position at the door. Christina continued to hug the little boy. She could hear Frank's footsteps upstairs as he walked from room to room.

17.00 hrs. Brynmawr, Wales.

Sandy Fishwick was seriously considering handing in his resignation.

Sandy loved old black and white movies. The older the better – you could keep your Marvel and your Bond, as far as he was concerned. He was looking forward to his shift being over, because then he could clock off, jump in the car and head home to Bristol for his day off. If the traffic was kind, he could be home in time to put the kids to bed, then he and the missus could call out for an Indian and crank up an old Hitchcock on Netflix.

The colonel, as everyone in his guard detail referred to him, was comfortably the least likeable principal he'd ever had. Worse than the Saudi sheikh who'd insisted on hookers of three different nationalities – 'one white, one black, one yellow' was his regular order – every night for a week. At least he'd tipped them a month's wages for carrying out the grim nightly task of standing outside the door of his suite at the Savoy, listening to his nocturnal entertainment. Worse than that leftie leader of the opposition. He'd been a real peach, constantly slagging off the police and the armed forces in Sandy's presence, conveniently forgetting that Sandy was wearing body armour because he'd be in the line of fire if somebody took a pot shot. Worse even than that odious businessman who'd been afforded government protection because MI6 had credible evidence of a threat against him, and who expected Sandy to fetch him cups of tea and even – get this – shine his shoes.

The colonel was worse than all these. Boorish, aggressive and pretty much always arseholed, he took out the frustration of his enforced incarceration on his bodyguards. There was never a word of thanks. Never a word of anything, except a slurred put-down. The colonel had his first slug of whisky with his cornflakes and it was downhill from there. So yeah, Sandy was seriously considering taking the advice of that dark-haired SAS man who'd turned up with the chick from MI6 the other day, and getting himself a different job. There were plenty of freelance opportunities out there, he reasoned, where you could be your own boss and turn the gig down if the principal wasn't showing you the proper respect.

He frowned at the memory of the SAS guy. He'd met a few of those Hereford boys and they were generally a laugh with their black humour and callously cynical way of looking at the world. This one was different. Super-serious, even grim. He'd managed to put the shits up Sandy when he emerged from his meeting with the colonel and told him to keep his weapon cocked and locked, asked him if he had kids and to consider getting himself put on to another job. It didn't work like that, of course. You did what you were told to do. But Sandy was a little more alert over the next twenty-four hours. Every creak of the house made him jump, every shadow concealed a threat. But none of his fears had materialised and now he felt more at ease.

He and the other two members of his team were in the habit of rotating their positions. It eased the monotony, kept them more alert and meant that nobody perpetually had the chore of standing outside the colonel's drawing room, as he called it, during the day, or in the corridor outside his bedroom at night. The other positions were at the iron gates in the charming old perimeter wall that surrounded the colonel's residence – his word again – and here, half a mile from the house, on the only road leading up to it. He'd parked the Range Rover across the road and at right angles to it, so that nobody could pass. And nobody did. Nobody had even approached, apart from the SAS man and his MI6 companion. The colonel was not a popular man.

Sandy was sitting in the Range Rover now. The radio was on low and his weapon – locked but not cocked, despite the SAS man's warning – was on the passenger seat next to him. His phone was mounted magnetically on the dashboard. He had the car heater on to keep him warm. The snow that had fallen during the week had thawed, and now the weather was dramatically different. It had been dark all afternoon, the bubbling clouds overhead a deep grey. Occasionally there were heavy droplets of rain, but Sandy couldn't help feeling the sky was holding something back. The storm was rolling around the surrounding hills, belching its distant rumbles of thunder. Silent flashes of sheet lightning occasionally pulsed across the sky, but this was just a prelude. The main event, when it came, would be spectacular. Sandy hoped he would be home by then.

He was occupying himself by watching a couple of spring lambs follow their mother uphill on an adjacent field when he saw the glow of headlights from the south-west. A vehicle was approaching.

Sandy put on his woollen hat and holstered his weapon across his chest and under his windproof coat. He exited the vehicle, walked round from the driver's side and stood in the middle of the road. He blew on his hands and stamped his feet. The road turned out of sight to the south-west about fifty metres away. He only had to wait thirty seconds for the vehicle to reappear. It approached at a steady speed and stopped about ten metres from where Sandy stood. The headlights were on full beam. They made him squint and illuminated tiny droplets of moisture in the air. And when the door opened and a figure emerged, it was slightly silhouetted and Sandy couldn't quite make out its features until it was a couple of metres in front of him.

It was a woman. Sandy recognised her face but couldn't immediately place it. 'Hello again,' she said, and it was her voice that did it.

'I was just thinking about you,' Sandy said. 'Have you dyed your hair?'

'Change is as good as a rest,' said the woman . . . 'Do you like it?'

'I'm a married man, love. Not allowed to have opinions like that.'

She gave him a flirtatious look. 'Doesn't matter where you get your appetite, as long as you dine at home. Isn't that what they say?'

'That's not what my missus says,' Sandy replied, hoping he was successfully disguising how flustered she'd suddenly made him feel. 'Your friend not with you today? The big fella?'

'No,' she said. 'He's otherwise engaged.' She nodded in the direction of the house. 'He's expecting me, I think. I'd like to get in and out before this storm hits.'

'Ah . . . I haven't heard about that,' Sandy said.

'We just need to go over one or two security matters. Nothing major. You'll be out of here soon, I should think. A day or so at the most.' Sandy hesitated. Her kittenish manner had rather scrambled his brain. 'Go ahead,' she said. 'Call the office, they'll confirm. It's fine, I'll wait.'

'I . . .'

'Bethany. Bethany White.'

'Right,' Sandy said. 'Of course. If you wouldn't mind just . . .'

He turned his back on her.

Sandy wasn't expecting the attack, so when it happened, he really stood no chance, even though he was stronger and was carrying a loaded weapon. He saw it all happen in the side window of the Range Rover. As soon as he turned his back, the woman stepped forward and hooked her left arm around his throat. She was strong, and the grip was tight. Her right arm wrapped itself around his waist. She was holding something. A long narrow filleting knife. Its tip was towards his stomach, the blade pointing upwards. He tried to push the woman's arm away, but the momentum was already with her as she plunged the blade into his belly.

The knife felt icy as it slipped through his skin and guts. Then the tip touched his spinal cord and the pain was extraordinary: white-hot, like nothing he'd ever imagined. His body went into spasm, but he was still looking down and saw her yank the handle of the knife up towards his chest, like someone engaging a hand-brake. The blade, still deeply embedded in his bowels, sliced through layers of skin and tissue, taking with it the folds of his shirt and coat into his abdomen.

His knees went. She withdrew the knife as he collapsed. The headlights of her car were still shining behind him, casting his shadow very distinctly on to the side of the Range Rover. He was clutching his stomach now. He looked down to see atrocious quantities of thick, almost-black fluid spewing from his belly. He felt his face screwing up in puzzlement. Surely it was too dark for blood. Maybe it was something else. The contents of his stomach, or . . .

Or . . .

He collapsed on to his front.

The world was spinning. He felt like he should hang on to something. That way he could stop the spinning, and if he could stop the spinning, maybe he'd have a chance of seeing his kids again. They could watch a movie together. He'd even let them choose Marvel. And eat popcorn.

Yes. If he could just crawl forward and grab the Range Rover's tyre. That would steady him. It was very close. A metre, if that. But he couldn't make his limbs move. His arms. They wouldn't move. Not an inch, no matter how hard he tried, and the world was spinning even faster, and the lights behind him were so bright, and he didn't know where he was any more, and he just couldn't work out why.

Danny hadn't seen a single person since the CO walked out of the holding cells. He'd sat for hours on the plastic stool, staring at the opposite wall, waiting. He smelled bad. It occurred to him that the last time he'd washed was at the embassy in Beirut, and his face was still stained with blood. He remembered how he approached Bethany, he in his towel, she in her dressing gown, and put one hand on her hip. And how she removed his hand and said, 'Look but don't touch, Danny.' At the time, he thought he'd misread the signs, but now he knew he hadn't misread them at all. Bethany White had played him just right, and he felt suddenly furious at his own naivety. The woman who'd killed three SAS men had been there, in his grasp, and he'd been too blind to see it.

He didn't intend to make the same mistake again.

But now he was in the hands of the head shed.

They would come, eventually. The question was, would it be too late?

He heard thunder outside. Thoughts circled in his brain. There was still a missing piece to the jigsaw. If Bethany White had been on a killing spree, why was she targeting the MISFIT team, and not the IS assassins who had tortured and killed

Ibrahim Khan? It made no sense to him. No matter how crazed Bethany White truly was, she wasn't the type to do something without a reason.

So what was it?

That question was circulating as the door to the holding cells opened. The CO entered. He looked troubled. 'What is it?' Danny asked.

For a moment the CO didn't reply. 'I spoke to a contact in Vauxhall. They agreed to check Bethany White's schedule.'

Danny stood up. 'And?'

'Ben Bullock's body was found in Dubai on January 13. Estimated time of death, somewhere between 20.00 and midnight on January 12. Bethany White took leave between the tenth and the fourteenth.'

'You don't say,' Danny muttered.

'Liam Armitage was found dead in Ghana on February 3. According to MI6 records, White was out of the country then too, meeting a potential contact in Tunisia.'

'And Ollie Moorhouse?'

'Found in Palm Beach on March 6. And on March 4 . . .' The CO pinched the bridge of his nose.

'What?' Danny said.

'She called in sick.'

Danny stared at him in disbelief at the brazenness of it.

'Flu,' the CO added. 'Or so she said. It was March 7 that they put her under close protection.'

'Plenty of time for her to fly back from Florida,' Danny said.

'Plenty,' the CO agreed.

'Boss,' Danny said. 'You've got to let me out of . . .'

He didn't finish his sentence. The CO's phone rang. He answered it immediately. 'Yes, I'll hold,' he said. He put one hand over the mouthpiece. 'It's Sturrock,' he said. 'He says it's urgent.'

Somewhere outside, the thunder rolled again.

Bethany watched the guard die. Face down on the ground, he muttered something about popcorn as his body twitched and a dark pool of blood spread out from his belly. She felt nothing as his final breath noisily left him. Death, she realised, was completely mundane to her. Even violent death like this. How many was it now? The three SAS men. The girl in Beirut. She had to count to remind herself that this was number five.

By the end of today, she would have more than doubled her tally.

She'd managed to keep her hands free of blood, but the blade of the knife was sticky and covered with gore. She wiped it clean on the back of his coat, then returned it to the glove compartment of her rented CR-V. She removed his handgun from its holster – somehow it had remained free of blood – and placed it in the footwell of the passenger seat. She hurried back up to the Range Rover and took the wheel. The seat was still warm from her victim's body. The heat was blowing, the radio playing softly and the keys hanging in the ignition. She took the phone from its magnetic holder and switched it off. If anyone called it, it would go straight to voicemail and they'd assume, to start with at least, that he was on another call. She switched off the radio, pressing the on–off switch with more force than was necessary because for some reason the sound of it profoundly irritated her. Then she started the engine. She turned the vehicle ninety degrees so it was parked up by the side of the road, then pocketed the keys. She exited the Range Rover and walked back to her CR-V, barely looking at the dead man as she passed. Back behind the wheel of her rental car, she moved the vehicle forward. The tyres crunched over the body of her victim. She lurched with the movement of the vehicle, but her hands didn't move from the ten and two position on the steering wheel, and her eyes stayed resolutely on the way ahead.

She drove carefully and, as she approached the gates to the colonel's residence, used her engine braking rather than her brake pedal to slow down. The tyres gripped the surface sufficiently, and she came to a complete halt ten metres from the iron gates.

She let the engine idle as the headlights illuminated the gates. The second guard appeared on the other side. He was a stocky fellow with a grey woollen hat and a black coat that didn't hide the holster across his chest. He peered through the iron gates, half frowning, half squinting in the headlights' beam. Bethany didn't take her eyes from him, but stretched out her left arm to open the glove compartment. This time she took the smaller knife with the curved blade. She could conceal the handle in the palm of her hand, and the flat part of the blade with her forefinger. It was just the right size.

The guard on the other side of the gates pulled out his mobile phone, dialled a number and put the handset to his ear. Then he looked at the screen. It was obvious that whoever he'd tried to call hadn't answered. Bethany lowered her window. She leaned out. 'His wife called,' she said.

The guard squinted again, but seemed to relax at the sound of a female voice. He walked to the side of the gates and tapped a code into a keypad. The gates opened and the guard approached. Bethany almost smiled. He had that swagger she recognised so well. The swagger of a man about to patronise a woman. The sort of swagger that her Ibrahim would never have displayed. The guard drew up alongside the CR-V, rested one hand on the roof and bent down to look in. He only managed a single sentence – 'What can we do for you tonight then, darling?' – before Bethany struck.

The hooked end of the knife sank into the flesh of his neck almost without resistance. All she had to do next was yank it back towards her. The curved blade cut deep into him. It was only when the tip connected with his Adam's apple that she had to yank a little harder. The blade emerged, bloodied, from his neck, bringing with it a trail of artery and tissue. The man staggered back, one hand pressed against the wound. Blood pumped hard through his fingers as Bethany opened the driver's door and stepped outside. Her victim was trying to reach for his gun, but he was also clearly trying to stem the bleed with his dominant right hand. His left hand clawed awkwardly at the holster, but he seemed to have lost control of his grip, and a moment later he'd collapsed to his knees in any case.

With her left hand she held a clump of his hair. With her right, she inflicted another wound on the opposite side of his neck.

He was struggling to breathe now, and his skin was turning waxy. There was a catastrophic quantity of blood gushing down his front and he was staring at it in shocked horror. He seemed to have forgotten all about the gun. Bethany leaned down, pulled open his coat and removed the weapon from its holster. The handle was sticky and she held it between her thumb and forefinger as she took it back to the car and dumped it in the footwell of the passenger seat where she was gathering quite an armoury. There was movement behind her. She looked back. Her victim had fallen forward and was now face down on the road, blood spreading from his neck. There was no movement in his body. She wasn't certain he was dead, but he was surely only seconds away and she had work to do.

'Go ahead,' said the CO.

He stared intently at Danny as he listened to Sturrock at the other end of the phone. His face was expressionless. He listened for thirty seconds, then said, 'Roger that.' He killed the phone call. 'The DNA result came through from Beirut. MI6 had Bethany White's on file. They ran a comparison. It's not her. They've put out an all-ports warning.'

'It's too late for that,' Danny said. 'Get me out of here.'

The CO nodded. He disappeared into the guard house and reappeared with the duty guard who unlocked the holding cell. Danny pushed his way out. 'Can you get a chopper in the air?' he said.

'Negative,' the CO replied. 'Not from Hereford. Our assets are currently in London.'

'We need to get a team moving,' Danny said, as they stormed through the guard room and into the open air. It was dark. Sheet lighting flashed across the sky. 'Shit,' Danny hissed. Weather like this would only serve to delay a chopper.

'Since when were you giving the orders, Black?'

Danny stopped and turned. 'Boss, I've been in that fucking holding cell all day while MI6 stare at their navels. Trust me, Bethany White is in the country. She's killed three SAS men that we know about. She compromised my team in Syria. Her next target is probably the colonel and after that it's Christina Somers – she'll do her last because she'll want to disappear with her kid. We need to get on the blower to both their close-protection teams, tell them to move their principals immediately.'

The CO nodded. 'I'll tell Sturrock.' He dialled a number and put his phone to his ear as he marched across the asphalt to the main Regiment building. There was a sudden, torrential downpour, and the two men were soaked before they got back inside.

Bethany wiped the knife clean on the back of his coat. She felt inside his pocket, recovered his phone, and switched it off before dropping it on the ground beside him. Then she climbed back into the CR-V. She quietly closed the driver's door, stowed the knife back in the glove compartment and drove through the open gates.

As soon as she crossed the threshold, the rain started. It was end-of-the-world rain, heavy and impenetrable. All of a sudden, Bethany could barely see the house, even though it was no more than twenty-five metres away. She killed the engine. The headlights died. Rain thundered deafeningly on the roof of the CR-V. It suited Bethany, because it camouflaged her approach.

There was now only one guard between her and the colonel. Just a few minutes and they would be face to face.

Danny followed the CO into his office, a sparse room with a few framed pictures on the wall of Williamson with various assorted bigwigs. The CO put his phone on speaker and placed it on his desk. 'You're on with Black,' he announced.

Danny didn't expect any word of apology from Sturrock, and he didn't get it. Just a terse update. '*My people are making contact with the close-protection teams now.*'

Silence.

Then . . .

'*Fuck . . .*'

'What is it?' the CO demanded.

'*The lines are down to the safe house.*'

'What about the colonel's CP?' Danny demanded.

'*We can't raise them. Their phones are switching to voicemail.*'

'All three?'

'*All three.*'

A moment of silence.

'*You've made a pig's ear of this situation . . .*' Sturrock started to say.

The CO leaned over and killed the call in mid-sentence. He looked at Danny. 'Well?'

'She'll target the colonel first,' Danny said.

'How do you know?'

'Because her kid's with Christina. She'll do her last and then try to get away with the boy.'

'She's insane if she thinks she can do that.'

'Maybe,' Danny said. 'But everything's gone the way she wants it so far. I think she's got something else up her sleeve.'

'You know her best,' the CO said. 'What do you need?'

'Get a team out to the colonel's place. Scramble the chopper from London to Christina's safe house.'

'What are you going to do?'

As far as Danny was concerned, he'd already answered that question. From here, he could be at the colonel's house in an hour, the safe house in ninety minutes. If he wanted to catch up with Bethany White . . .

'I'm going to the safe house. Boss, I've got to move.'

The CO nodded. He put his hands in his pockets and removed a set of keys. 'Take my car.' He opened a drawer in his desk, withdrew a Sig 9mm handgun and handed it over, then gave Danny his phone.

Danny turned to leave. But before he reached the door he looked back at the CO. 'Boss, MI6 are covering something up. They need to tell us what's really going on.'

'I'll get on to the DSF,' Williamson said. 'He has more clout.'
'Good.'
'Black?'
'Yeah?'
'She killed three of our guys. Make sure you find her.'
'I will,' Danny said, and he left the room.

21

Colonel Henry Bishop put another log on the fire. He took his empty whisky glass from the mantelpiece and walked across the drawing room to the drinks trolley. There was a flash of lightning and it must have caused a power surge because all the lights in the room went dim for a fraction of a second, and the Goldberg Variations faded momentarily. He thought, in that instant of darkness and silence, that he could see lights through the windows that looked out on to the front of the house. Car headlights, or was he imagining it?

The lights in the drawing room lit up again. Bach returned. As the colonel staggered towards the windows there was another crack of thunder and, as if somebody had turned on a switch, a torrential downpour of rain started. It was so loud it drowned out the music. The colonel peered through the window and could barely see more than a couple of metres. There was no glow of headlights, however. He had probably imagined it. He looked disconsolately into his empty tumbler and turned back to the drinks cabinet again.

It was early in the evening, so he was still indulging in the pretence of small measures. He poured himself a couple of fingers of Scotch, turned up the music, then returned to his comfortable armchair by the fire, took a sip, closed his eyes and let the Goldberg wash over him. Whisky and Bach truly were the only things that kept him sane.

How long he sat like that, he couldn't have said. A couple of minutes, perhaps? He was on the third Variation when he heard the door creak open and he immediately felt his temper rising.

Those bloody close-protection people had no sense of personal space. 'Can't you bloody knock before you enter?' he growled. 'How many times do I have to tell you?'

'Do you speak to all your girls like that?' said a voice.

A female voice.

The colonel spluttered, opened his eyes and stood up. He felt a moment of semi-drunken dizziness and had to grab the back of the armchair to steady himself as he looked at the figure in the doorway. She was very wet. Her hair was dripping on to the carpet. The colonel was confused. He recognised her, but not entirely. Then he twigged. 'You've dyed your hair,' he said.

Bethany White raised one hand to her hair. 'Do you like it?' she said. 'Last time I was here, you said you preferred brunettes.'

'Did I?'

'You did,' said Bethany, and she smiled at him in a way no woman had smiled at him for many years. Through the fog of booze and anxiety, he detected an unfamiliar stirring of desire. 'May I come in? I have some good news for you.'

'Those bloody close-protection people should have let me know you were here,' the colonel said.

'They recognised me,' Bethany said. 'And anyway, you won't be needing them any more.' She smiled again. 'They found him.'

'What?'

'They found Ibrahim Khan. He was holed up in a filthy little flat in south London. He's on remand in Belmarsh as we speak.'

It was only in that moment that the colonel fully appreciated the stress he'd been under. The sleepless nights. The constant worry. All that fell away in an instant. He exhaled a profound sigh of relief. 'Well,' he said. 'Well, well, well. Thank the Lord for that. May the powers that be throw away the fucking key. I think this calls for a drink, don't you?'

'I think it calls for more than that,' said Bethany, and the colonel had to clench his free hand to hide that it was shaking with the little thrill that just darted through him. She really was a fine-looking woman. The brown hair suited her, and he liked the way it clung to the side of her face because it was wet.

'What will it be, my dear?' he said. 'I might have some sherry somewhere . . .'

'I'll have what you're having,' she said, and stepped a little further into the room.

The Director Special Forces marched through the anonymous corridors of the MI6 building in Vauxhall.

He'd been here to discuss the continued deployment of the SAS in a training role to the Kenyan government. When the call came through from Hereford, he excused himself from the meeting. And when Mike Williamson filled him in, he headed straight to the fourth floor where Sturrock's office was situated. He barged past three secretaries, who all wittered that he really mustn't enter unannounced, and a guard who knew better than to challenge the DSF, to find Sturrock sitting behind his desk, staring across the river through the floor-to-ceiling windows on the far side of his office. An electric storm was flashing over the London skyline. When Sturrock turned in his swivel chair, the DSF saw his face was as white as the lightning.

The two men looked at each other across the office. 'I have two SAS teams in transit,' the DSF said. 'One is heading to Colonel Bishop's house, one is heading to the safe house. So far this clusterfuck has cost me three men. Either you tell me what the hell's been going on, or the next conversation I have is with the PM.'

Sturrock stared at him. 'It's complicated,' he said.

'I'm smart,' said the DSF. 'Try me.'

The rain was relentless. Visibility through the windscreen of the CO's BMW, no more than five metres. Danny's urge was to floor it, but to do that risked colliding with an unseen obstacle up ahead, or coming off the road. He was aware, but only vaguely, of pedestrians on either side sprinting to get out of the rain. He kept his attention on the road.

The colonel handed Bethany half a tumbler of Scotch. They were standing by the fire. She downed the drink in one and closed her eyes as the warmth from the spirit spread through her torso. 'That's good,' she said, and she opened her eyes.

The colonel was a truly pathetic presence. He reeked of stale alcohol, for a start, and his mixture of sexual nervousness and anticipation was evident in the way he kept licking his glistening pink lips, and by the film of sweat on his forehead. His face, already red from the booze, was now truly flushed with anticipation. 'I . . . I was a bit of a pig, I suppose,' he said. 'Last time you were here, I mean. This damn Khan situation was getting to me a trifle, I won't deny it. Shouldn't have said that thing about you being a, you know, a dyke. Hope I didn't offend.'

'It takes more than that,' she said, 'to offend me. You're a brave man, Colonel. We girls like that. Sometimes we even club together to show our appreciation. Do you understand what I'm talking about?'

'Yes,' said the colonel. 'Yes, I think I might.' He licked his glistening lips even more enthusiastically than before.

'Aren't you hot in that jacket?' she said.

'Yes,' said the colonel. 'Yes, a little.'

'Why don't you take it off?'

The whisky glass jangled against the mantelpiece as the colonel put it down nervously. He wriggled his way out of his tweed jacket and slung it over the back of his armchair. 'Perhaps, uh . . . Perhaps you'd like to . . . uh . . .' He made an airy gesture to indicate that she should do the same.

Bethany giggled. 'You're a naughty boy, Colonel. I never would have suspected it of you.' She stepped one pace closer to him and gently placed the tip of her left forefinger on his forehead. Then she brushed it slowly down the centre of his face, down his ruddy nose, over his moist lips, across his chin and down his Adam's apple, which wriggled under his podgy skin as he swallowed. She continued to the top button of his shirt, deftly undid it, then moved down to the next. She was acutely, horribly aware of the bulge under his trousers. She felt as if every cell in her body was recoiling from it. That bulge was far more offensive to her than the butchered corpses lying in her wake. But she continued to undo his shirt nonetheless.

Ibrahim had been naked when they killed him, so she wanted the colonel to be naked too. It was more humiliating that way and he was, after all, a big man. Better to get him to strip quickly and voluntarily than struggle with his corpse after she'd finished with him.

It was as if Sturrock couldn't bear to look the DSF in the eye as he spoke. He spun round in his chair again and looked back over the stormy London skyline. The DSF could clearly see his reflection in the window, however. His expression was haunted.

'MISFIT was our best intelligence source since 9/11,' he said. 'There's no question about that. Some of us wondered how long it could possibly last. More than once, we thought he might be close to exposure and we'd have to engage our extraction procedures. Pull him out of Syria, give him a new identity and a decent pension and make sure he lived a long and happy life. And we'd have done it. No question. We do look after our people, you know. We're not monsters.' As he said this, he clenched his left hand into a tight fist and put it momentarily to his forehead. 'We're not monsters,' he repeated, as if to persuade himself of that fact.

Sturrock paused, cleared his throat, then carried on speaking.

'Six months ago, a little longer perhaps, the MISFIT source provided some solid gold intelligence. There was to be a meeting of high-value IS targets. Local commanders, decision-makers, and four or five top dogs high up on both our watch list and the Americans' – people we had difficulty locating at the best of times, let alone having them all in one place at the same time. They were congregating to discuss the fall of their damn caliphate, and to establish ways of reinvigorating it by upping their terror campaign against the West. It was too good an opportunity to pass up. There were fifteen targets in all, and if we could take them out in one hit, there was a high probability we'd deal Daesh in Syria a near-fatal blow. It was discussed at the highest level and the decision was made, rightly, that such an outcome would dramatically decrease the security threat level in the UK.'

Unbidden, Sturrock spun round again. 'I don't think you understand,' he said, his voice dripping with accusation. 'Our people uncover threats from these bastards in the UK three or four times a week. Ninety per cent of these threats originate in Syria and Afghanistan. To take out fifteen Daesh commanders would . . .'

'I get it,' the DSF said, choosing not to remind Sturrock that half of the threats he'd just referenced were dealt with by his men.

Sturrock frowned. 'It was discussed at the highest level,' he repeated. He plainly wanted the buck to be passed further up the hierarchy. 'Number Ten was fully aware.'

'Aware of what?' the DSF said.

Sturrock looked at him as if he was an idiot. 'Of the air strike,' he said.

The colonel's shirt was off. He wore a yellowing vest underneath it. It smelt musty but went some way to camouflaging his paunch. The skin on his arms was pasty. Greying hair protruded unpleasantly from his armpits. It occurred to Bethany that everything about this man was different from Ibrahim. She remembered his lean, muscular arms and flat, smooth torso. She remembered the way he used to hold her, confidently and safely. And for a moment, just a moment, she let her mask slip as the injustice hit her: that her Ibrahim should be dead, and this foul excuse for a human should still be alive.

'What is it?' the colonel asked.

And instantly, the mask returned. She fixed him with her most seductive gaze, reached out, and started to unbuckle his trousers.

That kept him quiet.

'So you took out a target with fifteen Daesh commanders,' the DSF said. 'What's the problem with that?'

'It's more complicated,' Sturrock said, and he scowled.

'How so?'

'For a start, *we* didn't carry out the air strike.'

'The Americans?'

'No,' said Sturrock. 'The Russians.'

The DSF widened his eyes. 'Last time I checked, we weren't really on speaking terms with them.'

'Of course we bloody well aren't. They're poisoning people in the bloody provinces. But they also have an FSB agent embedded in the service. We know who he is and from time to time it suits our purposes to leak information back to the Russians. It was far too politically difficult for us to launch a strike from Syrian airspace, but the Russians were in bed with the regime and we knew they wouldn't be able to resist. They had the precise time, they had the exact coordinates of the meeting. All we had to do was sit back and wait for them to do our work for us.'

'It sounds like a perfect strategy. What's the problem?'

'The problem?' Sturrock replied. He removed his moisturiser from his pocket and rubbed a little into his hands. 'The problem,' he said, 'was the children.'

His trousers were round his ankles now. He was kicking off his shoes and stepping out of them. He wore Y-fronts, baggy enough to contain his excitement. Bethany raised her right arm and gently took hold of his chin. He was breathing heavily. She could feel his hot, whisky-soaked breath on her face. And now he was down to his underwear, she could drop her pretence. She wrinkled her nose and turned her face away in disgust.

It was then that the colonel appeared to twig that all was not as it seemed.

He looked down at her hand. It was still holding his chin. He appeared to notice something he hadn't seen before. He grabbed her hand and looked at it. There, between her thumb and her first finger, was a smear of red. It was unmistakably blood.

'What the bloody hell's going on?' the colonel said. He staggered back, bumping into his armchair. The bulge in his Y-fronts had deflated. Bethany made an extravagant show of noticing this and looked at him with a grumpily kittenish expression.

'Don't you love me any more?' she said.

'Where's my close-protection team?' the colonel demanded. He bent down to grab his trousers, but Bethany placed one foot on them before he was able to. He stood up again. '*Where the bloody hell are you?*' he shouted. '*Why did you let this woman in without checking with me first?*'

Bethany put a hand to one ear. 'Do you know,' she said, 'I'm not certain they can hear you.'

He stared at her.

Then he ran.

'What children?'

Sturrock turned again to look back over the London skyline. 'The Daesh personnel were meeting in a school,' he said. His voice cracked as he spoke. 'An infant school. Thirty children under the age of ten. It's a common strategy of theirs. Whenever several high-value targets congregate, they do it at a civilian target. They know it's unlikely to prevent an air strike from the Syrian regime or their allies, but Western powers are more reluctant to accept collateral damage. Agent MISFIT knew we were unlikely to order a direct hit on a school. He had another plan. He was known to some of the targets. His calculation was that, once they'd congregated, he'd be able to gain access to their private meeting and . . .'

'And what?'

'Eliminate them. Single-handedly.'

'That risked blowing his cover,' the DSF said.

'Indeed,' Sturrock replied, 'if he was unsuccessful. But he wanted out anyway. He was offering to make this his last job.'

'One guy against fifteen?'

'Our assessment,' Sturrock said, 'was that he was . . . unlikely to succeed. We elected to proceed with our original plan.'

'Did you tell him you were going to do that?'

Sturrock didn't immediately answer. When he did, his voice was very quiet. 'It was discussed at the highest level,' he said.

'Did you tell him?'

'We did not. Communications with Agent MISFIT were difficult and intermittent. He presented us with his plan as a fait accompli, and we were unable to warn him of our change in strategy. Moreover . . .'

'Moreover what?'

'Ibrahim Khan was an idealist. Our assessment was that there was a very real risk he would arrange for the school to be evacuated if he thought the children were in danger. We couldn't allow that to happen. The opportunity was too great to hit IS where it hurt.'

'So Khan was in the vicinity when the Russians hit the school?'

'He was.'

'And there was a high chance he'd be taken out in the strike as well as the enemy targets.'

A beat.

'It was discussed at the highest level.'

'Yeah,' said the DSF, unable to hide the disgust in his voice, 'I bet it was.'

'But Khan wasn't hurt,' Sturrock said. 'At least not physically. The strike was a success. All fifteen Daesh targets were eliminated.'

'And how many kids?'

'Between twenty-five and thirty. Estimates vary.'

'When did you next have contact from Ibrahim Khan?' the DSF asked.

'Two days later,' said Sturrock. 'He . . . he wasn't happy.'

Wearing nothing but his socks, his underpants and his vest, the colonel burst through the door that led from the drawing room to the hallway.

He stopped.

One of his close-protection men was lying on the floor, face up. The colonel couldn't even remember the fellow's name. Not that it mattered now. He lay in a pool of his own blood, which was still seeping from his neck. The cause of the wound was a long-bladed filleting knife which was still embedded in his neck, the handle sticking up into the air. The colonel stood over him, his legs paralysed with shock. He looked over his shoulder. She was there in the doorway, and she had a gun in her hand. She looked at the body. 'Whoops,' she said.

He found the movement in his legs and started to run towards the front door, but he stepped in the pool of blood and it was more slippery than he expected. He fell, then staggered to his feet again, his hands and knees smeared with blood. He was aware of her shadow, cast by the overhead light, approaching him. He ran towards the door again but before he reached it there was the sound of gunshot. It was shockingly loud and for a moment he thought he'd been hit, but then plaster fell from the ceiling, showering him with a mixture of powder and lumps. He looked back to see her pointing the gun in his direction. 'Put your hands on your head,' she said, and he had no option but to obey.

He could hear the rain falling outside, and a crack of thunder boomed over the house. She kept the gun pointing in his direction as she walked over to the dead body. She put one foot on the corpse's chest and, with her free hand, tugged at the knife. It looked like she had to pull hard, as if the tip was firmly embedded in the CP man's throat. But it came free after a few seconds and the colonel saw that about an inch and a half of the tip was smeared red.

She pointed with the knife towards the drawing room. 'Get back in there,' she said.

'When you say he wasn't happy,' the DSF insisted, 'what exactly do you mean?'

'I wasn't party to the conversation. Agent MISFIT took the unusual step of going over the head of his regular handler . . .'

'That's Bethany White?'

'Yes. As I say, he went over her head and directly contacted the ultimate head of the MISFIT operation. The person who identified Khan as an asset in the first place and who persuaded him to infiltrate Daesh.'

'The colonel?'

'The colonel. He was furious with Bishop. He was raving. He was . . .'

'What?'

'He was threatening to go public. He'd worked out that we'd leaked the intel to the Russians and he said he'd go straight to the

UK press and reveal everything: not only that we'd duped the Russians, but also that in doing so we'd given tacit approval to a strike that killed thirty innocent children.' He pinched his forehead, as though suffering a tremendous headache. 'Can you imagine it? He'd been undercover with Daesh for years. He'd have absolute credibility. The story would run and run. There'd be *books* . . .' He spat the last word as if it represented the very worst possible outcome.

'What did he want?' the DSF asked.

'Want? He didn't *want* anything. That was the whole problem. He was going to do it.' He hesitated for a moment, staring into the middle distance. 'We couldn't let it happen,' he said.

The DSF didn't say anything. He could see where this was going. He waited for Sturrock to continue talking.

'In that one communication with the colonel, Agent MISFIT went from being our most valuable source to our greatest menace. If he made good on his threat, the possible repercussions were too immense to consider. There was a very real chance of the UK being dragged into direct conflict with Syria and the Russian Federation, not to mention the irreparable damage that would be done to the service. The PM would have to go, of course, and she wasn't keen on that idea.'

'And so would you,' the DSF said.

Sturrock sniffed. 'Quite,' he said. 'None of us liked the call we had to make, but it was . . .'

'Discussed at the highest level?'

Sturrock nodded. 'Conversations took place,' he said. 'We were on the point of bringing you in to arrange a special forces operation to eliminate Agent MISFIT, when an alternative proposal was mooted.'

'Go on,' the DSF said. He felt slightly nauseous.

Sturrock closed his eyes. 'We leaked the fact that Agent MISFIT was a double to Daesh,' he said. 'We knew they'd take the appropriate action. The end result would be the same as if we'd eliminated him.'

'The end result would *not* have been the same, and you know it,' the DSF said.

'It was approved at the highest level.' Sturrock barely whispered his refrain. As soon as the information was leaked, we received no more communications from Agent MISFIT. We assumed he had been eliminated.' He frowned. 'But then the killings started, and Khan's DNA turned up in Palm Beach, Florida. We knew then that something had gone very wrong. We drew the only conclusion we could: that Khan was still alive, that he'd found out what we had done and that he was eliminating everybody who had been indoctrinated into MISFIT.'

'But you were wrong. Khan *was* dead.'

'When I heard Danny Black's story earlier today, it sounded like cock and bull. For Bethany White to have had a child by one of her agents would have been the grossest dereliction of duty. And that one of our own agents – and a female agent at that – should have been responsible for killing three former Hereford men.' He shook his head. 'Highly improbable.'

'But true,' said the DSF.

'So it would seem.'

'How did Daesh find out about Bethany and the kid?'

'By torturing Khan, I imagine. You know as well as I do that everyone breaks eventually, if you apply the correct pressure.'

'When we first met Danny Black in Hereford, you said you were personally unaware of Agent MISFIT's true identity until the third killing.'

'Correct.'

'So who leaked the information to Daesh? Who made the call? Who grassed him up?'

'I'd have thought that was obvious.'

'The colonel?' asked the DSF.

'The colonel,' Sturrock replied.

The colonel was back in the drawing room.

He was naked now – she had forced him to remove the rest of his clothes – and was sitting on a high-backed dining chair. The twine that bound him to the chair was thin but very strong. She had wrapped it about thirty times round his arms, torso, and the back of his chair. Strain as he might, it was impossible for him to break free of it. He had his back to the fire and it was uncomfortably hot. The woman was standing directly in front of him. She had the gun in one hand and the knife in the other. It was the knife that terrified him the most. He couldn't take his eyes from it as she stood there in terrible silence, staring at him. When she laid the gun on the side of his armchair – well out of reach – and approached him holding just the knife, his bladder weakened. Warm liquid spread over his inner thighs and dripped noisily from the chair on to the hearth rug.

'Have we had a little accident?' said Bethany White.

'Please . . .' the colonel whimpered.

She put one finger to her mouth and hushed him. 'I'm going to ask you some questions,' she said. 'You know what will happen, don't you, if you lie?' For emphasis, she placed the tip of her knife against his Adam's apple, at exactly the point from which he had seen it protruding on the corpse outside.

He nodded.

She stepped back. 'Was it you,' she asked, 'who betrayed Ibrahim to IS?'

The colonel couldn't hide his surprise. 'How did you know?'

'Was it you?'

'It was discussed at the highest . . .'

'Was . . . it . . . *you*?'

A beat.

'Yes.' He stared at her. 'How did you know?' he repeated.

She gave him a bleak smile. 'He told me,' she said.

'What are you talking about? That's impossible.'

'Not in person, of course,' Bethany said. She cocked her head. 'How long do you suppose they tortured him before he told them everything? I think a week. It looked to me like his beard had about a week's growth, when I saw him on the video footage.'

'What . . . what video footage?'

'The video footage of him being tortured and killed. The one his killers sent me. He'd told them all about me, you see. And all about our son. Do you know, I think they were almost more angry that he'd married a Western woman than they were about his betrayal of them.'

She took a step forward and the colonel shrank back in his chair.

'He told me all about the strike on the school, of course. About the children we killed. And that MI6 had betrayed him to Daesh. He didn't know exactly who made the call, so he didn't mention you by name. But I imagine he had a fairly good idea who was responsible. Don't you?'

The colonel nodded mutely.

Bethany nodded along sarcastically. 'Men like you,' she said, 'are everything that's bad about the world.'

'You . . . you don't even know me properly,' the colonel stuttered.

'I know enough. You and my father were cut from the same cloth. Pillars of the establishment, and as dirty beneath the skin as the terrorists you pretend to fight. There's not an authentic bone in your body. Ibrahim was worth a hundred of you. A *thousand* of you.' Her eyes flashed, then she smiled again. 'I don't want you to think it's all bad news, Henry. The *good* news is that we don't have a week for torturing. I can't stay for much longer. But I do want you to understand the reason for what is about to happen. Are you sitting comfortably? Are you listening?' She spoke as if to a child. The colonel found himself unable to reply. 'At the beginning of the tape they sent me,' Bethany continued, 'they made him explain in advance what they were going to do to him. First, they removed his ears, so he could no longer hear the words of his infidel masters. I inflicted that part of his punishment on Ben Bullock. Ibrahim often talked about how that man had offended and humiliated him. Next, they removed his fingers, so he was no longer able to fight for the infidel. That punishment became Liam Armitage's. After that, they removed his genitals, to unman him and punish him for lying with a Western woman. It wasn't easy to inflict that punishment on Ollie Moorhouse. He really did put up a struggle. But I managed it.' She paused. 'Would you like to know what they did next?' she asked.

The colonel shook his head.

'They took out his eyes,' she said. 'They did that *before* they burned him alive, because they wanted him to witness his other punishments.' She stepped closer. 'In a way, you're lucky, Henry. I'm going to take out your eyes before I kill you, so you won't have to watch me do it.'

The colonel, suddenly unable even to beg for his life, made a pathetic, strangled sound at the back of his throat. As Bethany reached forward and put the tip of her knife under the lid of his right eye, he leaned his head back to recede from the knife. Bethany merely followed the path of the eye. Now that his head was all the way back, there was nothing for him to do: if he moved it forwards, he would puncture the eyeball of his own accord.

'Goodnight, Henry,' Bethany said. 'This is for Ibrahim.'

She inserted the knife through the lower eyelid quite slowly. The colonel felt it slide easily through the skin, but it encountered some resistance as it touched the eyeball itself. Bethany pushed a little harder. The tip of the knife found purchase, and entered.

The colonel screamed. The pain was like nothing he had ever known: profound and infinitely sharp. The vision on his right-hand side flashed with an electric white light, then turned muddy as a warm flow of viscous liquid dribbled over his cheek. He felt the knife twisting in his eyeball and he screamed for a second time.

The process of removing the knife hurt even more than its insertion. The pain was so intense that he couldn't scream. He shook his head from side to side in a desperate attempt to stop her piercing the other eye, but she just grabbed his hair, held him still, thrust the knife into his left eye and twisted it again.

The agony was unspeakable. He gasped noisily for air and involuntarily sucked in some of the fluid that had dripped from his eyes. He choked as he felt the knife leaving his left eye.

Even though he was blind, he felt the room spinning. Somewhere on the edge of his awareness he could hear the woman talking, but he couldn't make out what she was saying. The pain was everything. It permeated every part of his body and every ounce of his awareness. He was shuddering with it, and he felt the chair to which he was bound jolting and rocking with the movement. His mind shrieked, and maybe his body did too, he couldn't tell any more.

And then, he felt it in his belly: the knife slipping easily through the layers of fat and into his stomach, and the keen torment of the blade's slow movement up towards his chest.

In that corner of his conscious brain that was still active, the colonel was glad he couldn't see, because he knew what he could feel: his innards, spilling out over his genitals and slopping on to the floor.

After that, it took him a full minute to die. Was she standing there watching him? Did she intend to inflict any more horror on him? He didn't know. He had the vague sense that the knife was still sticking out of his torso and for a moment he had the sensation of being out of his body, looking down at himself, bound to the chair, wounded eyes bleeding, guts vomiting slowly from inside him like the movement of a giant snake.

Then he felt his bowels loosen. And then, finally, the pain disappeared, and it was the end.

22

The DSF stared at Sturrock. He didn't bother to hide his contempt.

'That man risked his life for you. Day in, day out. For years. And you betrayed him to IS like that?' He snapped his fingers.

'We all have to make unpalatable decisions,' Sturrock said. 'We didn't know Bethany White would turn out to be a monster.'

'You made your own monster,' the DSF said. He pulled out his phone and dialled Hereford. 'It's Attwood,' he said. 'Get me the CO.' Seconds later, Mike Williamson was on the line. 'Update me.'

'*We have a four-man team approaching the colonel's house by car. An airborne team are in transit to the safe house from London.*'

'And Danny Black.'

'*He's driving to the safe house.*'

'Does he have back-up?'

'*No. He's on his own.*'

'Keep me informed.'

'*Roger that.*'

The DSF was about to kill the line, but Sturrock said: 'Wait!'

'What is it?'

'When they find Bethany White, I want her taken out.'

The DSF didn't take his eyes from Sturrock. 'Did you hear him?' he said into the handset.

'*Roger that,*' said the CO, and the line went dead.

The four-man Regiment unit had been despatched from Hereford with haste and briefed by the CO himself over the radio while they were on the road. '*You're to provide support to Colonel Henry Bishop's three-man close-protection team. You have his coordinates. We've reason to believe that an attempt on his life is imminent. Put a ring of steel around the principal and extract him from his location if possible.*'

'What do we know about the hitman?' the driver asked. His name was Matt Bussington, but everyone called him Busby.

'*We think he's a she,*' said the CO.

Busby glanced left at Billy Forman in the passenger seat, then at Kieran Clark and Joe Cleghorn in the rear-view mirror. They all had the same expression: a raised eyebrow and a faintly sarcastic sneer. Busby knew what they were all thinking. It was Cleghorn, a Geordie lad who never let anything pass unsaid, who vocalised it. 'Fucking hell boss, you telling us we need plate hangers and Diemacos to stop some chick giving her Rupert boyfriend what for? What did he do, bang his secretary?'

'*We think she's responsible for the deaths of Ben Bullock, Liam Armitage and Ollie Moorhouse, so save me the lip.*'

That silenced Cleghorn immediately. The guys in the SUV sat up a little straighter and Busby gave it more throttle, despite the intense rain. Sheet lightning illuminated the sky and there was a crack of thunder. '*Her name is Bethany White. If you find her, put her down.*'

'Roger that,' Busby said, and the team settled into a grim silence.

The elements battered their vehicle as they drove through deserted lanes south of the Brecon Beacons. Each time a flash of lightning lit up the air, Busby became acutely aware of the flinty, square-jawed expressions on the faces of his companions. He wondered if they were thinking the same as him: that the unpleasant prospect of nailing a woman was just about balanced out by the thought that this was someone responsible for the death of three of their brothers. So bring it on.

The approach to the colonel's house on the outskirts of Brynmawr was a single-lane road that zig-zagged through the countryside as it approached the target location. Busby was obliged to have the lights on full beam just to see through the torrential rain. The thundering of the water on the roof of the car was a distraction that forced him to concentrate on the road even harder. He hit the brakes quite suddenly as the headlights reflected off the brake-light glass and number plate of a Range Rover on the side of the road. There was something about it that didn't look right. It was parked at an angle, the front of the vehicle almost nudging into the ditch at the side of the road. It had been parked carelessly or in a hurry. And it was only when he came to a complete halt that his headlights picked up the body lying in the middle of the road.

'Fuck,' Billy Forman muttered.

The team automatically slipped into a wordless routine. Each guy opened his door. Billy, Kieran and Cleghorn engaged their weapons and panned the area, while Busby – instantly saturated by the rain – ran up to the body. It was lying on its front. Busby rolled it over on to its back. The man's face was fixed into a grin of horror. The skin was waxy and ice-cold. Busby quickly scanned down the body and clocked a vertical cut through his clothing and into his abdomen. The wound was a sickening mess of rainwater, blood and innards. Lower down the body he saw that the legs appeared to be crushed beneath the knee. He could read clearly what had happened: a vehicle had driven over the body in its hurry to get to the house. He noticed a holster around his chest. It was empty. Someone had taken its contents. He sprinted back to the SUV and shouted at his mates to get back in. They were all soaked. Knowing the water would quickly condense against the windscreen, he blasted it with hot air and then killed the headlights so they had a better chance of approaching unseen. He hit the accelerator and the vehicle bumped as it drove over the corpse, crushing it for a second time.

The rain gave them one advantage: it camouflaged the noise of the engine as the SUV approached the house. But visibility was still poor and it wasn't until another flash of sheet lightning lit up the way that they saw the outline of a set of iron gates twenty metres up ahead. The gates were open and in the moment that the lightning flashed, Busby saw the dark shape of another crumpled figure on the floor. He knew, instinctively, that there was no point checking this one for signs of life.

He killed the engine. The unit swiftly exited the vehicle, climbing back out into the solid rain. Busby jabbed one finger at himself and Billy Forman. They advanced, weapons raised, to either side of the gates while Kieran and Cleghorn covered them from the SUV. Once they'd reached the gates, they waited while the others advanced past them. Cleghorn ran the twenty metres to the front entrance of the building. Kieran headed to an oversized stone holder with ornate feet and crouched on one knee in the firing position, covering the entrance. Cleghorn raised one hand to indicate that Busby and Forman could advance.

Busby couldn't have been wetter if he'd jumped in a lake. He and Forman advanced relentlessly to the front door. It was ajar, and a dim light spilled from it.

The two blades entered together, quickly and silently. They checked to left and right of the doorway. Clear. They were in a long entrance hall. It was dark. No sign of personnel but, ten metres along and to the right, an open door into a room which was the only source of light. The light flickered somewhat: Busby could tell there was a fire in there.

They advanced in absolute silence. When they reached the room, each guy took up position on either side of the door. There was music playing – some classical shit – and looking in, Busby could see an overweight male figure sitting on a chair in front of the fire. He was tied there. His head was leaning back and there was something unrecognisable on the floor.

Kieran and Cleghorn were approaching along the corridor. Busby waved a finger at them to indicate they should check the house. They moved silently further along the hallway. Busby was a hardened soldier, but even he had an icy sensation in his blood as he and Forman entered the room, checking the corners for threats, and approached the figure in the chair.

'Jesus,' he whispered, and put one hand over his mouth and nose. Forman said nothing.

The corpse's eyes were two wounds. The eyeballs were still in their sockets but they were gouged and mangled. Blood had dripped down the cheeks and started to congeal in patches that made him look like a horrific weeping clown. His mouth was open, as though in a silent scream. The unrecognisable mass on the floor comprised the corpse's guts. Years ago, in Afghanistan, Busby had encountered a local woman with a bad stomach wound. Her intestine had bulged out like an inflated balloon and Busby had stuffed it back inside while he waited for the medics to come. There was no chance of that here. Intestines, stomach, even a flash of liver: the corpse's offal was more outside than in. The smell was unbearable. Somewhere in the background was a hint of stale alcohol. But the predominant stench was of semi-digested food and half-processed human faeces, warmed by the heat of the fire. It made Busby gag.

He moved over to the stereo system and killed the music. Now all he could hear was rain and thunder. Forman seemed weirdly transfixed by the sight of the corpse. And when Kieran and Cleghorn entered, their blunt professionalism was marred by their inability to keep their eyes from it.

'The place is empty,' Cleghorn said. He sounded distracted.

'You sure?' No reply. 'Cleghorn, are you sure?'

'A hundred per cent. There's nobody here. It's empty.'

Busby nodded. He looked at Kieran. 'Get on to Hereford,' he said. 'Tell them Colonel Henry Bishop is dead.' He frowned. He remembered the vehicle by the side of the road on the way in. But there was no second vehicle outside the house. The killer would only have approached such a remote location by car, and the CP team would have had at least one vehicle between them. 'And tell them Bethany White has left the crime scene. She's in a car. She has knives and at least one handgun. That's all we know.' He gave the corpse another disgusted glance. 'Photograph him,' he said, 'and the other bodies. And then let's get the fuck out of here.'

There was no let-up in the rain. The last time Danny made this journey, only days ago, it was through a swirling blizzard. The lack of visibility hadn't mattered then and it didn't matter now. He knew these roads intimately. He just wished he could push his vehicle faster.

But he was getting close now. The narrow road off Heol Beili Glas took a gentle swerve to the left, then sloped uphill. Before he reached the brow, Danny killed the engine. The safe house was situated in a gentle valley, about a football-pitch length beyond the brow of the hill. If he was to approach covertly, it would have to be on foot.

He checked his weapon, then looked at the CO's phone. No service. He checked the sky. No sign of the Regiment's chopper approaching. He wasn't even certain they would risk flying in these conditions.

Danny was on his own.

He exited the vehicle and approached the brow of the hill, back arched, weapon in his right hand. His clothes were soaked in seconds. Rain dripped into his eyes. He wiped it out then got on all fours and crawled, an invisible figure at the brow of the hill. He looked down at the safe house, fifty metres away.

The ground-floor lights were on. They glowed through the downpour. Danny wished he had some optics but he had to rely on the naked eye to survey the place. He squinted through the rain. There were two vehicles there, parked almost side by side. He could see they were both pointing away from the house, though he couldn't discern their make or model. He remembered his previous visit. The security guys' black SUV had been parked out front, but that was the only vehicle. Two cars meant somebody else had arrived. He had a good idea who that might be.

The night was dark and the rain offered decent cover. Danny moved on to the rough ground by the side of the road and started to jog down the incline towards the house. More detail came into view. The outline of the two cars. The door of the house, slightly ajar with a narrow strip of light escaping from the door frame. But the rain, which fell so hard now it stung his face, still blurred his vision. He couldn't make out everything he wanted.

Distance to the house: thirty metres. The door opened and a figure appeared. Danny hit the ground – sodden, marshy grass. He peered through the rain, trying to discern who it was, but his vision was too compromised by the elements. Male or female? He wasn't sure. The figure ran to one of the vehicles, opened the driver's door and started the engine. Headlights flared. The figure ran back into the house, leaving the door wide open. Whoever it was, they were preparing to leave.

Danny jumped to his feet again. He sprinted closer to the house, his clothes and boots heavy with rain. The other vehicle, the one whose engine was not turning over, was in his path. Only when he was five metres away did he see something lying alongside it.

A body, face down in the rain.

Movement at the doorway to the house. Danny scrambled down next to the body, where the vehicle blocked him from view. Carefully, knowing the sound of his movements was camouflaged by the sound of the rain, he turned the body on its back. It was almost as if nature wanted to provide him with a flashlight, because at that moment the sky lit up and Danny recognised Frank, the good-natured CP guy. His throat was cut, his eyes rain-filled and glassy. There was no point checking his pulse.

An immense crack of thunder split the air. Danny carefully peered round the corner of the car. He was just in time to make out two figures – an adult and a child. It was a split-second vision, but he had a sense of the adult hurrying the child towards the car before they slipped out of view.

His face was set, his jaw clenched, his fist clutching the handgun. Still crouching, he moved round the back end of the car. He was no more than five metres from the other vehicle, and the figures. The adult – Danny could see now it was a woman – had her back to him. She was leaning into the rear passenger seat, as though strapping the child into the back. She was unsuitably dressed for the rain – just jeans and a long-sleeved top – but Danny could instantly tell it wasn't Bethany.

It was the hair that did it. Bethany was blonde. This woman had dark hair. It was Christina.

Had she overcome Bethany? Was his target still somewhere in the house? He had to know. He stood up and silently strode over to where Christina was just straightening up.

He knew, as he put one hand on her shoulder, that he'd made a terrible mistake. The kid, tearful, was in the back seat, but on the far side. Whatever Christina had been doing, she wasn't strapping him in.

And as she spun round, it suddenly made sense. The hair was dark, but the face was Bethany White's. And she was spinning round not to reveal herself, but to provide her body with extra momentum. She'd grabbed something from the back seat – a heavy car jack – and was swinging it round into the side of Danny's face.

His reflexes were good, but not fast enough to recover from his initial mistake. Before he could block the movement, the car jack had connected with his cheekbone. Stunned and suddenly unable to focus, he staggered back. He felt her kick his hand. The pistol discharged harmlessly and the round went flying into the darkness. Then the car jack connected with his other cheek, even more forcefully.

The next thing he knew he was on the ground, lying on his side. His ears were ringing, and sharp pain drilled through his head as though his skull had been cracked. He fought through the pain and pushed himself on to one elbow, looking up. His vision was blurred, half from the blow, half from the rain, but he could tell she was standing over him, just out of his reach, one arm outstretched with the handgun, the car jack still in the other. She shouted at him above the rain: 'You should have died a long way from here, Danny Black.'

Everything started to spin. Danny tried to respond, but the words wouldn't come.

'You were out to kill him!' she screamed. There was a flash of lightning and Danny had a sudden sharp image of her face and her wild eyes. 'You're as bad as the others. He talked about you,

you know? He thought you were a good guy, but you were out to kill him!'

His vision was clearing. She raised the gun, which had been pointing at his chest, to his face. Danny knew he had a fraction of a second to respond. He lurched forward in a shaky attempt to tackle her legs, but the blows to his head had disorientated him and slowed him down. He fell short as she easily stepped back a pace. 'This is for Ibrahim!' she shouted, and Danny knew that this was it . . .

But then he sensed movement from the corner of his eye, and he heard a voice. A child's voice. '*Stop it, Mummy!*'

The gun stayed pointed at Danny's head, but the gunshot didn't come.

Then the little boy, Danny Jr, was there. He was standing between Danny and Bethany looking up at his mother, distraught and shouting: '*Stop it, Mummy. Stop it!*'

'Get in the car!' Bethany shouted. '*Get back in the car!*'

'I won't come with you,' the little boy shouted, his voice shaking with tears. 'Not if you hurt him. *Don't hurt him, Mummy. He's my friend.*' And he threw himself at his mother, knocking her gun arm away.

Danny realised he had one more chance. He lurched forwards, but his faculties were still not complete, his attempt to grab her unfocused. Bethany's counter-attack, however, did not come from the weapon. She pushed the child to one side and smashed the car jack into Danny's face for a third time, screaming with the effort. The impact was even harder than before. Danny heard the kid wailing, then collapsed face down in a puddle.

He must have passed out, but for how long he didn't know. When he came to, it was with half a mouthful of rainwater and the stench of exhaust fumes in his nose. His head had never hurt like this. Maybe something was broken. Certainly he was concussed. It was still raining hard and his body temperature had dropped. He wanted to puke, and moving his limbs seemed impossible. Somehow, though, he managed to push himself up on to one elbow and make some sense of his surroundings.

The exhaust fumes came from Bethany White's vehicle. It was ten metres distant and moving. Danny staggered to his feet as the vehicle accelerated away. He could just make out that there were two passengers: Bethany and the kid. And they were already too far away for him to chase on foot.

His brain was a mess. He knew that, but for the kid's intervention, he'd be dead. He looked through the rain up to the brow of the hill where his car was parked. Maybe he should run there, get the vehicle and make chase. Then he looked at the house. The door was still open. A sick feeling presented itself in Danny's stomach. Bethany had come here to get her son, sure. But she was here for another reason, too. She'd been eliminating all personnel indoctrinated into the MISFIT operation, and killing them in the same way Ibrahim Khan had been killed. He knew with cold certainty that Colonel Henry Bishop was now dead at home, without any eyes. And the final thing they'd done to Khan was to burn him. Alive.

He stared for a moment at the open door as that thought penetrated his reeling mind. Then he staggered urgently towards the house.

Danny burst in through the front door. His vision was still blurred, but the first thing he saw was another dead body – the second CP guy, sprawled on the floor of the hallway, his blood smeared up the wall, a remnant of the struggle he'd clearly put up. And now he was out of the rain, he heard screaming. Desperate, tearful screaming from the kitchen. He staggered in that direction and practically threw himself through the door. He had to steady himself with one hand on the door frame as he took in the sight that awaited him.

It was Christina who was screaming. The sight of Danny, bruised, bleeding and sodden, did nothing to calm her. She was tied to a kitchen chair. In her struggle to get away, the chair had toppled on to its side. As she screamed, she wriggled and writhed in an attempt to manoeuvre herself out of the kitchen, but really she was going nowhere. The old gas oven had been pulled out from the wall. Danny couldn't see the gas pipe behind it but he knew, from the faint smell of gas in the air, that it had been cut.

And he knew, looking at the other end of the kitchen, that he only had seconds.

A slim telephone directory had been placed in the toaster at the far end of the kitchen. As Danny looked at it, the mechanism popped up, but there was already a tendril of smoke rising from the burning paper. The telephone directory had ignited. The gas would blow at any second.

Danny thrust himself into the room. Christina's screaming was like a bell ringing in his agonised head. He bent over and lifted both her and the chair together. Spinning round, he saw the telephone directory burst into flame and he knew that any moment now the kitchen would be engulfed. He half ran, half jumped back towards the door, and he had barely crossed the threshold when the explosion happened.

The noise was not great: an extreme popping sound. The force, however, was immense. Danny was thrown into the hallway. Christina and the chair fell from his arms and landed, clattering, on the dead CP guy. Danny fell too, heavily and clumsily, but managed to push himself up again despite his unsteadiness. Already there was intense heat coming from the burning kitchen. He knew that with an ignited gas source a second explosion was imminent. There was no time to release Christina from her chair. He picked her up again and ran to the exit, bursting out into the rain just as that second explosion came. It was noisier this time and Danny could tell from the heat behind him that the flames had reached the hallway. He carried on running without looking back, only stopping when he was a good thirty metres from the house. Christina had stopped screaming now, but her panicked sobbing was uncontrollable as he put her down and turned to check out the house.

It was already an inferno. The rain did nothing to stop the flames licking from the ground-floor windows and the front door.

'*Oh my God. Oh my God . . .*' Christina was repeating the words to herself incessantly under her breath. Her dark hair was rain-plastered to her face, and she was shivering intensely. Danny looked to the road. He could see lights disappearing in the distance and he knew it was Bethany's vehicle, probably a mile away already. His urge was to run to the CO's car and make chase, but Christina was in shock. Exposure to these conditions could kill her.

She was bound to the chair with lengths of sturdy rope. The knots were wet from the rain and difficult to undo. It took Danny a full minute to release her, by which time Bethany's vehicle had disappeared. Still fighting the wooziness in his head, he pulled Christina to her feet. 'Can you run?' he shouted at her through the rain.

She stared at him, then nodded.

Danny grabbed her hand and pulled her with him as he started running up the hill towards his vehicle. Her pace was surprisingly good, or maybe his was unusually slow. As they ran over the brow of the hill, he experienced blurred trails in his vision. He closed his eyes and shook his head to clear it, then pressed on towards the car. He had to suppress a surge of nausea as he used his sleeve to swipe the shattered glass from the passenger window off the seat, before manoeuvring Christina into the car and taking the wheel. Rain pounded into the car through the broken window, but Christina barely seemed to notice. She was still shaking badly. She was also trying to speak, but at first could only manage disconnected words. '*Danny . . . Ibrahim . . . Dead . . .*'

'I know,' Danny said. He started the engine and put the heat on high.

'She . . . she . . . tried to kill me . . .'

'Yeah,' Danny said. 'Me too.'

She looked at him as if seeing him for the first time. 'You look like shit,' she said.

'Thanks.'

'Is . . . is Danny okay?'

'He's alive,' Danny said, 'if that's what you mean.' He found the CO's phone and gave it to her. 'Watch the bars,' he said. 'The moment we get any service, tell me.'

She looked at him, then at the phone, then back at him again.

'*What are we going to do?*' she whispered.

Danny looked straight ahead. 'We're going to catch her,' he said, and hit the gas.

23

Bethany White had expected to feel many things. Relief. Exhilaration. Contentment that Ibrahim had finally – *finally* – been avenged.

She felt none of these.

Her son was crying uncontrollably in the back of the car and it made her feel guilty. From time to time he attempted to open the back door, but it was centrally locked and he couldn't get out. She'd always known it would be difficult. How could little Danny possibly understand what he'd just seen, or what was happening to him now? But one day, soon, she would explain to him about his father, and he *would* understand, and respect what she had done.

She felt angry too. Angry with herself for listening to her son and sparing Danny Black's life. How the hell had Black got there? How the hell was he still alive in the first place? Two minutes after leaving, she saw a brief flash in her rear-view mirror of a burning building. Was Danny in there? She doubted it. The man was relentless. He never gave up. She should have hit him harder at the very least, because she was coldly certain he'd be following her as soon as he regained consciousness.

Which led to the other emotion that burned in her veins: fear.

She wasn't scared for herself. That sensation had been drawn from her over the past six months. She was scared for her little boy. Bethany was a target now. As long as Danny was with her, he was a target too. Because if she'd learned one thing about her former employer it was this: they didn't care who they killed to save their embarrassment and cover up their misdeeds. Bethany knew how to make herself and her son disappear. She had more fake passports stashed away, and covert routes out of the UK. But she needed twelve hours, and with Danny Black on her tail, those twelve hours were slipping from her grasp.

The windscreen wipers creaked on full speed. Although her visibility was poor and the road narrow and winding, her speedometer tipped fifty. Danny started crying more loudly and she felt the tension rising within her. Couldn't he just keep quiet? Couldn't he be his father's son? She was about to snap at him when she caught him looking at her in the mirror. That look made something burn inside her. Her little boy's expression was so like his father's that Ibrahim could have been sitting there behind her, urging her on.

She suddenly felt doubly resolute. She kept her eyes on the road and increased her speed.

20.00 hrs.

At first, Christina had not been strapped in to the CO's car. When she noticed the rate at which Danny was accelerating, it cut through her other troubles and she scrambled to plug in her seatbelt.

'Keep watching that phone!' Danny shouted. The roar of the elements through the open window was almost deafening.

They ploughed through the rain, speeding past the house. The flames had already reached the first floor. Black smoke was billowing from the conflagration. The rain made no difference.

The speedometer hit fifty. Sixty. Higher.

Danny was in the zone. He held the steering wheel lightly and handled every twist and turn of the road ahead with the skill that had been ingrained in him over years of training. He was driving dangerously but effectively. The terrain was hilly on either side, so she'd have to keep to the road. He knew there were no side roads off this one for at least ten miles. If he kept his speed high enough, and the vehicle on the road, he *would* catch her, eventually.

And then what? Where was she even heading right now? A port, maybe? Somewhere she could easily leave the country? Did she have contacts who could help her?

His face pounded with pain and a wave of dizziness crashed over him. He had to force himself back to full consciousness, and he realised Christina was saying something. 'Service! We've got service!'

'Give me that,' Danny said. He grabbed the phone and, with one hand on the wheel, dialled in to Hereford. 'Get me the CO!' he roared as soon as a voice answered. 'Now!'

Williamson was clearly waiting for the call. He answered in seconds. '*Go ahead!*'

'I'm on her tail!' Danny bellowed over the noise of the engine and the wind and the rain. 'Do you have my location?'

'*Yes.*'

'She's got her kid in the car. Christina's with me, but the two CP guys are dead.'

'*Same goes for the colonel and his guys. Stay on her and keep this line open if you can. We'll use it to keep tracking you.*'

'Roger that!' Danny shouted. He gave the phone back to Christina. 'Put it on speaker and don't hang up,' he told her as he nudged the vehicle a fraction faster.

Of all parts of the MI6 building in Vauxhall, the operations room in the basement was the most secure. Even Sturrock had to undergo three biometric identity checks before gaining access with the Director Special Forces. The ops room itself was an open-plan space with lines of workstations, comms desks and large screens against one wall displaying live footage from different parts of the world. Sturrock and the DSF marched straight through this part of the room, ignoring the surprised stares from the analysts and operators working down there, and into a private room on the far side. It was like the main ops room in miniature: a single operator, five laptops, and one screen on the wall.

'What have we got?' the DSF asked the operator.

'Hereford, sir,' the operator said. He pointed at one of the laptops. Mike Williamson, CO of 22, was visible on-screen. The operator tapped at his keyboards and some further imagery appeared on the wall screen. The screen was divided into three: a half, and two quarters. The picture on each section was dark and slightly grainy. One quarter showed the flight deck of an airborne chopper, clipping the side of the pilot's face and displaying most of the control panel. The second quarter showed the view in the main body of the chopper: heavily armed men, black-clad with balaclavas, helmets and helmet cams. Every five seconds the POV changed and the DSF realised he was looking at the helmet-cam footage from each individual member of the team. The half screen was an external camera. All it showed was the beam of the chopper's lights illuminating the driving rain in mid-air. The footage was eerily silent.

The DSF moved in front of the Hereford video link. 'What you got for us, Mike?'

'*Bishop's dead. So are both CP teams.*'

'Pictures uploading now, sir,' said the operator. Images appeared on the next laptop. The DSF only gave them a cursory glance. Five corpses on the ground and one brutal image of a man tied to a chair, blinded and excoriated. He noticed, however, that Sturrock couldn't take his eyes from that image.

'Bethany White?' the DSF demanded.

'*Danny Black and Christina Somers are on her tail now. She's in a vehicle and she has her son with her.*'

'Do we have her location?'

'*We're tracking Black via a mobile signal, but we think there's only one road she could be on. The chopper's moving to cut her off from the opposite direction.*'

Sturrock was still staring at the horrific picture on the laptop. 'Is the helicopter armed?' he said, and there was something in his voice that chilled even the DSF.

It was the operator who replied. 'Miniguns, sir,' he said.

Sturrock turned to the DSF. 'If they fire on the car, will there be any survivors?'

'No chance,' the DSF said. 'We have other options, Sturrock. The chopper can put down on the road in front of them. We have a team inside. We can take both of them alive.'

Sturrock wasn't listening. He turned to the operator. 'Get me the PM,' he said, and he grabbed a headset from next to one of the laptops.

'We're talking about a five-year-old kid,' the DSF said.

'*Get me the PM!*'

The DSF and the CO exchanged a long look over the video-conferencing screen. In the background, the operator was on the line to Number Ten. The images on the big screen barely changed: the pilot, the team, the rain.

'Give me the room, everybody,' Sturrock said. 'All of you.'

'I'm not going anywhere,' the DSF said.

'It's a direct order from the PM. Give me the room.'

The DSF and the operator filed out. They waited in silence in the main ops room, the focus of intense scrutiny from all the MI6 personnel at work down there. The DSF found himself remembering Sturrock's self-serving refrain. *It was discussed at the highest level.* Another of those discussions was taking place right now, and the DSF had a pretty good idea how it was going to pan out.

One minute later, Sturrock called them back in. 'The PM is in agreement,' he said. 'Instruct the chopper to fire on Bethany White's vehicle. Collateral damage is acceptable, given the circumstances.'

The DSF gave him a cold look. 'He's five,' he said.

'Just do it,' Sturrock replied.

'*Black? Can you hear me?*'

'Go ahead!' Danny shouted. The CO's voice was scratchy over the phone's speaker, but he could just make him out over the noise.

'*We have our orders from London. The chopper's going to make an intercept.*' A pause. '*Their orders are to fire at will.*'

'No!' Christina shouted. 'She's got a child with her!'

'*Danny, do you copy? Keep her hemmed in. Let the team deal with it . . . DO YOU COPY?*'

Danny didn't reply. He was remembering the little boy, tugging at his mother's arm while Bethany was preparing to nail him. He heard the kid's voice in his head. '*Stop it, Mummy . . . Don't hurt him . . . He's my friend . . .*'

Christina was looking at him in horror. 'They can't do this,' she whispered. 'He hasn't done anything. He's innocent.'

Innocent. Like his father.

'*Black! Do you copy?*'

'Kill the line,' he told Christina.

Her hands were shaking and the screen of the phone was wet. It took her a few seconds to hang up. 'What are we going to do?' she shouted.

Danny kept quiet. One hand was on the steering wheel, one on the gear stick. The vehicle felt slick on the wet road, but he was in control. He gave it a little more throttle and the car accelerated into the night.

Little Danny had cried himself into silence, though he was still distraught. And frightened. Bethany could feel the fear coming from her child in waves. She felt the urge to gather him in her arms and tell him it would be all right. But she couldn't lie to him. Not any more. And she was by no means certain that everything *would* be all right.

She was sweating into her semi-damp clothes. The car felt like it was slipping from her control. The engine was complaining, the suspension juddering heavily. Each time she turned a sharp corner, she felt every muscle in her body tensing up.

'Mummy . . .'

'*Quiet!*'

As she spoke, she saw two sets of lights. One set was in the rear-view mirror. A car, its headlights blurry and distorted in the rain, was gaining on her. Distance: seventy-five metres, maybe less. The second set was in the air, up ahead. Its lights cut through the rain. It was hovering, thirty metres high, a couple of hundred metres distant, its nose somewhat dipped.

She looked in the mirror again. She knew it was Danny Black, and she'd seen what he could do. The memory of his cold, efficient execution of Al-Farouk suddenly returned. Danny Black would kill her *and* her son, without hesitation. She *had* to get away from him.

Was the helicopter armed? She didn't know. But she was sure Danny Black was. She *had* to get away from him. She drove hard towards the helicopter. If she could get past it, she had a chance . . .

'She's accelerating!' Christina yelled. She was gripping the sides of her seat.

'Yeah.' Danny increased his own speed. His foot was on the floor. The gap started closing again.

'They're going to open fire on her. They'll kill them both!'

'She doesn't know that. She thinks I'm going to do that.'

Christina stared at him. 'You're not, are you?'

'No,' Danny replied. And then he added: 'Not both of them.'

The gap was closing quickly. Twenty metres. Ten. But they were approaching the chopper fast. A hundred metres. Fifty. '*They're firing!*' Christina screamed.

And she was right. Bright orange muzzle flashes burst from the guns on either side of the chopper. Danny was five metres behind Bethany's car and the gunfire was ripping up the road almost directly ahead of her. She was heading straight into the line of fire.

The engine of his vehicle screamed, and so did Christina, as he manoeuvred to the right-hand side of Bethany's car and sharply yanked his steering wheel to the left. The two vehicles connected with a brutal jolt and immediately swerved off-road and away from the chopper's line of fire. They hit a rough field and Danny saw Bethany's car roll a full 360, before coming to a sudden halt at ninety degrees to the road. He felt the axles going on his own vehicle and hit the brakes as sharply as he could, drawing to a stop barely five metres from Bethany's car.

'*GET OUT OF THE VEHICLE!*' Danny roared at Christina. He opened his own door and stumbled out. Christina did the same, and she ran further into the field, because she could see the chopper was turning in their direction and slowly approaching. Its guns opened up again. The muzzle flash returned and the rounds followed a trajectory leading up to Danny's car. They smashed into his vehicle, ripping it to shreds.

And Danny was directly in their path, standing between his vehicle and Bethany's, both arms raised.

'What the hell's happening?'

Sturrock was staring ashen-faced at the screen. The chopper's external camera showed minigun fire tearing through the rain and into the half-demolished vehicle. A man was standing beyond it, rain-soaked, face bruised and bleeding, arms in the air. 'Black,' he whispered.

'Hold your fire!' the DSF roared. He strode over to the operator, grabbed his headset and bellowed into the mike. '*HOLD YOUR FIRE!*'

The miniguns stopped. Danny Black seemed to stare directly into the camera. The men in the ops room stared back in silence.

Then the SAS man turned his back on the chopper and walked towards Bethany White's vehicle.

The rain drummed hard on the chassis. A clap of thunder rolled overhead. The rotor blades of the chopper beat loudly behind him.

But as Danny opened the driver's door of Bethany's car, it was strangely silent inside.

For a moment he thought Bethany was dead. Her arms were by her side, and though her eyes were open, her expression was listless. But then she turned to look at him.

'Get out of the car,' Danny said.

She looked over her shoulder at Danny Jr. The poor kid had the thousand-yard stare, but he was alive. 'It's going to be okay, sweetheart,' she said. Her voice was monotone.

'Get out of the car,' Danny repeated.

Behind him, he could sense the chopper landing. He leaned into the vehicle, undid the seatbelt, and forcibly pulled her out. In his peripheral vision he saw figures: Regiment men from the chopper in their black gear, weapons at the ready, swarming around the car. He pushed Bethany up against the side of the vehicle.

'Look but don't touch, Danny,' she said.

He gestured to one of the guys to approach. Danny had no idea who it was – he wore a black balaclava – but that didn't matter. He was properly tooled up: a fully stashed ops vest, a helmet cam, an assault rifle and a pistol. 'Give me your sidearm,' he said. The guy handed over a Sig 9mm. 'Get me Hereford.'

While the guy arranged comms, Danny was aware of one of the other SAS men roughly manhandling the kid out of the car and hustling him over to the chopper. Pistol in hand, he turned his attention back to Bethany. Rain streamed down her face and her blonde hair was matted to her skin. 'He remembered you, you know,' she said. Her voice was hoarse.

Danny raised the pistol to her head.

'He was going to walk out,' she told him. 'Out of training, out of the army. The way they treated him, it almost forced him out. Then you turned up, and he realised not everyone was like that.' She stared directly into his eyes. 'He was a good man. He didn't deserve what he got.'

Danny knew she was right. But then he thought about Bullock, Armitage and Moorhouse. He thought about the innocent woman she'd killed in Beirut. He thought about the colonel and, more acutely, his CP team. He thought about Frank and Alec, the bodyguards at the safe house. He thought about Christina, and how lucky she was to be alive.

'It's Hereford,' said the guy in the balaclava. 'We have the order to take her out.' He stood a couple of metres to Danny's right, watching.

'You're not going to kill me, Danny!' Bethany shouted through the rain.

Danny put the gun to her head. 'You heard the guy!' he shouted back. 'I have my orders.'

She smiled. 'You're a rare beast, Danny,' she said. 'You think first and shoot second. So think on this. There's video footage of Ibrahim being tortured and killed.'

'I've seen it.'

Bethany noticeably suppressed a look of surprise. 'Then you know before they killed him, he explained everything to the camera. That the British government leaked intelligence of an IS summit to the Russians, knowing they'd happily perform an air strike on a school full of children. That it was MI6 who leaked Ibrahim's real identity to IS when he threatened to go public?'

Danny must have let some surprise at this revelation show on his face. 'You didn't know that?' Bethany actually laughed. 'You only saw the edited highlights? And you were going to kill me anyway? Maybe I was wrong. Maybe you don't think first.'

'You got anything else to say?' Danny demanded. But he didn't feel as resolute as he sounded. He was remembering Ibrahim Khan, and thinking of everything he'd risked, and feeling nauseous at the idea MI6 might have betrayed him.

Bethany spoke again, but as she did so, she turned so that she was looking not at Danny, but at the SAS guy to his right. Danny realised she was talking not to him, but to the other guy's helmet cam.

'There are ten copies of that tape!' Bethany shouted even louder, and there was a glint of triumph in her eyes. 'Each tape is in a safety deposit box. Each deposit box is in a different country. I make a phone call once a month. If I fail to make that call, the tapes get released. Everyone – *everyone* – in the world will know what the British government did. Do you hear that, Sturrock? *Everyone* will know.'

Silence. Bethany's shoulders were heaving. Danny kept his weapon raised. Another clap of thunder rolled overhead.

Sturrock stared up at the screen. The audio feed was poor, the voices distorted by the rain and the thunder. But they'd all understood Bethany White's words. The operator was staring into the middle distance, as if he wished he was anywhere but there, and that he hadn't heard what he'd heard. The DSF was staring at Sturrock. The MI6 chief's face was pallid. He had a sick, rictus expression.

'It's your call, Sturrock,' the DSF said.

Sturrock didn't reply. He just stared.

'Alan, you have to make the call. Danny Black needs his orders.'

Sturrock whispered something. The DSF couldn't make it out. 'What did you say?'

'The bitch,' he repeated himself.

'What are his orders?' the DSF pressed.

Sturrock's eyes narrowed. He turned to the operator. 'Can she hear me?'

'I can make that happen, sir,' he said.

'Then make it happen,' Sturrock said.

The boy had started to cry again. His wails were just on the edge of Danny's hearing. The barrel of his handgun was centimetres from Bethany's forehead. His arm was perfectly still and he was ready to fire. Bethany was staring straight at him. She looked almost serene, and it unnerved Danny.

'*Can you hear me?*' The black-clad SAS man was holding up a chunky radio handset. Sturrock's voice was reedy and distorted as it came over the speaker.

Bethany turned to look at the soldier's helmet cam again. 'We can hear you,' she said.

For a few seconds, nothing came over the speaker except a scratchy hiss. Then it burst into life again. '*Black, hold your fire.*'

'I think your orders might be about to change, Danny.'

Danny lowered his weapon.

'*I don't trust you,*' Sturrock said.

'That makes two of us, Alan,' Bethany replied.

'*You'll be under constant surveillance, do you understand? If any harm comes to Christina Somers or to anyone – anyone at MI6 . . .*'

'Are you afraid I might want to pay you a visit, Alan?'

A pause.

'*If you're even a blip on our radar, we'll find you. If we don't find you, we'll find your son. He'll be taken from you. We won't guarantee his survival. Is that clear?*'

'It sounds like stalemate,' Bethany said contemptuously. 'Worthy of my father himself. How very MI6.'

'Is that clear?'

'Perfectly clear.'

'Then get in the car,' Sturrock said, *'and drive away now.'*

Bethany didn't move. Not immediately. She kept her gaze on the helmet cam. 'I hope you think of Ibrahim every night before you go to sleep, and every morning when you wake,' she said. 'He was worth more than the rest of us put together. I hope you think about what we did to him.' She looked at Danny. 'I know I will,' she added.

Bethany White turned her back on him, opened the car door and sat behind the wheel. The windows were misted with condensation. As she turned on the ignition of the battered vehicle, she was just a grey blur inside.

But then there was movement in the back seat. A hand wiped the condensation from the rear passenger window, and Danny Jr's face appeared. His eyes were raw, his expression frightened. Danny nodded at him. The kid nodded back. It was a peculiarly adult gesture, and for a moment it was as if the ghost of Ibrahim Khan was staring out at him.

The blur in the front that was Bethany White seemed to turn, but her face was still obscured, and Danny couldn't tell if she was looking at him or not.

Then the vehicle moved. It trundled slowly across the sodden field, and returned to the road slowly. It turned back the way it had come, away from the helicopter and back towards the burning safe house. Danny watched its rear lights receding into the rain and the darkness. All around him, the SAS team were silently moving back into the chopper. Only when the lights of Bethany's car had completely disappeared did he realise that Christina was still standing in the rain, just by the CO's wreck of a car. The lights from the chopper cast her long shadow across the field.

They stared at each other. Did Christina feel the same about this grubby compromise as Danny did? He couldn't tell. It didn't matter anyway. It was what it was. It had been discussed at the highest level.

'Will I see him again?' Christina asked. Because of the rain, Danny couldn't tell if she was crying or not.

He shook his head. 'No,' he said. He walked up to her. 'We need to leave.'

She reached out and brushed her fingertips against his cheek. Then she looked at the blood she'd wiped from his skin. Danny's whole face throbbed and his body temperature was suddenly dropping. He took Christina lightly by the elbow and together they headed back through the rain to the helicopter, which was waiting to take them away.